THE
ASTRONOMER
WHO DIDN'T LIKE MAGIC

Joe Bergeron

Book One of the Endurian Universe

Endurian Press

The Astronomer Who Didn't Like Magic is a work of fiction. Names, places, and incidents either are products of the author's imagination or are used fictitiously.

Copyright © 2015 by Joe Bergeron

ISBN: 978-0-9914005-2-2

Acknowledgement:
Excerpt in Chapter Fifteen is from the poem "Tigermine" by Conrad Aiken. Poem copyright © 1977 by Mary Hoover Aiken.

Cover illustration by Joe Bergeron.

Published by The Endurian Press

www.joebergeron.com

For all my friends from the Grand Canyon Star Party, the Winter Star Party, and Stellafane.

Chapter 1

The Light in the Hills

Horns cried somewhere in the distance, thrilling him, calling him on. The air was cold and clean, the wind carrying ice crystals that stung his face. He turned, taking in the great panorama around him: the fantastic pinnacles, the misty valley, the sky surging with an aurora that flowed upward from the horizon like an inverted cataract of jewel-colored water. He felt exalted, exhilarated, alive.

Blackness then blotted out this splendor. Silence and sullen heat absorbed it. Vast, luminous horizons collapsed into the interior of a small camping trailer.

The dreams of Leonard Ronar were colorful, if elusive, belying the greyness of his appearance and demeanor.

Lately he abandoned his dreams only with reluctance. He'd worked all night, as usual. Now the hands of his clock were converging on noon, which was like four in the morning for someone on his schedule. Sunlight was turning his trailer into a sheet metal oven. Though the windows were shuttered, enough sun leaked through to provide a dim chiaroscuro lighting. A fly buzzed around the cracks of the door, seeking escape.

Despite the heat and the stale, dusty odor, Ronar lay there staring at nothing, feeling no compulsion to rise.

Life on Kitt Peak National Observatory consisted mainly of gathering data and performing such self-maintenance as was possible and necessary in so austere an environment. A few hours would be enough time to prepare for tonight's observations, a small effort easily deferred. There wasn't much to do in the meantime.

Eventually willing his ennui into submission, Ronar swung his legs off the bed and stretched. He couldn't stretch while lying down because the bed was too short. When he stood up, he had to crouch to avoid whacking his head on the ceiling.

The trailer was the worst part of working at the Peak, except perhaps for the boredom. If not for his inverted sleeping schedule, he'd have been more comfortable just camping out in the open.

His trailer was still superior to the Quonset hut that housed everyone else on the mountain—at least it offered privacy. He flung open the door to admit light and air. Pawing through a pile of clothing, he selected a set of khakis which he deemed clean enough for at least one more wearing. Laundry facilities had yet to make their way to Kitt Peak, and in any event, Ronar was rather indifferent to such things.

Once dressed, Ronar scrubbed his face and teeth at the tiny steel sink and gave himself a quick appraisal in the mirror. Here, he supposed, was a face unlikely to set feminine hearts to fluttering. It was lean, with a rather hard mouth, grey eyes glinting beneath a harsh brow, and thick iron-grey hair in need of combing. His nose, he had to admit, was too fine for his taste: long and narrow, almost delicate, save for the odd Roman bump at the bridge.

Still, he approved of the overall severity of this face. He lifted his razor, stared at it, shrugged, and put it down again. Who was he trying to impress by shaving every day?

Ready for the world, Ronar lurched out into the crisp mountain air. The sun glared overhead like a bright copper rivet, banishing all shadow and stirring up a wind that spent itself trying to wring clouds from the desiccated air. The mountaintop was an unruly garden of granite outcrops bleached white-tan by the Arizona sunlight. It was softened by tough-barked evergreen shrubs, cool and lush compared to the desert growth on the plain far below.

The Peak's raw beauty improved Ronar's mood, though not to the point where the emotion actually registered on his face. All too soon he'd have to descend to Tucson, where he pictured himself explaining to puzzled undergraduates the differences between Mean Solar Time, Universal Time, and Sidereal Time. His stints on the Peak always took on an added glamour from the perspective of his duties at the University.

Ronar paced over to the Quonset hut and threw open the screen door. A partitioned area inside served as a makeshift commissary for the thirty or so people inhabiting the Peak. There a hefty Papago woman served simple meals laden with spices and grease. Ronar sat at a table, solemnly ate a plate of bacon and eggs topped with salsa, went back outside, and commenced killing time. He sat atop a pile of boulders, skimming journals and staring out over the landscape, so pensive and remote a figure that he did not attract the fellowship of those few who noticed him on his perch.

A family of tourists wandered by, their children yelping and cavorting. A tiny blonde girl broke off and approached Ronar, staring up at him as he tried to ignore her.

"What do you look like?" she asked at last.

Ronar felt his face contracting into a frown of perplexity. "I look like this," he said, waving at his face.

"No, I mean without your sunglasses."

Ronar removed the glasses and regarded the girl, who said nothing.

"It's the best I can do," said Ronar, replacing the sunglasses.

"You look mean. Don't you ever smile?"

"Of course I—" Ronar broke off, realizing he was snapping at the child. "Yes. I smile from time to time."

"I wish you would. What are you reading?"

"It's about variable stars."

"What are valuable—variable stars?"

Ronar closed his book and addressed the girl with greater attention. "They are stars that change greatly in brightness. Sometimes they're very bright indeed, while at other times they're not very bright at all."

"Oh. You know what? Sometimes my daddy says that about me when he sees my report card."

Without really intending to, Ronar laughed.

"That's better, " said the girl, smiling.

"I'm sure your daddy is very proud—"

At that moment the girl's father strode up, looking wary and put-out.

"Guess what, Daddy? I'm a variable star."

"That's nice, baby. Come on now. I'm sure this man is very busy."

Ronar remained silent as the father and daughter returned to their brood.

When Ronar wanted to show kindness to his fellow men, he did so by staying away from them, especially when he was in such an odd mood as now. An inexplicable dissatisfaction chafed in his chest and throat. When the sun finally declined he returned to the commissary for a solitary dinner of chili and tortillas. The radio blared out tinny, cloying ballads from some Mexican station. Ronar got up to tune in a news broadcast, ignoring the cook's half-stifled annoyance. He caught a story about the newest Soviet Sputnik to alarm the Western world.

Ronar was amused by the announcer's prattle about man's "conquest of space". So far, he reflected, mankind had conquered space to a lesser extent than a nearsighted swimmer paddling in the surf had conquered the sea. He shook his head and went back outside, neglecting to re-tune the radio to suit the cook, earning him a glare to which he was oblivious.

As evening approached, Ronar marched toward the 84-inch dome, a dazzling white hemisphere on the southern-most edge of the summit. Ronar disapproved of the look of the new dome, with its hangar-like equipment bay on the south side, and a squarish aluminum entrance gallery which offered tourists a glimpse of the instrument. It lacked the classic simplicity and beauty of the Palomar dome. He glanced to the east, where loomed the colossal inverted checkmark of the McMath solar telescope, the other major instrument on the Peak. Its design, though modernistic, was stark and unadorned enough to please him.

Ronar entered the observatory, confronting another family of tourists with their noses pressed against the viewing window. They looked at him rather sheepishly.

"Aren't we—supposed to be in here?" asked the wide-eyed mother.

Ronar became aware that he might be frowning at them for no good reason. He tried to reshape his expression into a smile, an effort as successful as all his other forced smiles, as he could see by the dismay in their faces.

"No. That is, yes. You're supposed to be in here. Sorry. Thank you."

Ronar sighed and turned away. So much for public relations. He escaped into the shadowy interior of the dome.

He did not linger at the telescope. Sunset found him on the catwalk that circled the big dome. He wore a beat-up green parka against the imminent chill.

Ronar's hands rested on a unique binocular which hung from his neck. Made in Germany during the war, it was a prototype incorporating the most advanced features of its time. The body was machined from aluminum brushed to a snow-like whiteness. The lenses glinted sapphire blue. The glass was unusually large—only Ronar's big hands kept it from being impractical.

Ronar leaned against the dome, staring moodily to the south at remote mountains whose summits were divided between rich golden sunlight and blue shadow. In the lush evening light they seemed citadels of mystery, inviting him to approach via the paths he blazed with his eyes.

It had been a long time since he'd had a chance to lose himself in the wild. True, there were day hikes and week-end trips when he found the time, but nothing he'd done in the past ten years compared with the adventures of his youth: the winters in the Colorado Ski Patrol; his participation in the Olympics of 1936, his curious return to Germany in 1941; and of course his boyhood discovery of Comet Ronar, an event which had set him on the road to Kitt Peak.

It hadn't worked out as he'd imagined as a boy. The grand romance of astronomy had been buried beneath the adult concerns of surviving calculus, writing a dissertation, finding a job, gaining tenure, grading examinations, and publishing regularly. His love of astronomy had not diminished, but something was missing. His restlessness, made more poignant by the sunset and the distant mountains, overwhelmed even his anticipation of the superb starry night to come.

Something had to change. How had it taken him so many years to realize that?

Something in the distance caught his eye.

Far off, near the summit of some nameless peak, a star of reflected sunlight danced in the unsteady air, a fiery point redder than the sunlight itself. It wavered in the silence, a lonely, beckoning wonder.

Ronar caught his breath, captivated by its mystery and beauty. He raised the binocular, but it revealed nothing more, only brightened the glare until his eyes watered.

Something tentative moved in his mind, like a call just beyond the range of conscious hearing, so fleeting it faded almost before he became aware of it.

He lowered the lenses and stared bare-eyed at that far-off glimmer. Unfamiliar feelings welled up within him. Suddenly he was a man of sadness and loneliness, rather than the self-sufficiency that had defined him up to now. He felt a pang of nostalgia, as though this remote flicker were signaling the end of his old life, or unlocking the door to a new one.

As the sun declined, the reflection began to dim, until it died with a final blood-red beam.

Ronar shuddered and released his breath. Blinking, he took a moment to weigh the emotions that had been so unexpectedly aroused. Unable to make much sense of them, he shook his head to dismiss them. But the feelings lingered, a mark on his mind and spirit.

He pulled a compass from his pocket and took a bearing on the place where the reflection had flickered out moments before.

The sun had set, but Ronar was in no hurry to enter the dome. Trailing the sun was a crescent moon, which must also set before the sky would be dark enough for his purposes. He remained on the catwalk, pondering that strange reflection, staring at the darkening hills as if he hoped it might flare up again.

Ronar stood in darkness while electric motors opened the dome's slit. The interior was lit by the dimmest of red lights, allowing the telescope's general form to be discerned. It was a steely clockwork thing, a thing of gears, wheels, trusses, and pylons. The mirror's short focal length gave the entire instrument a compact look belying its impressive light gathering power.

Tonight the telescope was equipped to photograph galaxies for which he'd already obtained spectra in the previous nights. By measuring their red shifts he could estimate their distances. With enough of these measurements he could piece together a picture of the distribution of galaxies in the universe.

Standing by the wall, Ronar called out to the night assistant, unseen in the small control room at the side of the dome. "Hector. Please slew to the first object. Do you have the coordinates?"

"I do. Are you clear of the telescope?"

"I'm clear."

"Stand by for slewing."

With a buzzing sound the telescope swept from its parked position to its first target, a remote galaxy cluster high in the sky. The dome rotated to follow, clacking and booming on its track.

"On target, Dr. Ronar?"

Ronar went to the finder, an instrument considerably larger than any he had possessed as a youth. He peered up into the eyepiece, pushing aside the stepladder, which was needed only by astronomers of lesser height.

"On target. I'll prepare for the exposure."

"Roger."

Ronar shot an annoyed glance toward the control room. The jargon of the nascent space program was only the latest fad to muddy his native, and favorite, language.

A small motor hummed and clicked as it moved the telescope to track the stars. Ronar sat beneath the guiding eyepiece and looked up into it. Barely visible were the dim flecks of galaxies peering back at him from a chilling distance.

"I have a guide star. All right, douse the reds."

The interior of the dome settled into an inky blackness. Ronar peered into the guiding eyepiece and watched until he was satisfied that the telescope was tracking well.

"I'm beginning the exposure. Three hours." There was a click. Now a beam of focused starlight was falling onto the glass photographic plate which would record its secrets.

For the next three hours Ronar was almost glued to the eyepiece. Then came a brief break to reset the telescope to the next object, beginning the whole cycle again.

Guiding was tedious. He had only to watch the guide star, and when it wandered from the cross-hairs nudge it back with a touch of the buttons on the hand paddle. It was hardly a task requiring his full attention. He'd learned to cope by allowing his mind to rove through waking dreams.

Tonight came the image of that flickering red light in the hills.

After nine hours and three successful exposures, with the onset of twilight not far off, Ronar decided to end the evening with a bit of self-indulgence, a special reward for his diligence.

"Hector. One final object. Slew to twelve hours fifty-four minutes, plus twenty one degrees fifty seven minutes."

"All right. Are you clear, Dr. Ronar?"

"I'm clear."

Ronar heard the annoyed sigh that came from the control booth. When the telescope stopped moving, Ronar wrestled the plate holder free of its mounting brackets. Replacing and realigning the camera was a delicate job which Hector or one of the other technicians would have to undertake in the morning. But, that was what they were being paid for, thought Ronar.

Ronar screwed a small adapter into the telescope's back plate, into which he inserted an old eyepiece. Its barrel was scratched and marred, but the lenses of this relic of his boyhood were lovingly maintained and unblemished. Ronar perched himself on the observing stool and applied his eye to the glass.

After hours of guiding, he felt the need to really *look* at what he was studying. Somehow it made the whole exercise seem less academic, more real.

Tonight he'd chosen to view the Black Eye Galaxy in Coma Berenices. Centered in the dark grey circle of the eyepiece field, it was a softly luminous ellipse, bright in the center where the suns were most tightly massed, partly obscured by the curious feature which gave it its name, a dark patch of cosmic dust superimposed against it. It stared back at him with a mystic impersonality.

Ronar's glance was worthless scientifically, but still, it seemed to him, important to real understanding. Ancient starlight falling on the seven-foot mirror was directed into his eye, able to impress itself upon his consciousness across such a gulf of miles and years. That was worth the occasional reminder.

These quaint practices irritated some of his colleagues, who felt that the time of giant telescopes should not be spent so frivolously. Or so he had heard. No one had ever voiced these complaints directly to his face.

The following evening found Ronar on the catwalk again, keeping an uneasy eye on the sky, the sun, and the hills. His observing program would probably come to a halt tonight. Rafts of high clouds covered most of the sky, wave clouds and mare's tails of icy cirrus. The forecast called for the passage of a quick front.

But it wasn't the prospect of losing a night's observing that bothered Ronar. He was concerned that the clouds would prevent a second view of the mysterious reflection that had so caught his imagination. He watched fretfully as diffuse cloud-shadows crept over the distant mountains.

He heard the door swing open, then footsteps on the catwalk's steel deck. He glanced down and to the side; there stood Stanley Cohen, an astronomer from the University of North Carolina, studying the sky with wan hope.

"Well, Leonard, I'd hoped that your loss might be my gain. But I can see there won't be much astronomy done on this mountain tonight."

"Probably not," said Ronar shortly. Just now he had no desire for company.

Cohen was small, his balding head reaching the level of Ronar's biceps. He'd recently lost several observing nights to a spell of bad weather, and was hanging around hoping to make up some of that lost time. His work in stellar spectroscopy could proceed under poorer skies than Ronar required.

Ronar stiffened. A dim gleam of reflected sunlight had appeared in the mountains somewhere out beyond Baboquivari. His companion forgotten, Ronar stared at the light. It was much dimmer than it had been yesterday, even though a lucky gap in the clouds was shedding full illumination on the area. With the sun sliding southward in its descent toward winter, the angle of the reflection was changing; the beam now almost missed the dome. No doubt the reflection was visible from this spot for only a few evenings each year.

He became aware of Cohen, whose puzzled glance shifted between Ronar's intense gaze and the flicker of light that was its target.

Grudgingly, almost against his will, Ronar muttered, "What do you make of that, Stanley?"

Cohen waved his hand toward the horizon. "That out there? That glint? Some kind of reflection. What do you make of it, Leonard?"

"A reflection. Nothing more."

Cohen shrugged.

Ronar wanted to take a second compass bearing, but he didn't want to call that much attention to his interest in the light. For some reason, this was something he wished to keep to himself. The reflection soon disappeared, leading Ronar to relax a trifle.

The two men watched the deepening twilight for a while longer. The moon was hazily visible through the clouds.

Cohen stretched and said, "I guess it'll be an early night for me. Have to try to find something to do until I can fall asleep. Maybe I'll just drive into Tucson. I've heard you can have a good time there if you know where to go."

Ronar only grunted in answer. If Cohen was hinting for company he got little satisfaction.

"Well, I'll see you tomorrow." Cohen turned and ambled away.

As the darkness gained strength, a fresh wind swept thickening clouds across the sky. Ronar left the dome and picked his way among rocks and scrubby trees, finally alighting on his favorite boulder. From this vantage Ronar gazed into the south, where not one speck of light marred the blackness. The strange loaf-like peak of Baboquivari, sacred to the Papago, was lost in the night. Somewhere to the right of it, and well beyond it, was the anonymous hill that bore a tantalizing secret.

For long hours Ronar sat there, pondering his strange restlessness, his turmoil, his sudden desire to feel the miles reel by beneath his feet. He had little patience for the vagaries of others, and still less for his own. All he'd ever wanted was to be an astronomer, or so he'd told himself repeatedly. Well...now he was an astronomer. He was reasonably accomplished and respected. What more did he want out of life?

Something more.

He considered his desire to seek out the mystery of the light in the hills. No doubt the thing had some mundane cause. If he found it, he would feel like a fool, hypnotized like a magpie by the glitter of sunlight off...

Off what?

By midnight his plan was made.

He spent the rest of the night in peaceful sleep, wrapped in blankets beneath the windy sky.

Dressed in hiking boots and khaki fatigues, Ronar stepped from the trailer into the sunlight. His eyes mirrored the heavy iron color of the thunderstorm in the west. The rising wind whipped his hair. The front had passed, promising clear skies after the thunderstorms blew themselves out.

On his back was a pack stuffed with hiking essentials. With the binocular slung around his neck he set off with a long, rapid stride for the south face of the mountain.

Only as he drew abreast of the dome did it occur to him that some might think him erratic were he to simply disappear. He brought up short, looking over his shoulder. The storm backed the dome like a field of ink, briefly thinned by submerged flashes of lightning.

After a moment's thought Ronar turned aside and trotted up the walkway. He entered the dome and stood quietly, allowing his eyes to adjust to the gloom. Presently the structure of the telescope became visible.

The instrument stood idle, slumbering in cool shadows. Night was its natural environment; daylight must be held at bay until the sun and its concealing glare had gone. Then the dome could be opened to reveal the contents of the night. Ronar looked at the great reflector with sudden appreciation, even a bit of reverence.

Beyond the telescope was a desk. There sat Dr. Cohen, poring over the densely printed columns of a star catalog. Ronar walked up and stood over him.

"Stanley."

Cohen started, sending charts and papers skittering over the desktop. He looked up at Ronar, grabbed the reflector of his gooseneck lamp, moving the cone of light up a broad, flat torso, seemingly into the upper reaches of the dome before finally reaching Ronar's face.

"Leonard!" Cohen fumbled with his glasses. "Why are you wearing that costume? You—seem to be equipped for a lengthy expedition."

"It's good news for you, Stanley. Fine night coming up. Put it to good use."

Cohen blinked. "You're...giving up your time on the telescope?"

"Yes. I'm going on a hike. Should be back in five days, maybe four. I'll be seeing you."

With that, Ronar turned on his heel and set out for the exit, feeling Cohen's stare on his back. He got halfway out the door before Cohen cried, "Leonard, wait! What are you talking about?" He caught up with Ronar and put a hand on his arm.

Ronar halted at the threshold and looked down at Cohen, feeling a mix of irritation and embarrassment.

"It's only a hike. Not—a big deal."

"A hike. Leonard, your telescope time has been scheduled for the better part of year. How can you just wander off and abandon it?"

Ronar shrugged. "I already have most of the data I need. I just need to clear my head. Need to move a little. Need to *live*." Ronar blinked, taken aback by the vehemence of his own statement.

Cohen stared at him in mystification. "But don't you have classes to teach before then?" he asked quietly.

"Hmm." Ronar considered that for a moment. "Hell. I'll tell the university I've taken a sabbatical." He cracked a smile, even uttered a quick laugh. If only it were that simple...

But it was just that simple, if he really wanted it to be.

"I really don't give a damn."

He turned again, stepping out into the sunshine, bounding down the stairs, a bemused Cohen following in his wake.

The dome was perched on the steep southern face of the mountain. Cohen glanced down the precipice and back at Ronar, apparently drawing the inference that Ronar meant to descend that way rather than via the road.

But Ronar now felt no great hurry to depart. He leaned against a boulder that seemed only precariously rooted to the mountaintop. He smelled electricity in the air as the thunderstorm approached. The wind gained strength, rushing up the face of the mountain, lofting ravens which then folded their wings to slip back down into another updraft.

Ronar looked along the ridge to the great stone thumb of Baboquivari, twelve miles away. Beyond it, the mountains of Mexico looked like nearby hillocks in the clear desert air.

Feeling oddly unsettled, he turned to his colleague. "Stanley, you're more familiar with my work than most. How would you assess its quality?"

Cohen seemed ill-prepared for this non sequitur. He shrugged and loosened his collar despite the falling temperature.

"It has always been excellent—purposeful, methodical, a very real contribution to the field. You'll have real influence on our ideas of large-scale structures."

"But would you call it a work of genius?"

Cohen fiddled with his tie as he thought that over. "Well, no, I could not honestly call it that."

Ronar nodded, a little wistfully, a little ruefully. "I know. Yet I stay with astronomy because I love it. It's the highest calling I know—no pun intended. My research may not be revolutionary, but I have hopes for it, and I'll continue it however I can. Don't worry; science hasn't lost me yet."

Cohen paused, then extended his hand with a curiously moist look in his eye. "You've quite a reputation in our field, Leonard...even aside from your work." He flashed a quick, embarrassed smile. "Now it seems there's more to you than I may ever get a chance to discover. Goodbye, Leonard. Without you, life will be less of an enigma, and a little less intriguing."

Ronar looked at him with wry perplexity. "You're overreacting. I'll be back." But even as he spoke the words he wondered if they were true. They shook hands solemnly.

Ronar turned and started down the slope, leaping from rock to rock with natural athletic grace.

Now the thunderstorm loomed over half the sky. A steel-blue shadow enveloped the mountain. Ronar scrambled down steep faces of bare rock, heading toward the sheets of rain that swept across the desert.

Cohen stood looking after him for a while, the wind whipping his thin hair and throwing dust in his eyes. When the first fat drops spattered against his glasses he turned and retreated into the dome.

That evening, as he stood on the catwalk watching the sunset, he spied a fleeting glint of reflected light in the hills, and frowned as if at some great mystery.

After the initial difficult descent, Ronar worked his way toward the west and Horseshoe Ridge. From there the ridge line extended south toward Baboquivari. Trails left over from the days of the Civilian Conservation Corps were overgrown but usable. The country was pleasant, green with scrub oak. Ronar opened his stride and made good progress.

The sun went down as Ronar approached the monolith of Baboquivari. The crescent moon provided enough light to let him continue for a while before the darkness grew too deep. He lit no fire as he camped at the foot of Baboquivari. The mountain belonged to the Papago, and their god Ee-Ee-Toy was said to inhabit the caves at its summit. Ronar felt no threat from the god, but the Indians might object to a white man camping so near their sacred place. Better to leave the darkness undisturbed.

Ronar lay back, wrapped in his sleeping bag against the chill. Coyotes whined somewhere in the arroyo down below. He could barely make out the shapes of kangaroo rats as they scampered at his feet.

The sky was thick with stars, crusted with stars, powdered with and shivering with stars. The Milky Way arched overhead like a bridge of pale frost. Ronar let his eyes rove over constellations that studded its smoky glow with scattered points of brilliance. Cygnus the swan took wing along the Milky Way's starry cirrus; beside it gleamed the delicate harp of Lyra. Farther south, astride the great dark rift that intruded into the star mist from the west, flew Aquila, the eagle.

The stars gave him the peace to let him find sleep.

Deep in the south, Mars stood near to Antares, two dire red beacons in the heart of the Scorpion.

Chapter 2

The Bronze Portal

The next afternoon Ronar traversed a pass a few miles from the Mexican border. A few final peaks rose up ahead. The Quinlan Range, of which Kitt Peak and Baboquivari were the high points, was petering out. Behind him, Kitt Peak was a trapezoid of purple haze on the horizon, while Baboquivari loomed tall and enigmatic at much closer range.

Lacking a map, Ronar was limited to compass-based dead reckoning on his trek to the mystery mountain. But he wasn't worried—the landmarks were distinctive enough that he was sure he could find the way.

A largely sedentary life had taken its toll on his endurance. He'd managed to find time to hike and explore around Tucson, but not often enough, and seldom farther than fifteen or twenty miles at a time. In the past few years, his annual pilgrimages to the Rockies had left him with sore muscles and blistered feet. Now he was sweaty, thirsty, sunburned, and tired. He berated himself for ever having let indolence and inertia reduce him to such a state, and vowed to take whatever steps were necessary to prevent it in the future.

Despite these discomforts, Ronar enjoyed his walk. The Sonoran landscape was silent about him, harsh and elemental, a tawny wilderness in which even the sheep of the Desert People found too little nourishment to be worth the effort.

The day had turned hazy. A diffuse sun hovered in the western sky, its rays bathing the mountains with a smoky afternoon glow. As Ronar scrambled around a fin of rock, he saw at last the peak he'd studied with such care from the observatory. It was neither tall nor distinctive, but to Ronar it had the look of a numinous place, a look enhanced by the silence of the desert. He scanned its flanks with the binocular, but its secrets did not yield to so easy a probe.

With a mixture of anticipation and self-deprecation Ronar tramped forward to begin his climb, skirting a low rise that stood between him and his destination. Again he was sure his search would end in anticlimax, with the discovery of some bit of shiny trash—an old icebox, a wrecked pickup, or the windows of an abandoned sheepherder's hut. He hesitated, suddenly unwilling to confront this inevitable disappointment, which threatened to dash hopes so vague he could not even name them.

Well—as long as he was here, he might as well continue, farce or no. What did he have to lose?

Dusk lay thick and purple on the land. The moon was a pale crescent floating in the rosy western afterglow.

He had found nothing, not a bit of glass, not a scrap of tin.

The northern flank of the mountain was gentle, with sparse vegetation, easy to climb and search. He had crossed and recrossed it until the sun was set and he knew every major rock on its slope.

He sank down to sit on one of the smaller boulders, located at what should be the very spot from which the reflection had shone, as near as he could tell. Could his goal lie on one of the neighboring mountains? No: from the observatory, he had noted tilted strata that marked the correct slope, and this was it.

He looked past the nearby swell of land, into the distance to Kitt Peak. The observatory dome was a barely visible nub on its rim. He chuckled. Suddenly he laughed, a sound like cobblestones clattering down the slope.

Well, he'd had his little adventure. He'd told Stanley he'd be back in four or five days, a good estimate as it turned out.

Trying to ignore the persistent spark of disappointment within him, he opened a can of beans, scooped them cold into his mouth, then spread his blankets in the dusk and lay down. Another night or two of freedom...and then...and then...

Sometime during the night, with Orion sprawled on the eastern horizon, Ronar awoke suddenly, sat up and said "What?"

But the dream that had prompted this had already escaped him. He lay back and soon slept again.

In the morning he was packed and ready to travel within five minutes. Still chagrined, he strode straight downhill, determined to at least see some different scenery by taking a different route back.

As he approached the base of the hillock that lay just north of the "mystery mountain", he noticed the remains of a trail leading up it. It was rather wide, but nearly invisible from age and disuse. Curious, he decided to follow it. It was rutted in spots, as though carts or wagons of some kind had once used it. The track continued up the slight rise, switchbacking in the steeper sections. Ronar kept his eyes cast downward, looking for any sign of recent use, but finding none.

The sun rose into a sky brushed with streamers of bright golden cloud.

The slope leveled out; he'd reached the summit. He encountered some upended slabs of granite. Engraved on their surfaces were old petroglyphs, including a large and impressive Man-in-the-Maze. Here the old road or path disappeared in grass and scrub.

Ronar straightened up, perplexed, and took a drink from his canteen.

There was something odd about the light. A reddish glow filled in the shadows on his hand.

He turned to the left. Tucked in among the narrow standing stones was something that glared in the morning sun.

He dropped the canteen, his gaze alternating between the glare, the distant observatory, and the mountain he had thought was his destination. How had he made such a mistake? Of course: from the observatory, this hillock appeared superimposed against the more distant mountain. From a distance, the two appeared merged, the lesser height blending into the greater.

Heart pounding, Ronar approached the goal of his journey.

He did not understand what he was seeing.

All he could determine was that it was cubical in outline, about fifteen feet on a side, and made of copper or bronze.

And that it was impossible.

Ronar circled it slowly, keeping a wary distance.

The side he was facing was, in itself, comprehensible enough. It was the entrance to a tunnel, stretching into a distance not penetrated by the twilight. The walls angled in somewhat, giving the impression of a squared-off funnel narrowing away into the darkness.

The trouble was, the other three sides looked exactly the same. Four openings, all leading inward at right angles to each other, all vanishing into the distance—all in a fifteen-foot cube.

Cold awe burned in Ronar's breast. Here was something beyond the experience of mankind as he knew it. Step by step, he approached the anomaly, put out his hand and touched it. It was old, weathered; flakes of verdigris came off on his fingers.

Here was proof that human thought had missed major aspects of possibility, had not yet uncovered whole branches of fundamental knowledge. Were he to walk away right now, never to return, his view of reality had already been forever changed.

The doorways beckoned. Ronar picked up a pebble and pitched it into one of the dark gates. It traveled a long way before hitting with a dull clank, somewhere within the cube's paradoxical depths. What about the top? He lobbed a chunk of malachite onto it. It struck nothing. No sound ever reached him from that stone.

It was obvious and unavoidable that he must explore this thing at once. For all he knew, it might fade like mist at the next sunrise. Or maybe it appeared only once per century, like Brigadoon, or maybe once every hundred million years.

But he doubted that. Its surroundings were undisturbed. It stood mute and impassive, as much a part of its environment as the rocks and the sage.

Ronar broke handfuls of twigs from a nearby creosote bush. He tied them to a long stick of tesota wood and struck a match to it. With this torch in hand, he turned to face the black gape of the Portal.

He entered the dusty bronze corridor, the sound of his footsteps echoing around him. A few paces took him beyond the cube's fifteen-foot outer dimension. Where he walked now, he could not say.

He detected no reaction to his presence, no sign of danger, no sign indeed that anything larger than a lizard had come this way in years. Nevertheless, a feeling of wrongness began to bother him as he advanced. He came to an abrupt halt as he realized what the trouble was.

Despite the evident narrowing of the tunnel, it seemed no smaller here than it had at the entrance. But how could that be? Looking ahead, it was clear that the walls, ceiling, and floor were indeed converging at a moderate but obvious angle.

He looked back and started in surprise. Though he'd come no more than a hundred paces—three hundred feet at most—the opening, as well as he could make it out in the last light of dusk, looked at least three times farther away.

Ronar accepted this with a subdued laugh. He measured the tunnel's width by pacing it off, and continued on.

Soon it was apparent that the shaft was indeed changing in size; it was growing. Unless he were shrinking—he couldn't dismiss the possibility, but it did strike him as unlikely.

As he walked, the walls and ceiling gradually receded into the gloom. The echo of his footsteps took longer to reach him, then died away completely.

The torch burned brightly at first, but faded as the twigs blackened and fell away, leaving only the smoldering tesota stick.

Now he could no longer see the walls at all. Turning, he discovered he couldn't see the entrance anymore, either.

Ronar stopped short. The thought of wandering without landmark or guidepost in this dusty dark void was unappealing. An uneasy feeling rose up in his gut, overwhelming his desire to explore further.

He retraced his steps, following the barely perceptible track he'd left in the dust and litter on the bronze floor. But ten minutes passed without the reappearance of the entrance.

Impatiently, he left his path and angled off to the left, planning to find the wall and follow it outside.

After another half hour, he had to admit that not only had he lost the opening, but the walls themselves.

His world was a circle of weak torch light glimmering on an infinite plane of bronze. His own shadow, long and distorted, was the only moving thing within his vision. All else was blackness and silence.

Ronar swayed. He had rarely been lost before; this experience redefined the concept. He was dizzy, disoriented. His sense of balance found no reference points in the emptiness around him. He fought off the feeling by concentrating on his feet planted on the floor.

Belatedly he thought of the compass in his pocket. The general direction to the exit should be East, since he'd entered with the glow of sunrise at his back. He took out the compass and held the torchlight close, but the needle wandered aimlessly, indicating nothing more than the steel knife sheathed at his hip when he brought it near.

Having no better plan, he chose a random direction and walked as straight a line as he could manage. Stealth seemed pointless, so he lengthened his stride to cover the maximum distance before his torch gave out entirely. He could only hope this was a meaningful action. His mind offered the image of an ant marching around and around the rim of a jar until it dropped from exhaustion. Was he as incapable of understanding and escaping his situation as the ant?

The torch failed at last. He flung it away. The motion fanned its embers into spiraling red stars that vanished when it clattered down some distance away. He walked on.

The radium face of his watch told him that hours passed in this way. But could he believe it? Perhaps this place distorted time as much as distance. Perhaps he'd really been here just a few seconds, or had toiled through many years.

It was interesting, he reflected, to be in a situation where such fanciful thoughts were actually apropos. He had to admit, they provided a certain giddy exhilaration that partially compensated for the fear.

Ronar thought he'd seen blackness before, in the space between the stars. But here was a darkness more absolute than any he'd ever imagined. He thought back to mysterious moonless nights of his boyhood, when a favorite game had been to walk alone in the woods without a light, guided by nothing but a dim strip of sky between the branches overhead. Now that same strip of sky would seem to him like a blazing highway.

Ronar's other senses reached out, trying to compensate for the futility of vision. But they revealed little—only a faint musty odor, and the echoless beat of his footsteps. When he called out, the darkness blotted up the sound with oppressive finality.

Suddenly his foot caught on something that clattered away with a dry, brittle sound. He danced to keep his balance and managed to stay on his feet. His heart pounded in reaction to this unexpected break in his half-dazed, robot-like march.

He found a match in his pocket and struck it. The flare-up revealed a skeleton, now disarrayed, wrapped in a few scraps of Indian dress. Ronar thought he recognized the style as Apache, a tribe that had not walked the hills outside this place for fifty years.

In the brief light, he bent down and lifted the skull, regarding it solemnly.

"Hey, old warrior," he whispered. "Where did you think you were wandering? In the land beyond Death? As good a theory as any. Maybe you were surprised to find you could die there, too."

The match went out. Ronar set the skull down and resumed his course, wondering if he would be able to avoid joining the Indian in his rest.

At last he noticed a change. The floor was sloping upward, gradually steepening as he went on. After interminable hours of wandering, any change seemed promising. He proceeded directly up slope. Now at least he had a goal—he would climb until either he escaped, or dropped. Resolved on this, he charged ahead like some walking machine.

He needn't have worried about the floor flattening out again. By the time he'd climbed a thousand feet the way had gotten quite steep indeed. The slope seemed to increase by a few degrees with every hundred feet he went forward. His pack threatened to pull him over backwards. He had to lean well forward to balance it.

Stubborn as he was, he had to admit it was hard going. He'd already walked at least thirty miles since yesterday afternoon. Soon though there was no more question of continuing upward. The floor was pitched as steeply as the roof of a house. Ronar was in danger of slipping and falling blindly downhill. He would have to retreat.

Moving carefully, he began to crab-walk to the right, searching for a gentler slope on which to resume his ascent. But the tilt increased in that direction too. Forced onto hands and knees, he crawled back to the left.

With a sickening feeling of unreality, he realized the angle was now steeper to the left as well. It was nearly forty five degrees, a wall as much as a floor. He flattened out, fighting off the vertigo that threatened to rob him of all sense of orientation. He seemed to taste the metallic flavor of the slick bronze beneath him—after all, his face was pressed up tightly against it. Sprawled there, striving to master himself, he tried to think things through.

Gingerly, he began to creep downward, sticking as close to the bronze as he could.

It was worse than useless. The slope was steeper in every direction. Wherever he was at any given moment was the flattest part. He tried to envision a surface whose shape could account for that, but his mind only swam with topological absurdities.

Clinging as much by force of will as by the friction of his body, Ronar grew keenly aware of the capacity of the hard rubber toes of his boots to grip the metal, and how very near they were to letting go. Sweat soaked him, lubricating his arms and palms.

He shook with a hard, ironic laugh, though he knew it might send him sliding. How had he gotten into this unbelievable mess? Hiking out of idle curiosity, he'd wound up clinging like a fly to an incomprehensible wall lost in some insane extradimensional space.

He began to mutter to himself. "Students, leave your papers on the desk as you leave. I hope they're more carefully thought out than your last batch. A late paper means a reduction of one full letter grade. Bad math means failure."

He chuckled. He had to admit it—this situation made teaching undergraduates look pretty damn good.

He saw two alternatives. He could stay where he was until he could no longer maintain the muscular tension that held him against gravity. Or he could get it over with and let the bizarre topology of this place have its way with him.

"To hell with this." Seeing nothing to be gained by remaining, he decided to take his chances. Lifting his feet and palms, he skidded down into limitless night.

The Carrollesque logic of the place did not disappoint him. In seconds, he lost contact with the wall completely, and simply fell through space.

It didn't occur to him to scream or panic. He simply fell, and after a while it didn't seem so fearsome. He discovered he could control his speed, either diving like a falcon or spreading himself on the cushion of the wind to slow down. He must have long since reached terminal velocity, but he couldn't remember what that was for a human body—over a hundred miles per hour, he was sure. He'd been falling so long he was surprised the air pressure hadn't increased from the loss of altitude. But he noticed no difference. At least his ears weren't popping.

That was one minor mystery to add to the multitude.

There was no sign of the wall. No matter how Ronar reached, rolled, or twisted, he found only pitch-colored nothingness around him.

His fate had two possible extremes. He might make an abrupt landing in the next millisecond, or he might fall eternally. Between those was a whole range of possibilities. He doubted he'd end up in the center of the Earth, or anything as mundane as that. This miraculous structure must have been built for a purpose. If it turned out to be a mere pitfall for stray, wandering humans, he would be intensely disappointed in the essential rationality of the universe.

In the midst of these musings, Ronar became aware of a subtle change. The wind seemed a little louder, a little more turbulent. Something was nearby, deflecting his wind stream, reflecting its sound.

Ronar tentatively put out his hand. At first he found nothing, but then, reaching farther, his fingers encountered and were seared by a vertical surface racing by at high speed. He jerked back his hand and stuck his fingers in his mouth.

More prudently this time, he took a pencil from his pocket and touched its point to the smooth metal face that whispered by so swiftly.

The wall was coming back. Very gradually, it was angling away from the vertical. Ronar used the pencil to monitor its progress as it came ever nearer. Eventually he allowed it to come into contact with the seat of his pants.

He was very careful about this—on such a slide, at such a speed, if he so much as touched the bronze with his boot heels he'd go flying end over end.

The slope continued to decrease. Soon gravity was actually holding him to the surface rather than merely keeping him in its vicinity. The bronze was smooth, but his speed was great, resulting in friction that toasted the seat of his pants. He leaned back to let the pack take some of the punishment, and even dared to drag his heels a little.

The cosmic luge-run began to flatten out faster. Ronar shed so much speed that G-forces weighed him down, like a pilot coming out of a loop. He had momentum to spare. The slide began to seem as interminable as the fall. But the slope was now more like a floor than a wall. Finally, inexorably, almost grandly, he slid to a stop.

Ronar sat for a moment longer to collect himself. He felt shaky and light-headed when he stood up. Having just free-fallen a distance he could not guess, he decided to forgive himself the weakness. He started forward with an unsteady, lurching gait. The floor flattened out completely within a few hundred feet.

He halted and drew in a sharp breath. Far ahead, just at the limit of vision, glimmered a tiny, dim square of light. He stared at it warily, uneasily, not even thinking to raise the binocular to confirm what his naked eyes were promising.

Shaking his head to clear it, he stepped forward. Soon it was obvious that he had indeed found a way out. But he did not breathe easily as he approached the exit. He didn't know what to expect. In fact, he hardly dared to expect anything at all.

Thus he was not totally surprised to step forth and behold above him the strange constellations of an alien world.

Chapter 3

The Tower of Sha Totek

Ronar gaped at something which, to his knowledge, no other astronomer had ever encountered: a totally unknown sky full of stars.

But what might be more immediately present? Prudence eked out a victory over curiosity, and he carefully searched the horizon. The night seemed blacker than any he'd seen on Earth—he could make out little of his surroundings.

He stood upon an almost featureless plain. The soil, when he bent down to feel it, was dry and dusty in his fingers; the air was thin and cold, with a sun-baked desert smell lingering in its stillness.

Only a single landmark was visible: a straight-sided tower of some sort, black against the stars. He had no way to judge its distance, and thus its size too was a mystery. It might be half a mile away, or half a hundred; forty feet tall, or forty thousand. What was it? A smokestack, a silo—perhaps a telescope?

At first it was as dark and featureless as the Portal beside him. Then a line of scarlet fire darted along its top edge.

Ronar flung himself flat behind the Portal, half expecting to hear a bullet bite into the bronze.

Nothing happened.

Ronar peered out. The bright line still ran along the top of the tower, but now its color was a hot acid-green, throbbing and wavering with a life of its own. Through the big 10x60 binocular, the line resolved into tongues of light, apparently a row of windows. The color settled into a languid pinkish-purple-orange which gradually faded and vanished.

Though Ronar had no idea what these prismatic glows might mean, they presented no obvious threat. The question of who or what lived in that tower could wait for tomorrow. He raised his head to address himself to more exalted matters.

Ronar's first impression was of a sky not much different in character than that of Earth. Therefore, he gathered he wasn't near the core of a galaxy or in a globular star cluster. The brighter stars were reddish or golden in color, indicating they were generally older than the stars near Earth. That in itself was enough to put him thousands of light-years from home.

His eyes fell upon a spot of contrasting color, a fuzzy blue-green disk half the size of Earth's Moon, glowing at the end of a straggling line of stars. It was a planetary nebula, a shell of gas puffed off by a dying sun.

"If I were setting these stars into constellations," said Ronar softly, "that dim line would be the Serpent, with the nebula marking the eye."

Full of anticipation, he raised the binocular. The nebula was a lovely sight with its swimming pool colors. But scanning the wider heavens caused sharp disappointment. The glass revealed only a few stars that were not already visible to the unaided eye. Few suns faint and distant powdered the field, as they would have in any part of the sky of Earth. Here he found only an occasional spark flickering between the stars that made up the naked-eye constellations. Evidently, this was a lonely corner of space.

In fact, he could draw only one conclusion. He was somewhere among the sparse and ancient suns that wander between the major galaxies. Perhaps this was a thin cluster in the halo of old stars that surrounds many galaxies, or perhaps a dwarf galaxy. He shivered as he revised his estimate of the minimum distance to Earth to tens of thousands of light-years.

The chill intensified as he realized the implications of this. Raising the glass, he inspected the spaces between the stars with more care, and saw his prediction fulfilled.

The sky was sprinkled with tiny patches of light, round and elliptical and spindle-shaped, arrayed in loose lines and groups, in clusters and in arcs, alone and in multitudes, all across the sky. Here were galaxies, in such numbers as could never be matched by Earthly skies.

From Earth's vantage point, the plane of the Milky Way formed a "zone of avoidance" through which no external galaxies could be seen. The dust of the galactic plane was nearly opaque beyond a few thousand light-years, hiding not only other galaxies, but the core of the Milky Way itself. No man had ever seen the nucleus of his home Galaxy. It was better hidden than the center of the Earth.

But in this ancient, used-up family of stars, space was truly transparent, free of the clouds of gas and dust that left Galactic space murky by comparison.

As Ronar scanned, a mighty galaxy slid into his field of view, big as an ocean liner amid a flotilla of tugs. He lowered the binocular and found it easily visible to the unaided eye, much more easily than it was from Earth. For he recognized this galaxy—M31, in Andromeda, though of course here there was no Andromeda. Ronar thought for a moment, then turned a few degrees away, where he found the dim, blurred spiral of M33, another member of the so-called Local Group of galaxies. They looked much as they did from Earth, though brighter due to the absence of galactic dust.

The conclusion was straightforward. The Milky Way must be relatively nearby. That it was not visible could only mean it was presently beneath the horizon. But at some time, in some season, it must rise, and it would be very large.

Ronar was half dazed by the possibilities. This world was a magic platform which not only allowed an unhindered view of a universe of galaxies, but an opportunity to extract the secrets of the Milky Way itself by studying it from the outside. If the Galaxy was like a forest hidden by the trees, this world offered a fire tower's view.

It was obvious that he must find a way to erect a telescope here, wherever he was. It did not occur to him to wonder whether anyone else might already have done so.

The astronomer put down the binocular and shrugged off his pack. He kicked some of the biggest rocks away from a stretch of ground and unrolled his sleeping bag. His spent body lay down almost of its own volition.

His mind seethed with ideas and experiences so strange and concentrated that they felt like his whole previous life crammed into one day. He still hadn't come to terms with the fact that the soil beneath him was not that of his home planet. That realization would have to wait; there was no way he could sort out anything that big just now.

Though he was exhausted, his eyes stayed open. The motion of the stars was apparent within ten minutes; the rotation rate of this planet couldn't be too different from Earth's. He kept glancing eastward, hoping to witness the rising of the Milky Way. He'd seen no sign of it before his attention was captured by something else.

Overhead, a medium-bright star had shifted noticeably among the others. Grabbing the binocular, he saw a misshapen speck of dirty reddish-grey. Here was a tiny moon, at full phase and near the zenith, which told him he'd timed his arrival on this new world to coincide with the Witching Hour.

Ronar watched its slow, quiet course across the stars. He frowned. A perfectly innocent bit of rock it seemed, and yet he was aware of a growing unease. Something was strange about this moon. The hair on the nape of his neck was doing its best to bristle.

He blinked. This was disconcerting—why such an irrational reaction to an astronomical body? He lowered the glass, rubbed his eyes, and tried to sift through his feelings. The tower, which was nearby and rather ominous-looking, aroused no such sense of loathing. What was it about this little satellite—why did it seem to peer down at him with such a malign and inescapable gaze?

Puzzled, and in some doubt about his mental well being, he shook his head and sank into sleep.

The tiny moon eventually set. All night, the plain was peaceful, disturbed only by the breeze, with its smell of sun and dust, and by the occasional colored glows emitted by the stark monolith of the Tower.

Ronar's dreams sorted themselves into an impression of ruddy light that bathed his consciousness. He opened his eyes. Overhead was a sky of limitless violet with a few frosty clouds scrawled across it.

Poised on the horizon was a monstrous sun, a swollen brick-red globe dappled with crimson and vermilion and vague streaks of darkness. It was awesome, an overwhelming hovering presence, a thing of majesty. But though impressive, its total light appeared not quite equal to that provided by Earth's sun. Ronar wondered if he had come upon a world of perpetual twilight. Then he noticed a white glow on the horizon near the red giant. It brightened and spat out a second sun, fierce as burning magnesium next to the giant's subdued light. Tiny compared to its companion, the white star looked about half as big as the sun he was used to. The two together gave at least as much light.

They made a strange pair, he thought: one large and sullen, the other small and blistering. He could stare in fair comfort at the red sun, at least now when it was low in the sky; but not the white one, from which he averted his gaze. The red sun's edge was indefinite, so that in the full light of day it was a scarlet brightening in a purple sky. As it rose higher, it gained more of a golden cast, yet it remained very obviously a red giant star.

Turning from the great binary, Ronar surveyed his surroundings.

The plain was littered with Indian-red rocks and dotted with scrubby vegetation—ordinary mesquite and yucca by the look of it. Barely visible on the northern horizon were a few hills.

Nearby glinted the Portal, as inscrutable as the one he'd entered on Earth, if indeed they weren't actually the same object in some obscure sense. Its eastern opening easily drank up the morning suns-light and gave no clue as to the mysteries of its interior.

In the dust, spots of green contrasted against rust. Ronar bent down and found the malachite he'd tossed into the Portal the evening before. It was shattered, as though it had fallen from a great height.

Then there was the tower. Through the binocular, it looked much as it had last night: smooth-sided, black, flat-topped, and featureless, except for the row of windows and overhang at the top. The surface was glossy and a bit translucent, like a shaft of obsidian, taking the light of the two suns and wrapping it around itself like an electric liquid. It was surrounded by thick, tapered walls of red sandstone perhaps thirty feet tall, topped with spikes and set with an iron gate.

Ronar considered his options. To find out where he was, the logical thing would be to go to the tower and ask. Surely he'd been seen by now, if anyone up there was interested. The inhabitants, if any, had shown no sign of hostility.

He stood there staring at the tower, trying to gain a sense of it, reluctant to approach it. It seemed utterly peaceful against the clear indigo sky, and yet it did not appear to be abandoned. Rather, it gave Ronar the sense that it was a place he wanted to avoid.

Better, then, for Leonard Ronar to seek his own answers than to rely on the help of dubious strangers. Ascribing this decision to prudence and not mere perversity, he turned and strode away. If he had not been interrupted, the chances are good that he'd soon have walked right back into the Portal, despite all the tempting astronomical possibilities of this planet, and so passed back into obscurity.

As it was, he'd taken only a few steps when he felt a hand on his shoulder. He spun, his sheath knife appeared—but nothing, no one, was in sight. Yet somehow, a voice hung in the air.

"No, don't go a-wanderin' off. You showed up at a bad time, and I'm right busy, but I'll take the time to jaw with you. It's mah job. Mosey on over to the Tower."

Ronar's eyes glazed over slightly as he pondered these words, spoken with a thick cowpoke accent mixed with undertones of other tongues. He elected to ignore them, continuing on his course as though he'd heard nothing.

The voice returned a few moments later. "Now, pardner, I didn't mean to put you off or nothin'. Come on over and let's talk things over."

Ronar shot an irritated glance over his shoulder. Didn't this man, whoever he was, recognize the choice of a free man when he saw one?

"No, thanks," he said in a low voice. "I'll go my own way if you don't mind."

"We-e-e-ell, as it happens, I do mind just a little bit. I can't have some stubborn greenhorn wanderin' around mucking things up when trouble's a-brewin'. Why don't I just help you along a mite. I promise not to hold you up too long."

"No, damn it, don't interfere with me or I'll—"

Ronar never got to complete his threat. A hissing red haze descended over his consciousness. In a few seconds he was unable to see, speak or think.

When the veil lifted, Ronar found himself standing in a garden within the walls of the tower. The tower itself reared up near at hand, casting a long shadow.

Ronar drew a breath, and beheld his host through squinting eyes.

Shorter than Ronar, he was a tall man nevertheless, with skin brown as saddle leather, and straight black hair bound in a knot on the back of his neck. He had a sharp nose jutting from a lean, youthful face, and a small black beard beneath a wide, mobile mouth. Sweeping eyebrows shaded eyes that shone with a black diamond glitter. He wore a scarlet kilt ornamented with gold, while around his shoulders was a mantle of iridescent feathers. His head was topped with a slightly comical scarlet fez ringed with topaz cabochons.

Grinning broadly, he offered his hand. "Howdy, stranger. I've lately been called Xa Toltec, but folks hereabouts have shaved that down to Sha Totek, which is okay by me. What's your handle?"

"Leonard Ronar," responded the astronomer. He stared coldly at his captor.

"So, what are you a gawkin' at, owlhoot?" asked Sha Totek. "Well, I'm probably doing a little bit of gawkin' myself. I know I raised a ruckus about you bein' here a minute ago, but really I'm right glad to see you. Been quite a time since anyone new has come through that there Portal. I was beginnin' to wonder if she'd rotted away over on the Earth side."

"It's in a lonely area. I found it by accident."

"That's usually the case. Well, my immediate function is to provide you with information, to help you overcome the inevitable disorientation you feel at finding yourself here. I mean—it's up to me to try to straighten out yore head so you don't go to thinkin' you done gone loco. To get you off to a good start, now that you're here."

"I want to know why you have brought me here against my will, and how soon you intend to release me."

Sha Totek blinked. "Simmer down! I don't mean no harm; I got a job to do and I ain't failed at it yet, nor neglected it, no matter how bad-tempered or dusty or smelly my guests happen to be. I repeat my offer of information. You'll be on your way soon enough, though if you keep on in the direction you were going, you'll be walking a hundred miles or three before you get anywhere."

Ronar considered him steadily. "Very well. A question. When will I be able to see the Milky Way?"

Sha Totek looked at him with pursed lips. "Lessee. The Milky Way. I remember that—the *Via Lactea; Arionrod*, the Silver Wheel; the *Kyklos Galaktikos;* the starry band that crosses the sky of Earth. I ain't thought of that in a dog's age. Used to be called the Girdle of Nut in my day. Can't be seen from here, galoot. Don't you want to rethink that question? The first one is usually 'Where the hell am I?' Or possibly, 'Where can I get a drink?'"

"I think I know where I am, at least within a few thousand parsecs," said Ronar.

"Do you now?"

"But I don't know much else. I admit it. All right— Where the hell am I? And who are you?"

Sha Totek smiled with satisfaction. "You have found the one way to the splendid world of Colibdis, wandering saddle bum. Me, I do a little hocus pocus, myself—might call me sort of a medicine man, a magician, or mebbe a—"

"Wizard?"

"Sorcerer. Got more magic than a trapper has fleas."

"I see."

"Hmm, you don't look convinced. I'm afraid the details will have to wait. As I let on earlier, I've got a lot on my mind these days. Come on in, and I'll explain things to you as I can." He waved Ronar deeper into the garden court-yard.

Ronar followed warily, shaking his head at the confus-ing rapidity with which Sha Totek's desert-rat dialect came and went. They approached the entrance to the Tower, an arch of black pylons springing from the ground like the tip of some vast buried mass. There Ronar balked.

"I will not enter this structure. I don't know what circus you escaped from—don't even know what I'm doing here—but I don't intend to follow you into this overgrown thermos bottle just on your say-so. Open the gate and let me go."

Sha Totek turned aside and studied him with sympathy. "Somebody's been jerking your chain pretty hard, haven't they, son? Or maybe I've just forgotten how it can be for newcomers; it's been so long. Well, I can see when a man's mind is set. You don't want my help, you needn't have it. Only one rule: don't try to go back through the Portal."

The gate shuddered open. Ronar pivoted and marched toward it while Sha Totek stood looking after him.

At the brink, Ronar halted, looking at the endless stretch of unknown and featureless desert before him.

After a long moment, he turned and eyed Sha Totek long and carefully.

"All right. I'll trust you. For now."

Sha Totek grinned broadly. "All I can say is, that's mighty big of you."

They entered the Tower. Sha Totek sauntered along, while Ronar warily looked in every direction. A spiral stair-case led upward from the shadowy foyer, but Sha Totek did not approach it. Rather, he stepped over to a yard-wide cir-cular hole in the floor. In the ceiling above it was a similar opening. Ronar leaned over and saw more holes piercing many levels above and many levels below.

Sha Totek raised his hand. Ronar felt it tugging at him, as though it had become a compact and intense source of gravity. The sorcerer lifted off the floor, followed by Ronar. The pull of his hand drew them both swiftly up the shaft.

Ronar contemplated Sha Totek's bootstraps as he tried to keep his skepticism alive. He looked down past his dangling feet at the receding landings, counting twenty seven before they reached the top of the shaft. There they stepped into a circular chamber occupying the entire top floor. Ronar was mildly offended by the decadent splendor of the room and its furnishings, but when his eyes fell upon its occupants, he flushed and went tight-lipped.

The room was littered with couches, benches, and pillows of every color and texture, which were in turn littered with an assortment of outstandingly naked women. Their tresses were like cascades of liquid gemstones—rich amethyst, honey-gold topaz, shimmering emerald—flowing over supple shoulders of sky blue, rose, lavender, and misty green. Some were giggling, others demure; some were sultry, and a few were bound and helpless, but seemed not to mind. All stared at Ronar with eyes huge as pools of dark water.

"What's wrong with you now?" asked Sha Totek.

"I—uh—" stammered Ronar stupidly.

Sha Totek gave him a narrow glance and marched into the room. "Begone," he said curtly. The girls dissolved into sprays of prismatic sparkles which soaked into the rugs and cushions, leaving only a stray giggle behind.

Ronar stood gaping helplessly, barely hearing the resumption of Sha Totek's monologue.

"You see, that Bronze Portal is the only way to travel 'twixt here and Earth. I guard it to make sure no one uses it to make trouble. A certain magical rival of mine—I mean, an ornery desperado named Namirnakh—has been trying for a long time to get access to the Portal. If'n he does, he'll attack the mother world. He rules his own country, name of Darteharnlandua; I usually just call it Darteharn. Some of the hombres around here even call it Darntown for short. Maybe they just can't work their jaws around the real name. Anyway, Namirnakh wants to extend the rule of magic over the peoples of the Earth. Then he's got a hankerin' to return to Colibdis to take vengeance on all his ancient enemies. Me, for example. He's been fairly quiet over the past few centuries, but I always keep an eye on him anyway. Lately something big's been stirrin' up his way. His armies are moving, and black magic has been wafting up from his castle like the stink from a drowned cow."

By now, Ronar's toe was tapping in irritation. "Look, all this is hard enough to absorb as it is. It would be helpful if you'd decide on one speech pattern and stick with it."

Sha Totek looked surprised. "You mean I'm not speaking standard English? I'm sorry—you must be confusing the magic that helps me adapt to different languages. It's wavering between providing the English I first learned from the tinhorns and sodbusters who live hereabouts, and the more formal, concise version you seem to favor. It'll probably settle down after a while. Any more complaints?"

Ronar stood in silence, studying the absurdly costumed man in front of him. He was, he realized, shaking, his body reacting to the unreal events around him in a way his mind hadn't yet caught up with. So far he was functioning much as he would in a dream—taking everything for granted, accepting impossible events, not asking too many questions. For now, that seemed like the best policy. He would humor this man, pretend all this might actually be real.

"No complaints. A magical attack on the Earth? Will Namirnakh's magic protect him against a tactical nuclear weapon?"

"Against a what? You'll have to bring me up to date on the progress of the American civilization as soon as we get a chance. But believe me, Namirnakh's a threat to any society made up of human beings. Set loose on Earth, he could unleash a flood of magical horrors that'd drown all but the strongest minds like rats in a whirlpool. He can call upon forces that feed on human madness, forces so dire that— that—" He paused, his glance darting around uneasily. "Something's happening."

Ronar privately agreed, although his only evidence was an intensified feeling of oppression. He joined the suddenly anxious Sha Totek at a window. A lengthening horizontal line of violet light appeared near eye level just beyond the walls of the compound. Sha Totek gasped as though it were a knife that had entered his flesh. He raised his hands and braced himself as if to push it away, but staggered back, seemingly overpowered. The line grew longer, wrapping itself around the Tower.

Ronar realized he was seeing the intersection of a plane with an invisible sphere surrounding the Tower. He leaned out to watch its progress. When the arc reached 180°, he knew the plane was intersecting the Tower itself, apparently at the level of the floor they were standing on.

The pressure on Sha Totek suddenly ceased, but the sorcerer did not appear to be reassured. He stared wildly at the floor, trying to take it all in at once. He spat out a string of explosive curses in many languages.

Ronar followed Sha Totek's gaze. The floor seemed ordinary enough, tiled with black and gold like a big chessboard. True, the tiles had a remarkable richness to them — the black ones looked so deep and flawless you could almost fall into them.

Through some warning instinct, the two men stepped from black tiles onto gold.

Suddenly perspectives changed. The black tiles seemed to fall away into infinity. An illimitable void opened beyond the squares of gold.

Tentatively Ronar extended his boot toward the nothingness where a black square had been. His toe slid beneath the level of the floor and was gripped by an instant numbing cold. He yanked it back. A fierce tingling climbed to his knee.

In that void, galaxies began to bloom like drops of oil spreading over stagnant water. They were not healthy galaxies, but sick and twisted, a collection of dying, spidery shapes in impossible, meaningless colors.

Ronar looked up, ready to demand some explanation for this madness, but he remained silent. Something outrageous was happening behind Sha Totek, and the sorcerer was unaware.

Silently, smoothly, a great tentacle, a glassy column thicker than a man's thigh, rose up behind the sorcerer. It was armored with plates and knobs of metallic green-gold; within its vitreous depths pulsed a vein of blue fire. It was lovely, gemlike, and plainly outside the farthest corner of Ronar's experience.

He tried to cry out a warning, but all he could get out was a quiet remark that sounded as if it came from a stranger's throat.

"Look behind you."

Sha Totek whirled. More tentacles rose from the blackness like a forest of magic beanstalks. The sorcerer leaped away, dancing across the room on the gold tiles. Unable to pass through them, the tentacles had to withdraw and rise up again in a nearby black square in order to surround him.

Chanting frantically in some guttural language, the sorcerer hopped from gold to gold. The tentacles harried him without pause; several times he was forced to start his spell over when he lost his place or was startled into some exclamation. Finally he cried out in exasperation: "In my own house he strikes at me! I need time to deal with this, time!"

The tentacles seemed unaware of Ronar. He felt paralyzed, watching someone else's mad dream through the mask of someone else's face.

But then the tentacles managed to trap the elusive sorcerer. Ronar saw death reaching for a man who had done him no harm.

The bright dagger appeared in his hand. He leaped at one of the tentacles, lashing out, but the blade only glanced from its slick surface with a musical chime.

Cursing, Ronar sheathed the knife and tried to wrestle the tentacle. He gasped at the contact with its space-cold substance, but ignored the pain and hung on, desperate as a sailor clinging to the mast of a storm-tossed ship. It flicked him off with contemptuous ease, sending him crashing against a wall. His left arm and shoulder dropped into the blackness. Stunned by the pain, he could barely control himself enough to pull it clear. His skin was blotched where small blood vessels had ruptured.

Dazed, he lowered his face to within an inch of the blackness and looked into that warped cosmos. The tentacles receded into space, converging on a distant mass of filaments which twisted and twined about each other like the tresses of some bodiless Medusa. Still more tentacles were on the way, and the central nexus itself was steadily drawing nearer.

Ronar looked up. Sha Totek was almost lost in a grove of glass serpents. One wrapped itself around the sorcerer's leg, dragging him down into darkness.

His spell forgotten, the sorcerer tried to claw his way back to reality. Soon he was immersed in blackness up to his waist. He took a death grip on a gold tile; even the act of clinging for his life submerged his fingertips in the deadly void.

Surging to his feet, Ronar ran to a marble bench and bent to lift it. His eyes widened as it defied his efforts.

He heaved at the bench, straining until awareness of his surroundings faded away, and the single task of lifting that bench dominated his mind. It simply could not be that heavy! His fury and disbelief soared as he forced even more effort from his body. He lavished his will on the bench, insisting that it rise, demanding that his body not fail him.

With a screech, the bronze pins that held the bench to the floor sheared away and it fairly leaped into the air under Ronar's urging. He held it overhead and turned toward Sha Totek, whose forearms only now remained in sight.

Ronar's back and arms convulsed. He brought the bench down like a meteor, full upon one of the tentacles where it trailed over a gold tile. Bench and tile shattered as though they were made of plaster.

With a high, musical *ping*, the tentacle split open like a length of worn-out garden hose. A thick clear liquid jetted out, smoking with cold, coating everything within range.

The rest of the tentacles quivered to a halt and began to waver aimlessly. Ronar pushed through them. He knelt and plunged his hand into the abyss, gritting his teeth at the pain. He grabbed Sha Totek's arm, clutched it with all his might, hauled him out and stood him upright. The sorcerer stood quivering, purple-faced and breathless. He forced himself to gasp out the rest of his spell, now in English:

"Guardians blue and Lanterns Green,
Your radiant light is rarely seen,
on these far shores of a foreign space
which has never known your race.
Guardians old and Lanterns bright,
Masters of the verdant light,
Let me wield now your might,
In brightest day, in blackest night."

Emerald light burst from his upraised hand—light that leaped upon the tentacles like a sentient thing, filling their substance with green radiance.

Ronar, shielding his eyes, glanced down. The nexus of the tentacles had become a glaring green sun.

Sha Totek's lair was filled by crashing, sizzling green energy, as well as by the sorcerer's wild laughter.

The light-storm died away, leaving Ronar's vision obscured by a brilliant pink afterglow that didn't clear for minutes. His ears rang from the din.

When he could see again, the tentacles were gone, and the floor was an ordinary floor once again. Everything in that section of the chamber was glazed with the substance that had spewed from the damaged tentacle. It formed a hard puddle on the fractured floor tiles, encasing fragments of the broken bench as if in white amber.

Sha Totek, Ronar was bemused to note, seemed undamaged, despite his rough treatment by the tentacles. He turned away from the sorcerer and went to a window, where he stared out at the sunlit plain, rubbing his arm.

Sha Totek collapsed onto a couch, alternating between bursts of manic laughter and yelps of pain as he flaked bits of the hardened glassy fluid off his skin.

"By Anubis, that was a hell of a stunt you pulled," he choked out. "I would have told you that bench was pinned down if my vision hadn't been going black at the time. But pinned or no, you managed to uproot it in the flick of a fly's wing anyway—glad to see you Earth men ain't gettin' soft. If I hadn't used the All-Purpose Viridian to touch up the damage that critter did me, I might not be so cheerful now. Ouch! The worst damage I took was when you grabbed my arm. I could feel the bones mash together. What a spell that was! Thrown all the way from Darteharn, slipped right through my defenses. It was two-dimensional! An immaterial knife! And that thing he sicced on us. Namirnakh must have penetrated three or four levels of divergence to come up with a monstrosity like that. He took me by surprise; I don't expect sorcery of such sophistication from him; he usually sticks to brute-force wizardry. He must be gaining wisdom in his adolescence. He actually would have gotten me if not for you."

Ronar shot him a quick look of exasperation. Was this man's mouth a perpetual motion machine?

The sorcerer continued. "Namirnakh must be on his way. He wouldn't have expended so much effort for any other reason. I'd better be ready…"

His words trailed off as he looked up and realized that Ronar was gone.

The astronomer left the compound and walked swiftly to the Portal. He regarded it with wild eyes, debating whether to step within and so return, somehow, to Earth.

He was denied the choice. Just as he stirred, uncertain whether he meant to enter the Portal or turn away, a silvery bubble flickered into existence and solidified around it. He applied his hand and found the bubble cold and hard. It reflected its surroundings with perfect objectivity, including the Tower behind him and his own angry face.

He shot a searing glance over his shoulder and went on walking. In an hour, the Tower was only a black finger flickering on the horizon, while the Portal was quite invisible.

He abruptly halted and sank down against an outcrop of rock. He sat there for a long time, squinting up at the two suns, or just staring at the horizon. His eyes were hooded and shadowed, even in the glare of the Colibdian noon.

Not until the last colors drained from the sky, leaving the sparse constellations to shine overhead, did he rise again.

A night breeze entered the unglazed windows of the Tower of Sha Totek. The sorcerer, himself as variable as night and day, sat quietly entranced.

Before him was a low checkerboard table on which he'd arrayed a geometric pattern of topazes and emeralds. Sometimes, very slowly, very deliberately, he would change the position of a stone or two and intently study the new pattern. His face was relaxed; his eyes focused on the distance, not on the table.

Eventually he lay back with a sigh, resting his forearm across his eyes. He was motionless for some time, and when he raised his head at last, he saw Leonard Ronar sitting in the shadows across the room.

He nodded at the astronomer and began scooping the jewels back into their velvet sack.

"I haven't offered you refreshment," he said. "Rude of me. Would you like anything? Beer, wine—better than you'd find in the saloons up north. Or something to eat? It's been a long day for us both."

"I almost went home."

"I know. I almost let you. May I ask why you so badly want to leave? You could prosper here. I'm obliged to you, and that's the opposite of what I can say about most of the owlhoots who scrounge around on this planet. What's gnawing at you? I spotted it the moment I set you down in the garden. It's something different than the fear that hits most of the folk who come through the Portal. You're not afraid, you're—disappointed?"

"If you're a magician, you have no basis for understanding what I'm feeling."

"Why don't you tell me about it and let me try to puzzle it out," said the sorcerer with some irony.

Ronar sat still, then nodded in the darkness. "I'll try. My—preconceptions have been badly strained since I entered the Portal. I'm an astronomer—a student of the stars and planets. Before yesterday, I believed that after centuries of study, mankind was beginning to see the basic truths of the universe. Not yet clearly, but in shadowy outline, with hope of filling in the details through more hard work. I glimpsed the possibility of a synthesis of all physical knowledge, based on a few fundamentals like causality, thermodynamics, and relativity. Now I'm faced with phenomena having no place in a rational view of the universe. The Portal itself, whisking me across incredible distances without time or effort. This world of magic, where great forces are summoned with a few chants and gestures—forces outside the boundaries of anything I know. Your enemy opened a window to another universe as a weapon against you. What does my knowledge mean in the face of that? On Earth, we learned the nature of the galaxies only a few decades ago. We've just begun to send objects into space. Our knowledge of the planets is mostly speculation. I see no path in science which could have led to a knowledge of magic, as I now know it to exist. I ask myself if science shows only the superficialities of nature, rather than its deeper truth. If so, maybe I've been walking the wrong road. I've never had such doubts before. I don't care for them."

Sha Totek sat in silence for several moments before speaking.

"I'm durned if I kin make out nary a word of that load of buffalo chips, stranger..."

Ronar got up to leave.

"No, I'm sorry, I'll try to restrain myself. I think you're a little confused. You overestimate the scope of magic. As far as I know, in our universe it's found only on Colibdis. Magic can exist on Earth only by direct intervention from here. Don't ask me why; it baffled me when I first arrived and it baffles me still. I've never learned anything from the study of magic but more magic. Magic is a means of manipulating nature, of circumventing it, not understanding it. As a sorcerer, I know something about the Beings of Power who exist in this universe and others. I call upon their might without necessarily sharing their wisdom. I can summon light, cheat death, and do many things. But if I let a rock drop from my hand, I don't know why it falls. A spell might make it float up again, but what does that tell me about why it fell in the first place? Maybe your science has a better chance of figuring it out than my magic. Magic has its wisdom, and its own logic, but they aren't at the core of reality. Don't be so hard on yourself. At worst, your knowledge is complementary to mine." The sorcerer sat back and gestured easily. Small lights flickered over the table at Ronar's side, hardening into a goblet of red wine.

Sha Totek drank from his own glass and laughed. "You know, before you came along, the last bunch to come through the Portal was a bunch of illiterate Mexican army deserters, drunk as skunks and not grateful for my guidance. That was forty-some years ago. The contrast between you is striking."

Ronar said quietly, "When I first saw the Portal, it called to me, when I might have turned aside. Did that call come from you?"

"No, friend. I summon no one through the Portal, because whether to enter it that first time is the only decision I allow anyone to make about it. If you felt a call, it came from within yourself, or from some source unknown to either of us."

After that the sorcerer looked at him, suddenly pensive. "And now I must ask you a question."

Ronar shrugged. "Go ahead. This seems to be the night for them."

"You say you know the nature of the stars."

"That is true."

"Might you share this secret with me?" asked Sha Totek hopefully.

Ronar was taken aback. "Secret? It's no secret, and I'll share it gladly." He stood up, holding Sha Totek's gaze for a moment before making his pronouncement. "The stars are other suns, immense globes of hot gas blazing in the vastness of space, each perhaps with its own retinue of worlds." He looked down at Sha Totek, awaiting the impact this revelation would have on him.

The sorcerer looked at him blankly as if waiting for him to continue. Finally he said, "Is that all? Do they not give portents? Are they not instruments of higher powers? Have they no significance beyond their gross nature as balls of burning gas?"

Ronar scowled mightily. "As to that last, I cannot say. But now that I think of it, their true significance need not be limited by their physical nature. After all, you and I are sacs of water held together by various carbon compounds, yet I daresay there's more significance in us than is implied by that."

Sha Totek laughed delightedly. "Let's hope so."

Ronar went to a window and gazed out into the night, where golden stars glowed in strange patterns. "You know, I think we might learn a thing or two from each other."

"Could be."

"I'll go now. I've got things to think about, and I do my best thinking beneath the sky."

"Now that's convenient, because I was just about to ask you to leave. I must try to spy out Namirnakh and his doings, and I'm afraid the nearness of your mind would interfere with the far-seeing spells. The magic is delicate, and your thoughts would distort the image like ripples on a pool of water. But I don't want you to think badly of my hospitality—hold on and I'll bring something that may interest you."

The sorcerer dropped down the shaft, quickly returning with a small globe of blue crystal mounted in a framework of silver. Its engraved markings shone with their own faint light in the dimness of Sha Totek's lair.

"This is from Eranior, a nation lying to the north. It's their attempt to portray the constellations, with due consideration given to lesser cultures and their concepts. Nevertheless, it may show a slight bias to the Eranian ideas."

Ronar took the globe and examined it. It was labeled in an archaic, somewhat corrupt Celtic dialect using Greek characters. Ronar's Gaelic allowed him to puzzle out some of the names. The star-figures ranged from human beings through a colossal insect to—a pressure cooker.

"A mixed-up lot of constellations here," said Ronar.

"It's a pretty mixed-up planet, pardner."

"I could use some water and a few sticks of firewood."

"You'll find them in the garden. Come on back in the morning."

Ronar shouldered his pack.

"Say…" said Sha Totek, "you don't have any *chocolatl* in that there rucksack of yours, do you?"

"Chocolate? No, I'm afraid not."

The sorcerer looked downcast. "Dang. I used to drink that by the bucketful back in…well, in a distant land. Can't get it around here…and I never learned to conjure it."

"Where I come from," said Ronar, "any child with a few coins in his pocket can buy chocolate whenever he pleases."

Sha Totek goggled at him. "Now that is truly a land of wonders!"

Ronar departed. In the garden, he filled his canteen at a fountain bubbling in the scented night. Nearby was an incongruous-looking stack of firewood, which hadn't been there before. He helped himself and left the compound. The gate swung closed behind him.

Burdened with crystal and wood, he headed away from both Tower and Portal, not stopping to set up his camp until he'd put a mile of desert behind him. With a fire lit, he feared nothing in this silent land.

Food hadn't been uppermost in his mind these past two days, but now he ate a meal of canned beef stew, dry biscuits, and raisins, which seemed a feast. When he lifted the canteen, his parched body did not let him lower it until it was nearly drained.

Turning his back to the fire, he began to teach himself the celestial signposts of this strange new world.

The globe showed no single northern pole star. Here, two bright stars flanked the pole at equal distances. They were "The Lever of Heaven"; its two stars were Eranized and Dartezed. Ronar easily located the real Lever, as it was set in an otherwise star-poor area of the sky. Dartezed was red, while Eranized was one of the few whitish stars visible in this ancient cluster. By the Lever's height above the horizon, he estimated he was only about fifteen degrees north of the Colibdian equator.

The globe's ecliptic was marked "The Road of the Gods"; apparently the local zodiac constellations were named in their honor. The celestial equator was called "The Road of Evil", passing through ominous-sounding constellations such as "Glorphos, the Ice Worm," that straggling star-group he'd noticed the night before, with its eye marked by the planetary nebula.

On the other side of the globe, in the quadrant marked "Summer", Ronar found the Galaxy. It straddled the equator, a gauzy spiral sprawling over no less than thirty degrees of sky. It was labeled "Colibdis, the Whirlpool."

So—the world was named after the most prominent thing in its sky, which was itself named for Charybdis, the great maelstrom of Greek mythology which nearly claimed Odysseus in his wanderings.

The Whirlpool, it seemed, was now in conjunction with the suns. Ronar would have to wait for the seasons to turn before he could behold the distant Galaxy with his own eyes.

Despite the physical and emotional exhaustion of the long day behind him, he went on scanning the pristine skies of this new world. He found a measure of peace in the dance of suns in this ancient cluster, and a measure of grandeur in the dim snowfall of galaxies behind them. Anyone within earshot would have heard a rare sound escape his lips—a chuckle of simple delight.

His sweeps were halted by a stranger among the stars of the Ice Worm—the tiny moon he'd noticed last night. As it crept along the Road of Evil, he realized again that something about this orbiting bit of rock was very wrong. Its wrongness eluded the eye, but was unmistakable to the mind. It seemed somehow unnatural.

"Whatever you are," he muttered, "you pollute the beauty of the night."

Ronar then stiffened in shock. He'd addressed astronomical objects before, but never had one actually responded.

It said, in a voice that went no farther than the confines of his mind: *I have not seen you before, but you call attention to yourself.*

Ronar stood gaping like a mooncalf. He shuffled, worked his mouth. "Indeed. And who might you be?"

I have more names than could be spoken in a night. It is enough for you to know that I am the god of man.

That claim was enough to silence Ronar, though he felt no inclination to prostrate himself.

You are interesting. Join me and those who follow me. We will remake the universe in the image of our minds.

"If you are what you claim to be, then surely the universe is already made according to your mind."

The moonlet responded: *You are misguided. It does not matter. One day you will come to me of your own will. Now I have other concerns.*

Blackness unfolded from the tiny moon. Dark tendrils spread against the grey luminosity of the sky, a ragged cloud that unfurled until it blotted out the nearby stars and hid the moonlet itself. It hung there, brooding, pulsating, peering down at the world spread beneath it like a spider in the strands of its web.

Feeling its scrutiny, Ronar felt his blood congeal, but he did not turn away.

Eventually the cloud-web detached itself from the satellite. The solar winds seemed to catch it, wafting it slowly starward, while the tendrils lengthened and spread into space like the barbs of a parasite attaching itself to its host.

The cloud blended into the deeps of space; the sky appeared unchanged. But Ronar was far from reassured. He found himself on his feet, rigid with tension. With a cry of frustrated wrath he raised his fist.

The tiny moon looked blankly downward like a newly blinded eye, unimpressed.

Utterly drained, Ronar threw himself down and lay trembling, burning inside, watching the stars crawl across the sky and feeling their wrongness.

Although it seemed impossible, sleep claimed him at last.

From beyond the western horizon, a lance of colorless radiance hurled itself into the void and vanished. The rocks and pebbles on the plain cast no shadows in its transparent light.

Ronar slept on, unheeding.

In the Tower of Sha Totek, the spectral lights did not fade from the windows.

Awareness returned slowly. He found himself in his trailer at Kitt Peak, which did not surprise him. The moon peered through the window at him. The sky around it was glowing purple and gold. The clock on the shelf gave the time: midnight. That did surprise him.

He arose from bed and stepped outside. He stared at the sky, feeling both wonder and apprehension. The sky was alien. Great curtains of gold-lit cirrus flowed and shifted like auroral wraiths. The sky was dim but growing brighter. A corona of magenta light glowered on the northern horizon.

The moon wandered about the sky. Ronar no longer needed his imagination to picture the Man in the Moon; it now had a real face, chalky and ghastly. It followed him, slewing across the sky to look directly at him no matter where he turned. Its round eyes and open mouth were full of dread.

It seemed to Ronar that he'd heard of skies like these, but had seldom if ever seen them himself. The phenomenon filled him with awe. The whole staff of the Observatory, as well as other people whom he hadn't seen in years, were also standing around looking upward. He wanted to go talk to them, but walking seemed difficult, and his thoughts were confused. The people looked fearful, their mouths agape, much like that of the moon.

A shadowy figure stepped up to Ronar. It was tall, but otherwise hard to describe. Its hair was odd, fine and white as spun sugar, but translucent. Its eyes shone with a light soft yet powerful, not truly white, but transparently colorless, a radiance that could illuminate without itself being seen.

"You must begin a journey," said the figure. "You and the other, the sorcerer."

"Where are we to go?"

"Go to where the light arises."

Ronar turned to the North. The scarlet glow had intensified, and now the sun, or at least something very like it, rose and swiftly mounted into the sky.

"Go north? Where exactly?"

"Show me your compass."

Ronar displayed it. The needle pointed toward the risen sun. But then it began to waver, and soon was drifting aimlessly in a full circle.

"Go there, as quickly as footsteps will allow."

Ronar looked again at the nighttime sun. It had stopped moving, but looked much dimmer than the ordinary sun, as though it were unreal. The moon continued to look at him mournfully. Ronar was upset. He wanted to ask the strange figure a question, but it was gone, and his mouth wouldn't work anyway. He suddenly felt powerless and insignificant.

Waves of flaming yellow cloud swept across the sky.

Chapter 4

The Road North

Sha Totek's mood was black. His spying and spells had led to nothing, certainly not to an explanation of this awful event. Now he was reduced to staring out the window, trying to penetrate the darkness where the evil cloud had vanished hours before.

A sudden feeling of presence tingled on his back. He turned to see what had joined him in his eyrie.

It was a black and looming figure, eyes aglow with a colorless transparent radiance that lit its surroundings without revealing anything of itself.

Sha Totek's strength gave way and he sank to his knees.

"Go north," intoned the figure. "Leave this place. Let the needle be your guide."

"It will be as you say," said Sha Totek, averting his eyes.

When he dared look up again, the figure was still there, but its light had vanished and it seemed to have slumped. Sha Totek watched for what seemed like minutes, and then could hold his tongue no longer.

"Er—excuse me? Aren't you going to dematerialize or something?"

"What?" came the confused response.

The sorcerer peered more closely. "Ronar—?"

"What the hell am I doing here?"

Sha Totek got slowly to his feet and gave Ronar a long, haunted look. "Oh, my friend. I think it is no accident you are here after all. It isn't every visitor who is used as a messenger by the gods."

"What are you talking about?"

"You just delivered a portentous message, in a voice not your own."

"My dream..." Ronar described his vision to Sha Totek.

Sha Totek eyed him moodily. "Indeed. It seems you've had an encounter with— "

"You needn't go on. There are gods on this planet. I saw one of them last night. Or two perhaps, if you count that damned black cloud."

Sha Totek looked at him in surprise. "How do you know that?"

"I—know no other name for what I saw. I felt intelligence and purpose in it, and great power."

"Yes—you dreamed one god last night, and saw another, or at least his cloak. The very God of Magic, that last. Of subtlety, of thought. He's hard to pin down, hard to fit with a name from the past. He fills many roles. Since I met the Assyrians, I've called him Ahriman. He is real and manifest, and we dare not ignore him!"

"I don't intend to. What does this thing want?"

"I don't know. He is a thinker. A schemer. His goals are like Namirnakh's, only more grandiose. He wants to extend magic far beyond the limits of Colibdis—to impose it on the entire universe, not just the Earth. That way he imposes himself on the entire universe. Only one god has what it takes to oppose him—power and inclination. That one is Varanu. His titles are Lord of Cosmic Order and God of Universal Truth. It is he whom you saw in your dream."

Unease written on his hawk face, Sha Totek collapsed onto a plush purple divan. "Don't loom over me like that; sit down," he said irritably.

Ronar perched on the edge of a wooden stool.

"And tonight," said Sha Totek softly, "not only has the Sorcerer God fled to work some mischief, not only has Varanu set out in pursuit, but that selfsame being commands me to make a journey north."

"Commands us."

Sha Totek ignored that. "I don't understand that business about a compass and a needle."

Ronar pulled his compass from his pocket and held it out to the sorcerer. "This needle always points north, no matter how the compass is turned." He demonstrated by slowly turning in it place.

Sha Totek looked baffled. "This is not magic?"

"No. The needle is aligned to an invisible field of force, the magnetic field of this planet. By its behavior, I suspect the field of Colibdis is weaker than Earth's, but strong enough, it seems."

The sorcerer looked around as if searching for the invisible field. "And what about the wandering needle? Where might that lead us?"

Ronar considered. "The needle wavered when I was in the Portal."

Sha Totek stared at him.

"It could be that we're meant to enter the Portal," continued the astronomer.

"That would only bring us to Earth."

"My dream was set on Earth."

"Not surprising, considering you've lived there all your life."

"We could readily cross."

"You could, if I were to allow it. I could not. My magic would falter there. I doubt Varanu could profit by my dispersal into dust. Even if he can, he'll have to see to it personally; I'll not cooperate."

Ronar said, "All right. Then consider this. The compass doesn't point to true north, but to the north magnetic pole. The two need not be identical. A compass is useless near the magnetic pole, as magnetic north is indefinite when you're right on top of it. That would make the needle wander."

"So we're directed to seek this 'magnetic pole'."

"It seems the best interpretation."

"Which would be near the true North Pole."

"Probably."

Sha Totek flung himself back. "By all the gods! Better a plague of spinsters than to make such a journey."

Ronar raised his eyebrows.

"Oh, come on!" said Sha Totek, seeing the question. "Think of the implications! A journey all the way to the North Pole? It's winter up there, and it'll be winter for a long time to come. The seasons last longer here than they do on Earth. And there are thousands of miles of dangerous country just to get to the edge of the Arctic! It's insane. We don't even know why we're supposed to go."

"Would this Varanu want to send us if it were impossible, or pointless?"

"Why not? I doubt that Varanu cares much for our well being. Is he concerned with good or evil? No. Order is his concern. The fates of men may seem fit to him only as they contribute to that order."

Ronar sat gazing into the distance. His usual sharpness was in abeyance, his dream vision still strong in his mind.

Sha Totek went on. "Besides. It's totally unthinkable that I should leave the Tower for any length of time. Who would defend the Portal?"

Ronar's vision focused. "Why does it need defending?"

"It always needs defending from Namirnakh. Especially right after he's made a serious effort to kill me."

"You're sure that was Namirnakh's doing? Why not Ahriman's?"

Sha Totek shuddered. "If Ahriman had tried to kill me, he would have succeeded, no matter how much furniture you might have thrown. We are beneath him."

"So you say. All right then, if you must make this trip, but the Portal must still be guarded, is there no one else who could do that?"

The sorcerer laughed. "Better for me to put a sword of fire in Namirnakh's hand than to admit some rival magician to my Tower. There are none I could trust, and very few fit to defy Namirnakh, in any case."

"Then you can't go."

Sha Totek's eyes bulged. "Are you mad? Never before have I been commanded by Varanu. Never before has he taken any notice of me, to my knowledge. I cannot defy him! I must go. I'll protect the Portal as best I can with spells of defense, deflection, and misdirection. I'll enlist magical creatures to range over the Red Plain. And if Namirnakh overruns it anyway? Maybe a final war between science and magic is the destiny of man." He shook his head. "But we must go."

Ronar shook his head also. "You must go, maybe. I want no part of this lunacy."

Sha Totek looked sidelong at the tall astronomer. "I had a hunch you'd be loco enough to say something like that. But what makes you think you have a choice? The god has commanded it."

Ronar bristled. "I always have a choice. I'm not in the habit of letting spooky figures in my dreams tell me what to do. No god yet has commanded me to do anything, and I'm not about to start with this one."

Sha Totek blinked, taken aback, studying Ronar as though debating how to handle a wayward, worrisome child.

"Don't you want to help the people of your planet and this one...?" he asked tentatively.

Ronar writhed on his stool. Blast it...what could he say to that? Suddenly he felt merely petulant. "Help with what? This storybook scenario you've described so vaguely? How can I help with that? The only thing about this planet that makes any sense to me is the sky overhead. The rest of it you can keep."

Sha Totek fidgeted, obviously weighing his words. "Well. You like our sky, do you? Do you think you'll like it as much if Ahriman stays out there, doing whatever it is he's doing?"

"No," said Ronar sullenly.

"Then you might as well come along with me. It's not like you've got anything better to do. I mean, you're stuck here, pardner. You ain't goin' back where you came from, and if I read you right, you don't really want to anyway. Just come along. If I can put up with you, you can put up with me. Maybe you don't feel up to it, but you'll find a way to make yourself useful. And if you can't, I'll just shake you off my boot heel somewhere along the way."

"What? You'd be a fool to refuse me. Of course I can help you. I'm intelligent, strong, and determined."

Sha Totek laughed. "Well, that's more like it. We ain't known each other none too long, but I'm inclined to agree with your self-assessment. And I applaud your lack of false modesty, which only holds us back, and forces others to waste time and effort discovering how grand we are on their own."

Ronar sighed. "If only you'd settle on one version of the English language."

"It's been a very long night. I must leave in the morning. Are you coming along, or not?"

Ronar considered. His senseless cantankerousness had gotten him into an awkward position. What, really, was his alternative? To put a knife to this man's throat and try to force him to open the Portal? Why should he struggle to get back to a place he'd been happy enough to leave a day or so before? Or should he just hang around in this desert, wandering in aimless ignorance?

Feeling foolish, he said, "I'll come."

Sha Totek nodded in satisfaction. "All rightey then. I suggest you try to salvage a few winks from all this turmoil."

Ronar was glad to comply. In the courtyard he found his rope hanging from the wall. Apparently Varanu had compelled him to scale the wall to deliver his message. Ronar felt a surge of resentment at the manipulation. He did not care to be used as a puppet by any so-called god, whether of darkness or of light.

His campsite looked peaceful enough. Yet as he lay down, the quiet sky and all the world seemed to seethe with weird, unseen forces and silent whispers. Sleep was long in coming, and real peace was unattainable.

Morning found Ronar back in the Tower, ready to depart, oddly eager to set out. Sha Totek took note of his revised attitude.

"Ronar, I'm puzzled. You've been about as trusting as a treed cougar ever since you got here. Why are you now so fired up to go gallivanting across the planet just on the say-so of your dream?"

Ronar hated being called out on inconsistent behavior. His adventurous mood soured somewhat. "It was my dream. I can't help but feel that the message came partially from my own mind. Besides, if Varanu is as you describe him, I must support him, at least in preference to Ahriman. Ahriman has already made himself my enemy by seeking to subvert the heavens. I'll see him destroyed, if I can."

Sha Totek looked amused. "Hmmm. How will you be armed in your opposition to the Sorcerer God?"

"Lightly, I'm afraid," said Ronar, oblivious to the irony in Sha Totek's question. "I only have this." He brandished his sheath knife.

Sha Totek appraised it rapidly. "This is a fine weapon, and valuable. Iron is rare on Colibdis. But you'll also need something heavier than this dagger. You packin' a six-shooter in your rucksack?"

"Actually, no."

"Really? Well, have you ever handled a sword?"

"A sword? Hardly. I'm a scientist, not a butcher."

"Good for you, but butcher or no, you ought to carry a heavy blade, if only for appearance's sake. You'll find it'll help folks take you a heap more seriously, although with your size and that buzzard face you might not have much problem there. Come with me, let's see what we can scrounge up for you."

He lowered Ronar and himself down the shaft from his eyrie. Ronar found the experience more jarring than he had the first time, now that his mind had had a chance to clear a bit. He bruised his thoughts trying to imagine what force Sha Totek could possibly be manifesting to levitate their bodies like that.

They arrived at a level lit by ceiling-mounted globes full of shifting luminescence. Beyond a doorway glittered what might have been a field of metallic wheat.

Ronar ducked inside the room, following Sha Totek. The globes brightened, revealing the blades and hilts of hundreds of weapons, each standing upright with its point embedded in the soft wooden floor.

"I'm something of a collector, and I never know when I might want to equip a small army," said Sha Totek. "Now, for you I recommend an Eranian great sword. You're certainly big enough to handle one, and you don't need too much skill to use one to reasonable effect. It's simply a matter of bludgeoning and hacking your opponent into the ground. You work on the assumption he's not big enough to hit you back as hard. In your case, I think the assumption is justified. How do you like this one?"

Ronar eyed it critically. "Bronze?"

"Well, I do have steel weapons, but I warn you, they can be more trouble than they're worth. A steel sword is the blade of a king. You're more likely to use it to defend it from thieves than to defend yourself."

"I'll risk it. If I must burden myself with a bar of metal it might as well be the best metal I can get. How about that one? It might suit me."

He indicated a sword that stood out even among its splendid neighbors. More than a yard long, the blade shone white as a moonbeam next to the bronze-brown blades around it. The handle, long enough for two-handed use, was wrapped with gold wire. The gilded pommel bore great emeralds, while the guard, which curved gracefully as the outstretched wings of a sea bird, carried a pair of garnets.

Sha Totek was taken aback. "That one?" He considered for a moment. "Sure, why not? It might be the perfect choice. But take good care of it—its value goes beyond that of the steel in its blade."

Ronar yanked it out of the floor and studied it. He had never before held a sword, or even seen one outside of a museum. He had expected something essentially like a big steak knife. Yet this object had a character unlike any mere piece of cutlery. The blade shimmered with a superb satiny finish. It had a magnificent edge.

"It seems—unusually fine," said Ronar.

"It is that."

Ronar wove its keen edge through the air. "It's lighter than I expected. A bit lavish with the gems, though, isn't it?"

"It would be a travesty to put a nondescript hilt on a sword like that."

Sha Totek fitted Ronar with an unprepossessing scabbard of worn leather to disguise the splendor of the blade. Ronar buckled it on and sheathed the sword, feeling self-conscious as it dangled awkwardly at his side. He was carrying a sword. He might be expected to use it. It was almost absurd enough for him to laugh.

"You're going to trip if you wear it like that. I suggest you sling it across your back," said Sha Totek patiently.

Ronar made the adjustment.

"Being as how you're so civilized, I don't suppose you've ever used a bow."

"Actually, I was quite a proficient archer at one time. It was an interest of my father's that we shared."

"Excellent."

They floated down to another storage level, this one packed with miscellaneous weapons: axes, flails, atlatls, lances, spears, tridents, and archery gear.

Sha Totek chose a heavy bow of bronze-bound yew while Ronar selected arrows from nearby bins. He took long black shafts with points of flaked white quartz. For all he knew, the bronze points might be superior, but he liked the look of the quartz, and Sha Totek made no objection.

The sorcerer cocked his head as though listening to a distant voice. "That's enough hardware. Let's get outside. Our mounts are almost here."

"Mounts? Aren't we supposed to walk?"

Sha Totek chuckled. "Your dream said to go as fast as feet could carry us. It didn't say whose feet."

They stood before the gate and watched a cloud of dust churning in the southeast. Within it, Ronar's binocular revealed a mounted man leading two tethered animals. They galloped through the shimmering heat with an odd, rocking gait.

"I contacted some amigos of mine right after you left last night, asking them to bring me these cayuses," said Sha Totek.

When the small train pounded to a halt in front of them, Sha Totek presented the lone rider to Ronar. "Meet Kosheeta, prince of the Eanda tribe. They live a couple hundred miles south—he rode like hell to get here so quick."

As Sha Totek introduced Ronar in Kosheeta's language, Ronar's attention was drawn irresistibly to the mounts. They were not horses.

They were reptilian, tawny-hided beasts, each at least as heavy as the largest draft horse, but built like a cross between a centaur and a Tyrannosaurus. Each had three pairs of limbs: four legs, long and fleet-looking, with splayed three-toed hoofed feet; and much lighter forelimbs, mounted high on the chest, each equipped with two great scimitar-like talons. When one of the beasts reared up on its hind legs to sniff noisily at the air, it stood nearly twice Ronar's height. Its huge, pointed ears swiveled toward him. Its blunt snout bristled with serrated teeth.

Kosheeta dismounted. The beasts seemed unruly; he had some trouble keeping them under control. Ronar backed off cautiously.

Said Sha Totek: "These are nehocks. They don't do well in cooler climates, but in this dry heat their speed and endurance is unbeatable. We'll ride 'em until we hit the first settlements up north."

Kosheeta spoke a few words in his liquid tongue. Ronar, really noticing him for the first time, found him very tall, thin, but well built. Among his weapons was a kind of method made of two vicious nehock claws bonded to an ivory handle.

The warrior addressed Sha Totek with deference but without fear.

"Kosheeta reminds me that the critters need to be conditioned if they're to accept us as their new masters. Follow my instructions and example. That big one with the grey leather saddle will be yours. Be careful; they're suspicious of strangers."

With that, the sorcerer slowly approached his nehock, looking it directly in the eye and keeping his hands extended, palms out.

Ronar moved toward his own beast in the same manner. In response, it released a cry like the whistle of a locomotive falling off a cliff.

"Careful!" hissed Sha Totek. Kosheeta stood back nervously.

Ronar continued forward, keeping his eyes locked on the fierce golden orbs of the nehock. It pawed and reared, its deadly forelimbs cocked and ready to strike, its ears laid flat against its head.

Ronar grew irritated. He'd never even liked horseback riding, and he could tell he was going to like dealing with these arrogant, recalcitrant monstrosities even less. What must it take to train such powerful carnivores to the saddle in the first place?

Sha Totek came as close to his nehock as he dared. "All right," he said tensely, "raise your hand, slowly, to his nose. Let him get a good whiff of you. Keep your hand limp."

Ronar complied. The nehock lowered its saurian head, drew in a few quick blasts of air, then expelled them in a thick charnel-smelling cloud.

Ronar choked and withdrew his hand. The nehock curled its lips and snapped its jaws shut a millimeter short of Ronar's fingertips. The astronomer's eyes blazed.

"Now, you've got to show him who's boss. Give him a wallop on the side of the head." Sha Totek gave his creature a mild backhanded slap.

"Anything you say," said Ronar, dealing his nehock such a buffet that it fell back clumsily, shaking its head.

Ronar rubbed his bleeding knuckles and eyed the rattled beast with disdain.

Kosheeta laughed uproariously and managed to get out a few words.

"He says: 'This milk-faced scowling one must be more gentle—nehocks are rare in this country and hard to replace'," said Sha Totek with a grin.

The nehock trotted up to Ronar with a new semblance of servility. Kosheeta was now careful to keep his distance from the animals.

Sha Totek said, "Nehocks are strictly one-man animals, unpredictable around others, even former masters. In fact, their former owners are often the most endangered, as if the beasts are contemptuous of anyone who would give up their reins. Or maybe they finally feel free to take revenge for old irritations."

"Do these things have names, or may I indulge my imagination?" asked Ronar.

Sha Totek put the question to Kosheeta. "Looks like these critters are numbered—oh, I get it—they're called by the number of warriors killed in their capture, followed by the totemic color of the highest-ranking man killed. Mine is called Two-Scarlet, while yours is Four-Ashen Grey. A formidable beast, that one."

Kosheeta also gave them gifts of food: a basket full of strips of dried meat, and a skin bag containing a stew of boiled grain, meat, congealed grease, and blood.

In return, Sha Totek gave him a box of carved ebony holding a collection of oddments: feathers, colored stones, figurines, and a tiny mirror. Kosheeta accepted this gingerly but gratefully, bowed to the sorcerer, and departed.

"The Eanda witchdoctors will use those magic gimcracks to help repel slaving raids from Ammon," remarked Sha Totek as they watched Kosheeta pass into the distance. He sighed. "I wish 'em luck."

The suns were standing down in a coppery afternoon sky by the time they were ready to set out. They draped the nehocks with saddlebags bulging with magical artifacts which Sha Totek claimed were necessary to give their unknown mission any chance of success. The rest of the cargo consisted of food, water, weapons, and camping gear. Ronar relied on the proven equipment in his backpack, which he lashed to the flank of Four-Ashen Grey, along with the sword and bow.

The prospect of exploring this unknown world held a dreamlike fascination. He was impatient to set out.

Less so was Sha Totek, who appeared reluctant to declare the preparations complete and climb into the saddle. He returned to the Tower, insisting on taking the time for "a last civilized meal", and then dithered still longer in a lengthy ritual of grooming and toiletry.

Ronar used the time to scrape three day's growth of grey spines from his own cheeks. He bathed in the scented fountain in the garden, then checked the lenses of the binocular for blemishes.

Still Sha Totek's procrastination continued, until Ronar was forced to find him and make a few pointed remarks.

With a melancholy sigh, Sha Totek performed a final reinforcement of his Portal-guarding magic, causing shimmers of unseen forces to ring both the Portal and the Tower itself.

Finally satisfied, Sha Totek wafted down to the garden court and out the gate, where they mounted the nehocks. The gate clanged shut behind them.

Sha Totek looked over his shoulder and said dreamily, "I've lived and prospered in that Tower for a span longer than the life of most civilizations. In all that time, I've seldom ventured outside the walls, though my vigilance has looked into many remote and secret corners of the world. Now as we set out on this journey, I feel the imminence of change. I wonder how much longer the shadow of Sha Totek's Tower will stretch across the world. I wonder how many more summers I'll be privileged to watch from my high windows. You know, wherever I happen to be, no matter how dull things there may seem, when the time comes to leave, I am always sorry to go."

Ronar, unsure how to react to this, said nothing.

An hour passed. Miles stretched behind them. The suns rested on the horizon.

The nehocks carried them swiftly across the plain, toward the Red Hills that bulked up in the distance. That distance was less than Ronar had believed—the horizon was close, indicating a planet a good bit smaller than Earth.

The gravity too was plainly less than Earth's. The nehocks bounded along more effortlessly than was otherwise plausible, and he'd been here too long to attribute the ease of his own movements to adrenaline alone.

As the suns set, the hills darkened from rust to a deep maroon, then faded to an undulating silhouette against a sky of luminous violet.

Ronar looked to the west. Suspended in the peach-colored sunset glow was a hairline crescent of silver. He pointed it out to Sha Totek.

"That's Sinanna, the bigger moon of Colibdis. The smaller, of course, is the Eye of Ahriman, which you've seen already."

Ronar studied the moon, wishing the nehocks were steady enough to allow him to use his binocular. It covered a full degree of sky, twice the apparent size of Earth's moon.

He turned to Sha Totek. "What's the relationship between Ahriman and his moon?"

Sha Totek shrugged. "He seems to live there, though why a god should need to hang his hat in any particular place is beyond me. The other Great Gods inhabit a spectacular structure, a kind of colossal shining saucer with a huge jeweled tower in its center. It lies far out to sea. Few have actually seen it. Some of the Islanders, with their seafaring canoes, have. They call it Larlaninulius, the 'Mirror of the Gods', and they call the gods themselves the Larlaninules, or 'the Mirrored Ones.'"

Ronar pondered this and asked, "Are you familiar with Christianity?"

"More or less. That there's a jealous god. I'd hate to mess with him."

"I doubt that these Larlaninules would satisfy the Christian definition of Godhood. They seem—too localized, and too specialized. In the Christian sense, a proper God ought to be omnipresent, and universal."

"Hmm. There aren't many on this world who would quibble about whether the Larlaninules are gods or not.

Limited they may be, but their limits are of a different order than ours."

Suddenly anxious to make the best possible time, Sha Totek kept the nehocks bounding along well into the darkness, even as they became increasingly difficult to control. Finally he was forced to call a halt. As soon as they were stripped of tack and baggage the nehocks raced off into the night, keening and wailing like fire sirens.

"That's part of the beauty of these critters," said Sha Totek. "No need to carry food for them, even in the desert. Just set 'em loose come sundown and they hunt for themselves. But if you ever meet another man's nehock in the dark, you'd better hope he gives you a chance to swat him on the nose before he makes you his dinner. And if he's wild, better look for a tall, strong tree. Or a potent spell."

"I'll be glad to be rid of the beasts," said Ronar.

The starlight was only slightly diminished when Ronar lit a fire of mesquite. He was bemused to find such a familiar plant in the soil of an alien world. A few seeds stuck to someone's boot as he came through the Portal would do it, he supposed. So far he hadn't seen any clearly alien plants to offer local competition.

They heated and ate the most perishable items in their larder, including Kosheeta's stew. Ronar found it innocuous, but Sha Totek reacted to each lump of unidentifiable meat with a prolonged sigh. In contrast, Ronar picked the grasshoppers out of his dish, while the sorcerer crunched his with pleasure.

Afterwards, Sha Totek managed to cheer himself with a flask from one of his indispensable saddlebags. He tipped it over two thimble-sized glasses and waited for the contents to ooze out in a sluggish stream that gleamed tarry-brown in the firelight.

Ronar sampled the cordial, which he deemed an unfortunate marriage of alcohol and pancake syrup. He put it aside, although he was grateful for the improvement it produced in Sha Totek's disposition.

Still, the sorcerer's melancholy was not fully dispelled.

"Ah—what a time I could be having if circumstances hadn't driven me from my sweet Tower. I could burn sticks of Yama in the braziers, and gaze into the beguiling Mists of Morluminar. Ectoplasmic females I could conjure: pliable, parti-colored creatures of real charm. And when at last I chose to sleep, perhaps I could summon even the Dreamfarer herself. Ah, Ronar, my friend. I have learned much during my long ages."

Ronar was only half listening to this wistful monologue. The major part of his mind was among the stars.

The firelight danced in the yellow gems on the sorcerer's fez, but his black eyes absorbed it totally as he gazed with an inner vision back across the millennia. Ronar thought he might have gone into a trance, but then he resumed speaking in a soft, distant voice.

"I am a man of Khemet, an Egyptian, as you would call me. I was vizier to Zoser, an early Pharaoh of the united Two Lands. I served him as architect, engineer, physician, scribe, priest, and sorcerer. To succeed as a magician on a world without magic you need a fast hand and a quick mind, believe me.

"One day, soldiers came before us and said they'd found a great marvel in the desert, over the cliffs and far from the Nile, where few men ever traveled. It could only be a work of the gods, they said, because it pained them even to look at it directly. It was beyond their power to make sense of it. It terrified them. Zoser sent me back with the soldiers to investigate, and to propitiate whatever gods were involved.

"I went expecting to find ruins left behind by some forgotten dynasty, but instead set eyes on the first of the Bronze Portals. It was already ancient, worn by the sands, but the desert of Khemet was so well suited to preserving the bronze structure that it stood for many centuries more.

"The Portal made a fearsome impression on me, but I could hardly afford to admit that to my men. I led them inside. When we became lost, it was only through my determination to maintain my authority that we found our way through the darkness. On the other side was a desert as unrelenting as the one we'd left behind, but it wasn't the same. Two suns burned in a purple sky. We felt strangely light on our feet. We were watched by hawklike birds that had arms like those of a man—living images of Horus himself. My men were convinced we'd died and gone on to the Land of Silence, and I half believed it myself.

"That night we trembled to see the very stars of Nut set in patterns no man had seen before, while the Whirlpool hovered above us like a spectre. We lit torches to drive back the darkness. A feeling of primordial chaos hung in the night air, as though great unformed forces were all around us, unseen but terribly present, hemming us in.

"Then a scorpion-like thing came into the camp, attracted by the torch light. It stung one of the men, who quickly died, as much from terror as from the creature's venom. It was obvious we were not all dead after all, for dead men in the afterlife don't die again. Dutifully, I began the chant to invoke Anubis, that he might weigh the man's soul and conduct it to be one with Osiris. There would be no embalming for this man, no grave goods, but it was the best I could do.

"When I looked up, the men were transfixed, staring glassy-eyed over my shoulder. I sensed an icy presence behind me. I gathered my faltering courage and turned my head. Looming in the shadows was a tall black figure, manlike, but with a jackal-head as fathomless as a midnight pool. Its eyes were long and narrow—my spine froze as they rotated in their sockets, examining us one by one. I was the most stupefied man in that circle as Anubis entered it and plucked the soul from the dead man. The god produced the scale and the feather. The soldier must have been a blameless man, for the feather was the heavier of the two. Anubis carried it delicately out of the firelight into the blackness surrounding us.

"When the god was gone we were left quaking and incoherent. After a while a man began praying to Ra and Thoth, and we all eagerly joined in. My own cynicism was shattered. We were all comforted by our devotion. It was as if the gods came to watch over us even as we spoke the words.

"In the morning we found the courage to cross back to Khemet. My reputation there was greatly enhanced when people learned I'd summoned Anubis, and I was almost deified myself. But when I told Zoser about the world of the Portal, his imagination failed him. He saw it only as a convenient place of exile for prisoners, lepers, and criminals, and it was used that way for years.

"I grew old, and more and more curious about the fate of all those undesirables who had been so painlessly disposed of. As my death approached, I went to the Portal, where my authority got me past the garrison that kept the exiles from returning. Then the disk of Ra shone on my back for the last time. I have never stepped on the soil of my mother world since that day.

"On the other side, I was pleased and surprised to find that the castoffs had prospered far beyond my expectations. They'd discovered a river valley much like that of the Nile, and had founded a nation, called Ammon. The people were vigorous and energetic. The diseased among them had been able to cure themselves with the simple charms that had been so useless on Earth.

"As for myself, I was delighted to discover that all my magic worked as well, and even then, it was considerable. All that mumbo-jumbo, all those spells that I used to befuddle and overawe the people of Khemet, all of it actually worked as intended, as long as I approached it consistently. With the extensive Egyptian canon of spells for life-preservation, I restored my youth, and later, as I grew more skilled, gained immortality. You won't believe it, but before that I was—small. Hell, I was a runt. But my magic enabled me to make of myself the bronzed demigod you now see before you.

"I promptly founded my own Pharaonic dynasty, and ruled Ammon for many years. I was a great sorcerer king. I designed and commissioned monuments unequaled by any in Khemet. Most still stand.

"The stream of emigrants from Khemet slowed as later Pharaohs recruited everyone in sight to work on the pyramids of the Fourth Dynasty. The very existence of the Earth Portal was forgotten. Only a trickle of wanderers and pilgrims stumbled upon it.

"Ammon grew fat with grain, and jewels. Life was a long afternoon of ease, languor, and magic. There were no other men to war upon. The gods were real and generally benevolent. The dangerous creatures native to the area were subdued.

"I eventually grew tired of rule—tired and disturbed by a mood growing among the people. They remembered that they or their fathers had been cast out of Khemet as pariahs. Now they had become a mighty nation, and they had magic. Some of the bitterest among them dreamed of pouring armies through the Portal to overwhelm the peoples of Earth.

"But I had known and loved both worlds for what they were. I placed my crown on the brow of my successor, went to the Portal, and built the Tower, where with my magic I enforced my current policy—that anyone may come through, but no one may go back. The would-be aggressors were frustrated. Over time, as the earliest generations died away, their dream of vengeance was quieted. Today only the scribes of Ammon know of Khemet, and even they scarcely believe in its reality.

"The Ammon Portal stood for no less than fifteen centuries of Earth. But the winds and sands took their toll at last. One day, what had been a black gate through the walls of space was only a meaningless, crumbling framework of bronze. For a while I thought we'd been cut off from our native world forever. But then I detected another Portal, operating on the Arctic continent later to be known as Hyperborea. I moved my entire Tower there by main force of magic, watching over the new Portal until it too wore away. Then another Portal came into being, and then another, until I had shepherded all the races of Colibdis to their respective lands: the Achaeans, and the Minoans; the Britons, the Jivaro, the Norsemen, and all the rest.

"In every case, I added the magic of the newcomers to my collection, with my own inventions and formulations tossed in. I synthesized the mass into a style of sorcery that is uniquely mine: elegant, clean, efficient, and severe. I have polished the roughness from a great chaotic body of lore and superstition. I have refined from it a power of streamlined logic, of clarity and ruthless internal consistency. I leave to the shamans and witchdoctors the arbitrary traditional spells, which in reality are as likely to strike the wielder as the victim."

Sha Totek mulled in silence for a while. His eyes were locked on a vista of time and experience which Ronar could barely imagine.

At length he chuckled and spoke again.

"Three Portals ago, I was ushering the Maya into their new home. They didn't know what to make of me, since I obviously wasn't one of them. They figured I must be a Toltec, so that's what they called me: Xa Toltec, 'The Toltec.' The Maya have always been a tad on the parochial side. Something about that name appealed to me, and I've used it ever since. You know, whatever power that is responsible for the Portals is wise. They placed the Maya on an island on the other side of the world, far from any other race. Their vision of the gods is nightmarish, even to me— no one else should be subjected to it. More importantly, their civilization has little resiliency, despite its beauty and grandeur. Any contact with a more advanced race would quickly destroy it. Even as they fled to Colibdis, their land was being overrun by Europeans. Now their culture has been preserved, for few fare far—excuse me; almost no one sails widely over the seas of Colibdis. Those slope-headed nitwits can go on assuming any stranger is just a member of another, inferior tribe."

"Maybe the gods set up the Portals. Seeking worshippers," said Ronar sleepily.

"I don't think so. I believe there were no gods before men came."

The embers were flickering, the night was chilling, and they sought refuge in their sleeping bags. Ronar watched centuries and civilizations march across the inside of his eyelids as awareness faded.

The last sound he heard was Sha Totek chuckling over the source of his name.

Chapter 5

Thunderbird

Ronar was awakened by a distant sound—a high, eerie wailing he recognized as the cry of the nehocks. He fell back to sleep, but awoke again a few minutes later when the nehocks trotted up and stared at him with baleful yellow eyes.

Ronar eyed them balefully in return, wondering what prey the beasts might have found on this apparently empty plain. He reached over to shake Sha Totek awake. The sorcerer only cast a bleary glance at the great predators and rolled over again.

Dawn was strengthening. In the east was the crimson nimbus that heralded the giant red sun. Ronar sat up, stretched, and crawled out of his bag to prepare a breakfast of tea, biscuits, honey, and dried beef.

Soon water was boiling in a small copper pot and biscuits baking in a covered frying pan. Ronar prodded Sha Totek again and did not relent until the sorcerer was sitting upright with a mug of tea in his hand.

As they ate, Ronar could not help but notice a certain diminishment in Sha Totek. He appeared smaller, somehow less colorful and vital, as though some mediocre actor were playing his role.

Ronar's scrutiny was not subtle, and at last Sha Totek could ignore it no longer. "It makes a feller nervous to have you squintin' at him like that. I'm okay; it's just that I lose some of my zing when I'm away from the Tower. This weak tea's ain't helping, neither."

The red sun rose. They were in the saddle before the white sun cleared the horizon. Ronar learned their names: Photos was the white sun, and Kudu the red; so Sha Totek named them, at any rate.

The afternoon heat found them traversing the passes of the Red Hills, an ancient range that partially encircled the plain of the Tower and Portal. The trail they rode was gentle and well established, the first sign of human habitation they'd seen.

"I don't let anyone settle within fifty miles of the Tower", said Sha Totek. "I like my privacy. Sometimes the locals come into these hills to graze sheep, but I don't mind that. We won't run into any real settlements until we cross this range."

"Settlements?"

"Sure. Mostly Indians, of course. Tohono, Pima, a few Apache. A stray Mexican or three. And Americans. They call their country Thunderbird."

"And they live just as they did before? Cowboys and Indians, unchanged after all these years?" asked Ronar.

"'All these years?' Fifty or sixty? That's nothing. How much change could you expect in that time?"

"In that time, the lives of Americans have changed so completely that the days of the horseback frontier might as well be the Middle Ages."

"That's hard to believe."

"Then listen."

Sha Totek caught up with Earth history that day as Ronar's precise, low-pitched voice sketched tales of world wars and nuclear weapons, television and supersonic flight.

He also described the circumstances of his own flight through the Portal, to the sorcerer's amusement.

"You mean to say you just hightailed it—without a look back—because you saw a funny light and had a hankerin' to stretch your legs?"

"Basically."

"That's one thing about the Portals," said Sha Totek, shaking his head. "You populate a world that way and you wind up with the worst lot of misfits and drifters you can imagine. You'd be surprised how few contented clerks and pastry chefs find their way through."

They passed the night in the hills. In the morning they topped the northernmost and final ridge in their path. Spread below them was Thunderbird, a country glistening with fleeting dew. By afternoon the Red Hills were only a blur on the horizon behind them, their color muted by a li-lac haze of distance.

They rode northeast into the tawny heart of Thunder-bird. The land was less barren than the Red Plain of the Tower, though still semiarid. Ranch buildings appeared in the shadows of sandstone buttes. They entered range lands where long-horned cattle picked at the tough vegetation. Sometimes men on horseback drove the herds across their path as the nehocks moaned and whistled at the sight of so much vulnerable meat. The cowboys flashed them looks of resentment, but did not come near.

No one approached them until they came within sight of Two Suns City, the capital of the territory. As they rode beside a shallow stream, a young boy looked up from his perch beneath a cottonwood growing from the bank.

With a shout he scrambled up the cottonwood's roots, his crude fishing line left dangling in the water. He ran alongside the riders, looking at them with eager eyes.

"My name's Martin! Who're you? Bet my maw would like to borrow those purple duds you're wearin', mister! Haw! Haw!"

Sha Totek leaned down from his saddle and fixed the boy with a malign grin. "Men call me Sha Totek, boy, and I use pups like you as poker chips when I gamble with Namirnakh!"

Martin tripped over a rock, rolled back to his feet undeterred, and sprinted to catch up to the sorcerer again. "Gosh! Sha Totek hisself! What are you doin' in T-Bird, Mr. Totek? Somethin' to do with that black fog that spewed out of the Devil's Eye the other night, I reckon. I was asleep when it happened, but the next morning my Pa was green as a pickled frog over it!"

"That's right, boy. I've come to Two Suns to tell the Mayor it's up to him to slap Old Scratch back into line."

Dismayed, Martin dropped back a little to parallel Ronar's nehock. "And who are you, mister? Some magic demon Mr. Totek's conjured up, maybe?"

"I don't think so. My name's Ronar. I've just come from Earth."

"From where?" the boy asked, uncomprehending.

"Earth. Arizona."

At the mention of Arizona, Martin's face went slack with awe. He breathed the name as if Ronar had claimed residence in Valhalla. "Arizona—! All my life I never seen a day like this. Two strangers ride into town, and one of them's the Gatekeeper, and the other's an honest-to-God man from Arizona. You from Tombstone? Yuma? Tucson? I bet my teacher'd like to speak to you. You ought to write a book while you're here. Are you packin' a Colt? You can stay at our ranch if you've a mind. Or I can tell you the best hotels. Does Mr. Totek sleep on a bed, or does he just kinda float?"

Martin continued his chatter as he ran along. His many questions left little time for answers, although Sha Totek managed to slip in a word here and there. Ronar noted how readily the sorcerer slipped into the Western dialect as he talked to Martin. He let the two of them carry the bulk of the conversation. Sometimes he tried to describe the wonders of contemporary Arizona. His stories received a respectful hearing, but he had the feeling Martin viewed them as tall tales. He soon gave up, and even Sha Totek eventually let the boy's monologue go uninterrupted. Presently Martin ran out of breath and fell back, to Ronar's relief.

Two Suns turned out to be a larger settlement than Ronar's experience with ghost towns and Western movies had led him to expect. It sprawled and rambled, boasting buildings of four and even five stories. They halted the nehocks, whose breath came hard. This gave Martin a chance to catch up again, still chattering and laughing.

Ronar raised his binocular to a neat cluster of structures standing on a mesa just outside of town. Most were of brick, and many had classical facades of pink sandstone, looking rather incongruous in their rustic setting. Ignoring Martin's prattling, he pointed out the complex to Sha Totek. "What's that up there? Looks almost like a small college."

"They call it Thunderbird University."

"Really? A university in the middle of this great anachronism? What do they teach, calf roping?"

"Now you just come down off your high horse for a minute. Thunderbird U is where you'll find some of the brainiest brains on this planet. Scholarly dudes from all civilized nations come here to study, write their books, and have them translated and published. Thunderbird books are found in every land. I've written a few tomes for the list myself. The T-Birds are mighty proud of their tradition of learning. Even young Martin, the son of an ordinary rancher, can likely hope to attend the University in due time. Ain't that right, boy?"

"I anticipate so," said Martin with surprising gravity.

"I am impressed," admitted Ronar.

"Thanks! Gee, these are some fine mounts you got; may I pet yours, mister Ronar?"

It took Ronar a few fateful seconds to realize what Martin had just asked. By the time he reacted, Martin was already reaching for Four-Ashen-Grey's flank.

"Get back, these things are dangerous!" he snapped, but it was too late. The nehock lashed out, laying Martin's forearm open to the bone with one quick flash of teeth.

Martin went to his knees, holding his wrist, staring at his wound as it rained blood on the dry soil.

"Damn you infernal devil!" cried Ronar. Leaping from the saddle, he ripped off his shirt and hastily wrapped it around Martin's wound. The crude bandage soon grew heavy with wetness. Martin began to sag, his face white, his eyelids fluttering.

Sha Totek dropped down and took Martin's head between his hands, looked him hard in the eyes, and pronounced a spell with quiet intensity. The boy went limp, his face relaxing, even smiling a little.

"I've called upon Hypnos to ease the shock and the pain, but death is not far from this boy. To pull him from that brink by my own power would drain me too much. If he is to live, the help he gets must come from other agencies, whether human or divine."

"I'll stick with human agencies for now," said Ronar. He sprang back into the saddle; Sha Totek handed the boy up to him. Ronar scowled at the sorcerer. "We are fools. This boy knew nothing of these creatures, and we weren't smart enough to warn him. Now he pays." He slammed his heels into the flanks of Four-Ashen-Grey.

"Meet me later at the Olympus Saloon!" called Sha Totek as Ronar thundered down the road.

Supporting Martin with one hand, Ronar lashed the reins with the other, demanding speed from Four-Ashen-Grey, who did not argue the matter. The nehock's sprint was not smooth, but it was very fast.

As they approached the outskirts of Two Suns, Martin opened his eyes and asked weakly, "Mr. Ronar? Why did the monster bite me?"

"Because he's a predator—a wild beast of the plains. It's his nature to see others only as a potential threat or a potential meal. The men who trained him are wrong to force such beasts into the role of riding animals. They should be left to their own ways."

"I forgive him. I bet he's sorry."

"He's not sorry. It's not in his nature."

They entered the city. Ronar yanked the reins and brought his panting mount to a halt in the middle of a busy street. Horses cried out and backed away from the towering nehock who, though exhausted and trembling, glared at them with blazing eyes.

The inhabitants of Thunderbird stared at Ronar's harsh, dust-shrouded figure, chest smeared with the blood of the limp form he carried like a broken doll.

A small sunburned man stepped forward and called angrily, "Git that goddamn nehock off the street, you dumb son of a bitch! You lookin' to git somebody kilt?"

Ronar's anger flared like sunlight breaking through storm clouds. "You tell me where to find a doctor for this boy, you fool, and I'll worry about the bloody nehock!"

The man blinked. "That one of them Jordan boys? Five blocks down and two to the left; that's Doc Joachim's office!"

Ronar sent the nehock pounding through the streets. He found the address, jerked savagely at the reins, leaped down and tied Four-Ashen-Grey to the hitching post in front of Joachim's building.

The doctor opened his door at the sound of the nehock's cries. He was a slender young man with serious eyes and a dark mustache who immediately stepped forward to take Martin from Ronar's arms.

"This is Marty Jordan. He's had his arm torn open by this nehock."

"Let's get him inside."

"I'll join you in a minute."

Ronar turned back to Four-Ashen-Grey, meeting its defiant golden stare with his own gaze of frosty grey. He laid his hand on the hilt of the steel broadsword whose scabbard hung from the saddle, hesitated, then drew the weapon. He raised it clumsily. The nehock blinked at him, then seemed to gather some inkling of what lay ahead, but by then it was too late. Ronar brought the blade down as hard as he could. It bit halfway through the beast's powerful neck and lodged in the spine. The nehock's convulsion yanked the sword from Ronar's hands. Its mouth gaped in a horrid silence, its tongue protruded, the great body collapsed, twitched, and writhed. Like candle wax congealing, the fire of its eyes became opaque.

Ronar stood over the carcass, shaking. "I'm sorry, great hunter. You came to this end through the foolishness of men . But I can't permit any animal to get away with what you did to that boy."

It was a bitter, sickening thing to have hacked this creature to death, wretched brute though it had been. He eyed the sword, hoping he would never find it necessary to so mangle and slay a human being.

He noticed that the nehock's death-spasm hadn't been entirely in vain. One of its great curved talons had caught him just behind the left collarbone, leaving a deep gash. Ronar nodded, almost in satisfaction. It was fitting that he pay some price for what he had just done.

Leaving the sword lodged in the nehock's neck, Ronar entered the office. Dr. Joachim had laid Martin on an examining table and was unwrapping the makeshift bandage.

Martin, while conscious, was dreamy, detached, and unconcerned about the procedure.

"The boy's in a strange state," said Joachim. "Even though he's suffered a major trauma, he's in no pain. I'd call it deep shock, but his pulse is fairly strong."

"Sha Totek placed some kind of a spell on him."

Joachim looked up in surprise. "Sha Totek! What's he got to do with this?"

"We're traveling together. He's probably here in town by now. A problem has arisen on your world."

"I'd guessed that, judging by the display the Devil's Eye put on the other night. Must be serious for the Gatekeeper to be on the move. But what did you mean, 'your world'? Are you an Earthman?"

"I am. A recent arrival. Name's Ronar."

"Pleased to meet you, I suppose."

Joachim peeled the last layer of Ronar's shirt from the boy's wound. Blood flowed thickly at once. The doctor shook his head. "That's real ugly." He packed the wound with white towels.

"Are those towels sterile?"

"Sterile? If you mean are they going to have babies, then yes; they're sterile."

"I mean are they free of bacteria."

"Hell, you mean those Pasteur bugs? Come over here and look close. See those red streaks running up the boy's arm? If you're worried about infection, he's got plenty already, probably from the filthy teeth of that nehock of yours."

The bleeding under control, Joachim assembled surgical materials. He bared Martin's arm again and swabbed out the wound with a solution of hydrogen peroxide, then had Ronar hold the edges of the slash together while he stitched it with catgut.

"Well, that's all I can do," he said, binding Martin's arm in strips of a cottony material. "If he hasn't lost too much blood, and if the infection doesn't get him, he'll be all right. If the circulation in his arm is messed up too much, he might lose his hand, but I hope not."

Ronar winced at that. "Can't you give him a transfusion? You know, replace his lost blood with someone else's?"

"Now, you let me be the doctor around here. That'd probably kill him right quick."

While Joachim tended to Ronar's shoulder wound, Ronar described the basis of blood typing and also told all he could remember about processing penicillin, which unfortunately wasn't much.

The doctor listened skeptically and said, "Bread mold, eh? What kind of magic is that?"

"No magic. Chemistry and biology. You must have at least a little chemistry around here." He tapped the bottle of peroxide with a fingernail.

"Yeah, a little. Though we wouldn't have no peroxide if we didn't happen to have a good source of barite nearby. The stuff is used in bleaching paper too...oh, but you don't care about that."

"Actually, I do. It's all part of the heritage of scientific advancement you left behind when you came to this planet."

"Hmmm. Well, you can't rightly blame me for that. My daddy came over in 1897, leaving me without much choice of where to be born. Daddy used to tell me that things back on Earth were really changing just before he was driven, er, just before he came over. All kinds of new inventions—telephones and electricity and big steam engines and all. I suppose they must have made a real impact by now, maybe even reached the West. I wouldn't know."

"Well, if your science is limited, why can't you take advantage of this—magic—that's so pervasive here to help Martin?"

"It ain't that easy. I don't know much about science, but even less about magic. We're at a disadvantage—we don't have enough magic to rosin a cricket's leg. We just don't have a cultural history of magic to draw upon. We've tried to work out a few spells, but it takes time to learn the rules, and it's not the sort of thing that folk from other countries are anxious to share. Besides, most of us don't want a thing to do with the heathen gods of other lands. The Indians, now, they've got plenty of magic. One of their medicine men could cure young Martin here by waving a couple of dried lizards at him. But most of the white folk resist having too much contact with Indian ways. Somehow though I never hear any of our farmers complain when the Thunderbird spills a little rain on their land.

"As for you, don't go climbing too many ropes with that arm for a couple weeks and you'll be fine. And for the public good, I offer you the use of my facilities. You're about the dirtiest, sweatiest, bloodiest, smelliest thing I've ever seen that hasn't been picked over by coyotes."

Ronar accepted the offer. He bathed, shaved, and then gave Joachim a 1955 buffalo nickel from his pocket. The doctor admired it, assuring Ronar that an actual coin from the United States was a more than adequate payment for his services.

"Goodbye, Doctor. Maybe you should look into the properties of moldy bread, as long as you're uncomfortable with those of dried lizards."

"Maybe I will. Good luck to you."

Outside in the late afternoon suns-light, Ronar freed his pack and saddlebags from the carcass of Four-Ashen-Grey. A crowd had gathered to gape at the remains of the outlandish beast. Ronar did his best to ignore them as he fished through the pack and came up with a red flannel shirt, the closest thing he had to a clean garment. He put it on, drew his knife, and bent to cut out the nehock's great foreclaws. These he stored in the pack.

Quite belatedly, Ronar noticed that the sword was gone. He smacked his fist into his palm and cursed. He'd insisted on carrying that particular weapon merely because it struck his fancy. Sha Totek had entrusted it to him, even though it was worth a king's ransom. But he, Ronar, had used it only to kill a hapless beast, and now he'd foolishly allowed it to be stolen.

The onlookers regarded him with some alarm.

Ronar closed his eyes tightly and shook his head. Things were getting out of control. With a forced calm, he said, "Please. Did any of you see who stole the sword that was stuck in this animal's neck?"

"Nope.

"Not me."

"Didn't see a thing, stranger. You want that carcass? He's got a good hide on 'im."

Ronar made a pained gesture of acquiescence to this request. Then he stood there a moment longer, willing his thoughts to be still, trying to let tension and frustration drain away. He hefted his baggage and walked off, leaving Four-Ashen-Grey lying in a pool of crimson mud. A few voices muttered behind him, but thankfully he was allowed to withdraw in peace.

Forcing himself to be fully aware of his surroundings for the first time since the boy was attacked, Ronar found himself on a residential street lined with two-story houses of brick or sandstone. In some yards American flags spangled with only 46 stars waved in the breezes of a world many thousands of light-years from the nation they represented.

Further along, things were less prosperous-looking, but still generally clean, except for the inevitable leavings of horse traffic in the street. Adobe replaced brick in rows of small, simple houses. Their yards were dry, scrubby with desert plants, some of which he recognized, and some which he did not. The people appeared well fed and decently dressed. In fact, they looked a good deal more respectable than Ronar did himself, despite his recent scrubbing.

After a few blocks Ronar turned onto a busy commercial street. His first impression was of a movie set onto which actors from various films had wandered, for among those wearing spurs and leather were people in archaic robes, cloaks, and tunics — a dress rehearsal for a very confused historical picture.

About one business in five was a saloon. Separating them were hotels, banks, stables, restaurants, dry goods stores, and even a pet shop.

Less predictably, reading material was everywhere, with competing newspapers hawked on every corner. No college town on Earth could have exceeded the number of bookstores.

Ronar entered one at random and gratefully dumped his mule-load in a corner. A girl sat behind the counter, reading. She glanced up at him, smiled. He gave a nod and looked around. The store was lit by broad windows or ripply greenish glass. It smelled of wood and leather, with a spicy undertone. The shelves were filled with splendid volumes, leather-bound and gold-stamped. The store was a node of tranquility which inspired Ronar to close his eyes for a moment, tilt back his head, and release a shuddering breath.

Scanning the shelves, he selected a volume called *Wild Plants of Eranior,* written in the same archaic Welsh dialect he'd seen on Sha Totek's star-globe. The writer defined "wild plants" as those native to Colibdis, rather than those that had found their way over from Earth. The text was descriptive and practical, concentrating on the uses of the various species in local folk magic. The illustrations were elaborate but highly stylized, probably not very accurate in scientific detail, but perhaps adequate for identification. Following the Eranian version was the same text in English.

The book was nicely designed and printed. Ronar found this indicia on the last page:

This volume is published by
Whirlpool Books
printed on paper milled in
Biter's Canyon, Alpine County
bound in leather from the great
Thunderbird Tanneries,
Apache Corners, La Luz County

The Whirlpool Book Company
Two Suns City, Thunderbird Territory

Ronar replaced it and ran his gaze along rows of richly colored bindings. "These books are beautiful," he said quietly.

"Thank you, sir," replied a clear female voice. "I don't believe I've had the pleasure of serving you before—?"

Ronar turned to the shopkeeper. She was a slim young woman with misty green eyes, honey-colored hair falling to her shoulders, and an expression finely balanced between decorum and an indiscreet interest. She wore a floor-length blue dress whose simple lines gracefully avoided any hint of severity.

Confronted with Ronar's silent appraisal, she ventured a more direct tactic. "Are you new to Two Suns? Perhaps a trapper or a range rider?"

Ronar averted his gaze. "I'm new to the planet. Been here only a few days."

The girl looked puzzled for a moment, then clapped her hands in delight. "How wonderful! An Arizonan! We haven't seen any for so long. Thank you for coming to my store. Welcome to Thunderbird! My name is Phaedra Holder. And you are, sir?"

"Leonard Ronar."

"Oh, you must know Sha Totek, being a recent arrival. I've met him; he's such a brilliant man. He's written some of our finest books."

"Yes—I know him. He's—my traveling companion."

Phaedra's eyes grew wide. "Really! He's in town then? That doesn't happen often, the scamp. What brings you both here?"

Ronar briefly described the circumstances of his visit to Two Suns. When he finished his spare account, Phaedra was left luminous with care and concern, which made Ronar endlessly uncomfortable.

"I'm so sorry," she said. "All those grisly things happening in the first few days of your stay! I do hope your life here will take a more pleasant turn from now on…"

"I—suspect I can deal with the situation," muttered Ronar, feeling inexplicably foolish. He turned to inspect the shelves again, his ears burning as he felt her gaze lingering on his back.

Eventually he selected three titles: *Stars and Constellations,* written by Gwyddno ab Emlyn, described as court astronomer to the king of Eranior; *An Outline of Colibdian History,* by Sha Totek himself; and *Wanderings of Hamadan,* which appeared to be a myth-cycle based on the exploits of an ancient Colibdian demigod. He considered several books on magic, but they all seemed superficial, describing the powers of various races and individuals, but with little information on the basis or nature of their magic.

A tentative question reached his ears. "Do...you enjoy reading, Mr. Ronar?"

"Enjoy it?" answered Ronar absently, his eyes not leaving the page. "I love it. Books are the purest, most refined record of human thought. Without these accounts of human wisdom, I don't think I'd be able to summon much respect for my own species."

"I feel the same way! Life can seem so sordid without such reminders that people can also think of things that are great and good. I enjoy writing poetry, myself. And silly little stories. Romances, mostly." Phaedra smiled and fluttered her hands in self-deprecation.

"Is that so?" said Ronar, fearful that she might offer examples. He found a paper clip in his pocket. "Young lady—I have no local money. Would this steel item be of any value here?"

She took it from his hand and regarded it in wonder. "Some kind of hair pin from Earth? Of steel? Yes, I'd be happy to accept it for those books. I do hope you enjoy them."

Somehow her delighted expression only made Ronar feel guilty for foisting a worthless paper clip on her in exchange for these fine books. Grimacing, he rummaged through his pockets and brought forth a handful of change. From it he selected the three shiniest pennies.

"Please take these coins as well. They're from Earth too."

"Thank you! How wonderful."

Phaedra did not seem anxious for him to depart. She looked into his face and began hesitantly, "Mr. Ronar—I keep a modest but comfortable home—I wonder if, in view of your trying experiences of late, you might not join me there for dinner tonight?"

Ronar started, studying this creature with her luminous gaze. What could such a lovely girl possibly want with him? Did he really look so hungry that she was compelled to offer this act of charity?

"I think not," said Ronar stiffly. "I really ought to try to find Sha Totek."

"I see…"

Ronar stowed the books and shouldered his many burdens. As he stepped through the door, he stopped, and without looking back said, "But I thank you for the offer."

"It was nothing."

Outside in the dusk, Ronar found most of the other stores darkened and locked up tight. Phaedra had obviously kept her store open past the usual closing time.

Ronar marched off rapidly, trying to shake off the persistent feeling that he'd just made a profound error. Sha Totek was probably in no great hurry to meet with him. Let him enjoy his decadent comforts while he had the chance. Ronar had no inclination to share them; certainly he had enough to occupy his mind without having to worry about pleasing some silly—he shook his head angrily and cut off that line of thought.

Desiring solitude, he resumed his wanderings. Soon the peaceful lavender light of twilight quieted his mind.

Ronar entered a neighborhood that was older and more decrepit than those he'd seen so far. There his attention was drawn to an unusual house. It was one of the few wooden structures he'd encountered, built along the lines of a Victorian mansion. The house was in ill repair, its paint grey and peeling, the grounds overgrown with spiky shrubs. Whatever beauty it might once have possessed must have been of a neurotic sort, like the genteel psychosis of a Heironymus Bosch painting. It was all askew, with wings, dormers, porches and verandas weirdly attached so that no two parts of the house seemed to be at quite the same level. Parts of the roof changed pitch for no apparent reason. Spindly towers, with dull black woodwork and corroded weather vanes, rose to various heights. Their dark windows looked in on tiny, useless spaces.

Ronar leaned against a dead tree, idly watching the old house as it faded into the night. A voice quailed at him from somewhere nearby: "Don't stand there a' gapin' too long, stranger; that's the Despard house!" Ronar looked around, but could not find the speaker.

A few minutes later, in the very last light, the pale face of a dark-haired woman appeared at a window and looked at him with an unreadable gaze. Ronar wondered what misfortune had reduced this obviously once well-to-do creature to such a state. Not wishing to interfere with her privacy, he walked away into as lonely a neighborhood as he had ever seen. It was a relief to stretch his legs again after days in the saddle. But soon, no longer able to ignore his hunger, Ronar returned to the business section of town to choose a restaurant, many of which bore ornate facades. Not wishing to deal with the niceties of formal dining, he pushed through the swinging doors of an unprepossessing-looking place called the Moon Room Saloon.

The most lunar quality of the Moon Room was the murky lighting provided by wagon-wheel chandeliers, their candles shaded by blue-glass chimneys. Ronar supposed the resulting indigo pallor was thought to lend atmosphere to the place, and conceded it might be restful to the eyes of men used to the pink-actinic fierceness of the Photos-Kudu pair.

The saloon's patrons were not noticeably subdued by the "moonlight." A scruffy group of cowhands and towns-men with a few exotic foreigners tossed in, they surrounded the bar like a dusty picket fence, shot glasses rising and fal-ling with speed and regularity. A few looked over their shoulders as Ronar approached the bar. They squeezed aside to admit him.

The bartender's immaculate costume was quite out of place amid the rustic furnishings, his white shirt and apron luminescent in the blue glow, his ostentatious jeweled stickpin glittering with icy points. His hair was oiled, his sweeping mustache heavily waxed. He regarded Ronar with polite reserve. "Will you drive a nail in your coffin, stranger?" he asked, cordially enough. He lifted a bottle of whisky, ready to pour into a tumbler.

"You have food here?"

The barkeep looked blank. "Food?"

"That's right, food. Physical sustenance. The staff of life. Vittles. Grub."

Tilting back his head, the barkeep shouted, "Hey Pepe! We got any food back there?"

A voice called back, "Well, I dunno; it depends on what you're plannin' to feed it to."

"What do we have that's fit for an impatient-looking gentleman about six-and-a-half feet tall?"

"We got beef. And parts of a cow some might be willin' to call beef. Also beans."

"Those will do," said Ronar.

"Yessir. Why don't you take a table."

"Bring me beer as well, if you have it. A large quantity."

Ronar selected a rickety table in the quietest corner of the room. Doffing his pack, he fished out *Stars and Constellations* and tried to read it in the dimness.

The food and drink arrived before long. Ronar found both plentiful and adequate, though the blue lighting colored the meat an unappetizing grey. The "beer" was a bizarre brew made of...he couldn't say. Maybe hops or some other normal ingredient had never made it over from Earth. He ate and drank, still poring over the shadowed pages of his book.

The dim light aggravated his slight farsightedness. With a sigh of resignation he took steel-rimmed reading glasses from a side-pocket on his pack and put them on.

A large, sour-smelling man, picking his way among the tables with exaggerated caution, managed to catch a toe under one of Ronar's saddlebags and fall heavily on his face. Ronar glanced at him and kicked his luggage farther under the table.

The man hauled himself erect, leaned unsteadily over Ronar, and growled, "Yuh'd better tell me you're sorry, mister."

"Sorry for what?"

"Fer trippin' me."

Ronar did not look up, but said in a low, irritated voice, "I'm sorry you're a clumsy, drunken fool."

"What'd you say?"

"Make that a clumsy, drunken, deaf fool."

"Four-eyes, nobody who sits there drinkin' that skunk piss instead of a man's likker ain't man enough to be callin' ol' Snake Eyes a fool."

"'Four Eyes,' eh? Interesting," said Ronar. He removed his glasses and regarded them for a moment, then looked up at Snake Eyes. "How many eyes do you see on my face?"

"Two, but them's two more in your hand."

Ronar looked at the glasses again. "I see. You consider these disks of glass to be eyes. Probably you regard other disks of glass in the same way. So when you're drinking your 'man's likker' and you get to the bottom of the glass, you see eyes there—slimy, staring eyes, soaking in your whisky, plucked bloody from human faces. Is that about the size of it?"

Snake Eyes stared at him in horror. His jaw worked and loosened, and his pallor went beyond even what the blue lighting could account for. At the last moment, Ronar pushed him away. He toppled and vomited up a quart or so of dark liquid.

Ronar turned and tried to conceal his mirth, but didn't completely succeed. Much as he relished giving this lout a hard time, he suspected he'd just bought himself a fair amount of trouble.

When Snake Eyes managed to find his feet again he was less foggy than before, and much angrier. "I reckon you're one of them smartass perfessers from the goddamn University. I said you weren't man enough to bad-mouth me, and I aim to prove it."

Ronar suddenly no longer felt like playing this game. His voice grew cold and sharp. "Yes, I am a smartass professor from a goddamn university. However, I could sit here drinking chocolate milk while wearing silk stockings and still be man enough to call you a fool. Now take your foul breath and your prized stupidity and back off."

Snake Eyes chose instead to swing his heavy hand in a backhanded arc that caught Ronar hard on the jaw.

Ronar was willing to accept this single blow, but no more. When he unfolded from his seat like a fast-growing redwood, Snake Eyes showed a brief uncertainty. His bloodshot eyes grew round as Ronar grabbed him by his collar and belt and hoisted him smoothly into the air.

Ronar looked up at Snake Eyes's frozen expression and explained carefully, "If you touch me or my possessions, you forfeit your right to bodily well-being. I'm now going to save you a lot of trouble by ejecting you from this saloon. You will stay away for as long as I am here."

With that, he walked to the door and pitched Snake Eyes into the street without unnecessary violence. Returning to his seat, he felt the respectful glances of the other patrons. Someone came out to mop up the mess on the floor.

Ronar resumed his meal with an internal sigh of relief. He winced...his wounded shoulder was giving him some nasty twinges. He'd been lucky—if he hadn't overawed Snake Eyes and the others with his feat of strength, he might have been in for a more difficult time.

A few minutes later, an old man sat down across from him and stared at him with large, watery eyes. Ronar began to wonder if he'd really handled the Snake Eyes incident so well after all. His apprehension vanished when the stranger solemnly produced an empty beer mug and placed it before him.

Ronar filled the mug from his pitcher and studied his guest. He was small and lean, his weathered face almost lost in a cloud of dirty-white beard. He wore a floppy-brimmed leather hat, a red bandanna, and a suit of clothes so caked with dust that their true color was a matter of speculation. He peered out between the brim of his hat and the rim of his mug.

They regarded each other silently for some time. Finally the bemused Ronar ventured a greeting. "Hello. Nice night, isn't it?"

"Uh-huh."

"I—notice some chisels and a rock pick in your knapsack. You're a prospector?"

"Yep."

Ronar sat back, wondering how to deal with someone even more reticent than himself. But then the old man broke the silence on his own. "Are you from the Other Side?"

Ronar looked up with interest. "That's right. How did you know?"

"Them steel specs of yours, fer one thing. Wouldn't find their like around here. But mainly it was your muscles. They ain't gone to hell the way those have what was born here. Only an Earthman could've pitched ol' Snakeface out the way you did. I oughter know. I was born on Earth myself; came over in 1893. Name's Ephrem Salazar."

"Ronar."

Salazar's taciturnity melted into eager questions about his old haunts in Arizona. Ronar described a few of the changes of the past sixty-six years. The old man was fascinated by tales of the cities that had grown up in place of adobe villages, and of the mammoth water projects that had brought orange groves to the desert.

"Well! Dams on the Colorado you say!"

"Yes. Too many of them, actually. Now there's hardly anything left of the Colorado by the time it empties into the Gulf."

"Sounds like Arizona's done pretty good for itself."

"I suppose it has. Some of the towns are getting a little too big for my tastes though, especially Phoenix."

"Phoenix! Sleepy little Phoenix?"

"Not so sleepy anymore. Between the cities and the dams and the crops and the lawns, it seems like the people of Arizona are busy trying to turn it into some other state. Still, Arizona's one of the few states I'd want to live in. It's mostly quiet."

Ephrem's jaw dropped. "State? Arizona's a state?"

"Yes, since 1912."

Ephrem looked crestfallen. "I'll be damned. Arizona a state! I reckon Thunderbird's the only territory left in the Union. Too bad the President can't see how good we're doin' over here. He might think we was good enough for statehood too," he said wistfully.

Ronar blinked, wondering how to respond to this. "He might. Considering what you've got to work with, I think you've accomplished a lot. Especially with your University and publishing industry."

Salazar nodded enthusiastically. "We done more than that, too. Miners from T-Bird straighten out the tanglefoots in other countries and help find new ore deposits. Myself, I spent years redesignin' the iron mines up in Tíuheimr fer them yella-haired mooncalves afore I got too old. I even learned to suck down that fermented whatever-it-is they swill up there. Had to, just to keep from freezing to death. I swear, maybe other lands are stronger than we are, what with their magic and their grand armies, but they've all come to rely so much on hocus-pocus that they can't figger out a new way to nail two boards together. Even Sha Totek, right smart feller that he is, ain't immune. I saw right off that that Tower of his is sittin' on a mother lode of iron ore, not the best maybe, but enough to put a steel sword or even a revolver on everybody's hip. And I don't think he even knows it."

"I don't think he does either. He has a bronze age mentality. Iron ore may be just so much rock to him," said Ronar.

They talked for another hour before Ronar decided to check on Martin. He paid his bill, left Salazar with a fresh pitcher of beer, and resumed his burdens. All eyes were on him as he stepped into the frosty night.

Chapter 6

The House

Ronar's long stride carried him towards Dr. Joachim's office. The streets were windblown and dark. Possibly the people of Thunderbird were of the early-to-bed-early-to-rise school of thought. Or maybe the recent activity of the Eye of Ahriman had encouraged them not to linger outside after dark.

He hunted along the Road of Evil and spotted the Eye, its vision dimmed since its master set out spaceward to work his mysterious mischief. Ronar tried to imagine the struggle between Ahriman and Varanu that Sha Totek had described—a conflict between the personifications of Order and Reorder, between Nature and Intervention.

He detected something more subtle than a war between gods, something so ephemeral he wouldn't have mentioned it to anyone. It was too subjective, too close to fantasy.

Ever since childhood, he'd been aware of a kind of music, pervasive but elusive, faint enough to be drowned out by any kind of clamor or turmoil. Only in moments of peace and solitude could it be heard. He had thought it was the song of the stars. When he was attuned to it, it seemed a flowing, majestic tapestry of quiet chords, a musical analog of the gentle fall of light along the star-stream of the Milky Way.

Now the song was calling attention to itself, though he had neither peace nor real solitude. It had become strained, slightly discordant. It was getting worse, though he could no more hear the actual change than he could watch a leaf sprouting from a tree.

For some idle reason he decided to walk past the "Despard" house again, it being the most interesting structure he'd seen. Its fantastic outline soon loomed up out of the night. He did not slow his pace, but he turned his head to look into the windows as he passed. He did not see the woman he had noticed earlier. Someone else met his gaze though...a forlorn-looking boy, face glimmering behind a window in a high tower.

Ronar continued on his way, brooding over the fate of Martin, picturing the staff of that damned bookstore he'd visited. But his steady march slowed as something occurred to him. He halted and turned to study the now-distant Despard house.

Feeling an unusual uncertainty, Ronar trudged back toward the house. He stood before the gate and once again peered into its many windows, seeing nothing, no one, not even a light.

With a shrug he opened the gate and passed through. The face of the House seemed to expand and enfold him as he approached. The veranda stairs creaked beneath his weight. He raised his hand, hesitated, then rapped on the double door with a knocker shaped like a repugnant face.

For some time there was no response. Ronar was about to turn away when the doors swung open, revealing the woman he had seen earlier, or at least a similar shadowy form. No lights shone upon her. She tilted her head, facing him silently.

"Good evening, Madam," said Ronar, feeling awkward and foolish. "My name is Leonard Ronar. I was wondering if I might speak to you for a moment."

"You have my attention, sir. I am Mrs. Elizabeth Despard." Her voice was languorous with a New Orleans accent. Her tone was guardedly polite.

"I—arrived in town just today, and met a local boy named Martin Jordan. He was badly injured by my mount. I carried him to Dr. Joachim for treatment."

"Oh?" said she.

Ronar hesitated, then plunged on. "I know this will sound ridiculous, but as I was passing your house a few moments ago, I saw the face of a boy in a window. I eventually realized that he looked very much like Martin Jordan."

Mrs. Despard's attitude did not change. "And...?"

"And, I returned to ask if the boy might have been brought here for some reason," said Ronar, resentful of being forced to state something that was both so obvious and sounded so foolish.

"No, we have no such child here."

"But I did see a boy."

"I daresay it was my son Barlow whom you saw. Will that be all? Good night to you then." The doors began to swing shut.

Ronar stepped forward, blocking them. "I—may I meet your son?"

Again the shadowy figure took a moment to study him. "You are a rather forward man, Mr. Ronar. If my husband were present, I expect he would take you to task for your boldness."

Ronar felt himself flushing. "I'm sorry, Mrs. Despard. I ask only for a moment of your time, to ease my mind. Then I will leave you in peace."

"Very well then. You may enter. Leave your baggage on the veranda, if you please."

She led the way inside. The dim light of the street seeped into a foyer finished with peeling wallpaper and un-lit candles in wall sconces. From there they proceeded to a larger room which was dark except for what little light managed to pass the curtained windows. Elizabeth Despard's form merged with that of a chair. "Please be seated, Mr. Ronar."

"May we have some light in here?" asked Ronar, peeved that he must request such a simple courtesy.

"You may light a candle or two if you wish."

Luckily, the silhouettes of a pair of candelabra were visible before a window. He produced matches and lit one candle on each holder.

It was a sitting room with a dusty parquet floor and dark green velvet wall hangings. Elizabeth Despard occupied a high-backed chair with wine-colored upholstery. Her face was pale, heart-shaped, with large dark eyes. Waves of coal-black hair spilled over her shoulders. Her dress was also black...a dress of mourning? The amount of décolletage it displayed seemed to indicate that it was not.

"Please do sit. I'm sorry I can't offer you any refreshment. We have little luxury here since my husband's arrest. The servants too are gone."

Ronar took a seat across the room. Impelled by an unusual fascination, he prompted, "Your husband was arrested?"

"Yes."

"For what?"

"My goodness, your inquisitiveness will be the death of you yet. Frankly, I'm surprised you haven't heard the tale around town already. He was arrested for worshipping something other than that insipid, invisible Christian god they favor around here."

"Really. I'm sorry to hear there is so little religious tolerance in a country that models itself after the United States."

Elizabeth's expression grew even more sour. "Tolerance in Thunderbird has some distinct limits. The fools."

"And you...you share in his religious preference?"

She nodded. "Indeed. But I was left in peace, since none of the townspeople wished to become responsible for orphaned children."

Ronar, leaning forward in his chair, blinked and started, realizing he had forgotten the reason for his visit.

"Would you call your son now, please?"

She made a negligent gesture. "He has come already."

Ronar followed her hand and started again, having been unaware of the entrance of the boy who stood regarding him so solemnly. He wore knickers and a little pinstriped jacket, and was about eight years old. Though he resembled his mother, Ronar supposed he might have confused him with Martin given the poor lighting at the window of the tower.

Ronar nodded toward the boy. "Hello, Barlow."

"Hello there, sir." The boy's demeanor was subdued, but Ronar supposed that was to be expected with his father in jail.

Barlow's mother dismissed him. "So then Mr. Ronar, are you satisfied that we have not kidnapped your young friend?"

Ronar stood up to leave. "I am indeed, Mrs. Despard. I'm sorry to have troubled you. I hope your husband will be free to return to you soon."

"That is highly unlikely," she said bitterly. "The penalty for this sort of 'crime' is hanging."

"What? When is the execution?"

"It has already taken place, alas."

Ronar's jaw dropped at that. What kind of a situation had he stumbled into here? Hang a man over religious differences? His indignation began to flare up. He just might have to look into this business himself.

He was about to announce his intention to seek justice for the Despard family when another sound, the wail of a distressed child, stopped the words in his throat. For a moment Ronar had the impression that Mrs. Despard was staring at him keenly. But when he looked at her, her expression had returned to one of boredom and distraction.

"Mrs. Despard, what do you make of that sound?" he asked.

She looked around vaguely, as though she hadn't noticed it. "Sound?"

"It is the cry of a disconsolate boy."

"Do you think so? That would be Barlow, I suppose. He is so distraught by the loss of his father."

They listened for another few moments until the cry resolved into recognizable words.

"Maw! Paw! Mr. Ronar! Where am I? What's happening to me?"

"That's Marty!" snapped Ronar.

Elizabeth Despard made a dismissive gesture. "How could that be?"

"That's what I want to know."

"Oh, come now. You're being extremely fanciful. It's quite late. I'm tired. I'd appreciate it if you'd take your leave now."

Ronar stared at her, astonished by her lack of reaction to these strange events.

"That is Marty Jordan calling to me," he said slowly, as though explaining to a child, "and I will not leave until I find him and get him out of here."

Elizabeth Despard fluttered her hands around her face in vexation. "Didn't you say the boy was injured? Sometimes the spirits of the weak or recently dead are drawn to this house. It's the nature of the place."

"Woman, what in the name of five lurid hells are you talking about?"

Now she too got to her feet. "Really, sirrah, what could be more plain? I think I have had my fill of you. Remain in my house and search for your young friend if you must. I have other matters to attend to. Please close the front door when you do finally depart."

Ronar was about to roar out a command for her to stay right where she was when renewed sobs distracted him. He looked around to try to judge their source, heard a door close, and looked back to find himself alone. For the first time he noticed how many doors led out of this sitting room. He had little chance of picking the right one and catching Mrs. Despard.

Martin's cries faded to whimpers and then were abruptly cut off.

Ronar surveyed the doors. Well, he would find that bizarre woman soon enough. Her house was big, but finite. He would find her, or Martin himself with any luck.

Grabbing a candelabrum, he chose a door at random.

The door opened onto a few stairs leading down to a low-ceilinged corridor with walls of brick. Ronar almost chose another door. But the incongruity of it—a door in an elegant, if faded, sitting room leading to a featureless brick corridor—drew him on. The single lit candle dispelled a fraction of the darkness with its wavering yellow glow. Cobwebs formed a series of veils through which he must pass. Shapes scuttled off them as he approached. It was hard to be sure, but they seemed to have too many legs even for spiders.

Reaching the end, he ducked through a doorway that led to the next chamber. This was a larger, loftier room, with portraits hanging far up in the dimness. Ronar raised his candle and looked at the pale, motionless faces. They gazed back at him like so many unsympathetic jurors.

Ronar threw open the drapes that covered the tall windows. Housekeeping at the Despard home was poor indeed. Dust wafted into the room as he disturbed the velvet drapes, but at least a small amount of light entered the room.

Ronar turned and started. A great horned owl perched atop a wing-backed chair, watching him. A streak of dark liquid marred the upholstery. Had the owl caught a rat, or whatever passed for a rat around here? A portrait hung on the wall beside the owl. It depicted a dark, sardonic-looking man wearing an archaic costume. The face was vividly rendered, but the pose was stiff and unnatural. Perhaps no talented portrait artists had found their way to Thunderbird or had yet been spawned there.

The room's main feature was an ornate staircase leading up to the next level. All right then, finally he was getting somewhere. He padded his way up the carpeted stairs, finding himself on a landing which gave onto three radiating corridors of impressive length. Each was curved, preventing him from seeing to their ends. Choosing the middle one, he crept along until he was arrested by the sound of sobbing coming through a door.

"Martin?" Ronar opened the door onto a lightless room. His candle revealed Barlow Despard sitting on his bed, blinking up at him with reddened eyes.

Ronar stood there, an intruder in the bedroom of a young boy he had just met. But the boy did not appear to fear him, or to resent his presence.

"Hello again, Barlow," said Ronar with a surreal feeling. "Are you all right?"

"I miss my father," whispered Barlow.

Ronar nodded, sat in a wooden chair. "Sometimes I miss mine as well. How long has your father been dead?"

"For a long time now. Is yours dead too?"

"Actually—I don't really know. He disappeared—both my parents did—when I was younger."

"That's too bad."

"I often hope they're in a better place, wherever they are." Well...that was the first time he'd ever spoken of *that* to anyone. "I'm sure your father is better off too," he finished lamely.

"I'm not so sure." The boy would not be cheered up so easily.

"Barlow—I've come to your house looking for another boy. His name is Martin. Have you seen him?"

Barlow nodded. "Yes, he's here."

At least this child was capable of giving a straight answer! "Where is he? Why is he here?"

"I don't know where he is. My mother brought him here. She wants to give him to her god, like all the rest."

Ronar froze, uncomprehending. "Give him to her god?"

"Yes sir, you know, his spirit."

A chilling premonition came over Ronar.

"Barlow, which god are we talking about here?"

"You know. The one my parents like. The bad one."

"Which one is that exactly?"

The boy pointed his finger at the ceiling and moved it to describe a course across the heavens.

"The one who looks down from the Eye?" whispered Ronar.

Barlow nodded.

"And...do you like this god too, Barlow?"

Barlow shook his head. "No, he scares me bad. Sometimes my big sister says that Mama will give me to him too, if I don't start liking him."

"What exactly do you mean when you say your mother wants to 'give' you or Martin to the god? What would the god do with you?"

Barlow shrugged. "I think he eats people up. Their spirit parts, I mean."

Ronar shuddered, working to keep revulsion off his face.

"All right, Barlow. Stay here. I'm going to find your mother and talk to her about Martin. And I'll get you away from here too. I won't let you fall victim to that devil."

Barlow looked up at him with round, moist eyes. "I'm not allowed to leave the house." He suddenly brightened. "Would you play a game with me? My father taught me how to play chess." He leaped over to a table where a chess set stood ready. He sat behind the white pieces and looked up with a hopeful expression.

Ronar approached the table, staring at the board. A game of chess. A few moments of distraction to defer the bizarre task that engaged him. A chance to sit with this troubled, neglected boy, a child who was restrained and dignified enough to be tolerable.

He pulled out the chair. Its legs screeched across the floor, sounding like some outraged beast. He sat down.

Barlow pushed his king's pawn forward two squares.

Ronar reached out to make a response, hesitated, lowered his hand. Barlow looked at him with puzzled expectation.

"Barlow...I would like to play our game later, if we can. Right now, I must find Martin. He's in trouble and I need to get you both away from here."

Barlow nodded, disappointed. "I understand, sir. Also, you want a chance to figure out how to respond to my strajidy, I expect."

Ronar looked at the boy for a few moments before he understood it was a joke, albeit one made with a perfectly straight face. Ronar produced a grudging smile.

"That's right. Don't rearrange the board while I'm away. I will see you later."

He turned, stepped out into the hall, closed the door behind him, stood there collecting his thoughts.

Time to find that woman, and end this farce.

He peered up and down the curving corridor, deciding to open every door in search of Elizabeth's bedroom. The thought of that invasion flushed his cheeks once more, but it could not be helped.

Or maybe it could be helped, if he simply couldn't find her. Most of the chambers were bedrooms with cell-like furnishings, all unoccupied. Some served no function he could envision. One was empty except for a truncated pyramid of stone in the center of the floor. A breeze issued from another room . Inspection revealed three ducts in the walls, each covered with a wicker grate painted a dull green. Cool, dry air wafted from the central duct. The one on the left exhibited a bit of suction. The one on the right was stagnant, but carried a scent of decay. Otherwise, the room was empty, except for a piece of paper in the corner, a sketch of a frightened face.

As Ronar crept along the curving hallway he was confronted by a wavering figure carrying a candelabrum. A nervous tingle flooded through him. Then he realized he was seeing himself in a tarnished copper mirror at the end of the corridor. His chuckle of relief was weak and forced.

Backtracking to the junction of corridors, he chose the left hand one, with similar results. But at its end he found a stairway leading up. Perhaps Elizabeth Despard kept her widow's chamber somewhere on the third floor.

At that point Ronar became disoriented. He wandered through a maze of meaningless chambers, dead end passageways, stairways spiraling to nowhere, and pointless changes in level and direction. It was like a run-down carnival funhouse built along Victorian lines. One step might take him from a drawing room with gold-inlaid furniture to a dungeon of no apparent use other than to contain more doors and stairways. It would have been interesting, even appealing in a dreamlike way, if not for the task that kept him here. He could not guess what philosophy would lead to designing a house like this. He doubted it was one he would ever share.

Even the windows only revealed brick walls, or looked into adjacent rooms. He knew the exterior of the house had plenty of windows; could he really wander so far without finding any of them?

Just as Ronar was beginning to suspect that the House was as boundless and pathless as the Portal itself, he entered a room with an outside view, a view that carried its own surprises.

He was assaulted by hot white light. Dropping his candle, he shielded his eyes, squinting out from between his fingers. The room was a gallery furnished in scarlet and gold. Daylight? Could he possibly have been wandering here all night long?

From the windows Ronar beheld a macabre scene.

A scaffold loomed in the morning suns. A hooded hangman placed a noose around the neck of a lean, black-clad man. Ronar recognized the victim's pinched, high-browed face from the Despard family portraits. His dark eyes glowered at his captors, a grim crowd of Thunderbirds.

The condemned man was not heavy, so the hangman tied a sandbag to his feet to assure a cleanly snapped neck. Satisfied with the arrangements, the hangman gripped the lever that would open the trap door and send his victim to his death. Ronar shook his head in bafflement. Despard? Wasn't he supposed to be already dead?

A magistrate climbed onto the platform, where he opened a black-bound book while casting uneasy glances at the condemned man. As the crowd muttered below, he inflated himself to maximum size, cleared his throat, and addressed the prisoner, who gave him a sidelong look of casual contempt.

"Damon Despard, years ago, you and your wife crossed to this new world of ours the same as the rest of us. We can't say what stigma may have driven you into the desert to stumble across the Gateway. By common consent, such shadows of the past are not spoken of here. We have all made the same passage for our own reasons.

"Over the years, you made no secret of the fact that you had chosen as your object of worship the spirit-creature known as Satan, or as Loki or Ahriman in other lands. Under the freedoms guaranteed by the Bill of Rights, we could not interfere with your religious preference, although we could not bring ourselves to respect it unduly."

The magistrate slammed the book and continued passionately. "But the Constitution does not provide the right to abduct innocent children for sacrifice in perverted rituals to Satan or to any other spirit. You have been tried and found guilty. Your crime is so abhorrent that our consciences, and our fear for our remaining children, permit no other sentence than death. If our Christian God exerts his power on this strange world, may he condemn your soul to no worse a circle of Hell than it deserves. Have you any last words before sentence is carried out?"

Damon Despard looked at him with a mild, distracted expression. He said, softly, reasonably, "Your God will not condemn me, for he does not exist on the face of this planet. Nor in my opinion did he ever exist on Earth, except in the minds of the ancient Hebrew tribesmen who imagined him, and their successors. So I have always believed. Thus you may imagine my surprise when I came here, to find many gods not only real, but sometimes conspicuous.

Of these, Ahriman is the most human, the most accessible to mortal minds. Like us, he has desires and ambitions, and he wishes intercourse with other thinking beings. By contrast, the other gods are scarcely more than localizations of impersonal natural forces. You'll find no comfort in them. Only Ahriman welcomes our worship. Only he cares for those of our small, ephemeral kind. In that, he is something like your Yahweh, but unlike Yahweh, Ahriman is not so quick to condemn us for being what we are. To oppose Ahriman is to support the mindless, inevitable running down of the universe like some untended clock. To deny Ahriman is to deny your own humanity."

The magistrate turned away and motioned to the hangman, who sent Damon Despard plummeting to an abrupt end.

Ronar stared at the swinging corpse, filled with admiration for the composure with which Despard had faced his death, and with distaste for his ideas. He much preferred a mechanistic universe to one controlled by the whims of any intelligence, however sublime. Only in the predictability of nature were peace and sanity to be found...

Ronar's hypnotized musings were interrupted by a sudden shove and a screech of despair. He fell, hitting his head against a marble table. The room seemed to sway as he looked up to see who had taken his place at the window.

It was Elizabeth, hair in disarray, face drawn into a grimace as she stared out the window. "Oh, don't, oh don't hang my husband, oh don't oh don't oh please don't." As Ronar watched in horror, she tore away the bodice of her dress and raked her chest with long nails, drawing a bloody network that drained down between her breasts. Her head jerked back and forth as she tore at herself, her movements becoming more and more frenzied, until strips of flesh hung from beneath her nails. Soon the whitish sheen of exposed tendons appeared beneath her clawing fingers.

Ronar could stand no more—he roared at her to stop. She ignored him, whirled and fled the room, leaving a trail of gore and a hopeless shriek that seemed to echo in the very atoms of the air. The door slammed behind her.

The daylight slammed off too, leaving Ronar in a darkness as sudden and overpowering as the glare had been. He got to his feet and groped for the door, fumbling in his pocket for a match. He didn't find one until he'd stumbled through the door. Before he could strike it he'd bumped into something soft and heavy.

Leaping back convulsively, he dropped the match but managed to find another and struck it. His fingers went nerveless at what the flaring light revealed.

She hung from a chandelier, a cord wrapped about her neck. Her bosom was wet with blood and lymph. Her lifeless eyes stared with a kind of lunatic oblivion.

The match fell, hissed in the dust, went out. Numbly, he fumbled for the dropped candelabrum, found it, and lit all three candles. He lurched back into the next room, which was still plunged into night.

Dead, a suicide! What a disaster for Barlow and the other children He should have guessed, should have restrained her, should have forced some sense of responsibility into her mind. If only he'd realized that the execution she'd spoken of was imminent, and not in the past!

He placed the candelabrum on a shelf and went to the window, shaking and confused. He looked out upon the remains of a garden, silver-blue in the light of Sinanna.

Low stone walls formed walkways among plants like tangles of ribbon. Time had laid a withering hand on them long since. Scrub grew in the flower beds. A one-time pool was only a depression in the dust.

The four headstones did not look out of place in this desolation. Ronar could barely make out their inscriptions. The largest one read:

Elizabeth Despard
1837-1865
Gone to her god—
before we could send her ourselves

The other stones marked the three Despard children: Chloe, Barlow, and Eliza. All four bore the same date of death.

Ronar turned away. He lifted his head, closed his eyes, and stood still for several long minutes. His chest felt like it was full of cold mud.

Ghosts. So, it was a house full of ghosts. Even that boy, Barlow.

An inner voice whose wisdom he respected was urging him to flee this place of madness. How could he deal with this situation when his only weapons were strength and rationality? The ghosts would not be impressed by the strength of his arms, nor could his rationality have much effect on their actions.

That window was tempting. It would be easy to open or break it, climb out into the sweet cool air of sanity, and disappear into the night. He stood there with his palms pressed against the glass, looking out at the ghost-free world only an eighth of an inch away. A few shadowy figures moved beyond the fence. Had someone seen him entering the house? Someone spotted him standing there, flinched away. Very probably, the sight of any figure in the windows of the Despard house was not welcome.

Perhaps he could call out to them, tell them to bring Sha Totek, who was surely better suited to handle this situation than he was. He would try.

As he clutched the window frame to open it, he teetered with a sudden dizziness. When it passed, a fog of unreality fell away from his sight and from his mind. As the last shreds of illusion faded, he beheld a house which was not merely shabby, but filthy and decrepit with age.

Ronar shoved his elbow through one of the window-panes. Someone outside screamed at the sudden clatter. Ronar lowered his head to shout through the opening. "You out there! Find Sha Totek, the sorcerer! Bring him here! Tell him Ronar is here. You'll find him at the Olympus Saloon."

A horrid voice mocked the pacing and intonation of his words, the yammering of some lunatic. The screaming outside became more general. Ronar fell silent, then tried again. Again that hateful gibbering interfered with his words, to the point where Ronar couldn't hear himself speak. Could anyone? His mouth snapped shut. He peered outside. The small crowd was scattering, falling back.

Now Ronar grew angry. There would be no escaping out the window for him. He retrieved his candles and returned to the next room. Elizabeth's body was gone, but her gallows-chandelier was not. Ronar kicked the dust away from beneath it. A crusted brown stain obscured the grain of the floorboards.

He lit a fresh candle, turned and regarded the portraits by its feeble light. He was glad of the wrath that had awakened within him. It kept him from being too uncomfortably aware of what he was facing.

"All right then, Despards," he growled. "You wish to play a game with me. I will play. I am coming for you now."

The prim smile on one of the portraits seemed to widen the least amount.

Ronar plunged into the house, barging through doors, pounding up stairs, doing his best to disturb the peace. He found himself in the main corridor of the second floor. He recognized Barlow's door, placed his hand on the knob. Suddenly he quailed. What truth might lie within the room where he had sat and conversed with the boy?

Setting his jaw, he flung open the door and rushed inside. The room was as he remembered it, minus Barlow, with the addition of dust and filth. The chess board was set up. The white king's pawn was advanced two spaces.

Ronar shuddered, stumbled into the corridor, and slammed the door. There he leaned against the wall, laughing raggedly at himself for letting that small detail unman him so. He wondered what would happen if he went back in and made a move in reply, then decided he wasn't ready to find out.

Ronar peered down the curving corridor. One of the doors was open. He studied it for a few long moments. No door had been open there before. He suspected he was meant to be enticed into that room, to enter it. He shrugged. Very well, he would.

His heels rapped on dust-free floors; no cobwebs wafted in the candlelight. The plaster walls were white and clean, the furniture decorated in cheerful colors. An ornate rocking horse stood in one corner, flanked by toy chests bright with clowns with winking eyes of black glass. Toys were strewn about: a wooden merry-go-round; a bank in the form of a monkey eating a banana; a doll whose cheeks were rosy disks on an ivory face.

Ronar cast a bleak glance on the one incongruous object in the room: a butcher knife, point stuck in the floor near two heaps of clothing . The blade looked stained in the uncertain light of the candles.

Two little girls sat at a table, one twice the size of the other. Both wore frilly party dresses of pale yellow. The younger girl had hair of dark gold; the older girl's was black. They sat before a miniature tea set, empty cups in hand. The fact that the room had been lightless before Ronar entered with his candles did not seem to trouble them. They looked up at him quizzically, their pale faces defined by shifting shadows.

"Chloe and Eliza?" asked Ronar quietly.

"I'm Chloe," said the older girl. "Who are you, and what are you doing in our room?"

"My name is Ronar. I'm here looking for a friend of mine, a boy named Martin. Have you seen him?"

"No."

Eliza, who looked about five years old and had a ribbon in her hair, giggled and said, "Oh, yes we have. Don't fib, Chloe."

"Hush!" said Chloe, sternly. "Anyway, I wasn't really fibbing. We haven't seen him yet. We just know he's here."

Eliza was not cowed. "I want to play with him."

"Yes, Eliza, we both do. But Mama needs him for serious reasons."

"Serious raisins! Ha ha. Mama is too serious for me."

A cold, sickly sweat trickled down Ronar's back.

"You girls are ghosts, correct?" It was most difficult to speak.

"We are not," said Chloe.

"Are too," whispered Eliza. "I told you to stop fibbing, Chloe. I've been little like this for such a long time. You never get any older either. We're dead." She patted her thighs and belly. "I feel real though." She looked up at Ronar, smiling. Her two front teeth were missing. "Hey, you tall funny man. You're not a ghost yet. Do you want to see if I feel real?"

Ronar shook his head.

"No?" Eliza's face fell. "It's been such a long time since we had someone to play with. Mama never lets us keep them for very long."

Chloe was studying Ronar with narrowed, suspicious eyes. She looked perhaps eleven, a slender miniature of her mother. "You can't have Martin back, Mr. Ronar. We need him."

"Need him for what?"

Eliza giggled. "Our god is going to eat him up."

"What does that mean?"

"Make Martin a part of him. Consume him. Merge with him. You know," said Chloe.

Nausea began to replace Ronar's cold sweat. "And why hasn't he 'eaten you up' too?"

Chloe grinned broadly and squirmed in her chair. "Oh, he has. I feel him inside me all the time. He makes me so much bigger than I was before. Usually I'm only a tiny part of him, and then I don't even know who I am anymore. But sometimes, like now, he sets me down and I'm myself again, for a while."

Eliza's round face showed a kind of uncertain wonder. "I think I feel him inside too. I thought it was just me being bad."

"I'm not going to let your god eat Martin," said Ronar.

Chloe laughed. "As if you can stop him. You'll be lucky to get out of here yourself. You should have left when you had the chance."

Eliza brightened. "Why don't we play with Mr. Ronar, Chloe? We can have lots of fun."

"Good idea, Eliza."

The children set down their tea cups and stood up, facing him, their white hands outstretched.

Ronar flushed, resisting the impulse to flee these horrid ghost children like some panicked dog. His gaze darted around, taking note once more of the knife in the floor and the piles of rumpled clothing.

"Why is that butcher knife here, girls?"

Chloe gave it a resentful glance. Eliza stared at it open-mouthed, as if she'd never seen it before.

"You know, if you two are ghosts, that means you died."

"Golly, really? You sure are smart, Mr. Ronar," said Chloe, rolling her eyes.

Ronar continued inexorably. "You died awfully young. How did you die, girls?"

"The townspeople killed us," muttered Chloe.

"I don't think so. Your mother committed suicide when your father was executed. I saw that in a vision of some kind. She was not yet even under arrest, yet she killed herself. What did she do first? I don't believe the people of this town would have gone after a bunch of children. Who killed you?"

Eliza whimpered. Tears flowed from her huge, reproachful eyes. Ronar hesitated, stung by remorse.

"I don't like it when people make my little sister cry," said Chloe quietly.

"I think she'd have a good reason to cry even if I weren't here." Ronar walked over to the heaps of clothing, kicked at them. "Look at this. Two bloody little dresses. Do they have anything to do with that knife, do you think?"

By now Eliza was sobbing. Her hands fluttered up to her throat. Chloe gave Ronar a murderous glance, winced, and held her own throat.

Eliza's sobs broke off into choking. Her hands dropped. A wide pink slash had appeared at her throat. She fumbled with it, held it open, inserted her fingers. Ronar fervently wished he had never started this.

"Where's my blood?" Eliza rasped. "I don't have any blood. Chloe, where's all my blood?"

"Don't be silly," panted Chloe. "We're dead. We don't have any blood."

"But where's my ghost blood? I have a ghost body. Why don't I have any ghost blood?"

"You just don't, that's all," snapped Chloe, clearly irritated by her sister's hysteria. Chloe's hands still circled her throat.

"It was Mama! Mama! She let out all my blood! Chloe!"

Chloe dropped her hands to stroke her sister's hair, revealing that her head was half severed from her body. Then she whirled on Ronar. "You think you're so smart," she spat. "But I know what ghosts can do to people who are still alive." Again she reached out with a colorless hand that seemed to radiate cold.

She jerked back when Ronar's dagger appeared in his free hand, gleaming in the candlelight.

His voice came low and hoarse. "Mind your manners, you brat. Remember how it felt when your blood flowed, set loose by cold metal in your throat—I'll bet you don't want to feel that again. Not so soon."

Eliza wailed and ran to huddle in a corner. Chloe hissed in frustration and backed into the shadows, where she clung to her sister.

"You can't do that to us," whispered Eliza. "You aren't our parents."

"I just want to get Martin and get out of here."

"You never will," said Chloe.

They turned to the nearest door and passed through it like the wraiths they were, still hand in hand. Eliza looked over her shoulder and whispered "Bye" as she passed from sight.

They carried the room's illusion of cleanness with them. The walls went dingy. The shape of the furniture was blurred by dust.

Despite his resolve, Ronar could not endure what he had just experienced without some reaction. He shook uncontrollably. Simultaneously came a near-hysterical relief—he doubted his dagger could have had any effect on the ghost children. Only the memory of their grisly demise had saved him, sparing him from whatever they considered "play."

That did nothing to make him feel any more manly about threatening two little girls with a knife—even dead ones.

Ronar forced his thoughts outward to the stars, which are unmoved by the fates of the tiny beings on whom they shed their light. In them was a permanence and a serenity that would outlast whatever mayhem might befall him. Their beauty would go unblemished, despite whatever failures or triumphs he might contrive in his brief lifetime. He must draw strength from that.

That is — unless Ahriman had its way among them.

Another emotion grew: a deep-seated rage. Those children had been born innocent; perhaps they still were, after a fashion. The masters of this house must account for many crimes.

He followed the children's pattering footsteps along dark corridors, down staircases, through hushed, shadowy rooms. They faded as he entered a dead-end hallway. At the end of it, hairlines of ruby light formed a square on the floor.

Ronar dropped to his knees. The square marked a trap door. He grabbed a metal ring and pulled it open against the stiffness of long disuse.

A rock-walled shaft led downward, a wooden ladder set into one wall. Far below was an opening that admitted flickering red light into the shaft. Murmuring voices echoed faintly from the depths.

Ronar extended a foot to test the ladder. It sagged at the first pressure, unfit for use. Lacking a rope, he decided on another method of descent. Bracing his back against one wall of the shaft and his feet against the other, he began to make his way down. On Earth, he'd climbed mountain chimneys in this manner; in this reduced gravity the descent was almost easy.

The shaft didn't end at the red-lit opening, but continued down to depths he couldn't guess. He clung to the walls, just above the reach of the wine-colored light, listening to the throaty chanting of Elizabeth's voice, sometimes broken by a chorus of childish voices repeating some strange prayer as they would a nursery rhyme.

Delay served no purpose. He grabbed the sill of the opening and prepared to fling himself in. But something halted him—the lazy waft of air from the black depths of the shaft, its musky scent, its hint of strange murmurs. Its mystery fascinated him, drew him on to explore.

But this was not the time to discover what Morlocks might inhabit the interior of this planet. He had work to do—work he'd be delighted to put off or abandon, but could not.

And so he swung into the reddish light, landing on a stage or platform of polished black obsidian.

He was in a cave, a convoluted volcanic bubble, apparently natural and almost unadorned. Opposite him was a black altar that seemed a mere extrusion of volcanic glass, crudely dressed to provide a more-or-less planar top, but without any ornament or symbol that Ronar could see. The light came from freestanding braziers flaming with a spectrum of reds: carmine, magenta, vermilion, maroon, cherry, and rose.

A strange, watery cry brought Ronar's attention back to the altar. Shapes were shifting within it, dimmed and refracted by irregularities in the glass. Ronar squinted, trying to make out what he was seeing. Only when the image passed behind a flatter area of the altar's surface could he recognize the face of the boy, Martin. It was most uncanny to see him submerged there like that. The blasted altar must be hollow. This "explanation" wasn't very successful at easing Ronar's mind, to his regret.

"Mr. Ronar! You came here to save me? Can you get me out?" The boy's voice was oddly liquid and distorted.

"That's right, Martin," said Ronar, his voice artificially confident. "I came to get you out of here. Be brave for a few more minutes and you'll be on your way home. I promise you."

A tinkle of icy laughter came from the shadows beside the altar. The spirits of the house lurked there, becoming clearer as they moved toward him. The three children looked at him with varying expressions. Chloe was narrow-eyed, resentful. Eliza looked coy and mischievous. Barlow was—smiling a friendly smile. His eyes kept darting between Ronar and Martin, his grin broadening.

Ronar ignored them for the moment in favor of their mother. She was much as he had seen her before, her face pale and beautiful, her chest slick with gore. Only the red rope-burn around her neck was new to him.

"Hello again, Mrs. Despard," said Ronar quietly.

Her voice was remote, edged with anger, yet the languor of her New Orleans accent persisted. "Mr. Ronar. My, how you do get around. Have you visited my boudoir as of yet? I'd hate for you to miss anything."

Ronar was too unnerved to engage in banter. "Release Martin. We will then depart, and you may complete your ceremony without our interference."

"That is kind, Mr. Ronar, but I fear it will not be convenient. For the god of man is beleaguered. He defies the tempest, stands against the earthquake, braces against the tide. He requires human souls during the struggle, to add their strength to his. The boy must contribute."

Ronar snorted. "This is ludicrous. I'm afraid your god will have to do his defying, standing, and bracing without Martin's help. Release him, woman, or I will see to it that you regret it."

The ghost-woman laughed derisively. "And how will you do that, braggart? We are beyond your power. You cannot hinder us while we attend to his transmigration."

Ronar bared his teeth, his heart pounding. "Why pick on a helpless boy? Why not try your luck at sending my soul to that wretched demon you worship, you witch?"

"Perhaps we shall."

"Yes...why not?" Barlow's face was alight with a sudden hope. "You could stay with us then, Mr. Ronar...be like us. It's not so bad, really. If you stay, maybe...maybe you can be my new father."

Something crumpled inside Ronar at this plea.

Elizabeth laughed again. "We'll see about that later, Barlow." She stepped over to the altar, where she seemed to captivate Martin, quieting his restless thrashing. His small face gazed raptly into hers. "Look deep, boy. Let dark dreams send you to your new master."

Ronar roared and lifted one of the braziers. The hot metal seared his flesh, but he ignored the pain. "Turn, damn you!"

The ghost-woman turned.

He thrust the brazier into her face. It seemed to meet momentary resistance, but then passed through her as through a fog. The flaming liquid spilled onto the floor and spread into a pool of ruby flame. Ronar cast down the brazier in disgust.

"Alas, Mr. Ronar! We are spirits and worshippers of Satan; how can you expect his fires to harm us? What will you do now?"

He stared at her, working to keep dismay from showing on his face. What could he do? Not being Sha Totek, he couldn't simply mutter "abracadabra" and cause his opponents to dissipate in the breeze.

The only aspect of these phantoms he could hope to influence must be their minds. Perhaps he could gain some control over the situation if he could make her lose her arrogant self-assurance.

Unfortunately, psychological warfare between the sexes had never been his forte.

"Button your dress, woman. You remind me of a frog I once dissected in school. You make me want to puke, and you're too damn immaterial to clean up after me."

She looked back at him imperiously. Her self-inflicted wounds drew in on themselves, sucking back the blood and gore, healing so rapidly that within seconds her chest was white and flawless as marble. She thrust out her breasts, making no move to close her bodice. Her appraisal of Ronar became distinctly challenging.

For an instant Ronar was flustered, but then he barked out his unpleasant laugh. "You're a ghost, woman! Good Lord, aren't any of you capable of advancing beyond the state you were in when you died? If I understand correctly, seduction requires two parties, both of whom are living."

"I can seem remarkably alive to you, given the chance."

Ronar shook his head in wonder. Then it struck him— they could indeed not change from the way they were at their deaths. Barlow still missed his father as much as ever.

Eliza was still little more than a toddler. Elizabeth still tried to get her way using the body she no longer possessed.

What exactly was he facing here? He had fallen into the use of the word "ghost" easily enough, though it was an imprecise term. Was the magic of Colibdis making it possible for him to see spirits that would have been invisibly present even on Earth? Or were they dependent on that magic for this strange half-existence? Were these captive souls, or unnatural shadows of once-living people?

Ronar, realizing he was staring at Elizabeth's breasts, tore his gaze away, directing it at her face. "I—I haven't yet seen your husband, Mrs. Despard—at least, not since I witnessed the memory of his hanging."

"Nor will you see him. The good townsfolk would not suffer him to be buried within their community. Thus he no longer walks within these walls."

"My absence has not been entirely involuntary…"

The ghosts and Ronar alike looked around for the source of this new voice.

A dark figure stepped out of a shadowed corner. "…and I believe I must now make an exception."

"Damon!" Elizabeth said, wide-eyed. She raised a hand to her mouth.

The children trotted up to their father, crying "Daddy! Daddy! Look what Mother did to us!" They tipped back their heads to reveal their opened throats.

Despard sighed. "Yes, children, I know. Your mother has always been prone to impulsive actions. I will speak to her about it later. Now, my former wife, listen to me. Your efforts to procure the child for our god are laudable, but we can do more. Ronar himself is the greater prize, and we must take him."

Elizabeth responded with a doubtful glance at Ronar.

"Yes, wife, I have studied Ronar since his arrival in Thunderbird, and he is formidable. He is not like the weak and ill people we have preyed upon before. But then, he is right here in our house, among us. If you had tried to defeat him in the way you intended, he would have—embarrassed you. Cover yourself. There is another way."

"You'll never beat Mr. Ronar," called out Martin. "Heck, I bet you couldn't even handle that ugly horse of his, let alone him."

Barlow laughed, then cast a guilty look at his father.

The lunacy of the situation was taking a toll on Ronar's self-control. He fought down an urge to compliment Despard on his wife's mammary development. Instead he said, "You're right, Despard. That blasted thing you call a god would like to get its hands on me."

Despard bristled, drew himself up. "And how would you know that?"

"It told me itself."

"Indeed?"

Ronar noted indignation in Despard's taut face.

"That's right. It initiated a chat with me almost as soon as I arrived on this planet of yours."

"I find that quite improbable." Now Despard was actually trembling. Ronar continued his probe.

"It tried to recruit me to its freakish cause, but naturally I told the disgusting spook to go to hell."

"Be damned to you!" Despard burst out.

"What's the matter, Despard? Hasn't your little god ever taken the trouble to address you, despite your many years of devotion to it?"

Despard's mouth worked; he seemed on the verge of some new outburst while his wife and children watched in fascination. But gradually his eyelids lowered and his mouth grew firm.

"There is no need for words between us. We are one. I know his will, and he knows all there is to know of me. His asking you to join us was a kindness. I know your kind. You are solitary, arid of spirit, devoted to an esoteric discipline offering little warmth or comfort. I might easily have been like you. But look at the life I gave myself by making other choices. Look at my magnificent wife. You admire her, I can see it in your eyes. And well you should. Her spirit is a liquid fire, the most piquant spice imaginable. Look at my beautiful children, each more clever and delightful than the rest. You, on the other hand, are emotionally unassailable. You are a bleak and hopeless fortress, proof against whatever love the world might offer you."

Ronar looked at him in disbelief. "Must I point out that you and your family all died well before your time? That your delightful children were murdered by your magnificent wife? That you yourself were executed for your crimes?"

"Yes, that is true. But while we lived, we lived in full. Even now, we have an existence in the shared being of our god. What do you look forward to, however many your years? I can tell you. Isolation, loneliness, a struggle to find some meaning in your life. And then, oblivion. You will have nothing better. Perhaps it suits you. Let us have the boy, if you will not join us, and go your way. What does he mean to you? People are only troublesome abstractions to you, after all."

Ronar's reply came without effort. "This isn't about my nature. It's about Martin's. He smiles, he laughs, he is full of joys and enthusiasms. Maybe I am as you say. But I'm not such a megalomaniac as to think that everyone should be like me. I am not so deluded as to suppose that my own flaws and lacks are universal, that my faults devalue everyone else. Others may be happy and untroubled, and they bring light to the world. I will not leave one such person in your grasp merely because I am not one of them."

"Very well. We have given you numerous chances to leave. Now it seems we must take you after all."

Ronar gave another raw laugh. "You can try. Frankly, after getting a good face-full of you and your family, I'm not afraid of you anymore. I know your kind too, Despard. If you were still solid enough for me to take a swing at you, you'd be plying me with polite talk until you could stick a knife in my back."

Despard did not flush in his anger; perhaps that was too lifelike a reaction to expect. He did step forward, his hands darting out to clamp onto Ronar's shoulders.

To Ronar's surprise, he felt the contact, though not as the touch of living hands. Instead, a deep, stunning cold spread out, diffusing though his body, seeping into his head. In his fading vision the ghosts lost their illusion of solidity, becoming grainy, like over-enlarged photographs. That was his last sight of the world for a while.

He entered a blackness devoid of any sensation. Though he saw nothing, he was aware of the presence of the Despards—all five of them, if he was not mistaken.

Flecks of crimson light appeared, swirling silently, an attractive if meaningless display. After a few moments their movements became more purposeful, each shred of fire slipping into place to build up curves and planes of luminosity.

Soon the basic pattern was obvious: a human face. When the final fragments came together, he confronted a mask he knew to be an image of Ahriman.

Ahriman looked at him with a dispassionate stare that flickered occasionally into an expression of malicious triumph. The god was lean-cheeked and saturnine, with a high forehead and prim, ascetic features. In fact, Ahriman looked almost exactly like Damon Despard. Ronar studied the image more narrowly. Its features blurred momentarily into androgyny—more like those of Elizabeth than Damon. He even caught glimpses of the children as the face blurred and flowed. It smiled at him, looked superior. For one unforgettable moment the face of the God of Evil and Magic petulantly stuck out its tongue.

Ronar's contempt flared high. The Despards must have no clear idea of what they were worshipping—or at least no consistent one. If anything, they seemed to view their god as a grandiosely magnified version of themselves.

Very well then. If the Despards could somehow haunt his mind and share their visions with him, he could do the same for them. But what sort of images might dismay or baffle them?

The answer occurred to him all at once. With a disembodied smile at the appropriateness of it, he summoned an image of space to surround his consciousness, billions of light-years of it.

The Despards drifted as filmy outlines of human beings, now spectral in every way. They looked around, awed by the immensity around them. A great wilderness of stars burned amidst banks of glowing mist, tiny points of light beyond counting, daunting them with the knowledge of an infinity of worlds. There was nothing to hold them there, but neither was there anywhere for them to go. They cringed as if seared by the naked starlight that rained upon them from all around.

To enhance the effect, Ronar summoned an image of Saturn, its grand geometry as perfect a paradigm of natural order as he could imagine.

Their thoughts were palpable. They had never conceived of a setting so remote from man, so independent of human deeds or artifacts. Never had the Despards dreamed that human beings could be so tiny, so utterly lost. It was unthinkable that they could ever find their way back to sanity through this stunning vastness.

They had entered Ronar's mind full of cunning; now they had only a desperate desire to escape this monstrous intellect and its mad creations.

And yet Ronar felt that what he had shown them so far was not enough. He had a vague yet growing sense of the god they worshipped: the anthropomorphism of its nature and desires, the pettiness of its ambitions. The cosmos Ronar presented to them was grand indeed, yet he sensed it was merely the breath of something still grander: an underlying reality, a god so ineffable as to make this Ahriman appear nothing more than an absurd prankster. Ronar could never hope to understand or express this reality using words or concepts; they were far too limited. But he felt something great: a peace, an inexpressible fulfillment, dissolving his mind in a sea of cool radiance. If he could feel this, so too must those who had intruded into his being. Later, his only regret would be that the ecstasy had been so brief, and his recollection of it so poor.

The first sound he heard as he returned to the world was that of his labored breathing, gradually slowing and becoming more controlled. His body tingled with blood flow resuming. He lay weak and helpless on the floor of the volcanic cave. One by one his other senses returned.

When he was able to see again, he beheld the ghosts, now transformed.

Damon, Elizabeth, and Chloe moved blindly about the room. Their dry lips were drawn back from their teeth; their jaws hung loosely . Their ears were like flaps of colorless leather, and their sunken noses leaked flakes of dry tissue from within their skulls. Lank hair fell over eye sockets that contained nothing but dried crusts. Chloe and Elizabeth moaned and gibbered, unable to form words. Mortality was catching up with them at last, thought Ronar, watching their decay with morbid fascination.

Barlow and Eliza were in an altogether different state. They were beaming, radiant, holding hands and smiling.

"Goodbye, Mother, Father," said Barlow. "You've held us here long enough." He turned to Ronar. "And farewell to you, Mr. Ronar, sir, and thanks."

"Goodbye, Barlow."

"Goodbye, Mommy and Daddy," laughed Eliza. "I hope you're getting what you wanted. Bye, Chloe."

Elizabeth wailed. The two children disappeared in a bright wind that extinguished some of the flaming braziers.

Damon Despard was still able to speak, though dust and bits of debris spurted from his mouth as he did so.

"The boy is free. Get out of here."

Ronar lurched to his feet. The altar where Martin had been imprisoned was empty. The house trembled.

"Let go of your vanity, you fools," said Ronar. "Follow after your children, if you can."

Word of the madman who'd invaded the House of Despard had spread throughout Two Suns. A crowd was gathered in front of the mansion. They carried lanterns, defying the night, the cold, and their fears.

A collective cry of dread went up when the doors boomed open to reveal a tall figure, dark and menacing.

Ronar stepped off the veranda and walked toward them with an unsteady stride.

The crowd, not entirely reassured, parted before him, but then promptly forgot him as a small moan escaped from Martin's lips. The boy's parents and Dr. Joachim hovered over the boy. Ronar tottered up, looked down at the boy. "How—how did Martin get—"

Dr. Joachim looked up at him in wonder. "It was his spirit. I've had Martin's body with me the whole time, even as the Despards pried loose his soul and summoned it to them. Now body and soul are reunited. How you managed that I doubt I'll ever understand."

Ronar frowned, then lost his train of thought. He turned and looked back at the house. "Well," he announced to no one in particular, "those spooks won't be trying this again anytime soon." Then he collapsed in the street.

And suddenly Sha Totek was there, robes flapping in the night winds. His gaze seized upon a slender figure who wore a paper clip dangling from a ribbon around her neck.

"Phaedra Holder," he commanded, "Take care of this man. He is some kind of a hero."

Phaedra instantly came forward and knelt beside Ronar, cradling his head in her lap, stroking his hair.

Ronar opened his eyes and dimly saw the sorcerer standing nearby. He began to mumble. "These people...they are all souls..."

He paused to lick his lips.

"Those spirits in there...trapped by magic...kept from passing on despite their deaths...it's not dignified. I'm not sure...how I like this magic of yours, Sha Totek."

Then he turned to look up past the gentle swell of Phaedra's breast. "You are beautiful...as sunlight falling... on fields of...green grass..."

"He's delirious," declared Sha Totek. "Young lady, take this hotel room key. Help him to the Olympus and put him to bed."

"Anything you say..." she said dreamily.

Somehow Ronar found the strength to lumber away with Phaedra.

The crowd began to disperse. Soon only Sha Totek remained, standing beneath the stars of midnight, studying the house, and waiting.

Eventually, a man stepped up to him and placed a vane of shining steel into his hands.

"Here's that feller's sword, Mr. Totek. I can't steal from a feller who'd take on the Despards like that. I'm right sorry."

Sha Totek nodded and the man departed.

The sorcerer looked around, spying the steeple of a Christian church peeking up above the rooftops.

"I truly hope you won't mind if I call in some outside help on this," he whispered. "I have to make do with what I know."

The sorcerer sighed and invoked the most ancient of all magics.

When the incantation was complete, the Jackal-Headed God stepped forth from the folds of the night, its great eyes rolling in their sockets as they surveyed the house.

Sha Totek shivered as Anubis went to perform the task it had performed through vaults of time very nearly as deep as his own.

Anubis passed into the house. Sha Totek knew that no one would ever hear from the Despard family again. Even if the Despards were unwilling to depart on their own, Anubis would see to it that they did. Sha Totek looked up, grateful that the Eye of Ahriman was not open to look back at him. What he and Ronar had done tonight would not go well with that one.

Chapter 7

Town Meeting

The main room of the Olympus Saloon was bright in the morning. Tall windows admitted suns-light to shine on white tablecloths. Brass fittings gleamed. It was already a lively place, although only a few of the harder cases were drinking hard liquor at such an early hour. Celebration over the downfall of the Despards continued from the previous night. Sha Totek held court at one of the most boisterous tables, presiding over a group of local dignitaries, trying with some sincerity to deflect their efforts to credit him with the ghost family's demise.

Two of the sorcerer's companions seemed to take the name of the establishment too seriously — middle-aged men wrapped in the himations of Classical Greece. The silver-plated six-guns belted around their waists glittered splendidly, though they added an odd note to the Periclean dignity of their bearers.

Sha Totek kept an eye on the grand staircase that led to the rooms above. Someone descended: Phaedra Holder. He turned to her with a smile that died when he saw the tight, controlled expression on her pale face. Her eyes were moist and glittering. Looking neither left nor right, she left the saloon.

"You know, that Phaedra is a fine young woman," drawled one of Sha Totek's tablemates. "I'm inclined to take a poke at whoever put that look on her face."

The sorcerer winced. He was more subdued when he returned to his conversation.

Presently the babble of voices died away as the patrons, bartenders, dealers, waitresses, and prostitutes took note of another figure descending the stairs. His garments were rumpled and filthy. His face was unshaven, his iron-grey hair wild and unrestrained. He paused on the stairs, looking down at the faces bobbing in the brass-and-crystal sea of the saloon. He looked numb, uncertain, perhaps a little lost.

Someone called out, "Who's that mangy desperado? Get him the hell out of here!"

"Quiet, you idiot, before I turn you into a tree frog," snapped Sha Totek. He stood and walked toward the staircase, his jeweled costume incongruous among the drab outfits of the male guests of the Olympus. He climbed up, grabbed Ronar's elbow, and guided him back upstairs. "You look like hell," he said out of the side of his mouth. "Why didn't Phaedra clean you up before she left?" He felt Ronar bristle beside him. "Er, maybe she needed to open her store. Never you mind."

Sha Totek didn't care for Ronar's silence, or for the distracted look on his face. He spoke reluctantly: "Ronar—if you need to—the world probably won't end if we stay here a day or two."

That woke the man up a little. "No. I've had enough of this town. When are we leaving?"

Sha Totek blinked. "I've got to address a town meeting at noon. Warn the T-Birds about what's going on, and tell them what to expect from Namirnakh."

"Very well."

"Would you do me a couple of favors?"

"Possibly."

"I want you looking presentable. I'll send a tailor up to your room, and a barber—in an hour."

Ronar frowned. "What for?"

"Because I want you to speak to the crowd too, and here's what I want you to say..." Sha Totek laid out his plans.

Now Ronar's frown was a full-blown scowl. "Not a chance in hell. I'm not spouting any such nonsense. I'm heading out of town. You dispense your bullshit and catch up with me when you're done."

Sha Totek blinked. "Ah, Ronar, it's really important to give these people some hope..."

"Look, do you want my help with this escapade, or not?"

That was loud enough to again silence the carousers down on the floor. Sha Totek waited until they resumed talking to continue.

"Ronar..." He halted at the obdurate look on the astronomer's face. He sighed. "Let's keep it down, all right? Yes, I want your help."

"Then I'll meet you north of town." Ronar stalked down the stairs and out the door.

Sha Totek rolled his eyes, but did not budge. His mind flew into furious activity. Ronar's stubbornness would ruin his scheme unless Sha Totek could think fast.

At the appointed hour, Sha Totek found himself behind a lectern facing a crowd of Thunderbird notables and not-so-notables, their expressions darkening with his every word.

"Namirnakh may send foot soldiers through here on their way to the Portal. If they do come through, you just get out of their way. I doubt you could do much to stop them."

That produced some grumbling, but it couldn't be helped. No amount of fervent patriotism would help against the grim troops of Darteharn.

"I think Namirnakh will send his main forces by sea. They'll come from the Dark Port and land somewhere in the Bay of Aegeos on your north coast. Some may come overland by way of Mersinea. I'm asking for two or three of you sidewinders to ride yonder and give 'em my warning."

"I'll go!"

"Same here!"

"Eat my dust, you varmints, I'm gettin' there first!"

Soon half the men in the hall were declaring their intention to make the trip. Finally the Mayor, who was one of those men affecting Mersinean dress, intervened by sending three of his cronies. They left immediately and enthusiastically.

His major purpose fulfilled, Sha Totek took a few questions, mostly to satisfy the Thunderbird regard for Democracy. The first one was unwelcome, but expected.

"Mr. Totek, sir, meanin' no disrespect, but if'n you're the almighty magic-man you're cracked up to be, why don't you just ride your broomstick up North, instead of goin' all that way on horseback?"

Sha Totek took a moment to implant a vision of the life led by a dung beetle in the man's mind before he replied. "Why, friend, I could be there as quickly as—this!" He snapped his fingers, blipping himself two feet to the left.

"But it would be a big mistake for me to do that. A big shift through space is difficult magic. If I were to snap myself all the way to Hyperborea, I'd get there all right, but I'd be more tuckered out than a lonely sheepherder's favorite ewe. Be scarce a whit of magic left in me. But you might think, if I get there soon enough, I could take it easy, rest up while I'm waitin' to see what's up. Well, trouble is, I'm goin' to a place not far from the dang North Pole. It's a cold winter night up there, a night that goes on for months. Right savage it is. No place for rest and recuperation. No, my best chance is to get where I'm a goin' with as much of my pep preserved as I can manage."

In addition, such a course as the man suggested would be contrary to the expressed will of Varanu. But that argument wouldn't impress these cowpokes. Sha Totek uneasily noted the dissatisfied faces before him. He'd left them thinking he was abandoning them in the face of a possible attack from Namirnakh. It was true enough.

Another man raised his hand. "Mr. Totek? Just exactly why must you go to Hyperborea?"

Sha Totek swallowed hard. There was nothing for it. "Varanu told me to go."

"Varanu? Ain't that one of them heathen gods?"

"You sure it weren't the good Lord what told you to go?" asked another man.

Sha Totek had never heard of a minefield, but he was learning about the concept now. "It may have been," he said carefully. "You know that here on Colibdis, the identities of the gods aren't quite as distinct as they were on Earth. Here, one man's Varanu may be another's Jehovah. It's just a matter of names and perceptions."

That brought a long moment of chilly silence.

Sha Totek suddenly felt highly conspicuous standing before this Christian crowd, asking them to have confidence in what was, to them, a minor pagan idol. He hoped his questioners wouldn't realize he hadn't answered the question, that he had no idea of the purpose of his mission. Knowing the volatile folk of Thunderbird, that could send them running for a bucket of tar and a bag of chicken feathers.

This meeting must end on a positive note if the Thunderbirds were to have the heart to carry on in the days that might lie ahead. It was time to pull the rabbit out of the hat. With an imitation of glad surprise, Sha Totek looked down the aisle at the doorway. Everyone in the hall turned to follow his gaze.

A tall, grey-haired man entered, striding briskly toward the stage. He wore a pinstriped suit of charcoal grey, with a string tie fastened by a pin of smoky quartz. He was perfectly groomed. His jaw jutted out at a confident angle.

All eyes except Sha Totek's followed him as he walked down the aisle.

Sha Totek roused himself and announced: "And now — Ladies and Gentlemen! Meet the newest and greatest hero of Thunderbird, the man who single-handedly brought down the house of Despard! Let me introduce you, my friends, to a man direct from Arizona, straight from the great University at Tucson! My dear friend and companion, Professor Leonard Ronar!"

A storm of approval broke out as Ronar took his place behind the lectern. He looked out over the sea of faces as they voiced their admiration for this man who was not merely a hero, but an Arizonan.

"Fellow citizens of the United States of America—"
That was enough to provoke another outburst of enthusiasm. "Howdys all around, greetings from Earth, from the good old U.S. of A. It's rightly an honor for me to speak before you today. Ya know, although you folks of Thunderbird are separated from your countrymen, word of your doins' does git over to the President and the Congress. Yep, our good friend Sha Totek carefully eyeballs your progress, and communicates it regularly to Washington."

A sigh of amazement went up at the news.

"The President is mighty impressed by your great University, and the publishing business you've built around it. He's also tickled by your friendship with our Indian brothers. Of these achievements you can be right proud. Therefore, as an appointed representative of the Federal Government, it is now my honor to announce that by an act of Congress, Thunderbird has been admitted to the Union! Thunderbird is now the forty-eighth state!"

A cataclysm of joy erupted from the crowd, making their previous demonstrations seem half-hearted. Ronar thundered out, "Now let's show that sidewinder Namirnakh what good Americans can really do!"

A few individual cries could be picked out from the general uproar:

"Statehood! Statehood!"

"Ronar for Mayor!"

"Ronar for Governor!"

"Ronar for Senator!"

One man stood up and cried, "Hey, wait a minute! I just heard last night that there are already forty nine states in the Union! Wouldn't that make us the fiftieth?"

The celebration collapsed into silence.

"Ah…" said Ronar. "As a matter of fact…"

"As a matter of fact," piped up Sha Totek, "the vote that made Thunderbird a state was actually taken before those other two states were admitted. So, officially, Thunderbird is forty-eighth. We'd best be riding now. Vaya con Dios."

That was good enough to satisfy any doubters. The astronomer waved and nodded, stepped down and ambled out of the hall, with Sha Totek close behind.

"Good boy," muttered Sha Totek without moving his lips. "Now let's mount those nice horseys over there and ride on out of here."

"Sure, whatever you say."

News of Statehood flashed through town like fire crackling down a fuse. The citizens of Thunderbird danced in the streets as Ronar and Sha Totek rode north on Main Street. Dance hall girls flaunted their petticoats. Weeping cowboys pounded each other's shoulders. Children danced. Women looked at Ronar with glistening eyes. The crowd surged, yelped, and whooped. The Mayor fired a precious round from his silver-plated revolver. A few flags were hastily unfurled, each bearing a new star tacked onto a corner of the blue field.

Sha Totek glanced at his companion as he accepted the praise with an easy smile. They'd done a reasonable job in the short time available. Now the sorcerer could relax.

By the time they'd left the crowd behind on the edge of town, the man riding beside him no longer looked as much like Ronar.

"Good work, Big Jim. Now, you remember what to do now?"

"I sure do. I hightail it to Morongo or Vasquez Crossing, so nobody around here can recognize me. With this stake you done give me, I can get my own place."

"And you remember what'll happen to you if you ever spill the beans?"

Big Jim flinched a little. "Yessir. Don't worry, I ain't anxious to hunt around in my bedroll lookin' for anything that might have fallen off me during the night. Nosireebob."

"Good boy. Now, then, the suit. I want it."

"Awwwww..."

"Jim."

Tall dropped off his horse and started to strip. Sha Totek fished out the man's old clothes from a saddlebag and tossed them to him. In a few minutes Tall went loping off into the brush, while Sha Totek resumed his ride, leading the other horses.

He found Ronar standing in the road a mile farther along, holding his binocular. At least the man had shaved and bathed at some point.

"Who was that man you were with? Where did he vanish to?"

"Good news, Ronar!" grinned Sha Totek. "You've just declared Thunderbird the newest state!"

Ronar turned white. "What the *hell*—"

Sha Totek was saved from Ronar's explosion by the appearance of a wagon rolling toward them from town. It came clattering up, halted. Doctor Joachim was driving; riding were Martin, the boy's parents, and other children made on the same general lines as Martin. Martin lay on a stretcher, weak and sleepy, but clearly in no further danger.

When Martin saw the astronomer looming over him, he marshaled his strength enough to ask, "Mr. Ronar? Will you do me a favor?"

"If I can."

"The next time you see me, will you tell me what happened last night? I can't figure out what was a dream and what was real."

"I know what you mean."

Martin glanced at his mother, who was talking with the doctor. He whispered, "Did I—did I really see that naked black-haired lady?"

Ronar snorted. "No. You didn't see any lady, believe me."

Martin's parents thanked Ronar with what Sha Totek supposed was simple pioneer dignity, and departed. Thankfully, they didn't mention statehood, which might have overcome Ronar's strained efforts to be polite. Mrs. Jordan spared an envious glance for Sha Totek's purple finery as their wagon pulled away.

"Well, I'd say you've made enough of an impression on this town for now. Let's ride on out of here," said Sha Totek airily.

"I'm for that," growled Ronar. "And I expect an explanation for what you apparently told these people in my name." He approached his horse, eyed it warily, and mounted it without grace.

"Ronar, why must you be such a surly son of a bitch? You did something great last night. You rescued that boy, freed two other spirits, and faced down the remainder through sheer strength of character. Then you enjoyed the company of a delightful young woman. And yet somehow you remain meaner than skunk piss."

Ronar's attention focused to a sharp point fixed on Sha Totek. "If I can avoid spending another night dreaming about decaying ghosts leering at me in the night, I'll be a happier man. As for Phaedra—" He halted, sputtering, at a loss. "I'm..."

Sha Totek took note of the distress on Ronar's face. "Ease back there, partner. You don't want to talk about it right now, that's fine."

"It's surely none of your business. It's just that I never...I don't..."

Sha Totek's jaw dropped. "You're not a...funny boy, are you?"

"No! No. It's just that I don't have an...easy time with women. I don't trust them, and I don't trust myself with them. What about you? What did you accomplish last night? A series of encounters with the local prostitutes?"

"Alas, you wrong me," lamented Sha Totek. "I was confined with the Mayor and the Governor. While you were interfering with the religious observances of the Despard family, I was convincing those grave gentlemen of the danger threatening them. I admit I had not planned to spend the evening with two men dressed in sheets, but such was my lot."

Ronar raised an eyebrow at this, but did not dispute it.

"I hear you killed your nehock," said Sha Totek.

Ronar was somber. "Yes. I'll never ride one of those things again. We never should have used them in the first place."

"Perhaps not."

"I'm afraid I was in no state of mind to deal with the carcass. I left it on the street."

"Oh, don't worry about that. Someone skinned it and sold the hide to a tannery. Joachim removed the eggs—he thinks they may be viable, or at least tasty. The meat..."

"The eggs—?"

"Didn't you notice? The biggest, fiercest nehocks are the females."

"And what about these lies you told in my name?"

"That was for morale. These folks are facing a tough time. They've been yearning to be a state in that country of yours for years and years. They needed to hear the news from an actual American, not from me. Since you weren't willing to help, I did the next best thing. Between your doings with the Despards and the words I put in your mouth, your reputation in T-Bird is golden, in case you ever get back."

"It was a lie."

"Yes, it was a lie."

Ronar fell to brooding, which struck Sha Totek as an improvement over snarling. After a while Ronar said, in a more reasonable tone, "Why are you so sure the Thunderbirds will be helpless before Namirnakh?"

"They have no tradition of magic, and their god is the only one on Colibdis who never does anything noticeable."

"But don't they have guns?"

"Guns? Now, that would be interesting. But they do not have guns, or anyway, only a few antiques from Earth, worn as badges of honor by men like the Mayor and Sheriff. They cannot make them. A blacksmith cannot hammer out a gun. You've seen that Thunderbird makes many things, but guns require tools they do not have and cannot make. They can't even get steel in any quantity. No, guns are out."

They left the outliers of Two Suns behind and entered the range lands of northern Thunderbird. Later in the afternoon, Sha Totek turned at the rumble of thunder behind them. "Look back there. Learn something about this new state of Thunderbird."

Ronar drew up and turned about. Hovering over the distant city was a colossal thunderhead, blindingly white above, shaded to blackness below. Stratospheric winds sheared the cloud's peak into a hook like the beak of a bird of prey.

"A magnificent storm. Looks like an eagle."

"Symbolic, ain't it?"

All at once the storm extended inky wings of turbulent cloud, casting vast shadows over the landscape. It reached out with talons of lightning, crying with the voice of thunder. The Thunderbird soared, trailing streamers of rain over the parched country that bore its name.

"You've got to hand it to those Indian shamans. They really do it with style." The sorcerer shook his head in admiration.

"Are you telling me these Indians can conjure a thunderstorm in the shape of a bird, but they can't do anything against Namirnakh?"

"The magic of Namirnakh is very great. It is unsurpassed in all the world. Almost."

Chapter 8

The River Tal

Ronar awoke a few mornings later beneath a vault of indigo so pure that a few stars were still visible. The suns were just below the horizon. A line of high cirrus in the eastern sky was washed with that glorious light that is somehow golden and magenta at the same time.

Ronar's sleeping bag was beaded with dew, a small price to pay to awaken to such beauty. Sha Totek, on the other hand, could not be pried out of his magical tent. Glossy as silk, complex as a miniature medieval pavilion, each evening it unpacked and erected itself, a colorful web spun by some unseen spider.

The astronomer climbed out of his bag, pulled on his boots, and stretched the stiffness out of his joints.

The bejeweled hilt of his sword winked at him from its place among their piled gear. He pulled it out of its shabby scabbard and examined it closely for the first time.

He was glad to have it back, for it was truly a magnificent piece of craftsmanship. He had rarely seen gems as fiery as those that decorated the pommel and guard. The blade was fascinating. He had always imagined the blade of a sword to be like an enlarged jackknife, but this was a highly evolved work. A portion of the blade just above the hilt was dull; clearly, a hand could grip it here for greater leverage. Both sides of the blade had a small channel running its full length.

When Sha Totek finally poked his head out of his tent, the first thing he saw was Ronar sweeping the great blade through the air, its steel giving back the hot white light of the newly risen Photos.

"Very commendable," said the sorcerer. "But for both our sakes, I hope you'll learn to cut more than air with that weapon."

"Like this?"

Ronar sprang towards an odd tree that looked like a spiky wooden dandelion twenty feet tall. Taking the grip in both hands, he sent the blade whistling in with such force that the tree was cut through, forcing him to jump back as it toppled.

Sha Totek made a strangled sound. "That's an edge of mere steel! A few more whacks like that and it'll chip, or at least need a good sharpening. If you must do that, at least use the part of the blade closer to the hilt. It's stronger."

"I don't understand. I thought these things were intended for abuse. Chopping through armored opponents, for example."

"An opponent is one thing, a perfectly benign tree is another. Just be careful with the damn thing. I may fix you up with some lessons once we reach Eranior."

"You said using a sword like this is easy...?"

"It's like most things. You can use it crudely and get some use out of it. Or you can delve into the artistry of it and become much more effective."

Soon they mounted to begin the day's ride. The land continued to fall away from the high plateau of Thunderbird. Gradually it flattened into a horizon-touching expanse of knee-high grass, brown in the winter dry season. Sha Totek steered them onto a dirt track running northeast. This road often ran beside winding depressions, riverbeds cut off by the meanderings of some main channel. Wherever the present river might be, it must be full of sediments to have lain down these rich soils, in the process choking out so many of its former pathways.

"I can't imagine why no one lives here. It must be the best farmland on the planet."

Sha Totek shrugged. "No Portal nearby. I suppose someone will migrate here eventually. Might even make a nice fifty first state for that country of yours."

As Photos and Kudu passed their apex the two riders topped a natural levee and looked across the great river whose languorous course had shaped the landscape they had traveled most of the day.

Sha Totek swept his arm over the wide golden vista. "Here is the river Tal. In the highlands of distant Ammon it rises, watering that most ancient of human civilizations. In Eanda it joins with the River of the Grasses, and flows north for a total of no fewer than fifteen hundred miles. Here it veers to the west, to enter the Bay of Aegeos some hundred miles further on. At this point, it marks the boundary between the unclaimed lands to the south and Eranior to the north."

They rode down to the bank, where the Eranians maintained a ferry, a wooden barge tethered to a dock. A ferryman emerged from a thatched cabin and started toward them.

"How will that raft cross the river? It has no paddles, sails, or poles, and there's no cable," said Ronar.

Sha Totek smiled wanly. "We have left Thunderbird behind. You will now begin to get a fuller idea of the forces that drive Colibdis. By the way, don't be surprised if I assign myself a name you're not used to hearing. I'm less universally beloved here than I am in Thunderbird. And I don't want word of my travels reaching Namirnakh. Keep your sword under cover, or our friend will know we're not the simple magician and disciple I'm about to claim we are."

The ferryman met them with enthusiasm, for this was a lonely post. Ronar regarded him carefully, the first representative of a truly archaic culture he had met, except for Sha Totek, who could hardly be called representative of anything. A light-skinned man of medium height, the ferryman had dark shoulder-length hair, blue eyes, and a heavy mustache. He wore an earth-colored cloak over undyed woolen garments. His only ornament was a copper lion-head medallion suspended from a leather cord. He spoke a rolling, lilting version of Welsh, hard to follow since it incorporated elements of older Celtic languages, as well as some Latin. Ronar had had little use for Welsh as a boy, but now he was grateful for his father's love of obscure and dying languages.

The astronomer ventured a greeting, his accent revealing him as a speaker of English. Anxious to practice that language, the ferryman switched over, speaking it with an accent like thick porridge. Most of his infrequent passengers were Thunderbirds traveling on missions of scholarship and commerce.

"Did you see the foulness that leaked from the Eye of Evil last week? Perhaps the Renegade has at last seen the light of Belenus and has fled our world."

"Could be," said Sha Totek noncommittally.

They led the horses onto the ferry. The ferryman stepped to the center of the raft, raised his arms, and grandly recited the incantation that would carry the vessel to the opposite bank. When this produced no effect, his face fell in perplexity and embarrassment. Gathering himself, he repeated the words, to no avail. The well-used spell seemed suddenly useless.

"Damn," muttered Sha Totek. He took himself to a corner of the raft and stood facing the water.

"Please forgive the delay," said the ferryman. "I must have muddled the inflections of the operative verbs. I will try again." First he triple-checked that all lines were indeed free, and even ducked into the water to make sure the ferry hadn't grounded on some mud bar. Satisfied, he again offered up his spell, this time including a plea to Arianrhod, goddess of rivers.

The ferry surged out against the current. The ferryman looked relieved but still puzzled. He took the tiller to guide them across the river.

The Tal was very wide at this point, a stately brown flow moving smoothly but forcefully to the sea. Gulls and ospreys flitted in a sky of cornflower blue. Beside them were species unknown on Earth. Ronar studied these with his binocular. They were undeniably birds, a similarity Ronar found more startling than their differences. Some had rows of tiny teeth, like the fossil Archaeopteryx. Their wings were more simply feathered and less specialized.

The oddest thing about them was their arms. These were small and light, but perfectly functional, their needle claws a useful adjunct to the talons of the fishing birds, giving them a more secure grip on fish and making it easier to eat on the wing.

Sha Totek joined him in looking out across the waters. "In many parts of this planet the Earth creatures push the native Colibdians aside. Men would just as soon eliminate the wild creatures which once ruled this world. Too many of them bring memories of superstitions which haunted their forefathers even before they set foot on this world. Perhaps someday the native creatures will rally and drive out the invaders, both man and beast. There are many splendid animals here, and some, in their way, are wise. I would not see them pass into the realm of legend."

The sorcerer fell silent. He lounged along the railing, trailing his hand in the water. He lifted a palmful of it into the suns-light and let it trickle out between his fingers. His eyes misted over as he contemplated the falling drops, on their way to the sea after washing the feet of his descendants far to the south, as if each drop were a day from his long life.

Ronar left him in peace and resumed his birdwatching from the other side of the raft. A pelican cruised some six feet over the water, watching for a flash of fin to betray the presence of a fish.

Two great silvery claspers swept out of the water, meeting in the pelican's body like an iceman's tongs. The bird was pulled beneath the opaque surface as if it had never been. Ronar retained only the afterimage of spiny, segmented arms, like those of an aquatic praying mantis.

"Scissorfish," called the ferryman uneasily. "Nasty beast." He went on muttering in Eranian Welsh.

Ronar only smiled grimly at the blank face of the river Tal. It seemed the native life forms were indeed capable of an occasional act of revenge.

At length the ferry docked on the northern bank. The ferryman helped lead their animals ashore. Sha Totek suddenly turned and looked him hard in the eye.

"Friend, take heed. Keep your ferry moored on the south bank of the river. Burn it at the first sign of marchers out of Darteharn. Then flee to Mersinea or Thunderbird. Do not forget my words."

The ferryman paled. He looked about to question Sha Totek, but the sorcerer's manner forbade it. In the end he accepted the warning with a tight-lipped nod. Sha Totek paid the toll, and he and Ronar rode up the bank.

Ronar said, "I'm surprised you risked that warning. I doubt those were the words of a simple magician."

Sha Totek nodded. "I know. But if Namirnakh should come this way, it would be convenient for him to capture the ferry. Let the spell-spinners of Darteharn spend some of their own strength in crossing the Tal, as I had to."

"What do you mean?"

"Didn't you notice? The ferryman's spell was useless. My presence negated his petty magic. I had to improvise my own spell to drive the raft."

The sky deepened to the usual Colibdian indigo as they climbed out of the humid air near the great river. Ronar squinted up at Photos and Kudu. The red blur of Kudu was so close to its dazzling companion that it was nearly overwhelmed. "The suns have been approaching each other since my arrival. One will soon eclipse the other."

"Yes," said Sha Totek. "Once every two months, Photos is obscured by Kudu's bulk for a period of three days. Most people avoid open country during the Gloaming. It's said that Ahriman is in ascendancy when the red sun shines alone. Only a superstition, I hope."

Hazy on the horizon was a threat to observing this eclipse: a jagged mass of clouds. The clear skies Ronar had enjoyed during his week on Colibdis might be coming to an end. This thought changed to uncertainty as he studied the far-off clouds, marked, he now noticed, with streaks and patches of white...

"Mountain range!" he cried.

Startled out of some reverie, Sha Totek looked back at him in vexation. "Those are the Mountains of Twilight. It will be our lot for the next several days to struggle over their unkind crags, in cold, bitter air that tantalizes the lungs. Sinanna alone knows when next we'll see light, comfort, and civilization."

"The moon knows this?"

"Sinanna is a name of a moon god also, whose domain includes other barren, pitiless, places, such as the range we now approach."

"Are there any special dangers?"

"Only those that befall all who venture into high, wild places. Aren't those enough?"

The sorcerer moped for the rest of the day, his black eyes hooded and a little sullen. But Ronar felt keen anticipation as the peaks of the Twilight Range crept ever nearer.

The evening came while they were still twenty miles from the base of the Twilights. The pearly light of Sinanna, now nearing first quarter, shone on the veins of snow that defined the shape of the mountains.

A meteor pulled a line of greenish-white fire across the sky. It passed near a star notable only for its solitary reign in an otherwise empty part of the sky. Ronar angled his star-book to bring its pages into the light of the fire. It told him he had found Taralorne, the Lonely Star.

Sha Totek retired early to his miniature pavilion, whose colors seemed wan and futile in the austere light of Sinanna. Ronar lay beside the embers of their fire, which were occasionally fanned by sheets of chilly air sliding off the mountains. His mind wandered restlessly, but his eyes were locked on Taralorne, shining with sad splendor in the great northern wilderness of the heavens.

Chapter 9

The Gloaming

Again Ronar awoke beneath a clear sky of richest amethyst with no sun yet in sight. The brush and grass were ethereal beneath a dusting of frost. The horses breathed out small white clouds that barely moved in the still air.

The morning was so pristine and lovely that Ronar was moved to tempt Sha Totek from his funk with the best breakfast he could make. He re-lit last night's fire, waiting for the flames to subside into coals while he unpacked a slab of bacon (or some similar smoked meat) and cut some slices with his dagger.

A ruddy light rose in the east, pouring over the dagger's blade like blood. Ronar set aside his work and stared.

A single sun rose that morning. Photos was gone, and with its light went all semblance of this as an Earth-like planet. The ominous presence of Kudu as it climbed over the horizon was like the rumble of a deep bass note. Without the competing glare of Photos, Kudu was fully revealed for the first time. It was a far more alien thing than Ronar had first realized. Not even spherical, it consisted of a number of diffuse lobes which gave the impression of surging and bubbling, which they no doubt did, but not fast enough to discern. It looked like the star was barely holding itself together.

Subdued, Ronar went back to his cooking, adding parched corn, some kind of heavy cake, fruit jam, and Mormon tea with honey to the menu.

Sha Totek emerged looking with sour displeasure at the solitary crimson sun. "So begins the Gloaming, a time for dejection and dismay. It is said that more suicides occur during the Gloaming than during the darkest nights of winter." He ate without further comment.

Ronar did not understand this moodiness. He knew only that if he himself were in such a state, he would not welcome any intrusion into his brooding. Assuming that everyone was like himself, he forbore to ask Sha Totek what was troubling him.

By midmorning, the foothills of the Mountains of the Twilight rose up just ahead. The range stabbed out of the plain as suddenly as Ronar's beloved Front Range thrust up from the high plains of Colorado. Both were awesome natural ramparts stretching into interminable distances. But while the Rockies trended north-south, the Twilights ran east-west.

Sha Totek roused himself to say: "To the west, in Mersinea, the Twilight range comes to a dramatic end. Before it plunges into the sea, it gathers itself into one final monstrous summit, with the temples and theological academies of Pantheos clustered at its base. They call it, not surprisingly, Olympos. Pilgrims from all over the world try to attain its summit. Few succeed, for it is such a mountain, such an appalling monolith of rock and ice and raging wind, that only the most obsessed can endure it. Even the air is too bitter, too mean, to sustain life. You ought to go see it someday, Ronar. It might appeal to you."

Irritated by Sha Totek's mocking tone, Ronar asked, "Aside from the fact that it is there, what is the point of challenging this fearsome pinnacle?"

Sha Totek's answer came in a gentler voice. "Because, from the tip of Olympos, it is possible to perceive, on the edge of the horizon, a small glimmer marking the apex of Larlaninulius, the Isle of the Gods."

Ronar raised his eyebrows at this. "Maybe I will go see this Olympos one day."

The weird half-light of the Gloaming painted diffuse shadows beside every boulder. The road led between two tilted faces of rock, like colossal anvils embedded in the earth. It followed and sometimes crossed a stream that fell towards them down staircases of jumbled rock. The way became steep and winding. The horses picked their footing carefully among loose cobbles. Their speed was cut in half.

Still, after only an hour of this travel, the plain already seemed far below and far behind.

The reality of winter first touched them as they mounted these lower slopes. A slow, chill wind moved through the trees. The air wasn't really very cold, but patches of snow lay in the shadows of boulders and in the deep gloom beneath stands of evergreens. These trees looked like ordinary firs, but a closer look proved them to be alien, products of parallel evolution, mainly distinguishable by their fruiting bodies, which were white tendrils studded with nutlike seeds. A holly-like shrub was also common, with dark green waxy leaves, almost black in the Kudu-light, and ivory-white berries. They had an astringent smell that Ronar found invigorating. But attractive as these Colibdian plants were, he was delighted to come upon a stand of quaking aspen, leafless but unmistakable, for he had walked among such trees every day of his youth. He silently thanked whatever man, beast, or bird it was that had brought the seeds to this foreign soil.

182

Ronar remained fascinated by the somber splendor of the red sun. It wasn't dim, but he could squint toward it without much discomfort. Its redness was extraordinary. The typical "red" star, such as Antares, was really about the same color as a low-powered light bulb. But Kudu was truly red-orange, veined and spotted with vermilion and gold. Tentatively he assigned it to spectral class N, that rare group of very cool stars whose atmospheres contained sooty carbon compounds that reddened their light even more. As such, it was probably also a variable. He decided to ask Sha Totek if there was evidence for this, sometime when the sorcerer seemed more talkative.

The brooding beauty of the altered landscape seeped into him. The ancient, smoky light lay heavily on the land, infusing it with a rich melancholy, a smoldering sadness like a sunset that does not end. The sky had deepened to purple-black, a setting of amethyst for the great ruby of Kudu. Below and behind, the plain stretched away all rust and copper and terra cotta, to the just guessed-at valley of the Tal.

Ronar shuddered, but not from the cold. This chill was of internal origin. Something hidden in his mind was trying to emerge like a windflower straining to break free of March snows. Though vaguely disturbed by this insight, Ronar was not a man inclined to argue the course of a river or dispute the path of an avalanche. What he could not stop he would accept.

They halted long enough to unload sheepskin jackets from the packhorse. Sha Totek clearly did not admire the utilitarian buff-colored garment. The vividness of his regalia was lost anyway in the limited spectrum of Kudu's light. To Ronar the world resembled a sepia-toned photograph seen through reddish glasses. The main color contrast was in shadows on the snow, which reflected the deep purple of the sky.

The trail wound between upended slabs of rock which fused into a deep, narrow gorge. The stream echoed off the walls until the chasm was filled with its bubbling music. Foam glowed lavender in the light of the swath of sky overhead. Only when the gorge veered toward Kudu did the feeling of late evening leave it. Then the somber star grudgingly sent a few smoky shafts of amber-red light to catch in the mist of the waterfalls.

Eventually the trail climbed up the side of the gorge while the stream rambled off in its depths, depriving them of the wild cheerfulness of its company. The trail leveled off somewhat, which was just as well, for the horses were laboring. They had climbed hard with little time to adjust to the increasing altitude. Worse, fresh snow lay shin-deep on the road, with ice beneath it. Ronar was happy to ease his horse's burden by walking him up the steeper grades. He had more confidence in his own footing than in the horse's.

Stern peaks surrounded them, thrusting skyward, proud and solitary, unbowed by their mantles of snow and years. The sight of these great silent spirits straightened Ronar's back and kept his footfalls firm. They were giants of austere majesty watching to see that all who walked among them were worthy. Ronar would not falter before them.

The road, marked by cairns of rock, crossed the featureless sweep of a snow-covered moraine. Then it switchbacked briefly up a mountainside and leveled off to follow the mountain's contour, the roadbed laboriously cut into the rock. They entered a dense forest of evergreens. The sharp, raw wind was blunted, but their view of the mountains became intermittent.

By the time they reached the shelter, even Ronar had to admit it had been a very long day. The hut was a simple stone box built into the flank of the mountain, windowless, but equipped with a fireplace. A spring gurgled from a nearby cleft in the rock, flowing over bulbous ice formations before trickling out of sight in the woods.

According to Sha Totek, no one in their right mind would keep an inn in the Twilights, making these huts the only refuge available to mountain wayfarers. But Ronar had resorted to lean-tos of pine boughs and snow under worse conditions, and had no complaints.

They unloaded the horses. Ronar led them to a meadow downhill where he helped scrape away the snow, revealing brown, ice-crusted grass The horses, trembling with their long exertion, cropped up everything in sight as fast as Ronar could uncover it. To this meager fare he added some grain they had carried in.

Kudu lay poised on the horizon. Ronar paused to watch it ease its bulk behind the silhouetted mountains. There was almost no twilight; only a sudden black sky with yellow stars, and in the west a fleeting crimson afterglow. On the meridian, Sinanna was a coppery half-disk as it underwent a Gloaming of its own.

Ronar glimpsed some small animals, picas if not for their six legs, pale eyes, and owlish facial disks of white fur. Sha Totek had told him most forms of Colibdian life were safe to eat. Ronar was tempted to go for his bow, but he doubted it would be wise to bend it in this cold. So he merely peered back at the creatures with the goggling night-eyes of his binocular while the horses crunched their dinners.

Ronar opened the shelter door and led in the three horses.

"Must we share our quarters with the beasts?" asked the sorcerer peevishly. "I was actually beginning to think it was roomy, until you walked in."

"They'll be more useful to us alive than as frozen meat. Besides, I heard wolves howling in the distance."

Sha Totek looked annoyed. He cast a fiery gaze at the tinder in the fireplace; the wood he'd gathered blazed up brightly. "Firelight...a great improvement over the melancholy rays of the Lesser Sun."

They tied the horses out of the way as much as possible and went about preparing their supper. It was hard to ignore the horses's presence, but it couldn't be helped.

"The sunset was magnificent," ventured Ronar.

Sha Totek looked at him. "I thought so too during my first few Gloamings. After thirty thousand of them, I have become a man of extremes. I like things one way or the other. Up or down. In or out. Day or night. Not this nameless, indefinable murk of the Gloaming."

Ronar persisted. "I find it sublime. A quiet, reflective time."

Sha Totek shrugged. "Then again, you also like these mountains."

"Kudu is a very ancient star. Perhaps it is a reminder of death," said Ronar, probing for insights.

Sha Totek looked askance at the transparent ploy. "I don't fear death. I've lived more life than have any fifty men. Someday I will likely decide I have lived long enough, and end it. But if I am struck down before that, I will not cry out at the injustice of it."

Ronar nodded in the flickering of the fire. "I might have thought that five thousand years of life would give you a greater appreciation of natural beauty."

"I might've thought it would spare me the presumption of upstarts," snapped Sha Totek.

Ronar said nothing more, choosing to let the sorcerer sulk in peace. Perhaps Sha Totek's long life had only jaded him to the majesty of the universe, or perhaps his knowledge of magic had given him a false view of it. If the former, Ronar hoped not to live so long; if the latter, he hoped to be preserved from a knowledge of magic.

That night Ronar slept fitfully. He woke up often, fragments of uneasy dreams slipping out of reach. The only image he retained was that of his father, grey-eyed, tall as a mountain, dark hair shot with snowy white. The dream-father looked down at him with eyes bright as stars, asking sadly, "Where are you going, son?" Hadn't there been a reply of some sort? Yes, he recalled it now—a woman, with silver hair and great luminous eyes of solid mint-green, dressed in streamers of silver, ice-blue, and green. How could she see with those opaque eyes? The skin around them was purple-black, as though she had two permanent shiners.

She said: "He goes by a long, hard road."

Ronar awoke with tears smearing the red light of the embers. Angrily he blinked them away. He was losing patience with the emotional malaise afflicting both himself and Sha Totek. If it came from within, he wished it would surface so he could resolve it. If it came from without, say from Namirnakh or Ahriman, he wished they would reveal themselves so he could confront them.

In the meantime, he could internalize his will, banishing these specters, at least for a while. With cool discipline he visualized a quiet, starry void that brought him peace and sleep.

In the morning, he remembered nothing of this.

Ronar used a piece of bark and a pine bough to scoop up the impressive deposits left by the horses. He was glad the temperature had dropped below freezing, minimizing the impact of sleeping in a stable. He thought it best to clean out the hut before rousing Sha Totek. No point in giving him any more cause for complaint than necessary.

Housekeeping completed, he led the horses into a dim world of wild, forbidding beauty. Tiers of heavy cloud had moved in overnight, colored dirty maroon by the light filtering down from Kudu. A few inches of fresh snow had fallen, ornamenting the evergreens with faded rosy silver.

The spring had frozen over, but a couple of sharp kicks freed a trickle of icewater, numbing his face and hands as he splashed it on. He filled water bottles and waited for the horses to drink their fill. In the meadow, he cleared the snow with long sweeps of his arms.

Back at the hut, he found Sha Totek awake and brewing tea over a renewed fire. The sorcerer seemed a forlorn shadow of his former rakish self. His eyes were bleary, his face black with stubble, his hair in disarray. The garments that had once blazed with scarlet and purple were streaked with ashes and dirt.

He looked up at Ronar with sardonic weariness. "Lovely weather, isn't it? Grey and maroon is such an exhilarating color combination."

Even the tea wasn't very satisfactory. The water boiled almost as soon as the pot touched the flames, resulting in a tepid brew.

Their dreary breakfast completed, Ronar fed the horses from their store of grain to supplement the poor forage in the meadow. Sha Totek layered on every item of clothing he possessed. Ronar dressed more lightly. They rode off, the horse's hooves making small fluffing sounds in the feathery snow.

The day grew no brighter. A thin, keen wind came up to send dark clouds scudding by. Flurries fell in gauzy masses, obscuring the peaks like fog. Ronar examined the snowflakes that lit on his sleeve, appreciating the universality of the physical laws that had shaped them.

About midmorning the road veered around a keel-like formation, bringing into view a vast alpine vista. Mighty peaks encircled an isolated valley, a bowl cut off from outside drainage. Within it lay a dark evergreen forest ringing a lake whose frozen surface shone like a lens of milky glass.

This pocket forest was far below, while the summits of the surrounding mountains were even farther above. They could be seen only fleetingly, as clouds often shrouded their lofty heads. Spires of ice-coated rock swiftly dismembered the clouds that blundered into them.

One peak of this mighty company drew Ronar's special attention. A soaring pinnacle of stone and ice, its lower slopes consisted of vast snowfields and chaotic gorges choked with glaciers. A sheer diamond-shaped face of rock reared above all, stern and formidable, supported by black-ribbed bulwarks of stone. The summit was plumed by snow driven off by blasts of savage wind.

This mountain loomed tall in Ronar's mind. He raised his binocular and traced the road as best he could. It seemed to follow the rim of the bowl-valley, then wind out of sight around the base of his special peak.

"That mountain—" said Ronar, pointing, "what is it called?"

Sha Totek, aroused from his reverie, said. "Which? Oh, that one? How should I know? Perhaps it is called Mount Misery, or maybe Mount Ballbreaker. Or perhaps it is nameless. There are many peaks, and few to name them. Name it yourself, if it strikes your fancy." He tried to shake off the irrelevant interruption.

"This is a magnificent range." Ronar's hushed voice blended with the soft hiss of wind-driven snow.

Sha Totek looked around with bleak appraisal. "It is harsh and merciless, a place no magic has yet tamed. The god of the wilds walks upon these summits, judging all who pass."

Ronar shook his head. "Mountains neither forgive nor condemn. They only hold up a mirror in which men can judge their own worth."

Sha Totek looked surprised by Ronar's reckless flirtation with poetry. Prying himself from his brooding, he gave his companion a searching look. He said carefully, "Perhaps. But this mirror of the mountains is not for all men. In other aspects of life are mirrors for other kinds of men."

Ronar ignored this. "The road circumnavigates the mountain?"

"Yes. And on the far side is another shelter in which we shall spend the night."

"I'm going to climb that mountain."

Sha Totek's temper snapped. "Oh, by the iron balls of Hamadan! Are you crazy? We're on a mission from Varanu, not a pilgrimage for glassy-eyed zealots! What good will it do if we arrive too late to fulfill Varanu's plan?"

"We'll lose no time. I can be up and over this mountain as fast as you and the horses can amble around it."

"Are you sure? Can you do it?"

Ronar smiled easily. "I can go anywhere in the mountains. Day and night. Storm and shine."

Sha Totek regarded him with consternation. He started to renew his objections, but the light in Ronar's eyes was so steady and clear that he was deterred.

"Very well. Climb your mountain. I won't try to stop you."

"Excellent."

It took the rest of the morning to reach the base of the mountain. Ronar's eyes were fixed on it all that time, looking for routes, considering obstacles. As they neared the mountain, he felt it beckoning him even as its lower slopes hid the high sanctity of the summit from his view.

Ronar dismounted, taking only a bit of food and water, a rope, and a few souvenirs.

"You ought to take your sword," said Sha Totek tiredly.

"Nonsense. I need to be free to move, not burdened by that steel yardstick. Besides, I doubt there's anything living at these altitudes that could menace a healthy man. The most dangerous thing I'll encounter will be myself. I'll see you on the other side."

With that, Ronar sprang up the slope with appalling energy, disappearing behind a ridge in an incredibly few seconds.

Sha Totek looked up at where Ronar had been. The dreary light of the Gloaming glinted from ice crystals whipping by in the thin wind, biting into his cheeks. All around him towered the terrible, mindless splendor of the Mountains of the Twilight. Never had he felt so alone, or so forlorn.

He turned his gaze to the northwest, toward Darteharn, heard harsh words echoing from the peaks, realized they issued from his own throat.

"Namirnakh, you fly-eating scumsucker! This is your fault, I know it! Your mischief has forced me to leave my home to clean up after you, scoop your schemes into the chamber pot where they belong! When I get my hands on you I'll rub your nose in the mess. So swears Imhotep of the Two Lands!"

When this oath had been absorbed by the emptiness, Sha Totek felt some relief, but also embarrassment. He was glad he hadn't included any voice-carrying magic in the outcry, as Namirnakh wouldn't be intimidated by the tantrum of a miserable, dispossessed sorcerer such as himself. Besides, he had his flippant, devil-may-care image to maintain.

With a groan he nudged his horse, starting around the flank of what he had begun to think of as Mount Ronar.

Ronar flung himself up the mountain, sparing nothing in his desire to look out from its summit. It was a pleasure and a relief to allow his legs their natural stride. While his horse was an amiable beast, riding it was painful confinement compared to the loose and easy travel of his own legs. So far, even the snow wasn't much of a hindrance, since only the first few inches were fresh, with a hard base of granular snow beneath. His lug-soled boots gave good traction. He could go anywhere in the mountains, tackling slopes and surfaces that would balk anything else short of a bighorn.

He resolved to take full advantage of this surge of energy while it lasted. Despite his zeal, he had no illusion: he had perhaps six hours of murky daylight to climb and descend a good four thousand feet. Best to unwind as many miles as possible before the Mountains of Twilight noticed his presence and took exception to it. He marched up a huge snowfield that plunged on either side into savage gorges. The grade would have called for switchbacks on Earth, but the lesser gravity of Colibdis made it feasible to bull his way straight up.

The snowfield narrowed as he ascended. Within two miles the bracketing gorges had drawn close together. The snowfield dwindled to a mere ridge, a knife-edge that offered the only way forward. Across the great gap bisected by this ridge were jagged tongues of rock that must surely offer some passage to the summit.

Ronar proceeded with care. The ridge was icy in places, and parts were rotted and unstable. Bending low, he tested every foothold, ready to step back if a sheet of rock should go skittering into the grey mistiness below. Erratic winds swept across vast spaces of open air. They rushed at him from both sides of the peak ahead, split by the mountain like water cut by the prow of a destroyer. They slammed together madly along the crest of the ridge, whirling and

clashing from every direction. Ronar grabbed what handholds he could find to anchor himself against the blast. His
progress came by inches. There were moments when he felt
he must be swept away like some lost sparrow.

At last he was across. He looked back with some doubt.
This climb would be no lark.

Great slabs of stone rose before him, sheer, icy, and un-
scalable without technical gear. Luckily, between them
were easier slopes, small glaciers winding up the gorges
that broke up unclimbable rock. He began powering up the
nearest gorge, keeping mostly to the sides. There he could
sometimes walk on fallen rocks, avoiding any crevasses
that might be hidden in the ice.

The climb was steep and long, but the way was fairly
open. Ronar made good time. His initial enthusiasm had
quieted to a determination that drove him to tick off the
footsteps. He sucked the thin air in rapid lungfuls. Having
found his stride, he was comfortable in his exertion. He was
content, and yet a small nervous current tickled the back of
his mind. He knew that in making this climb he was keeping some kind of appointment with himself.

He climbed out of the gorge. The glacier spread out,
becoming a gentle, snow-covered shoulder of the mountain.
Above that was an obstacle Ronar feared he might not sur-
mount, a high wall of stone that looked as smooth as the
flank of a granite monument. He studied it in vain for a
route he might attempt without equipment. He bit his lip,
contemplating turning back, or seeking some tortuous route
around the obstacle.

The clouds beyond the wall cleared momentarily. There
loomed the summit, tantalizingly near, yet still veiled in
grandeur.

Ronar hesitated no more, but swept up the slope to the base of the wall, where a few seconds of reckless scrambling put him thirty feet up its side. There his instincts could do no more. He teetered atop a column protruding from the face, with no feasible way to proceed, and at least fifty feet of wall still above him.

Ronar fished around in his pack and brought out his rope and the four gleaming claws of Four-Ashen-Grey. He lashed them together, their points projecting at right angles to each other. Leaning back cautiously, he paid out rope until his grapple hung down about ten feet. He whirled it, releasing it as it reached its apex. It bounced off the cliff and fell past him. As it skittered down from the second cast it narrowly missed catching him in the same shoulder where the nehock had gouged him as its final living act. On the seventh cast, it did not come down again.

Ronar tugged at the rope, which proved firm. His over-confidence about the ease of this climb had been just shy of hubris, he realized. Now he was indeed about to risk his life. Yet he could not take the possibility of death too seriously. He did not feel it in the wind. His death, when it came, might well be as pointless as a plunge down some mountain face, but it would not happen now. Something else lay in wait for him beyond this place.

He shrugged and quickly hauled himself up the rope. At the top, he saw he needn't have worried. The grapple was wedged securely between two boulders. He gave silent thanks to the memory of Four-Ashen-Grey as he stowed the talons and the rope.

A redoubled wind stung his eyes and brought forth tears. He squinted up at the great massif of the summit, still a thousand feet above. The huge, diamond-shaped face on the south side was as inaccessible as last week. That was not to be his route. With a peculiar mixture of humility and exultation, he launched himself at the more manageable slopes. Soon he reached a height where the wind was so fierce and steady that the rocks were stripped of snow except in hollows where it had lain sheltered for dozens of years. Ronar breathed with difficulty. The air was thinner than it would've been at the same altitude on Earth. Unacclimated as he was, he could not remain long at this height.

At last he hauled himself over the final shoulder of rock. Buffeted by the wind, he stood on the summit of his mountain, where he beheld a vista as raw and wild as any he had ever seen.

The great realms of air around him were grey and murky, shrouding the distance with veils of snow and mist. Ragged grey-maroon scud clouds blundered into the sides of mountains and fled in tatters over the valleys. Above, an unbroken cloud deck flowed past like a foaming river inverted just overhead.

The mountains stretched to the south, east, and west as far as he could see, a silver-grey wilderness of massed peaks and deep shadowed valleys. To the west were monstrous crags, even greater than this one, so implacable that even he might not have dared them. On the northern horizon was a grey-green expanse he supposed must be the nation of Eranior.

The landscape, filled with roaring currents of air, seemed to recede before Ronar's tired eyes. He turned around just in time to see a billowing bank of cloud bearing down on him, smothering the summit in icy mist.

He found himself on his knees. The wind wrenched sobs from his constricted throat. Wild thoughts raced through his mind, pouring out of some troubled core where they had been confined.

What am I doing here? Where is the sanity in this? His confusion and dismay could no longer be weighed down by the accumulation of events. Was this the universe he thought he knew, this place where the essences of the dead could be called back after their demise? Where spirits schemed and did evil after the decay of their bodies? The memory of the Despard's probing of his soul came forth, bringing outrage and a spasm of trembling. His soul? He had never suspected the existence of such a thing. What else did its existence imply; what else must he accept? Were there really—gods—out among the stars, fighting over the destiny of the universe? To determine whether it would be governed by nature or by intelligent intervention? Was a power-hungry wizard really planning to dominate Earth with magic? If he, Ronar, fell asleep this instant, mustn't he wake up in the trailer on Kitt Peak?

That thought crystallized another realization. On some level, he had treated the suns and moons and stars of this world as though they were merely part of some elaborate planetarium show—beautiful and mysterious to be sure, but not real in a sense he could feel in his spine. Now fatigue, hypoxia and emotional exhaustion combined to induce a full comprehension of where he was.

He squeezed his eyes shut as the magnitude of that simple truth washed over him. No longer were the pinpoint lights of infinity mere abstractions to be photographed and measured and pondered. Now the winds of another world were at his back, a world lit by the declining light of a strange sun. No matter that he'd gotten here by stepping in one side of a bronze cuboid and out the other. He was here.

Ronar shakily regained his feet. He peered into the dim cloud-fog as though expecting some kind of instruction to issue from it. "What am I doing here?" he asked again. The wind gave back no answer.

He didn't know what he might ultimately face if he kept to this road. But from somewhere came a certainty: if he would prevent the madness that ruled this planet from laying waste to the universe, he must not falter.

The fog tore away in tatters. Ronar's trembling subsided. Day was failing. The clouds began to disperse. Beyond the rents sailed the waxing globe of Sinanna, now pearly-silver once again. The Gloaming would soon be over.

Ronar gave himself one last look at the vista he had worked so hard to attain. Pink-gold alpenglow bathed the surrounding peaks. The wind declined, but the cold gained a deadly edge. He must descend quickly. He hadn't expected to watch nightfall from the summit. Sha Totek must already be huddled in the next wayfarer's hut, giving him up for lost.

Behind him, the clouds opened in time for Kudu to cast a last bloody ray over the world. Before him, a billowing cloud drifted past. A human figure, vast and shadowy, materialized in the cloud's red-lit depths. It loomed before him, motionless, faceless, its head surrounded by a corona of scarlet and golden light.

Ronar smiled.

The Spectre of the Brocken had come to see him off.

Sha Totek sat on the stack of firewood and stared glumly into the hearth. He was ravenous, but somehow he couldn't bring himself to prepare a meal meant only for one. The sun had set more than two hours ago and Ronar had not returned. It seemed that the mountains he loved had claimed him after all. Sha Totek regretted the foolishness which had led Ronar to throw his life away, but at the same time he acknowledged the need he had seen in Ronar's eyes. Someday he would find the time to assess Ronar's brief but unforgettable role in his life—but not now. He sighed, trying to reconcile himself to the dreary prospect of going on alone.

But in the distance—an unexpected sound—the rising clump, clump, clump of boots through snow. He looked up in suspense as the door swung open. In blew Ronar with a blast of frigid air. He was breathing heavily, his clothing crusted with snow, but his eyes glittered with vitality.

"Good to see you again," said Ronar. "That walk turned out to be tougher than I thought."

Sha Totek sprang to his feet, dancing from foot to foot. "Ronar! By the Wayfarer's Womb! How did you find your way over that mountain in the dark?"

"Actually, I only reached the peak at sunset."

Sha Totek's jaw dropped. "You mean you descended that entire mountain in two hours?"

"I glissaded most of the way."

"You what?"

"Glissaded. Slid down the glaciers on my ass. Sinanna's light guided me well enough."

"You *slid* down the mountain—"

"That's right. Oh, I've decided what to name the mountain. I'm calling it the Brocken, in honor of an interesting optical phenomenon I observed from the summit."

"Ronar, you are a human avalanche."

"I was confused when I reached the road. I wasn't sure which way to go, but then I saw your tracks. Otherwise I might have headed back the way we came."

"I see no problem there! No doubt you would simply have proceeded around the world, approaching the hut from the opposite direction."

Ronar shucked off his wet overclothes. The horses nickered from one end of the hut. Ronar went over to inspect them.

Sha Totek hung a pot over the fire. Beans and bacon were soon boiling. Speaking offhandedly, he said over his shoulder, "Did you ever figure out why you wanted to climb that mountain so badly?"

"I had some things I needed to get out of my system. One thing I learned—" Ronar turned, went up to the sorcerer and unexpectedly grasped his hand. "—I'm in this thing with you for as far as it goes."

"Ha! Then let Namirnakh beware!"

Chapter 10

The Demon of the Bells

Sha Totek and Ronar squinted in the morning light, almost overwhelmed by the radiance of the emerging sun Photos. Ronar was impressed by how quickly he had come to accept the gloom of Kudu as the standard of daylight. He capped one side of his binocular and used the other to project an image of the white star on a blank page of a book. Sha Totek looked over his shoulder, remarking at the sunspots pocking the face of an object he had thought pristine. A third of the disk of Photos was still covered by Kudu. Both men relished the heat that soaked into their bones from the paired suns.

As they rode, Ronar was surprised and a little irritated that Sha Totek's humor did not improve much despite the end of the Gloaming. He couldn't imagine why the sorcerer had been so morose for so long. The ride wasn't bad. The cold wasn't severe, there was no real danger, and they had enough to eat. His impatience, still in conflict with his respect for the privacy of others, finally won out.

"You know—"

"All right! You've dragged it out of me. I can no longer endure your constant probing and questioning. I will try to explain why I look upon this journey with so little enthusiasm."

"If you wish," said Ronar, nonplussed.

"As I told you, when the Bronze Portal of Ammon finally crumbled, I moved to the site of the new Portal and resumed my watch. Well, it happens that the second Portal to become active was the one in Hyperborea. Having lived my whole life near the deserts of Khemet and Ammon, I thought I knew what desolation was. But when the appalling waste of the arctic continent confronted me, I was amazed. I had not dreamed that such an expanse of icy nothingness could exist.

"The air of Hyperborea is cold and dry, excellent for the preservation of bronze. That Portal stood and functioned for some five hundred years of Earth. For all that time I was virtually stranded in that cheerless place. Only the Inuit came through, so few I still remember all their names. They, and the white bears, and the wolves. I was not by choice so solitary a man, especially in those younger days. All those centuries without speaking to another literate human being brought me to the edge of sanity. Some might say they pushed me over. When that Portal gave way at last, I felt I had been delivered from the Land of Silence. I went wild with joy. I started talking to myself, just to regain the knack for when I again encountered human companions. I transported the Tower to the island of Kratoa and greeted the Minoans as they arrived...or was it the Assyrians? Sometimes I lose track.

"Never since then have I set foot on Hyperborea. To return there now without even the comforts of the Tower to sustain me seems a dismal fate. It may be childish, I grant. But to me this is a return to a nightmare that has haunted a corner of my heart. You have not heard the voices in the fearsome winds of that land. I am not grateful to Namirnakh for bringing this about. Only by the will of Varanu himself would I make this trip."

"You could have blown it up," said Ronar quietly.

"What?"

"If the Hyperborea Portal was as useless as you say, you could have destroyed it and saved yourself a great deal of hardship."

Sha Totek looked at him in wonder. "The ideas you get! No. The Portals were erected by powers beyond my knowledge, for purposes I cannot guess. I would not take it upon myself to inject my personal wishes into their designs."

"Really? Isn't that what you do by allowing only one-way travel? Did the builders of the Portals instruct you to do this?"

Sha Totek looked at him reproachfully. "You know, you have a way of making a man sorry that he tells you anything."

The road dropped rapidly for the rest of the morning. By mid afternoon they left the last ridge of the Mountains of Twilight behind. They rode over a rolling plain of short grass, interrupted here and there by outcroppings of rounded grey stone. Here they left the road, for they were too conspicuous upon it. But on the smooth turf they still made excellent time.

The air was cool and damp. Before long a flat sheet of drizzling clouds moved overhead, ending their brief reacquaintance with Photos. To Sha Totek the rain was merely a new source of misery. But Ronar found a quiet beauty in the undulating, misted landscape with its palette of greens and greys.

Just before dusk a few angular shapes appeared on the horizon. They halted while Ronar surveyed them with his binocular.

"It's a village. It looks empty. The buildings are crumbling."

"I guess the place was abandoned when the new road bypassed it," said Sha Totek. "Convenient. We might as well spend the night there."

They entered the village as the light was fading. Most of it consisted of post holes marking the outlines of wooden houses that had rotted away long ago. Only the few stone structures still stood. One in particular was more-or-less intact, a church made of blocks cut from the local limestone. The steeple was eight-sided, with a pointed roof of slate shingles. Gabled windows pierced its uppermost level. The belfry within was opaque with shadow.

The wooden doors of the church were little more than rotted slats. Still, Sha Totek halted before them and motioned Ronar to do the same. He chanted in singsong Latin, too fast for Ronar to follow. It served no obvious purpose, but the sorcerer seemed satisfied. "This church has been deconsecrated. The Christian god no longer dwells within it. I wouldn't enter it otherwise—he's a jealous god, that one. Come on, let's get out of the rain."

But Ronar was arrested by what he saw on the door. "What are these old—carvings? They seem to depict some sort of a—birth."

Sha Totek studied the crumbling wood more closely. "Why, so they do," he said quietly. "Perhaps there was a time when these people attempted to fuse their old ways with those of the Christians. Apparently the idea did not take hold."

In they went. Ronar gathered the remains of the wooden furnishings for a fire, feeling rather sacrilegious as he did so.

"Be careful what you burn," said Sha Totek. "Spare any icons or relics. Deconsecrated or not, we'll offer no needless insult to the Christ."

The firelight revealed an echoing space interrupted by pillars. Ronar examined the walls. Much of the plaster had crumbled, but on the intact areas were painted images of Christ and the saints, rendered in the rounded, large-eyed style of the ancient Celts. Some of the frescoes depicted the stations of the Cross. Piles of rock lay against the walls, the remains of statues. Ronar dug out and lifted a carved head which looked back at him with peace and dignity. Without looking away from it, he asked, "Are the Eranians Christians, then?"

Sha Totek looked up at the ceiling nervously. "Not any more. We're not far from the site of the Portal that brought the Britons here from their island. Their race had been converted to Christianity only recently. When they arrived, they soon received a convincing demonstration of the plurality of gods on this world. Many of them abandoned the Christ and returned to their ancestral faith as a result. This led to some nasty disagreements. The non-Christians migrated north. The Christians hung on in this region but eventually died out, to my knowledge."

Ronar set the head back down. He lifted a brand from the fire and went into the base of the steeple. The area smelled damp and musty. Nothing stirred, not even mice or rats, or whatever their local equivalent might be. A staircase wound up along the inner walls, but it was dangerously deteriorated. Ronar was tempted to try it anyway, but he had risked his life too recently for a repeat performance quite so soon. He raised the torch as high as possible. It shone on the rims of bells hanging high in the darkness.

When they had eaten, and finished caring for the horses, Ronar and Sha Totek spread their bedrolls near the fire. They dropped off to sleep quickly, lulled by the still air of the chapel and the patter of rain on the roof.

Sha Totek was awakened by the tolling of a bell. Its reverberations hung in the air as his eyes snapped open. In the light of the embers, he frowned with puzzlement. Ronar slept on, undisturbed. Sha Totek looked toward the bell tower with suspicion. Pinpoints of deep blue fire flared in the pupils of his eyes. He swept his gaze over the bell tower wall, and his frown blackened. He got to his feet as silently as a column of smoke rising from a flame, drifted out the door and on into the night.

A sharp wind hissed in the grass. The clouds had fragmented, passing in front of Sinanna, their edges silver-lit. Patches of moonglow chased each other over the moor.

Sha Totek stared up at the bell tower, at the figure that leaned from a window.

It might have been a gargoyle carved from the same grey stone as the rest of the church, its surface mottled with the same fungal patches that whitened parts of the wall around it. It leaned on the sill with pipestem arms, its fingers long and large-jointed. Its back was hunched, its torso a twisted column. Its beak flared back to form a crest, from which projected four polished horns. At first, only its eyes showed signs of life. They were narrow, red, and liquid, aglow with an unnatural light.

"Well, demon," said Sha Totek, "why have you awakened me?"

The demon rocked its head from side to side to peer at him with one eye and then the other. It spoke in a low, frog-like voice, its beak clacking as it formed the words. "I wished to see what game I had pointed out to my master."

"And what game have you?"

"I have done well. I have spied out Imhotep of the Two Lands."

"I will not deny it. But it seems unfair that you know my name while I am ignorant of yours."

The demon's laugh was a flinty, chopping sound. "I will tell you! I am not living; my name will give you no power over me. I am called Mauch Chunk."

"Of course you are. So then, you will report my presence to your master, Namirnakh?"

"I have already done so. I sent bats bearing word of your coming the moment the suns went down. They are now beyond your reach. I am not a fool, to alert you to my presence before my task has been performed. But your acuity as a sorcerer must be overrated, for you should have perceived me at once."

Sha Totek smiled pleasantly at Mauch Chunk, while behind this mask he writhed with vexation. Truly, his vigilance had grown shamefully lax. Or perhaps his powers had faded more than he'd anticipated. "A prudent precaution, Mauch Chunk," he said easily. "But what prevents me from blasting you to gravel this instant?"

"Nothing whatever! However, the damage is done, and I think you would not strain your waning powers to no purpose."

"Perhaps you underestimate the human quality of vindictiveness."

The two regarded each other in silence. Mauch Chunk's eyes glittered with smug triumph, but before Sha Totek's black-eyed stare it soon looked away. Finally the demon ventured a comment. "Assuming you set out from your black stone penis when Ahriman's Eye sent forth its exhalation, you have not made very good time. Where have you been loitering?"

"I stopped off at Thunderbird to dispel some troublesome wraiths."

Mauch Chunk chuckled. "You will pay for that when the Dusk Riders stoop down to pluck you up. You and your grey-haired companion, who is too inquisitive. Do you find him an effective bodyguard?"

"I suggest you make no effort to find out. I am so enjoying our little chat that I would not wish to see you whittled down into a votive statuette."

Mauch Chunk's expression creased into one of contempt. It leaned farther from the window; above its head two stony points emerged into the moonlight. Great grey wings unfurled, shading all light from the demon's body except for the molten glow of its eyes. "My long idleness here has not diminished me. Though among the least of my Master's servants, I am not so inconsiderable that I need fear a mortal man."

"Not even one who wields a yard of steel that was once carried by Bran himself?"

Mauch Chunk's wings quivered. "The Sword of Bran? A fat lot of good it did him! But still, it is a rare prize. My master would take pleasure in casting its shards at the feet of his fallen enemies."

Sha Totek shrugged. "Then take it. I believe it's among the gear at Ronar's side."

Demon and sorcerer stared at each other across the intervening darkness. Sha Totek shifted his weight from one foot to the other, but Mauch Chunk remained perfectly still.

At length Sha Totek said, "Well? What's keeping you? I won't interfere. I'll wait right here until you return with the sword."

But Mauch Chunk did not move or speak. Possibly its expression grew more hateful. At last, a single, choked word escaped its throat.

"Bastard."

The fire in its eyes died out, replaced by a black opacity.

"By the looks of him, I'd say you just did him a favor," said Ronar.

Sha Totek jumped. "How long have you been standing there?"

"A few moments. How did you stop that thing?"

"Actually, I did very little. I know these demons. They are constructs, things of the earth. Over time, they acquire the characteristics of the substances they contact. That one had dwelt in this church so long that the essence of the stone had seeped into its bones. In the darkness, in the moonlight, it wasn't hard to urge the process to its logical conclusion."

"I'm glad there was no need for me to fight it."

"I'd be gladder still if we'd discovered it earlier. Now we must leave at once, and ride with no thought of moderation. Namirnakh will be after us." The sorcerer sighed deeply.

They went about the task of saddling and loading the horses, which stamped and snorted with uneasiness. The atmosphere of the church was now charged with menace.

Sha Totek threw a stick on the fire and glared at it to produce a fierce blue flame.

"Hurry," whispered the sorcerer. "I underestimated Mauch Chunk. His spirit, such as it is, remains. And it is feeling unfriendly, to say the least."

Ronar scowled, glaring about with a look that might daunt anything except a dead monster that haunted a pile of decaying stone.

From the murk beyond the firelight came creaks and groans. Dust and grit sifted down from above. The flagstones beneath their feet began to tilt.

Sha Totek cinched up the last saddlebag and scrambled into the saddle. "A ride in the night air won't be too bad, don't you agree?"

Ronar nodded sharply and vaulted into his own saddle. "Let's get out of here! Hyah!" They ducked beneath the lintel as the horses bolted through the door. A chorus of rumbling protests broke out behind them. Ronar looked back at the petrified demon still leaning from the bell tower, great wings limned in moonlight. The church began to crumble. The bells tolled chaotically as the walls toppled and raced to meet the shadows cast by the moon.

Then it seemed that Mauch Chunk lived again. From the dust of the collapse soared a bat-winged shape. Ronar stared in amazement as the demon glided toward Sha Totek. He cried out a warning; Sha Totek wheeled just as the demon was upon him.

The warning saved the sorcerer's life, but his horse was knocked down, throwing him to the ground. Ronar swept out his sword, but the winged shape lay motionless in the grass. Ronar hopped down from the saddle and approached it cautiously. The demon's torso was sheared off at the waist. It showed no sign of animation. Apparently it had broken free in the collapse and sailed out like a child's glider. Inert though it seemed, he did not turn his back on it as he withdrew.

Sprawled on the turf, Sha Totek held his leg as he muttered a stream of curses that withered the grass and made Ronar's ears feel swollen and bruised. The astronomer went to him, swaying a little. "Tone down those blasphemies, will you? I'm starting to see spots in front of my eyes." He stooped to examine Sha Totek's injured leg, finding a deep wound, a gash from one of Mauch Chunk's horns or talons. The blood looked black in the moonlight. Sha Totek's mutterings turned to a quick shriek as Ronar's fingers plunged into the wound.

"In Ahriman's name, did you lose something in there?" gasped the sorcerer.

"I want to be sure no fragments remain before I...bind the wound. Don't go anywhere."

"Are you trying to amuse me?"

Ronar got up to rummage through their gear. Sha Totek yelped again as Ronar returned bearing a curved copper needle threaded with catgut. "I've got to stitch you up."

"Ahhh!"

"Come on, you just faced down Mauch Chunk, don't faint at the sight of this needle." He uncorked a bottle of carbolic. "This is the finest disinfectant Thunderbird has to offer." He poured the acid liberally over the wound.

"*Augh!*"

"Oh, for crying out loud. How about a little magic? Hocus Pocus Diplodocus, no more pain, you hairy locust."

A wave of fatigue washed over Ronar at these words. Was it just the lack of sleep catching up with him, or—? He picked up the needle and sewed up Sha Totek's wound. He applied more carbolic, then bound the sorcerer's thigh in a cotton cloth.

The sorcerer showed no further concern during this procedure. "Let me warn you," he said quietly. "You try a spell as clumsy and insubstantial as that to invoke a really big effect and you'll be in trouble."

Ronar was abashed. "You mean that was real magic I used?"

"That was your intention, wasn't it?"

"Not really. Is intention enough?"

"Most actions of any kind require intention, plus skill and knowledge. You had the intention, but lack the skill and knowledge."

Sha Totek got to his feet. His horse, they found, had suffered less than its master. They checked its load, mounted, and rode off into the night. The sorcerer steered them toward the road, there being no more hope of avoiding attention. The sky beyond the broken clouds began to pale just as they reached the cobbles comprising the road in this lightly settled region. The rising suns chased off the last fragments of cloud. Ronar and Sha Totek emerged from the darkness looking haggard and worn, like two ghosts caught in the morning sun.

Sha Totek turned a streaked and grimy face to Ronar. "There is an inn, a very hard day's ride north on this road. We must reach it before sunset, or Mauch Chunk's liable to have the last laugh."

The day passed in monotony, with hoof beats alternately sharp and muffled as they went from pavement to grassy stretches in between. Streams were frequent in the shallow valleys, all either fordable or bridged. Forage for the horses was abundant, when they dared stop long enough for the trembling animals to crop it. They were being badly used.

During a brief halt in mid afternoon, Ronar noticed black specks wheeling slowly overhead. He brought up the binocular.

"Eagles overhead," he remarked, "or possibly vultures."

Sha Totek's head snapped up to cast a glittering gaze at the circling specks. "No eagles, but Teratorns. Astride them are the Dusk Riders."

"Teratorns?"

"This is no time for lectures. Unless we get under cover, we'll be hearing from them at dusk."

They forced the horses to even greater efforts. Ronar tried to keep watch on the Teratorns, but it was difficult to observe them from a pitching saddle. If those birds were large enough to carry riders, they must be at a great height to appear so small. He wondered what kind of man could endure the rigors of such a steed.

The horses began to stagger with exhaustion. Sha Totek muttered a charm of vitality to keep them on their feet. The suns sank inexorably toward the horizon. No sanctuary appeared on the moorland ahead.

With brassy evening light on the moor, Ronar discovered that the Teratorns now appeared distinctly larger. Apparently the thermals that had held them aloft were fading. With dusk came their attack.

"The inn!" cried Sha Totek. Ronar looked ahead. A structure was on the horizon. The Riders must see it too.

"We're not going to make it," said Ronar grimly. "The Teratorns are almost on top of us."

Sha Totek spat a sulfurous curse.

"No time for that," said Ronar. "Come on, let's ride into that crater and make some kind of a stand."

"Crater" was an exaggerated term for the shallow bowl they entered, but it was better than nothing as a defense against swooping birds of prey. Both men leaped from their saddles. The Teratorns were even larger than Ronar had imagined. He debated whether to force the horses to lay down, making them more difficult targets for the great talons. He regretfully decided they'd have to stay up, to serve as shields for himself and Sha Totek.

The astronomer shouldered his quiver of quartz-tipped arrows and strung the heavy yew bow, berating himself for not having practiced with it. He transferred the sword to his back.

Sha Totek brought an opaque black vial from one of his magical saddlebags. A lemon yellow light shone from it as he removed the stopper. Using a small golden implement, the sorcerer scooped out daubs of glowing paste. He winced as he quickly painted six short stripes on each of his forearms. The glow faded from the paste as it dried, until it seemed merely a muddy paint.

The Teratorns gave out cries like the tolling of bronze bells. They dived toward the rim of the little bowl, then swept overhead, five in a row. The horses screamed in terror. Ronar was stunned by their size. Each had the wingspan of a sailplane. The very blast of their wings was nearly enough to knock him off his feet. Their cries were a deafening reverberation in the air.

The birds peeled away, wings scooping out great thunderclaps of air as they gained altitude. Ronar shook his head and stared awestruck as they wheeled for another approach. The last sunbeams struck purple and bronze iridescence from their black feathers. Their primary flight feathers, each at least a yard long, were edged with silver, as were their crests. Their hooked beaks were polished like black lacquer, while their eyes were fiery globes of yellow-green crystal, each the size of his fist. He couldn't help but speculate on what kind of vision such eyes must provide.

But Ronar was most startled by the arms of the Teratorns. These birds were not overgrown Terrestrial condors, but products of Colibdian evolution, as those well-developed, viciously clawed forearms proved.

The five Teratorns formed into a V-shaped phalanx and bore down on them like an arrowhead. Ronar jumped as a bolt of concentrated sunlight ripped out of the gloom behind him. It slammed through the air just in front of the lead Teratorn, which was singed, but only momentarily deterred.

Ronar looked at Sha Totek, whose smoking forearms now had only five paint-stripes each.

"Damn!" shouted the sorcerer. "I missed! Ronar! Quit that witless gaping and bend that bow!"

It was a tribute to Ronar's latent talents that he managed to nock and release two arrows before the Teratorns were upon them again. Both shots missed; he hadn't led them far enough. They barely managed to throw themselves down in time to avoid the talons. Ronar's horse wasn't so lucky. It was struck and hurled end over end, its side torn open, its back broken. Such was the impact that blood sprayed as though atomized.

"May Varanu pluck you!" yelled Sha Totek. He was back on his feet almost before Ronar's horse stopped tumbling. With teeth bared, he took careful aim at the retreating birds, then struck his forearms together to bring two more of the stripes into contact. Another sunbolt erupted, this time hitting squarely. One Teratorn went down in a mass of flame and oily smoke. "Hah!" cried Sha Totek.

Ronar nocked another arrow and sighted along it. He cooly dismissed all thoughts except those involved in achieving a ballistic path between his bow and the heart of his target. Satisfied, he released the arrow. Deflected by a last-second gust of wind, it penetrated a wing, bringing forth a scream of fury, but doing no real damage.

He nocked another, but the birds were back again. This time they hovered over the depression, their wings forcing down such blasts of air that Ronar, Sha Totek, and even the horses were knocked flat.

Ronar lay looking up at the Teratorn that had chosen him as its prey. Its wings hid most of the sky from his sight. Its fire-green eyes locked onto his. All four sets of talons reached out as the bird settled. Ronar grimaced in anticipation.

Then he grew puzzled. He still held the bow. He couldn't draw it fully since he was flat on his back, but he could still fire an arrow from point-blank range. Why didn't the bird get it over with? He waited with heart pounding, half expecting magical fire to blaze from the bird's eyes and incinerate him. But none came—the Teratorn continued to hover, although the strain of the maneuver was evident in its eyes. Finally, almost impatiently, Ronar raised the bow and released the shaft into the bird's breast. Instantly dead, it fell on him like a musky mass of autumn leaves. Its talons felt like railroad spikes against his skin. He heard a crash and glimpsed a quick yellow light as he struggled free of the dead bird. Despite its size, the Teratorn didn't weigh much more than he did himself.

He scrambled to his feet and got his first look at a Rider. Attached to the dead bird's back was an ovoid object about three feet long. The thing arched and pulsed as Ronar stood watching. Covered with overlapping leathery plates, it had no eyes, mouth, or other openings. In fact, its only obvious external structures were two tubes that entered the base of the bird's neck.

The Rider's motions grew more spasmodic. The connecting tubes ripped from the bird's neck, revealing rasping probes at the ends. The brown body flopped heavily off the carcass and heaved itself toward Ronar.

After a moment in which his vision seemed to swim, Ronar realized he had drawn his sword and hacked the parasite to bits.

With frantic strength he retrieved his bow from beneath the bird's carcass and whirled to take stock of the situation. Sha Totek plunged his dagger into the Rider of the second Teratorn he'd blasted. That left two: one crouched over the packhorse and tore out its throat; where was the other? Its whistling pinions gave the only warning as it dived at him from behind. Ronar flung himself down, and was up again so fast that the tail feathers brushed him. He sent a shaft after the great rushing shape. It sank deep into the Rider, to Ronar's savage satisfaction.

The bird's reaction wasn't what he'd expected or hoped. It stiffened and let loose an appalling shriek. Sha Totek looked up. "No! Don't shoot the Riders! If they're injured, they pump a poison into the birds that drives them mad!" He fired off two more sunbolts at the erratically plunging Teratorn, but missed with both. Ronar made two good hits with his bow, and Sha Totek's last blast finished off the tortured creature.

Ronar spun and cast a burning gaze at the remaining Teratorn, still preoccupied with the remains of the pack-horse. The astronomer dropped his bow and charged the bird. It spread its wings to lift off, but too late. Ronar leaped onto its back. His weight caused the bird to flounder to the ground. Ronar held tight and drew his dagger, a spike of gold in the fading dusk. The bird tried to surge upwards again, but Ronar cracked its skull with the hilt of the dagger. The Teratorn flopped down again, stunned. Quick as his hand could move, Ronar cut the tubes connecting the bird to its Rider. He lifted the cold bulk of the Rider and dismounted the bird. Hooks reached for him from the underside of the parasite, but they were too short to get a grip. He heaved it into the pyre of the nearest burning Teratorn, where it jerked until it swelled up and burst.

Not yet satisfied, Ronar cut the toothed tips of the two umbilicals from the bird's shoulders. The wounds looked clean and healthy compared to what had been there before.

The Teratorn slowly raised itself on all fours. It gave Ronar a long look from one brilliant eye.

Ronar glared back at it. "Now get away from here, and leave us be!" Then, seemingly beyond all caution, he thrust his face into the bird's and hissed, "And remember it was Namirnakh who made you a slave—and Leonard Ronar who set you free!"

The wrath in the bird's gaze was like a physical force. It snapped its beak like a bear trap, then vented a cry of rage. Ronar fell back. The Teratorn spread its wings, fifty feet from tip to tip. It launched itself skyward, and soon disappeared in the east.

Ronar stared after it in wonder. "I could swear that bird understood what I said ."

"Perhaps, perhaps," said Sha Totek breathlessly. "On this planet, there are birds, and there are Birds. The Teratorns aren't the smartest among them, but they're definitely the biggest. Shall we remove our assets from this place? Namirnakh might not grant us time to catch our breaths. Astonishing that we've survived the attack of five Teratorns without a scratch."

"Two horses were scratched," said Ronar soberly.

"I thought you didn't like horses."

"They were gentle creatures and served us well."

"We haven't far to go. Those long shanks of yours must serve for now."

Night pressed close around the inn. The stone structure's few occupants stared nervously at the blackness beyond the shutters. Certainly no one had forgotten the spine-freezing cries which had rung out in the distance just an hour before. It was yet another of the unsettling events that had troubled their land of late. Reports of monsters leaking over from Darteharn, word of witch conclaves in the foothills of the Mynd Bannock; all these following the dark vapor which had erupted from the Evil Eye some days past.

They watched the darkness lapping up against the windows, taking what comfort they could from the sputtering peat-fires on the hearth.

They heard footsteps on the threshold. Somehow they knew that whatever was out there was beyond the ordinary and would do nothing to lessen their fears. They stared at the door to see what evil the night would bring them.

The door slammed open, admitting a wave of chilly air. Two apparitions stood outside. One stepped into the light,

wild-eyed, quick and flamboyant despite his grimy clothing
. The other remained in the shadows, looming like some
silent, watchful spirit.

The wild-eyed one stalked into their midst. His hands
wove webs of tinted fire in the air while his jet-black eyes
scanned the pale faces of those around him.

"I am Sha Totek, the Barrer of the Way, come back
among you after all these centuries! Wake your children;
tell your wives that the legends of old are abroad again. Tell
them their milk will sour and their sheep give birth to
prodigies! And I bring you—" His pause was merciless,
bringing his listeners to a painful edge of anticipation. "I
bring you—" he flourished a hastily-wrapped paper package—"I bring you some roast fowl for your meager table",
he finished quietly. He tossed the package of Teratorn meat
onto a table and collapsed onto the nearest bench.

Chapter 11

Ring of Fire

They didn't stay long enough to trouble the dreams of the other travelers. They ate, claimed three hours sleep, ate again and cleaned themselves up as best they could. They were back in the saddle before midnight, riding horses which Sha Totek bought with a few small jewels he'd carried. Their owners had been happy to expedite the departure of such unwelcome guests as the Barrer of the Way and his silent companion.

Sha Totek was certain that other agents of Namirnakh, slower than the Dusk Riders but just as dangerous, would soon be on their trail. For a while he fretted with indecision. Then, reining to a sudden halt, he invoked certain powers of vigilance, erecting a web of magic designed to tweak his consciousness should other magical beings venture within it. He regretted each use of magic he was forced to make, but small ones now might keep him alive for large ones later.

The next few days were an uncomfortable blur to Ronar. They rode hard every day and evening, stopping at inns only long enough to replace their horses and snatch enough rest to let them sit upright in the saddle. Sha Totek was more and more driven. He grew more drawn with every mile that fled beneath them, and more humorless, except in a feverish, ironic sort of way.

They'd reached mid-northern latitudes; here the hand of winter was ever more apparent. The dun-colored moor was sometimes streaked with snow. The farming villages they passed were dormant, drawn into themselves. Threads of smoke from their chimneys were the only sign of life they showed.

A mountain range appeared on the western horizon, a jagged grey haze. "That is the Mynd Bannock," said Sha Totek. "It forms the boundary of Eranior and Darteharn. This is the most populous region of Eranior; several cities are nearby. A day farther north lies Myrddin, capital of Eranior. We'd best avoid these places. We can't afford the kind of delays we found in Thunderbird. Anyway, my reputation among these people is ambiguous at best."

That night they visited a roadside inn which was a far cry from the lonely outposts to the south. They entered a great low-ceilinged hall lit by marble fireplaces and lamps hanging from gilded chains. They sat at a carved wooden table, their cast-off jackets wet and steaming .

Ronar observed the other patrons with interest. He'd anticipated a crowd of hairy howling barbarians, but he now realized this was merely the prejudice of a "civilized" man. While there was no shortage of laughter in this common room, beneath it was an air of grave restraint which kept Ronar sitting straighter than he might have otherwise.

"Nice to be out of the weather for a bit," said Ronar.

Sha Totek eyed him with mock surprise. "What? Are you becoming effete?"

"Austerity is fine for strengthening and instructing a man. But an occasional dose of ease gives the contrast which lends the hard lessons their value." Such was Ronar's rationale as he enjoyed the sophisticated counterpoint of the string-and-reed band in the corner.

Sha Totek too seemed to be enjoying himself. He smiled easily, pointing out and identifying the non-Eranians in the room. These included a fair number of men from Tíuheimr, light haired, with blue eyes or grey. Their bearing was sober, their garments drab and severe. A few Mersineans wore heavy cloaks over woolen chitons. The only visitors who appeared to be from Thunderbird were Ronar and Sha Totek themselves.

The waiter arrived, studying them impassively as Sha Totek ordered food and drink. In a few moments the man returned and set down a wooden pitcher of beer and a pair of tin mugs. Sha Totek poured for them both. Ronar sampled it, was satisfied, and drained it. He set down the empty mug decisively.

"Have another," said Sha Totek.

"No, thanks. One is enough for me. I'm not a big drinker."

"Oh, come on; do you expect me to finish all this? Just one more."

"No. I don't enjoy the sensation."

"Oh, I see. I'll tell you what then. I'll use a spell to modify its effect on you, so you'll notice none."

"You can do that?" asked Ronar cautiously.

"It's very easy. May I?"

"All right, I'll try it."

Sha Totek refilled the mug, then sat whispering and staring at it with a peculiar intensity.

"There you go. Give it a try."

Ronar lifted the mug and sipped. "It tastes no different."

"It is different though, I assure you."

Ronar shrugged and drank off half the beer, set it down, looked around the room. The glamour and color of the crowd continued to impress him. He shook his head, pleased to have the privilege of witnessing this throng of interesting and worthy folk.

That glamour doubled when a new group entered, floating along like haughty lords, making all others seem like apes in comparison. They wore delicate garments of pastel colors, trimmed in silver or gold. Two tall, slender men with keen faces flanked a haughty, pale woman with silver curls piled atop her head. Her eyes also gleamed like silver. Ronar, finding himself gaping at her, withdrew his unseemly regard only with difficulty. The trio chose a large corner table.

"She's something, isn't she?" asked Sha Totek slyly.

"I should say so. She's the most ravishing creature I've ever seen," blurted Ronar. Chagrined by this utterance, he sat back blinking, wondering how best to withdraw from this uncomfortable territory. He took another few sips of beer. "What in the world are they? They don't look—quite human."

"They're Elves. Sometimes known as fairies."

"Fairies? I assume you mean of the folklore variety—?"

Sha Totek chuckled. "That's right."

"So, are they—real? Or are they magical constructs of some kind?"

"Oh, they're quite real. Quite human, despite their looks."

"And how does one get to be a fairie?" Ronar almost burst out laughing.

"Well, partner, it's something about the air on this planet," said Sha Totek. "Every now and then, magic seeps so deep into someone that it—changes them. They get a funny look in their eyes, turn away from the ordinary people around them, and are drawn to the land of Faerie, where they take their place among the other fey folk."

Ronar gave a grimace of doubt. "So why aren't you one of these fairies? You're more magical than anybody."

"No...I *have* more magic than anybody, but I *am* not more magical than anybody. There is a subtle yet important distinction between them."

Ronar snorted and reached for the pitcher.

Sha Totek continued: "It's unusual to see Elves out of their own country. They have their own little world there, where things are to their liking, and they rarely emerge. That filly you're admiring—she's a Cotavion, by the look of her." He shook his head, and his gaze moved inward. The name meant nothing to Ronar.

Ronar continued to eye the fairie woman. "Are we going their way?"

"Nope. No time to play with Elves on this trip."

When Sha Totek's voice resumed, it seemed to come from a distance curiously great.

"Got yourself a filly back home, Ronar?"

Ronar almost spit in his beer. "Me? Good God, no. I'm not exactly the type. Have you taken a good look at me? I frighten women and children. I am harsh. Women want handsome, sensitive, gentle men, not great shambling ogres such as myself. No, I don't trouble women, and I don't let them trouble me."

A glance at Sha Totek revealed the sorcerer's steady gaze. "Then what about Phaedra? She seemed to find you acceptable."

"That? Why, that was only…" Ronar's voice trailed off. "I don't know what it was. I think my heroic deed must have gotten to her. Surely a girl as radiant as that can have no real interest in someone like me."

They were both silent for a few moments. Ronar emptied his mug and filled it again.

"What do you want out of life, Ronar?" asked Sha To-tek softly. "To study the stars and peer out over the world in solitary splendor?"

Ronar flashed a look at him. "Now you sound like Damon Despard. No, not exactly that. I want what I suppose any man wants. I want the companionship of a beautiful woman, and a home where love and warmth fill the air. Rooms full of children. I want to look beside me as the decades pass and see the face of one who shares my brief journey through time. I would like to have a daughter, to marvel at her beauty and grace. I would like to have a son, to teach him not to live as I have lived. Or not entirely as I have lived, at least."

"Those seem like good, honest, simple desires."

"I never claimed to be especially profound. But, for too many years I made excuses. I was afraid. I glared out at the world in—solitary splendor. Now it is too late for me."

Ronar's vision dimmed until he no longer saw Sha To-tek.

"Every man is a universe unto himself, this much I know," he muttered. "We carry our own worlds within us, more vast and complicated than we can understand. To communicate with other minds, we have only words, incomplete and ambiguous as they are. Therefore we isolated beings move through the world, registering on each other only through the senses. We barely begin to understand even ourselves. Understanding others is an impossible task. The wonder isn't that I feel isolated, but that there are those who feel they are not.

"Women want to be treated kindly, with compassion. I observe them and see their lovely forms performing mysterious actions. I inadvertently bruise their feelings in the process of living my life, when I interact with them at all. Such a man is best left alone."

Ronar's awareness gradually returned. He sat there staring at his mug, wondering dully what had moved him to declaim in that embarrassing fashion. He looked up again, suddenly truculent. "What about you, Sha Totek? You don't exactly immerse yourself in society in that Tower of yours."

"This is true," said the sorcerer quietly. "For the first few centuries of my immortality, I maintained a few human companions. I would apply spells of long life to those whom I favored. But human relationships are always changing, and are unlikely to persist as long as I do. Eventually my friends and lovers found themselves forced to endure a person they no longer desired, simply so they would not be separated from the magic that kept them alive. And I tired of them, facing me with the choice of letting them die because my interest had waned, or continuing to sustain a growing collection of former friends simply because I had taken it upon myself to extend their lives in the first place. In the end I found it better not to involve myself with anyone to that degree."

The sorcerer excused himself and wandered off, apparently just another outlander in search of the nearest outhouse.

Ronar looked up at the approach of the waiter, who set down crocks of stew, loaves of bread, plates of greens, pitchers of cream, and dishes of cheese and butter. The man seemed ill at ease. When he'd finished he regarded Ronar with an eye of appraisal. Ronar wondered what was expected of him. Was he supposed to pay for the food now?

The waiter ended the suspense by clearing his throat and saying, "Sir, you appear an upright man, for all your wildness of mien and strangeness of device." He glanced at Ronar's binocular. "May I ask why you break bread with such a one as the Errant Mage?"

"Errant Mage? I haven't heard him use that title, if it's any business of yours."

"No, not if he's anxious to conceal the truth of the matter. But errant he is, and believe me, he is not to be trusted."

A kernel of indignation flared up in Ronar. "Why do you hold this view?"

The waiter sniffed. "Like all the sons of Eranior, I learned its history on my father's knee. It isn't my place to enter into a dispute with you. But beware of Imhotep. He has always cared for the other world more than for this one."

Ronar's patience evaporated. "I don't care for what you're saying. My companion is a great man, and you are ignorant. You are not fit to polish the ornaments on his hat."

The waiter looked first startled, then offended to receive such abuse. But Ronar's demeanor did not encourage him to press the issue.

Ronar glowered murkily at the waiter's retreating back. He was troubled as Sha Totek returned to his seat.

"Be as casual as you can," said the sorcerer with apparent amusement. "Take your time. Tell me what you think of those stolid gentlemen standing at every door."

Ronar appraised them: large men with bristling mustaches, each with a bronze torc around his neck. They all stood facing Ronar's table.

"Soldiers, or police," he said.

Sha Totek nodded. "Yes. I'm interested to learn their intentions concerning us."

They didn't have long to wait. At some imperceptible signal, the men left their posts and marched in their direction. Silence fell. Ronar moved to stand, but Sha Totek's hand on his arm kept him down.

In a moment they were surrounded by ten men with bronze swords at their sides.

"Gentlemen," said Sha Totek pleasantly. "My compliments on the service offered by this establishment. But I assure you, a single busboy will be sufficient."

The man with the most fearsome mustache looked at him impassively. "You are Imhotep, late of the Two Lands of Egypt, one-time Pharaoh of Ammon?"

"Maybe I am, and maybe I'm not."

"I am Cadwaladr ap Dillan of the House of Aneirin, Captain of the Sons of Wut."

"Pleased to meet you, I'm sure."

"His Highness King Sionyn requires you to meet with his representatives at your earliest opportunity. That will be tomorrow evening, no later, at the Skye Island. Do you know this place?"

"I think so; I may have built it."

"We will accompany you there. While we recognize that we cannot force you to comply, neither can we believe you would do our King the insult of passing through his lands without making your intentions known to him."

"Of course not. The thought never crossed my mind."

"Hmph." Cadwaladr frowned. "We set out at sunrise. We leave you to your meal."

Ronar and Sha Totek watched as Cadwaladr and his troops departed.

"You will comply with this arrogant demand?" asked Ronar.

Sha Totek spread his palms. "We might as well spare ourselves some trouble and go along. The Skye Island's not far out of our way."

The food was the best they'd had on their entire journey. But as hunger became less urgent, troubling questions weighed on Ronar's mind.

"Why do the people of Eranior distrust you so?"

Sha Totek's gaze flickered over Ronar. "Out of respect for you, I will briefly tell the tale, but then I will ask you not to raise the matter again.

"When the British Celts first crossed to Colibdis, two among them quickly rose in stature. One was the warrior Bran, called the Blessed, First King of Eranior. The other was Namirnakh. He was no Briton, but a self-proclaimed magician who had wandered to Britain from some Eastern land, Persia perhaps. He soon ingratiated himself to Bran, suddenly finding his magic useful for more than fraud and trickery. He bided his time, increasing his powers, and was soon second only to Bran in authority. Bran's people had wide lands to explore and colonize. Before long they had founded a great nation. In gratitude for his contributions, Bran made Namirnakh a great lord of Eranior. They reigned virtually together, side by side, their life spans lengthened by the depth and skill of Namirnakh's magic.

"But Namirnakh was ambitious, and was seduced by the god Ahriman, who was gaining in power at that time. Namirnakh betrayed and killed Bran in a particularly grotesque manner. For a time he ruled alone, with the crowned skull of Bran mockingly occupying the throne next to his. But many were outraged by this treachery, especially the house of Aneirin, which had been loyal to Bran even before they'd been harried off the Earth by the Saxons. They and their followers rose up against Namirnakh in civil war.

"The Aneirins begged me for help, but at that time I refused to interfere in the doings of the men of Colibdis. I thought it enough to take upon myself the function of Gatekeeper. As such, I did not allow any of them to return to Earth in search of aid. I would not let them enter their Portal, but otherwise I stood aloof.

"The bloodshed was hard to imagine, the destruction nearly total. But the Aneirins were able to drive Namirnakh and his forces westward, over the passes of the Mynd Bannock, to the gloomy moorlands beyond. That country became Darteharn. The Aneirins assumed the kingship of Eranior, and have ruled ever since. They have always worked to contain the threat of Darteharn. They have always revered the memory of Bran. And they have always resented and mistrusted me.

"Had I acted then, I could have swept Namirnakh away like an insect, for he had not yet come into the full force of his magic. But I did not act. I am reminded of my error every time I look at a map and see the stain of Darteharn disfiguring so much of the land. Yet you will notice that I am acting now. I have made myself into the nemesis of

Namirnakh. He hasn't since made a move I haven't helped to counter, whether the Eranians realize it or not. Only thus can I stifle his laughter at the memory of how I stood back and did nothing. Someday I will pull that whelp from his lofty throne and show him what two thousand years of regret does to a sorcerer."

He drained his mug of beer and looked around with glittering eyes.

To Ronar, this was a very different man than the flippant conjurer he'd met in the airy richness of the Tower. At first, because of the sorcerer's antics and dissolute habits, Ronar had thought himself the more stable, even the more mature, of the two. Now he realized with chagrin that stiff behavior and Spartan habits weren't necessarily the same as wisdom and responsibility. As he tried to grasp some part of the rigor of Sha Totek's five thousand-year vigil, he was forced to reassess many preconceptions. He wondered how well he would have endured the sorcerer's burden. Solitary as he was, the thought of Sha Totek's centuries of solitude, broken only by the next few stragglers to wander in through one Portal after another, daunted his imagination.

Ronar found the harried-looking man sitting across from him a sad contrast to the vital, confident figure who had dwelt in the Tower. He resolved to do all he could to see Sha Totek returned to those surroundings as quickly as possible.

For the present they were not yet halfway to their goal, with the wildest sections of their path still ahead. But tonight offered one small consolation. They suddenly realized they had nowhere to go before morning. They were free to claim their first decent night's rest in over a week.

They left the common room, Ronar having some difficulty picking a way among the tables. Like starving men who prefer a scrap now to a feast later, the thought of beds and comfort banished all thoughts of the future.

Despite his fatigue, Ronar's mind remained active after the lamp wicks in their room were snuffed out. He felt like talking, but Sha Totek preempted him as he drew breath for his first word.

"Please shut up. I want to get some sleep before the innkeeper becomes so scandalized by my presence that he evicts us."

Ronar complied.

A pounding at the door awakened them before dawn. "Sorcerer! It's time for you and your lackey to arise. We must be on our way."

Ronar was on his feet before that statement was complete. He flung open the door, grabbed Cadwaladr by the torc, and said in his best Eranian Welsh, "I want to make clear which of us is the lackey here."

Cadwaladr's hand went to his hilt, but Sha Totek called out, "Captain, if you force Ronar to hurt you, I will transform the rest of your men into newts. Irreversibly, I might add."

Cadwaladr relaxed; Ronar released him. "Very well, sorcerer. But I say again, prepare to depart. I will not allow your whims to interfere with the wishes of the King." The soldier shot a hard look at Ronar and departed.

Ronar closed the door behind him. "I'm tired of his arrogance."

"Perhaps you feel upstaged by it," said Sha Totek helpfully. "You should watch who you antagonize. You are no trained fighter. He could have gutted you, despite your indignation."

"Maybe." Ronar regarded Sha Totek with a look of stern reproach. "Last night you told me that beer would have no effect on me."

The sorcerer waved a dismissive hand. "Nonsense. I told you that you would not notice its effect. But be easy. My memory of what may have passed between us last night is fading fast."

Minutes later, in the common room, they were met by the full contingent of the Sons of Wut.

"Is it permitted that we break our fast, or is this deemed contrary to the will of the King?" asked Sha Totek politely.

"You may eat."

Ronar ate what was set before him and soon regretted it. Fatty sausages in a creamy soup occupied his stomach like five pounds of lard. Damnable headache!

They rode off before the shadows of the dawn had shortened appreciably. The morning was quiet and crisp. Northern Eranior was bleak and spare beneath the dun-and-white covering of winter. Snow lay deep on the north sides of scattered granite megaliths.

They passed through villages and towns whose windows were shuttered, their barn doors barred. Ronar wondered whether these rustics simply liked to sleep late on winter mornings, or if they'd been warned of the passage of Sha Totek and had their women and children locked up in fright.

After a few miles Sha Totek sidled over to Cadwaladr, who rode at the head of the circle of riders that surrounded them. "Captain, it would be wise for us to take a more evasive course. I regret to inform you that I'm being hunted by agents of Namirnakh. There's no point in making their job any easier."

Cadwaladr laughed derisively. "What nonsense! You're in Eranior's very heart, accompanied by the cream of the Sons of Wut. Namirnakh himself could not reach you here."

"Your confidence warms my heart, but nevertheless I think we should get off the road."

"We are expected at the Skye Island."

"The Island isn't that far from here. We won't be delayed."

"We keep to the road."

Ronar, overhearing this exchange, cantered up. "Cadwaladr, I'm not sure I even believe in Namirnakh, or Darteharn, or you, for that matter. But I do know we've already been attacked by a stone demon and a flock of Teratorns, all within the borders of Eranior. We're leaving the road. If you try to stop us, you must either die or explain to your King why you killed us."

"One tenth of that goes for me, too," said Sha Totek.

Cadwaladr studied them both. "Sorcerer, your companion shows rough manners. Greylock, in this land we do not deal with each other by constantly offering threat of violence. Are things otherwise in your land?"

Ronar was at a loss for words.

"Our friend Ronar is fresh from Earth," said Sha Totek. "He's a citizen of the land of the free and the home of the brave. It's their way."

Cadwaladr nodded. "Then he is of the same stock as the callow ruffians of Thunderbird. This explains much. Sorcerer, lead us as you will, so long as we arrive at Skye Island before sunset."

"Thank you." Sha Totek risked a single glance at Ronar's face.

They followed an erratic course, staying out of sight of the road, following stream beds, cutting over ridges. Soon even the Sons of Wut seemed disoriented. Sha Totek proceeded confidently until noon. Then, as they topped a rise, his ears seemed to prick up. He raised his hand to call for a halt.

He sat for a moment in silence. Then a low "No...he wouldn't dare..." drifted back to the others.

The sorcerer turned and faced his companions. "This is most interesting. Our friend Namirnakh has arranged a reception for us just ahead. How he knew our exact path I can't yet say. I doubt there's any graceful way to avoid the encounter, and frankly I'm not in the mood to look for one."

"Nor are we," said Cadwaladr. "No man of Aneirin will defer to Namirnakh in his own country."

Ronar said nothing. He merely bent his bow against his stirrup and strung it, checked his quiver, and loosened his blades.

They rode into a circular area ringed by earthen banks, perhaps man-made. Sha Totek jerked on his reins and wheeled about. His eyes were wild, his teeth bared.

Ronar's narrowed eyes swept the skyline. Three figures rose up beyond the far rim of the earthwork. They wore tattered cloaks and carried long, twisted staffs. Ronar raised his binocular. Aged faces filled the field of view. Their beards were grey, their gazes calm, if perhaps a bit vague and unfocused.

Ronar whispered, "Are those three old men all we face?"

"Wait," said Sha Totek.

More groups of three appeared, first at the four points of the compass, then filling in the spaces between. Soon more than a hundred ill-clad figures stood on the rim of the circular mound. They varied in age and gender, though all were younger than the first three. All were dressed in the same sort of rags.

"Where are they coming from?" rasped Cadwaladr.

Sha Totek shrugged. "Maybe from warrens dug into these earthworks. Or maybe from thin air."

Ronar sneered. "I'm sure it's the latter. How else could they have escaped the vigilance of the Sons of Wut?"

Sha Totek called out loudly. "I see that among the benefits of following Namirnakh, a fine wardrobe is not uppermost."

That produced a stirring in the ranks and low, brittle laughter from the aged triad in the north. They all let their tatters fall away, revealing robes of black, except for the three elders, who also wore scarlet mantles. A thin voice wafted over the morning breeze. "We wear the unsullied black of Namirnakh, and the scarlet of his Master, wily Ahriman, whom the upright cattle of Eranior call Teutates. Come with us now to Kharnarnithon. There our lord Namirnakh wishes to renew your acquaintance, which has lapsed for so many centuries."

Sha Totek sent forth his voice in the same quiet tone. "Kharnarnithon? Not yet. Those centuries you mention are not a third of those I have seen, though they amount to nearly the entire span of your upstart lord. Namirnakh will set eyes on me in good time, but the time and place will not be to his liking. Now clear the path, you spy, parasite, false priest."

"I say as well, clear the path, in the name of the Royal Torc of Eranior," said Cadwaladr. "These men are under the protection of the King. You must give way."

"Your mission is forlorn. If we were to open our circle, would you take your warriors and ride away in peace?"

Cadwaladr shook his head vigorously. "Only with the outlanders in tow."

"Then you must share their fate. Sorcerer, beware. You are not now protected by walls of black crystal."

"Nor do you witches have Namirnakh to wipe your noses or to hold your palsied hands as you cast your feeble spells."

A vibration of ire quivered among the magicians. Sha Totek worked hard to restrain a smile.

The voice that answered was tense and wrathful. "We have wondered why your Tower is in Namirnakh's color. Perhaps you are destined to become his servant, even as we."

Sha Totek set free his smile. "Symbols vary among various peoples. To you, blackness is a sign of evil, of malice and petty desire, treachery and deceit. To others it is a reminder of the great darkness that surrounds us all, and which ultimately renders our grandest conceits futile and ephemeral. To still others, it means a depth of time, in which wisdom and experience can accumulate to a depth far beyond what might be expected of apprentice witches and their sycophants."

"What of you, Greylock?" came a shriller voice from another quarter. "Why do you travel with this anachronism?

Are you a mercenary? Has he promised you riches derived from sorcery?"

Ronar's reply welled up without conscious thought. "I am Leonard Ronar, an Earthman. I have come to stop your stinking god from befouling my sky."

"Very diplomatic, Ronar," said Sha Totek from the side of his mouth. "Very subtle. Now that the mutual huffing and blowing is over, things may get more serious. I suggest you all back off a bit. They'll be concentrating on me, at least at first."

"Can you withstand them alone?" asked Cadwaladr.

"If at any point you see a way to make yourselves useful, feel free to pitch in."

The assembled witches drew themselves up and linked hands. "We will throw your heads at Namirnakh's feet and set your souls to wandering."

"We will throw your feet at Namirnakh's head and solely set you meandering," prated Sha Totek in an irritating voice.

A deep-seated groan came up from the earth. The ground quaked like pudding. Thin tendrils writhed into view just behind the witches. They climbed skyward, twisting and thickening, sprouting branches and limbs. The branches put out multitudes of twigs. Their quivering ceased.

A mighty circle of oaks now ringed Sha Totek's party.

"Ignore this," muttered the sorcerer over his shoulder. "This is just for effect."

Green buds popped into being on the trees. In seconds they unfurled into a canopy of foliage, incongruous in the winter bleakness. Their false summer was brief. The leaves flamed scarlet until each great tree possessed a crown of fire. Ronar recognized it as the fire of Ahriman.

A wind came up, swirling around the earthwork. It drew the fires into a vortex that roared into the heavens, a cylinder of flame that baked them with a penetrating heat.

The horses ran about with wide eyes. Ronar half-fell from his mount. Several of the others were thrown. Ronar squinted, raised his arms to ward off the spinning inferno. He shot an accusatory glance at Sha Totek.

The sorcerer shrugged and grimaced. "Pretty convincing, isn't it?"

"Sons of Wut!" cried Cadwaladr. "Attack! Cut through on the north side of the ring!"

They drew their swords and charged howling straight toward the firestorm.

"Are they crazy?" asked Ronar.

"Maybe not. Watch and see."

Ten warriors reached the flame wall, apparently none the worse for it. Just inside the ring were the servants of Namirnakh, also immune to the flames. The warriors wielded their heavy blades with deadly strength, hacking down several of the witches before they could react.

"The flames are a sham!" yelled Ronar. He drew his sword. "I'll join them!"

"No! The fires are real enough! And put away that sword!"

Ronar looked narrowly at Sha Totek. He sheathed the sword in view of the urgency in his voice.

The witches reacted. Scarlet meteors shot from the trees, embedding themselves in the flesh of the warriors, where they burned like phosphorous. Their screams were plain even over the roar of the flames.

"Fall back!" cried Cadwaladr. Only he and three others were able to flee. The others shriveled into charred husks, eaten through by the burrowing fireballs.

"The Sons of Wut are charmed against general magic. Only when the fire was directed against them as individuals could it overcome this protection," said Sha Totek grimly.

The remaining fighters, including Cadwaladr, had not entirely avoided the fireballs. They clutched at their limbs; smoke and vapor sputtered from their wounds. "Sorcerer, help us!" yelled one of the men.

"I can't! Not if I'm to save all our lives."

"Bloody hell!" Ronar snatched a water bottle from his saddle and ran to each man in turn, pouring water into the wounds. "Does this help?" he asked Cadwaladr.

"Yes—at least I think the damned things are extinguished."

"Hold still."

Before Cadwaladr could object, Ronar was probing his wound with the tip of his dagger.

"Don't worry, Captain! Ronar enjoys exploring other people's interiors, and is moderately skillful at it," offered Sha Totek.

In a moment, Ronar's blade flipped out a small object.

"What—what is it?" asked the ashen-faced Cadwaladr.

"It's a damned acorn."

"An acorn! I am struck down by an acorn!"

Ronar left the Eranians and went for his bow. Furious, he sighted on one of the three crimson-cloaked ringleaders. Their faces were slack, upturned, their eyes closed. He could hardly miss. Even if the wind should deflect the shaft, it would still strike some other member of the circle.

He drew the arrow, his target steady above the shaft.

The target remained steady. Ronar's release was usually automatic. He waited for it.

Nothing happened. His fingers still held back the string. His target flickered in the heated air beyond his deadly point of flaked white quartz. His hand began to tremble. He had to remove his attention from the target to force his fingers to let go. It was very strange.

The arrow hissed out, was taken by the whirlwind, and leaped into the breast of a woman to the left of the intended target. She didn't fall from the circle, for she was small and slender, easily supported by the witches on either side of her.

Ronar dropped the bow and cried out as the firestorm swept down upon him. The fierce hot wind brought stinging tears to his eyes. A fiery hand constricted his heart. In its way, his grief was as perilous as the storm of supernatural fire that raged around him. Yet he must live. He seized the bow and sent shaft after shaft at his enemies while he could still bring himself to do so. A terrible anger built within him, directed against those who had forced him to stray so far from his natural behavior. He sought, without realizing it, to avenge the witch's death by slaying as many of her companions as possible.

Arrows exhausted, he turned and screamed out, "Sha Totek! When in hell are you going to do something—?" He subsided as he beheld what the sorcerer had wrought.

He could no longer see his companions—not clearly, at least. They were obscured by—an area—a zone of space that was somehow different from what surrounded it. The field was not so much purple-grey-black as it contained the idea of purple-grey-blackness. Within it he made out the silhouettes of the men and the horses, all standing or sitting calmly.

In the heat and wind of the firestorm, Ronar squinted at that purplish something while absently brushing flaming leaves from his clothing. The field was expanding. Ronar stepped inside it.

A sense of complete relief flooded over him. The dark deeds and travails of Colibdis seemed as remote as the legends of Odysseus or King Arthur. Within this limitless mauve-colored haze, he was at peace.

He put out his hand and stroked the cool flank of his mount. "I'm glad to be away from that madness," he said calmly. "It was getting to be too much for me, towards the end."

Cadwaladr ap Dillan and his men sat nearby. "How are you feeling?" asked Ronar.

Cadwaladr shook his head slowly. "The pain is still there. But what of it?"

"Too bad about your fallen men."

"Life or death are much the same; neither is worth the striving." Cadwaladr gazed blankly into the limitless distance.

Ronar nodded in agreement. He stood there in that soft void, savoring the silence. How odd it had been, and what a waste...the pain and toil of life in that other world. His awareness of this truth had been late in coming, but was most welcome.

Sha Totek was neither calm nor relaxed. Sweat rolled down his face. His brow was furrowed, his eyes squeezed shut, his jaw muscles clenched. He sat on his heels, palms pressed together.

"What is this place?" asked Ronar.

"This is Morluminar," Sha Totek said tonelessly. "Don't get too used to it."

"I feel so—detached," said Ronar distractedly. "As though my previous life were but a well-remembered dream."

Sha Totek slowly unclenched himself and came to his feet, though his palms stayed locked together. He glanced around, his eyes calm and remote, like a cheetah eyeing distant prey. "I have set the expansion in motion. Soon Morluminar will engulf the Druids of Namirnakh, and they will see how their parochial craft fades to insignificance in the face of true sorcery."

"There's a difference?"

Sha Totek chose to answer the earlier question. "Out of sight, out of mind; so they say, and there's some truth in it. Our minds link themselves with the space and time in which they find themselves, providing our everyday experience with immediacy and reality. But this is Morluminar, a realm so unlike our own, so far removed from it in any meaningful sense, that our universe is for all practical purposes infinitely remote. Our minds can retain no connection across such a gulf, and thus our old lives seem like a dream. For us, they do not exist. Only the thread of my magic preserves any link between us.

"Look around more closely. There is no earth, no light, no air—not even any space as we know it. Yet we stand or sit, and we see, and we do not die; nor do we truly live. This place is so alien that these concepts have no meaning. We do not, could not, truly perceive our surroundings."

Ronar felt a new kind of awe.

"But Morluminar can be beguiling. We must not linger. Prepare for a shock."

Sha Totek jerked his hands apart. An instant's blue-white glare leapt out and exploded around them. Colibdis was restored, or they were restored to Colibdis.

Like a wave of cold grey surf, the turmoil and regret of Colibdis smacked into Ronar. He reeled; the sense of dislocation was nauseating. Strife and madness were all around. For a moment he bitterly longed to return to Morluminar.

Their enemies were in disarray. They milled about, their circle broken, their confusion evident. The giant oaks were gone, and with them all sign of the crimson Fire of Ahriman.

Sha Totek laughed at them. "When the waters of Morluminar lapped up around their ankles, their local magics faded like mist before the suns. The small-minded fools."

The witches rallied themselves, and a semblance of order returned to their ranks. The three elders drew together. One called out, "You haven't escaped yet, meddler! Ahriman himself will aid us. You will be struck down long before you reach your goal. The gaze of Namirnakh is far-reaching. Your meanderings confuse him not at all."

The snap of a bowstring punctuated that tirade. A black arrow buried itself in the throat of he who had uttered it. A moan of dismay came from the witches as their leader fell, his hands clutching the protruding shaft.

Ronar stepped forward in the grey gloom. "Ahriman can't spare much effort for you just now. Now crawl away before more of you are harmed."

Eighty hateful faces turned toward him. Staffs were raised, the ground trembled, and thunder muttered in the chilly air.

"That's enough!" shouted Sha Totek. "By Morgna the Incandescent, begone!" He raised his hand. An impossible light streamed from his fingers, azure and green and gold, a rainbow condensed into a single liquid radiance. Even under the circumstances, Ronar was ravished by the beauty of that gorgeous luminescence.

The witches produced sprigs of mistletoe to ward off the light.

Sha Totek laughed again. "Don't be ridiculous!" Pencils of scintillating brightness, a different color for every target, lashed out and incinerated the mistletoe. "And don't bother with those rags either!" The light leaped upon their discarded garments and washed them away in a flood of polychrome radiance. "No longer will you go disguised as priests or peasants. When you return to the villages you've been infesting, show your neighbors the finery of Namirnakh. What a reception you shall have! Perhaps you'd be safer wearing nothing at all!"

With a few final curses, the minions of Darteharn broke ranks and fled.

Sha Totek was flushed with victory. "Namirnakh underestimated me, to send against me so few, and they so unprepared." He sobered. "Still—somehow, they found me. They anticipated my path. That shouldn't have been so easy in this wide land. He has forced me to expend significant power. If Namirnakh can find me once, he can find me again." He shook his head, then busied himself with caring for the Eranians, whose agonies had returned with the dispersal of Morluminar.

Ronar found himself shaking. In truth, Sha Totek's defenses were at least as disconcerting as the witch's attacks. He forced himself to retrieve his arrows from their targets. They made sickening sucking and crunching sounds as he extracted them. His victims seemed frail and innocent as they lay bleeding.

A sudden thought stopped Ronar in his tracks. He was sure he'd emptied his quiver before entering Morluminar. Where then had he gotten the arrow he'd fired at the druid elder? Wanting with all his heart to lash out, he'd reached into his quiver and found the shaft. He counted the arrows as he retrieved them. Twenty-five, one more than he'd thought he possessed. He shook his head.

He came to his first victim, the woman. Her lifeless eyes were green, her hair auburn. Ronar stood brooding over her. He noticed Sha Totek there beside him.

"Ronar, let me guess. For all your bluster, all your threats of mayhem, you have never killed anyone before today, have you?"

For a moment Ronar was in doubt as to whether he could reply. Then: "No, I have not."

"I'm sorry to have been a cause of that experience."

"Was she evil, do you think?" asked Ronar.

Sha Totek smiled gently. "My friend, in my time I have learned that true evil, sheer malice for its own sake, is most rare. I'm not sure if even Ahriman is, in that sense, truly evil. This woman no doubt held a set of beliefs about how things ought to be in the world. She was quite willing to impose those beliefs on other people, even at the risk of their lives, or even her own. Surely she was ready to kill us. Is that evil? Yes, by our lights. But I'm sure she felt justified in her actions, although her rationalizations may have been a trifle tenuous. Don't dwell on it too much. We did what we had to do, and no more."

"Maybe we should have killed them all, to keep them from making more trouble," muttered Ronar.

"That is another extreme," said Sha Totek with the lift of an eyebrow. "These witches have been neutralized. They will soon be found out and dealt with. We need only reach our goal, not exterminate every person who gets in our way. Now help me get these men on their horses."

They went to the stricken soldiers and helped them to their feet. "Well, Captain, let's get you to the Skye Island, where you will have some reward for your valor," said Sha Totek.

Cadwaladr ap Dillan looked at the sorcerer unsteadily. "It occurs to me...that we are no longer in a position...to compel you to follow the King's wishes."

Sha Totek laughed in surprise. "Why, Captain! As you yourself pointed out, you never were in that position! Come on, then. If the King has something to say to me, I would be boorish not to hear it."

They rode north, leaving behind a scarred and blasted arena. For years to come it would quiver with the memory of the forces that had been unleashed within it.

Chapter 12

The Skye Island

A cluster of hills appeared on the horizon. "There's our destination, atop the highest hill," said Sha Totek.

Ronar frowned. "I thought we were heading for an island."

"We are. An island in the sky."

Presently they reached the base of the hills. A fair-sized village huddled at the foot of the highest one, a grey-white mound showing a few bones of rock. A few odd-looking structures could be glimpsed on its summit.

The village looked prosperous, with a variety of shops. Sha Totek's party turned off the main road onto the spur leading up the hill, well paved with blocks of schist. Bronze lamps mounted on pedestals of the same stone stood along the way.

The Skye Island came into view as they breasted the hill. Its structures turned out to be larger than Ronar has realized, and even more unusual. He stared at them blankly until recognition dawned. "This is an observatory!"

"That's right," said Sha Totek. "The royal observatory of Eranior. I thought you'd be interested."

The complex was beautifully landscaped, though winter had laid a sere hand on its greenery. Buildings were unobtrusive and rambling, built from native rock. The observing instruments themselves were dominant, some of them over thirty feet tall. They were not telescopes, but devices for measuring the positions of celestial objects as accurately as possible without benefit of optics.

An upended triangle of stone pointed due north, perhaps the gnomon of a huge sundial, or a device to monitor the position of the celestial pole among the stars. There was a rotating framework of bronze, a meridian transit, probably used to tell time by the stars. Somewhat isolated from the rest was a series of concentric circles of standing stones, similar to Stonehenge, except that these stones were capped with sighting points of bronze. Ronar guessed it was used to measure the rising and setting points of astronomical bodies, thus establishing a calendar. Interspersed among these major instruments were others, not always clear of purpose, but all made with grace, and elegance.

Coming upon this pristine Skye Island after days of flight and death was like awakening from a fever dream. Suddenly the air seemed crisp and pure rather than cold and cheerless. Ronar felt a profound relief. He sensed here the peaceful spirits of the long line of men, the Tychos and the Ptolemies of this other world, who had watched the stars from this summit. This place he understood.

They halted before the largest building in the compound, which was low-lying and unpretentious, as though not to compete with the celestial significance of the instruments around it. It was made of well-dressed blocks of schist, their green-and-grey swirls reminding Ronar of the eddies of distant nebulae. He and Sha Totek dismounted and helped the injured down from the saddle.

Three attendants dressed in dark blue appeared in the doorway. One guided the wounded soldiers into the building, while another took the horses. The third greeted Sha Totek with careful courtesy and led him and Ronar inside.

This man's sober expression and searching glance hinted that something extraordinary was afoot.

They walked along corridors of cool stone, past doors of intricately carved wood. They were met by a young man whose face was shaded by a green cowl, around whose neck gleamed a torc of gold and steel. The attendant bowed to him and departed. Sha Totek regarded their new guide in silence. They continued on to a particularly massive door. A servant passed within and lit a number of lamps. Ronar's party followed. The room's only occupant was an old man who sat facing the embers on the hearth.

The grave young man in green turned to Ronar. "Friend Ronar, permit me to present Gwyddno ab Emlyn, Royal Astronomer and Master of the Skye Island. You will have much to discuss. The sorcerer and I must confer. Someone will come to collect you shortly." He and Sha Totek withdrew, shutting the door behind them.

The old man beckoned Ronar to a seat next to his.

Gwyddno ab Emlyn's profile was fringed with a cloud of white hair that thinned to imperceptibility around the edges. His eyes looked sleepy, his head sunk between bony shoulders. He wore a colorful checked cloak pinned at the shoulder with a large brooch. Around his neck was a silver torc. He did not turn to face his guest as he spoke. "Young man, welcome to our Skye Island."

"Thank you, sir. It's good to be here."

"We hear you are an astronomer, a watcher of the skies like ourselves. Our Skye Island is said to be the greatest center of sidereal knowledge in the world. Please, as our guest, feel free to take advantage of this. How may we share our knowledge with you?"

It might have occurred to Ronar to respond to this offer with condescension, but somehow it did not.

"Sir, I'd be pleased to know whatever you've discovered about the skies of your world. As you may know, I'm from Earth, where astronomy labors under different conditions."

"From Earth! Then you have no magic to aid in the unraveling of your skies—or to hinder it. It is recorded that five wandering stars can be seen from Earth, while here we have none. Still, we have two suns to earth's one, and two moons, though one of those we could do without. There is said to be nothing in Earth's skies to compare with the Whirlpool."

"Actually," said Ronar carefully, "the Whirlpool can be seen from Earth, but from a different point of view. There we call it the Milky Way. We see it from within, since the Earth and Sun are part of it. Plus, we now know of nine planets in the family of the Sun. Still only one sun and moon, though."

Gwyddno ab Emlyn's head wavered slightly.

"I have your book," said Ronar gently.

"Which book is that?"

"*Stars and Constellations*. I haven't had time to read it through, but the bits I've read are fascinating. I've always been interested in constellations and their lore."

"You say the Earth lies somewhere within the Whirlpool?"

"Yes. You see, we've learned that the stars are distant suns. The Whirlpool is a fog of innumerable stars. The Sun is one of those stars. About your book—"

Gwyddno ab Emlyn sighed deeply. "Forgive me for interrupting, young man, but perhaps you'd better tell me what else has been learned by the scholars of the Mother World, before I make myself appear more foolish than I already have."

Two men gazed at each other across a bare wooden table. A single candle standing between them cast the only light in the room.

Sha Totek's black eyes glittered in the yellow glow. They had a strange intensity, a submerged amusement, but carried no trace of mockery or derision. It was as if he regarded a much-loved but little-seen nephew, a boy whose gravity seemed a little forced, but whose dignity he didn't wish to injure.

The man across the table returned the scrutiny with cleared-eyed openness. He had thrown back his cowl, revealing an unlined face with hazel eyes, sandy hair, and a heavy mustache.

Sha Totek said, "Your line breeds true, young king. You look much like your oldest forefathers."

Sionyn nodded. "We have ancient carvings which show this to be true. We also have a few depicting you, sorcerer, though most of those did not survive our early history. You have changed not at all, it seems, except in your manner of dress and the way you wear your hair."

Sha Totek chuckled. "I've had more guises and fetishes in my time than you've had moonturns in your life. They add variety to the passing millennia. But I'm afraid my recent travels have compromised my usual standards of appearance."

"The purpose of your travel troubles us more than its effect on your grooming."

"I'm on my north. Eranior simply happens to lie between me and my destination. Pay me no mind and I'll soon be gone again."

"Our seers are not oblivious to the signs. The Eye of Teutates is closed, and there is much movement and magic on the far side of the Bannock range. We believe Namirnakh is preparing an army to capture the Bronze Portal. Are you aware of this?"

"Not with certainty, but I did expect it."

King Sionyn paused.

"Then what can possibly account for your leaving the Portal unguarded at such a time?"

"I wish I could give a good answer to that. The truth is, I'm not sure. I know only that I've been ordered to go north by Varanu himself—Gwyn to you. Ronar believes we will ultimately be led to Hyperborea. Varanu spoke to him in a dream."

"You don't know why?"

"Not really. I can only offer speculation. I believe Namirnakh and Teutates are acting in concert to advance some scheme. You know Namirnakh's goals: the invasion of Earth and the conquest of Eranior. He may have found some route to Earth through Hyperborea—perhaps he's even rebuilt the Hyperborea Portal. That may be what Varanu has sent me to stop."

"Why should Gwyn care whether Namirnakh invades Earth? No god has ever shown concern for such things—except Teutates."

"Again, I don't know."

"What will be the result if Namirnakh does reach Earth, by whatever route?"

"Another mystery. According to Ronar, the men of Earth, while without magic, have otherwise learned much. Their subtlety does not appear to be great, but the sheer destructive power they command would seem to be gigantic. Namirnakh might still overwhelm them, in which case he would return with new weapons to overrun Colibdis. Or the Earthmen might win, and come pouring through the Portal to avenge themselves. Either would be disastrous for all concerned."

"What of this man Ronar? Have you found him a worthwhile companion?"

Sha Totek sat back, his face entering the shadows beyond the candlelight. "He is your senior by some fifteen of the Old Years, perhaps past his prime by that measure. He is unused to dealing death. He thinks too much at times. Yet when he does fight, he burns with wut, with the very furor for which your own people are renowned. In his way, he is dangerous. When he sets himself to a task, he is inexorable as the tide. If many Earthmen are like him, then let Namirnakh beware. But I think his kind is rare on any world."

Sionyn pondered for a while. "This conflict—this is the sort of thing you've been warding off all these years, by your vigil on the Portals—?"

Sha Totek nodded from the shadows.

A servant brought goblets of hot spiced wine, and they drank.

Said the king, "When the Romans first encountered my forefathers on the Other Side, they thought them children of demons, straight out of Chaos. If that was so then, our retreat from Chaos is now complete. Our lot is cast so far into the camp of Order that if Order fails, so too must we."

"I remind you that those same forefathers gave rise to the Darteharnians," said Sha Totek. "They don't consider themselves followers of Chaos. They see themselves opposing a sterile, pointless order which we view as right and natural. Who is correct? I propose to preserve the status quo until someone bigger than me comes along and takes the matter out of my hands. Even then—first I'll make him prove he's bigger."

Gwyddno ab Emlyn rested his head on the back of his chair. He seemed to gaze into a distance far beyond the patterns of copper and marble inlaid on the ceiling. "Here at the Skye Island," he said slowly, "we watch over the passing of the seasons and the phases of the larger moon. We know Colibdis to be a sphere. All but the most provincial know that the two suns are the center about which Colibdis revolves. We watch as the red sun slowly waxes and wanes. Over the centuries, we have even discerned the slow drift of the stars relative to one another. But we had no idea there was so much else to know! How have Earthmen uncovered all this?"

"Mostly by means of curved surfaces of glass, and substances sensitive to light." Ronar held out his binocular as an example of the optical art, but his host ignored them.

"Only that?"

"It's nothing that couldn't be done here. In fact, I hope to bring such tools to this world someday, once this madness is over. Colibdis offers possibilities for astronomy that Earth cannot match."

"Indeed?"

Ronar told him what he'd already learned with the help of his binocular. The old astronomer was particularly interested in the nature of the Whirlpool.

Gwyddno ab Emlyn chuckled. "Legend has it that the Whirlpool is a maelstrom which might someday swallow up our world. Now it seems just the reverse is true. It's the place from which we ultimately sprang."

"I know magic can enable one to see beyond the limits of normal vision. Why isn't it used to investigate the stars?"

"It's been tried. We might study the Eye of Teutates this way, should any of us wish to lose ourselves to the Sorcerer God. Beyond that, magic falters. Our priests tell us that the heavens are the domain of the gods alone, who do not permit mortal intrusion into their privacy. But I don't think it's anything so personal. When I weave the spells, they simply reach a boundary beyond which they do not go."

"Why not examine the Eye, now that Teutates is absent?"

The old man stirred uneasily. "We dare not. We dare not. The power of Teutates is growing, and I would not test his vigilance." He spoke in a conspiratorial voice. "I detect a discord in the heavenly music. I hear the dark chord of the Renegade among its strains, balanced by a purer note, that of Gwyn, perhaps."

Ronar felt a strange thrill at this casual expression of mystical ideas he had never dared to articulate. "On Earth we have a science called...'the actions of the smallest parts.' This theory questions the basic reality of the universe. In fact, it insists there is no objective reality, that the tiny particles which make up matter are inherently unreal. So, by extension, are all material objects. It also states that what we see as 'reality' is determined by our very observation of it; that we actually bring what is 'real' into existence by observing it. The implication is that if no one were around to watch, things would not be as they are. In fact, they might not be at all. It strikes me that Teutates might be trying to manipulate this somehow. If nothing is fundamentally real, then one apparent reality is as good as another. Perhaps a mind that perceives this clearly enough can alter reality to suit its whim. Perhaps that is the essence of magic. It might require only a subtle change in physical laws to change the entire universe into a slate onto which Teutates could write his will."

"You talk like a sorcerer."

Ronar shook his head. "That I will never be."

"Anyone who dabbles in magic soon learns that what we call reality is at most a convenient common ground for everyday interactions."

"I find that disconcerting. Take Varanu, or Gwyn—what does it mean to be a god of truth and order if the universe is basically unreal and in some sense unpredictable? Is he a Newtonian god who hasn't yet learned modern physics? Or is he a god who does indeed throw dice?"

"I'm afraid you've left me behind."

"I'm sorry. I'm just rambling," said Ronar.

"You have raised mysteries far beyond our power to settle. But other puzzles we might yet resolve. Let me show you something."

Gwyddno ab Emlyn rose stiffly and hobbled over to a chest of copper and wood which was covered with delicate ornamentation. Tiny faces, monstrous creatures, and abstract designs were carved or engraved into every visible inch, each picked out with a fineness of detail that Ronar could barely appreciate without his glasses.

Gwyddno opened the chest, revealing niches containing rolled-up sheets of parchment. He ran his fingers over them, selected a particular roll, and spread it on a table. "Now that you've told me the nature of the Whirlpool, perhaps this chart will mean more to us both."

The chart, its borders decorated with curlicues and arabesques, depicted the unmistakable form of a spiral galaxy, rendered in a fine pointillism that looked completely nebulous from a normal viewing distance.

"Is there enough light? Can you see well enough?"

"Yes," said Ronar remotely. "It is enough."

Here was something Earth-based astronomy might never be able to match. Ronar looked at the face of his home galaxy—the central condensation, the loosely wound spiral arms, less well defined than he'd expected.

And a bar. A central bar. The Milky Way was a barred spiral galaxy. In glancing at this old man's bit of parchment, he had learned enough to write a lifetime's worth of papers.

"Note the large star marked at the center," said Gwyddno. "It's usually the brightest star seen in the Whirlpool's cloudy face. Sometimes it flares dramatically over a period of a few hours. We have no idea what it might be."

Neither, Ronar realized, did he. No astronomer knew exactly what astrophysical monsters dwelt in the nuclei of galaxies. Until this moment, no astronomer had even known for sure that the Milky Way possessed such a nucleus.

"At rare intervals, new stars appear, then flicker out. They are marked, along with the dates of their appearance. I never saw one myself, but the astronomers of the Skye Island have been keeping watch for many generations."

"Those I recognize. We call them supernovae, stars that explode and destroy themselves." Ronar peered closely at the map. The galaxy was dotted with ten of the celestial pyres, all occurring during the twelve hundred year history of Eranior. Many would have been invisible from Earth, lost behind intervening clouds of dust. Ronar thought back to the few known historical supernovae: the Crab supernova of 1054, Tycho's Star, and Kepler's Star. Given their estimated distances from the Earth, and taking into account the light-travel time, he ought to be able to identify those three supernovae and find their true location relative to Earth. By triangulation, he could then determine Earth's exact place in the Galaxy, a feat that had eluded Shapley himself.

But wait a minute...

Ronar's mouth fell open. "I ought to be casting horoscopes. What an idiot!"

"What's wrong?" asked Gwyddno. But Ronar was too caught up in his thoughts to reply. He'd neglected to take into account the light-travel time between Earth and Colibdis! The light of recent supernovae would not reach this planet for many thousands of years. So much for that idea!

Ronar shook his head like a dog after a near miss from a speeding car. "Sorry to drift off on you like that. This planet has the habit of picking me up and shaking me by the heels every now and then."

The door creaked open; Sha Totek poked his head in. "Come on, you two stargazers. Our host requests the pleasure of your company for dinner. Ronar, do try to behave yourself." He vanished.

"Our host?" said Ronar. "I thought that was you, Gwyddno."

"Oh, no. Ordinarily it would be, but the King is here to meet with the sorcerer. Come, you'll want to wash before dinner. Take my arm, if you would. The servants often leave things laying about where I'm not used to finding them."

He stood up, and Ronar realized that the old man was blind. He was taken aback yet again. It was getting to be a habit.

The dinner was held in a small hall, twenty people seated at a rectangular table. Gwyddno ab Emlyn, occupying the foot of the table, lazily sipped honey wine. The senior astronomers of the Skye Island occupied one side, while the other accommodated the chief members of the King's retinue. All sat in deference to the King, for his chair stood on a platform at the head of the table. Ronar and Sha Totek were seated at his right and left hands.

The Eranians wore cloaks striped or checked in hunter green, maroon, and royal blue, fastened at one shoulder with pins or brooches. They wore torcs of copper, silver, or bronze, except for the King's, which was of gold-and-steel. Other than that, the King's costume was no richer than anyone else's. Ronar approved of that.

The two wanderers had done their best to make themselves presentable. Ronar had to admit that Sha Totek had done the better job. The sorcerer, having somehow restored the color of his flamboyant silks, was as flawlessly groomed as he had been at the Tower. He seemed lighthearted despite the suspicious and outright hostile glances of many of the guests.

Ronar had, of necessity, been more restrained in his sartorial efforts. He wore the charcoal-grey suit Sha Totek had acquired in Thunderbird, which in this setting appeared outlandish but dignified enough. Compared to the array of multicolored cloaks around him, Ronar looked as severe as an executioner.

Sha Totek said, "My lord Sionyn, may I present Professor Leonard Ronar of Earth, my companion for these past weeks."

The King nodded at the astronomer. "The sorcerer tells me you have been most helpful to him in his travels. He says you are becoming a considerable warrior, despite your newness to the profession."

Ronar smiled thinly. "Thanks, King. But I don't mean to make it a profession. If I can accomplish my aims without further killing, I will do so."

"That is admirable. And what are your aims, may I ask?"

"My immediate mission is to discover what task Varanu intends for us, and carry it out if desirable. I hope it includes the defeat of Namirnakh. If not, I will expand its scope to include that goal. Eventually I wish to destroy the god Teutates, who offends me."

Sionyn's eyes widened; Sha Totek smothered a chortle.

"I see," said the King. "If you can accomplish these aims without violence, I'll pray see you elevated to the pantheon of gods yourself."

A few of the king's lackeys laughed.

Ronar shrugged, falling into a perverse mood. He didn't care to be laughed at when all he'd done was answer honestly. The implication that he was becoming a warrior also troubled him. The killing he had done today was still a fresh burden on his spirit. The lifeless faces of his victims would haunt him for a long time.

He felt an impulse which he acted upon without question. Excusing himself, he abruptly left the table, collecting unbelieving stares as he walked out on the King. Sha Totek stammered out some lame excuse for his departure.

But Ronar soon returned to the makeshift throne, proffering a long, narrow object sheathed in leather. "I have something to return to you, King."

Sionyn took the sword. He grasped its handle, bright with gems, and pulled, revealing the splendid steel blade, mirror-bright.

A small, heartfelt groan escaped the sorcerer's lips. His eyes rolled back.

Ronar continued. "I overheard Sha Totek say that this belonged to a predecessor of yours called Bran. I carried it here from the Tower, where Sha Totek has had it squirreled away all this time. Now I return it to you, as I've had no good use of it."

Ronar changed into an enormous pop-eyed frog, but so briefly that nobody noticed, including Ronar himself. Sha Totek muttered ultraviolet curses under his breath.

The temperature of the room fell twenty degrees. Every sound, from the clinking of glassware to the crackling of the fire, fell silent. All stared in stunned disbelief.

Sionyn studied the sword minutely, passing it before his eyes inch by inch, brushing his fingertips over the gold wire wrapped around the grip and along the cold shining vane of the blade itself.

He said, his voice soft with reverence: "The Sword of Bran. I cannot doubt that it is true. Two such blades could not exist in all the history of man. We never dared dream we would have it back again. We thought it dissolved in the fury of the battle in which Namirnakh treacherously slew our First King. Sorcerer, you have been holding it against the day it should be needed again. Astronomer, you have borne it to us in the very face of our enemies. It is good that you return it now, when events are so uncertain, and Namirnakh is ready to rise up once more."

A tear rolled down Sionyn's cheek. Suddenly he looked less like a king and more like a young man bearing too great a burden. He cast a luminous gaze upon Ronar. "This is a great day. Ronar, you are truly my brother. Imhotep, let our differences be forgotten. In the name of Bran, I offer you both the fellowship of Eranior."

"We accept with gratitude, lord King," said Sha Totek quickly, before Sionyn's emotions could be overruled by a moment's rational consideration of what had just happened.

The King summoned a harpist who played a haunting, solemn tribute to the long dead Bran. Sionyn and his people did not spare their emotions, but wept freely, and soon joined in the music by singing, repeating the refrain in its eerie minor key. When the harp fell silent Sionyn made a toast to Ronar. He and his people radiated such love at the astronomer that a fair amount reflected from him onto Sha Totek. The sorcerer sat bemused.

When the dinner was over, the King asked Ronar and Sha Totek to await him in the same room where he and the sorcerer had conferred earlier. Off he went to round up the others who were to attend their meeting.

Sha Totek led the way. He and Ronar entered the room, lit a few lamps and seated themselves at the table.

Sha Totek turned a pained, wry gaze upon Ronar. "You know, you great juvenile oaf, you just did something whose consequences you neither understood nor considered. It was only our good fortune that it went so well for us. That sword was the trump card I might have used to extract co-operation from the King. It is the most revered relic of Era-nior."

"Did you give me that sword, or didn't you? It was mine to do with as I pleased," said Ronar in irritation.

Sha Totek flushed. "I put the sword into your keep-ing—but I did not make it your property. I intended it as a bargaining tool. The disrespect with which you put it into Sionyn's hands might have been the end of us."

"I don't disrespect the King," was all Ronar could bring himself to admit, his perverse mood still upon him. He was embarrassed by the reaction his gesture had caused, almost resentful that what he'd intended as an act of ill-conceived rebellion had backfired. He said no more.

Sionyn entered leading a party of three, all of whom had also been present at the dinner. One was a stern, keen-eyed military man. The second was quite a different type, fat, relaxed, peering with baby-blue eyes through pads of pale flesh. He toyed with his medallion, a palm-sized con-struction of bluish metal, fine and feathery as a snowflake, with a shard of icy green crystal in the center.

The third was a formidable-looking woman of middle age, grey-haired, her expression remote. She wore a green robe embroidered with silver and gold. The King and his party stood by respectfully while she took her seat, then found their own places.

The King made the introductions. "Imhotep, Professor Ronar; I present Fyrsal ap Garnock, a leader of my hosts; the witch Gromer; and finally Morwenna, High Sorceress of Eranior."

Ronar watched closely as Sha Totek greeted his fellow magicians. The potential for rivalry was implicit in the searching gazes they gave one another. Did something more electric pass between Sha Totek and Morwenna?

The King began. "The sorcerer has convinced me that his mission to the north, conferred upon him by the god Gwyn, must not be hindered."

Gromer turned to Sha Totek. "And just what is this mission?" he asked in a wary tone.

"That's not entirely clear. The message came to my friend Ronar in a dream, but I'm afraid it was rather cryptic. If not for the authority of the messenger, I'd have laughed it off," said Sha Totek, clearly uncomfortable to be unable to offer more.

"And Gwyn has made no offer to explain your task?" persisted Gromer.

"No, nor has he offered to shine my boots."

"It strikes me that intelligence may not be Gwyn's most outstanding attribute," said Ronar. This remark earned him six looks of amazement.

"Young man," said Morwenna, her regal head swiveling his way, "no one can speak of the intellect of Varanu with any real knowledge. But I can tell you something of his concerns. He is Lord of Cosmic Order and God of Universal Truths. He is not the god of keeping men abreast of his intentions."

"How is it that you know so much about Varanu?" demanded Ronar. "Sha Totek told me he isn't held in the highest regard by you people."

"Ahhh..." interrupted Sha Totek, "If I may say so without offering either flattery or offense, Morwenna is considerably older than she looks. She was a—student of mine, back in the days when I guarded the way into Eranior."

"I also know something of Gwyn, or Varanu if you will," said Gromer. "I grant that he is not concerned with the antics of men. Why then should he send these two to interfere with the plans of Namirnakh, whatever they may be? What can they possibly do that Varanu himself cannot?"

"I doubt he can do this." Sha Totek leaned forward, bugged out his eyes, and vibrated them back and forth. Gromer grimaced in disbelief.

Sha Totek sat back. "But I remind you, Varanu can't do anything while Teutates preoccupies him with their own conflict."

"I have been seeking to discover the nature of that conflict," said Morwenna. "But my efforts to observe the disharmony between order and magic have met with interference from a source I at first thought unaccountable. I have detected a focus of power forming somewhere near this world, approaching steadily through space. It is strengthening in such a way as to lead me to expect a climactic event of some sort, in about sixty days as I read the signs."

"And the target of this focus?" asked the King.

"It is Hyperborea."

Sha Totek leaned forward, his eyes brightening avidly. "That is most interesting. My compliments on your insight. What is the nature of this focus? Does it stem from Namirnakh, or Teutates?"

Morwenna frowned slightly. "Not from Teutates, I would say. Nor fully from Namirnakh, although I do detect hints of him in it. I would say it is a natural force which is being made to behave unnaturally."

"That's a general description of magic, isn't it?" asked Ronar.

"That is true of magic in some forms," said Gromer. "Others are quite beyond nature as we know it."

Sionyn turned to Sha Totek. "It seems to me, Imhotep, that your mission must involve this force which Morwenna has detected. If she is correct in expecting a climax in sixty days, can you be there in time? The journey into Hyperborea must be the most difficult in the world, even in the summer. And this isn't summer."

Sha Totek raised a finger. "There lies a difficulty, lord King. Namirnakh has demonstrated an ability to track me with precision, or to foresee my movements. If I'm harried thus all the way to Hyperborea, I may arrive too drained to accomplish anything, if I arrive at all."

Fyrsal ap Garnock spoke up. "You are in fact being tracked, sorcerer. My men have encircled the Island, and have been fending off enemy creatures on a regular basis. They seem to be popping up from nowhere."

"We have a few nests of them in our midst, I'm afraid," said the King. "Sorcerer, how is Namirnakh able to dog your heels like this?"

"I'm afraid I know. Though I've limited my use of magic since leaving the Tower, I am by now partly a creature of magic, so long have I sustained my life with my unique spells. This magic is now part of me, and I cannot abandon it without dissolving into a billow of dust. It must be this magic which the watchful Namirnakh can detect. He would thus be unlikely to confuse me with anyone else."

"This is true," said Morwenna. "I myself have been aware of your approach since you came down from the Twilight Mountains."

"Again I salute your acumen, my dear," said Sha Totek gallantly.

"But yours is not the only life-preserving magic in the world," objected Gromer.

Sha Totek flashed a bright smile at him. "No, but it is the finest. Morwenna's magic has preserved her, but she has, I regret to say, aged slightly since I saw her last. Namirnakh has transformed himself into an inhuman being to extend his life. I, on the other hand, appear not only perfectly human, but younger and stronger than when I first applied the spells."

Ronar had been staring down at the table; now he looked up at Sha Totek. "What route are you planning to take to Hyperborea?"

The sorcerer shrugged. "East around the Gulf of Kiruna, through the northern wilds, then over the ice, I suppose."

"Is there any other feasible route?"

"No."

Gromer said thoughtfully, "You might be able to go by sea."

Sha Totek raised his eyebrows in surprise. "By sea? But there's no outlet to the open sea except past Namirnakh's fortress at Larguc. It's either that or launch straight into the Gulf; either is suicide."

"Not necessarily. We've been devising ways of riding out the fury of the Gulf. We can encase a few men in a shell of strong but resilient plasms, and fill it with vapors of suspension to ease the buffeting. Then the maelstrom can be endured, and the tide will sweep us quickly past Larguc to the open sea."

"But that doesn't solve the problem. Namirnakh can track me as well over the waves as across the land."

"But what if there's a decoy?"

Ronar received a collection of puzzled looks.

"Decoy? Ronar, Namirnakh is hunting me, not a flock of ducks."

"Don't be fatuous. You say your immortality spell is unique. What if you were to apply the magic to someone else? What if that person were to travel to Hyperborea by the more predictable overland route, while you went by sea?"

Sha Totek considered. "There may be something to that. If I were to cast the spell on another, the freshness of the magic would make his aura temporarily stronger than mine. Namirnakh might well aim his pursuit at the decoy. I perceive that you are volunteering for this task."

"I am."

"What's this?" Gromer pulled himself up in surprise. "Friend Ronar, in view of your, er, gracious return of the Sword of Bran, surely none here can doubt your sincerity and good will." He said this with a heavy irony to which the King appeared oblivious. "But to take on Sha Totek's magic of immortality and set out on so arduous a journey seems rather a large task for a man newly arrived on Colibdis, with small knowledge of the affairs of this world. Don't you agree?"

Sha Totek acted quickly to break the ice forming between the two men. With a laugh he leaned over and slapped Gromer on the shoulder. "My friend, you haven't spent time with Ronar as I have. If you had, you'd know that if he decided to walk to the Greater Moon, you'd see his footprints on it a week later."

"We will send a dozen of our most hardy wilderness rangers to accompany him," said Fyrsal ap Garnock.

Ronar shook his head. "No thanks. I can travel faster and less conspicuously on my own."

Sha Totek studied him with the same respectful wonder he might reserve for some marvel of nature.

Sionyn gazed at him from beneath knitted brows. "Do you know what you propose? Can you do this? Can you find a path through the wild darkness?"

The King received a rare smile, stern yet gentle. Here at last was a situation in which Ronar felt neither lost, overwhelmed, nor perplexed The words came as if he'd been waiting to say them all his life.

"A man can find the way, if he has his wits about him, and the will."

Ronar swayed as the inlaid pattern of the ceiling swirled, fractured and blended kaleidoscopically in his vision. He shut his eyes, but the patterns remained, projected in green on the back of his eyelids.

"Will that spell really make me live longer?" he asked dubiously.

Sha Totek chuckled. "Oh, it may add a few years to your span, but it takes frequent treatments to add centuries, especially at first. You know, Gromer, fine man though he is, is known to display moments of cynicism from time to time. He suggested to me that the main goal of your plan was to benefit from my magic of immortality."

"Did he now."

"He did. Of course, I disabused him of such a wild notion. I'm happy he's to accompany me. He's wily and experienced, and powerful enough, though only a wizard, not a sorcerer."

"Someday you'll have to explain the distinction."

"Yes. When the night breezes of the Red Plain perfume my Tower once more."

They looked at each other in pensive silence, finally broken by the sorcerer. "So. It seems we face an unexpected parting."

"So it seems."

"Are you sure you want no companion on your journey?"

"I am. This will be a rigorous trek. I can't be concerned with the well-being of tagalongs."

"Ha! Of course. And what weapons will you carry?"

"I'll need a new bow. The wooden one would be too brittle in an arctic environment. That and my dagger."

Sha Totek sighed. "This is getting monotonous, but you really ought to carry a sword. Any sword, since you so magnanimously returned Bran's blade to his heirs."

Ronar shook his head adamantly. "I'm no barbarian. I will not use a weapon whose purpose is to sever men's limbs and spill their guts. Nor will I burden myself with one. I will be heavily loaded as it is."

"As you will. It's beyond my powers to persuade you. Now I think I'm off to bed. Sionyn's wizards and I will be on our way early in the morning."

"I won't be. The King has given me the run of the village. If I can monopolize the craftsmen there for one day, they can make me some equipment that should come in handy."

The silence settled down again.

"So now we part," said Sha Totek. He looked searchingly at Ronar, who returned a steady, grey-eyed gaze. "I suppose I must say this, since you never will. I doubt there's another man in the world who would accept the task you've set yourself. Follow that wavering needle. Come straight and swift to Hyperborea. You are needed."

Ronar looked down, his face reddening. "It'll seem strange to wander this planet without you at my side. I feel like we've been together longer than we really have. Take care of yourself. We'll meet again, and when we do, we'll put some pointed questions to Namirnakh and his stooges."

They gripped each other's hands. Ronar turned and strode from the room.

Sha Totek the Sorcerer looked after him, sighed again, and turned his gaze to the far North.

Presently there came a knock on the door, a hint of the perfume of Morwenna, and he was distracted.

The next morning Ronar harassed the artisans of the village with mysterious orders and instructions. He pestered weavers, tanners, seamstresses, basketmakers, carpenters, blacksmiths, cobblers, and cartwrights. Among the items he required were skis. Luckily, skis were used by the people of Tíuheimr, the eastern neighbor of Eranior, and thus were known to the locals, at least in principle.

On the other hand, his demands baffled the craftsmen at the village music shop. Puzzling over Ronar's sketches, makers of lutes and harps braided catgut, strung it over oval wooden frames, and varnished them. To their dismay, the strings produced only a dismal thunk when plucked. Nevertheless, Ronar appeared satisfied. To the astonishment of the onlookers, he tied the strange new instruments to his feet.

At Ronar's direction, a maker of tools and implements mounted the nehock claws in handles, after the fashion of the Eanda. A blacksmith hammered a serviceable ice axe from a bar of white-hot bronze.

At the cartwright's shop Ronar ordered a small sledge with a harness meant for himself.

Soon the entire village was humming with activity. Ronar tried to overlook no way in which the technology of this land could enhance his chances of success.

In late afternoon, as the chill of evening flowed down from the heights, he went from shop to shop to collect his goods. Half the villagers looked on anxiously as Ronar passed judgment on what they had made.

He was generally pleased, although he had to pry the sledge from the cartwrights, who felt it necessary to carve strapwork decorations into the runners.

That night he sat in conference with Sionyn, Gwyddno ab Emlyn, and a few others. They discussed Ronar's route, referring to maps that were useless beyond the northern-most shores of the main continent. Hyperborea was depicted as a vague mass, replete with fanciful drawings of strange monsters.

Oil lamps cast circles of yellow light on the table. Glittering there was some of the highest technology on the planet, including Ronar's watch. He'd opened the case and was using a jeweler's screwdriver to calibrate it to the length of the Colibdian day. The King said he'd never imagined a mechanism so complex or so minuscule.

The second item was a fine little astrolabe, a gift of the Skye Island astronomers. Between it and the watch he should be able to navigate, though the compass must be his ultimate guide.

The night wore on. The Royal Cartographer concluded his lecture with stern warnings. "Avoid the city of Nartar at all costs. It is a Roman colony, but something has gone badly wrong there, and the inhabitants are not what they used to be. Stay to the west of the city, along the coast. Avoid Nartar, skirt the River of the Doomed, shun the Glowing Hills.

"Also, beware the Ice Worms. They can snare your soul with just a look. Avoid the white bears. Steer clear of the Tinklechain of Shomderlee. Eschew all voices in the wintry winds."

Ronar lent half an ear to these admonitions as he fiddled with the watch. He glanced up at Sionyn. "King, have Sha Totek and his party set out yet?"

"They've gone to Myrddin, the capital. I expect them to depart from there tomorrow."

"Why the delay?"

"I gave Gromer a task to complete before they left."

"I see. Do they have the compass?"

"It was made as you directed, and given into the sorcerer's hand."

"If you don't mind my curiosity, what's become of the sword of Bran?"

Sionyn gave a small smile. "It is displayed in a place of honor in the Palace. I expect it will reside there undisturbed the great majority of the time."

With Photos and Kudu still below the horizon, Ronar set out from the Skye Island accompanied by the King and a cadre of the Sons of Wut led by Cadwaladr ap Dillan. Though still drawn and pale, that proud warrior was clearly on the mend, healed by magic unstintingly applied.

They traveled in chariots with bronze-tired wooden wheels which gave a bone-jarring ride on the cobbled roads. Ronar noted that centuries of the study of magic hadn't acquainted these people with the leaf spring.

They went swiftly over a series of ridges. From their summits Ronar could make out the curvature and concentricity of these landforms. The rocks were metamorphic schists and gneisses, a sign of enormous stresses sometime in the past. Ronar became convinced this was an impact crater, not unlike the Red Plain, though not as ancient.

By midmorning they topped the last of these ranges. Sionyn halted the chariots to let Ronar take in a staggering sight.

The hills sheared off into cliffs that plunged for thousands of feet, cutting through layers of fog and mist until finally drowning in an insane sea. This precipitous coast swept around in an arc that disappeared below the horizon on either side. Even from this height the wild violence of the waters below could be seen and heard. Great surges of grey water piled atop each other, crushing up against the cliff, trying to find their way over the lip of the crater. A thunderous booming and crashing rolled up as mighty waves collided with each other, sometimes building to mountainous heights, with deep holes between their chaotic crests.

For Ronar, the most fantastic aspect of this scene was the city that clung to the cliffs. For miles it adhered to every conceivable ledge or irregularity on the face of the precipice. Its towers and concourses, spires and halls, domes and arches, were like outcroppings of gold and marble crystals, vivid against the greyness of rock, cloud, and sea.

"There is Myrddin, my capital. The tide is going out. Raise your farseeing glass to the west, friend Ronar, and tell me what you see."

In his bemusement, Ronar obeyed without thinking. He discerned a tiny ovoid of light tossing on the wild waves of Kiruna. Soon it passed beyond his sight. "It looks like the magicians are on their way."

"May no god take exception to their mission," said the King.

Ronar peered into the misty distance that had swallowed his friend. He wondered what must pass before they would meet again.

"Kiruna used to be a calm and pleasant body of water," said the King. "Then Namirnakh threw down that part of the mountain wall that separated it from the sea. Since then, Llyr and Sinanna have warred over the waters twice a day. First the sea god sucks at the strait, and the basin is all but drained. Then the moon god becomes ascendant, and the waters come raging back in. Myrddin is our only coastal city that has survived. Even it must perpetually retreat as the waves eat away at the land. In the beginning our city stood on a gentle slope with a favorable harbor. That first city now lies beneath the waves. Still the cliffs retreat. Even now we are sometimes caught unawares, and we die when the cliffs give way and buildings topple."

Ronar looked at the surging water, its level dropping as he watched. "Abandon the city. What advantage is there to remaining?"

"No advantage," admitted Sionyn, "except that here is the capital of Eranior, which has never been conquered."

A stray Photos-beam stole through the clouds, shining on the ramparts of the city, setting them aglow with a creamy-lemon light. Steep staircases switchbacked down the cliff, terminating at piers of cyclopean construction that braved the waves and currents. It must have been there that Sha Totek and his allies had taken to the mad waters in their soap bubble of sorcery.

Ronar could hardly imagine the torrent that must exist at the strait where Kiruna met the ocean.

He looked across the gulf to a grey blur on the horizon. The binocular revealed little more—just a lonely pinnacle jutting from the face of the water. The central peak of the crater?

"What island is that?" he asked, pointing.

"That is Avalon," said the King.

Chapter 13

The Country of the Doomed

The hills trended north and south, sloping to flatlands in the east, falling in the west into the depths of Kiruna. Ronar had followed the rim counterclockwise along the shore of the crater-sea. Now he was headed in the direction he must follow to the end of his odyssey. The crater ramparts were mantled with Terrestrial conifers, with little sign of native vegetation. With the suns hidden by clouds, he could almost be riding through a boreal forest somewhere in the Yukon.

The road had petered out the day after he left Eranior. Now, three days later, even the trails had vanished. He had passed beyond civilization, beyond inhabited lands. Snow covered the ground, but the forest was too rocky and the snow too wet for skiing. He'd keep the horses until those factors changed, then set them free, hoping they'd find their way home.

On his left hand was a parting gift from the King, a massive gold ring set with a deep-red garnet. The gem glittered with facets so cunningly placed they gave the stone an apparent depth greater than that of the ring itself.

The ring had been bestowed and accepted with equal gravity. Ronar wore it despite his hiker's fanatical concern about unnecessary weight. It was, after all, a magnificent bit of jewelry.

The King had seemed relieved by his acceptance of the ring. He'd wished Ronar the grace of all benevolent gods as the astronomer turned to face the wilderness.

The ring felt strangely heavy on his hand. Ronar thought it a thing worth having.

Ronar paused on a rocky summit and sat looking out over the austere white-and-grey landscape. That wide vista showed no sign of man. Ronar expected none in the thousands of miles separating him from his goal.

So far he'd made excellent time, but this country was still fairly benign. He was a little daunted by what he'd volunteered to do. The cold north wind was a constant reminder of the magnitude of his task. If someone had set him down in Alberta and challenged him to march to the North Pole, would he have accepted?

His confidence hadn't been feigned when he made the offer. But now, faced with the reality of a vast, trackless wilderness, it was easy to reflect that it had been based on a few boyhood adventures: time in the Colorado Ski Patrol, training for the Biathlon, the infrequent mountain pilgrimages of his later years. Certainly he'd never attempted a trek of this magnitude before—if he had, he'd surely have made the cover of *National Geographic*.

Luckily, this was a smaller planet. A degree of latitude only forty eight miles wide was less imposing than one of seventy. Then there was that convenient reduced gravity.

He pulled a map out of his pannier. It showed a city some one hundred miles to the northeast, its name written in sepia: Nartar, only twenty miles east of Kiruna. He couldn't give it a wide berth even by staying in the hills— he'd have to creep along the precipitous coast, or make a wide loop to the east to truly avoid the place. Both options were unacceptable. Ronar couldn't guess how seriously he should take the warnings he'd received about the city. The Eranians had called its inhabitants creatures of terror, but there was no telling what sorts of unreasonable fears might have grown up over the years.

And beyond that—this pure and pristine land showed no sign of gods, magic, or madness. Here were pines and mountains, wind and snow—things he understood. Despite his recent experiences, it was hard to believe that evil magic was a factor he must consider in this trek. The silence of this forest encouraged serenity. Each morning he woke up, calmly navigated his way north through the daylight hours, and made a peaceful camp when the light was exhausted. If he kept that up he would eventually reach his goal while hardly realizing he had done anything.

The quickest way to bypass Nartar would be to descend to the plain where his skis would be effective. He'd pass close to the city, probably close enough to see it. By keeping to the west bank of the River of the Doomed and ghosting his way through during the night, the eyes of Nartar, whatever their nature, should remain unaware of his passage.

A flicker of motion caught his eye. Ronar halted the horses and reached for his new bow, a spar of whalebone. His quarry, a ptarmigan, was so unwary he was able to string the bow and shoot without alarming it. The bird fluttered and lay still. Ronar hopped down from the saddle, glad for a bit of fresh meat to supplement rations which might have to sustain him for longer than seemed reasonable.

He picked up the bird and found it to be two-headed. One head was only partly formed and non-functional, but it was a head nevertheless. He studied the bird for a moment, interested and faintly repelled, then eviscerated it and hung it from a saddlebag. He couldn't afford to let squeamishness deprive him of food. He put his foot in the stirrup to remount, hesitated, and returned to the ptarmigan. He cut off both heads and tossed them away. At least now he wouldn't have to look at them. In a moment he was on his way again.

Soon the silver-grey of the day deepened beneath a clearing sky. Ronar halted and gathered wood for a small fire. He plucked the ptarmigan and seared it on a stick. It seemed a feast, as will any food after a long day in the wild. Eventually he'd have to reconcile himself to eating his meat raw, Inuit style, but not yet.

As the embers died, yellow stars shone out unrivaled. Sinanna was waning and wouldn't rise until after midnight. The Lever of Heaven stood halfway to the zenith, but it still had a long way to go. By his own efforts he must boost the Lever to the apex of the sky. Only then might the compass needle start to wander, marking the end of his quest.

He descended the ridge the next afternoon. Once on the flat he unloaded the horses. With considerable misgivings he yelled and swatted them back the way they'd come. A few minutes later he watched them disappear among the trees. He was conscious of their loss for a long time. They were mild-eyed beasts, perhaps the only friendly creatures he'd encounter for weeks.

Now it was his turn to become a beast of burden. He loaded the sledge, tying each bundle in place, all the while aware of the silence and emptiness around him. Then he buckled on harness and skis and picked up the poles. With one good push he was on his way; the sledge moved easily.

The terrain, a windy plain with only an occasional shrub shading the snow, was excellent for skiing. He moved smoothly, leaving arrow-straight tracks.

The weather remained gentle. A low cloud deck gave glimpses and then long looks at the suns. Ronar's heavy clothing was still packed away in anticipation of more rigorous climates. For now the steady exertion of towing the sledge kept him warm.

At nightfall he halted for food. Still some fifty miles from Nartar, he felt no qualms about lighting a fire. Tonight his dinner included dried fruit.

After his meal he pulled on a cowled sweater of Eranian wool, buckled on the skis, and continued on into the night. Between starlight and airglow the snowy landscape was ghostly but clear. The route was fairly level, the snowpack uniform, the few obstacles stark against the luminosity of the snow. The temperature dropped, but as long as he kept moving it would take more cold than this to trouble him. The wind died off. He glided through an endless world of dim silence.

The night brought out its veil of mystery. Ronar's awareness of the proximity of Nartar increased. He wouldn't actually pass it until tomorrow night, but still he went cautiously. Somehow, with starlight shining like filtered ghostlight over the snowy plain, the threat of Nartar seemed less hypothetical.

He covered many miles before the clouds began to move in. As the light failed completely he halted between two hummocks and set up his camp. He flexed three long canes into inverted U shapes and poked their ends into the snow, overlapping in the middle to form the framework of a dome. Then he draped an oiled skin over the poles and staked it down.

Darkness became absolute as clouds covered the last patches of sky. He could see nothing but the greenish glow of his watch face, hear nothing but the squeak-crunch of his footsteps in the snow.

The tent wasn't quite large enough to stretch out in. The goose down sleeping bag supplied by the Eranians was a haven from the cold. He kept his dagger close at hand in case the area turned out to be prowled by wolves or Ice Worms or whatever. But he sensed that the silence was genuine. He lay there contemplating the vast darkness surrounding him, and slept.

He slept into the afternoon, waking to suns-light filtering into the tent. He emerged into a crisp and pristine world. Today Kudu was nearly invisible, for this was an anti-Gloaming, the time when Photos passed in front of its larger but duller neighbor. The small white sun hung in the southwest apparently alone, for the red giant couldn't rival its glare. Kudu showed itself as an irregular red nimbus only when Ronar occulted Photos with a fingertip.

Ronar prepared for dusk by waxing his skis and inspecting his other equipment. He rubbed soot on the exterior of a pot, filled it with snow, and set it in the sun to melt.

The concentric suns set soon enough. The indigo sky drained to black. Ronar broke camp and got into harness. He stood there with ski poles in hand, held back by a certain inertia. Tonight he'd test the watchfulness of the city of Nartar. All the hushed warnings suddenly assumed greater significance. The forested crater wall to the west now seemed quite attractive.

A small part of Ronar's mind berated him for foolishness. It was a part of him used to being ignored; presently it shrugged and fell silent. He set out with a steady distance-eating shuffle.

Ronar's apprehension faded as night unfolded in majesty around him. It was hard to take danger seriously when moving freely through such a landscape. He was fast and silent, and he was unheralded in a lonely wilderness. He believed those were advantages enough.

Before long he encountered a small river, frozen hard and smooth, the Doomed. It glowed in the starlight, brighter than the snow, as though it had a luminescence of its own. He was tempted to follow its smooth bank, but the map showed the river passing before the very gate of Nartar. He veered west and north again, keeping the Doomed visible on his right as a pale glowing line.

From time to time he slid to a halt and scanned the horizon with the big binocular. Their great light-gathering power rendered the snowy distances pale but clear. They revealed no danger. The silence and emptiness remained unbroken.

It wasn't the glasses that first revealed the Glowing Hills, but rather a sudden sense of a presence just over the horizon. Soon a dim undulating mass appeared ahead. He'd gone off course. In his nervous vigilance he'd forgotten to follow the stars and had simply paralleled the banks of the Doomed. The city of Nartar lay dead before him.

Raising the lenses, Ronar peered in fascination at the dread city.

It sprawled in a hollow of the Glowing Hills, vague and ghostly, silhouetted against their strange greenish light. The town was amorphous, with lanes of unresolved structures winding up the slopes of the Hills. In the center were walls and columns apparently made of the same glowing rock as the Hills themselves. They reminded Ronar of luminescent fungi he'd once seen in a forest at night. No spark of man-made light was evident. Though the hour was late, he would have expected at least a candle or two to mark the presence of any group of civilized beings. Perhaps Nartar was deserted, living only as a grim legend in the minds of its neighbors. It certainly looked like a city of the dead.

Ronar lowered the binocular and turned to put Nartar on his right. He would skirt the city—let this be his closest approach. He skied away to the northwest, going a bit out of his way, but no closer to Nartar. Somehow the wisdom of that choice seemed inarguable, if belated.

Figures rose up from the snow like columns of smoke. They solidified into black shapes defined by the grey glint of starlight on their armor.

Ronar gasped with disbelief and snowplowed to a halt. So, there would be no easy recovery from his error. Very well; these people would find him not easily turned from his path.

Faint, bubbling speech escaped from the figure he faced; it took him a moment to recognize it as Latin.

"You are careless. Or so it seems. Perhaps you wished to be intercepted."

Ronar's Latin was shaky. He took a moment to formulate a coherent response. "Not really. Let me go on. Do not try to stop me."

Another spoke. This voice was as dry and sibilant as a hand running over a tabletop. "You imply that you might be stopped. This surprises me. Perhaps we should attempt it, despite your protestations. You have unfinished business with Nartar."

Ronar thought carefully. "I have never seen any of you before."

A brittle chuckle came forth. "True enough. These Hills have not cast their glow upon you in many centuries. But our claim against you is not only as individuals. All the souls who have ever been cursed to be born in Nartar have a complaint against you."

The first man looked askance at Ronar's sledge and gurgled, "I must say, you have become ascetic in your personal habits since our forefathers knew you."

Ronar said sternly, "I am on a mission of the greatest importance. If I do not succeed, both this world and Terra may suffer great harm."

"When you live in Nartar, the prospect of harm to the rest of mankind does not seem appalling. Let both worlds burn. We have a grievance against you. You punished us in centuries past. Now you will release us, or die."

Cursing himself for slow-wittedness, Ronar said, "I am not Imhotep."

"Your present name doesn't matter. We know you as the Egyptian magus. It is craven to deny your identity. The aura of your magic went before you like the influence of a lodestone. You can be none other than the Magus. Although we are isolated, we are in communication with the dark powers. We know something of what goes on in the north. It strikes us that Namirnakh might be interested to know your whereabouts."

Words of protest froze on Ronar's lips. He abruptly realized he was fulfilling his mission at this very moment. If it would confuse Namirnakh, he must encourage this belief that he was Sha Totek. He casually shrugged off his harness and kicked off his skis. "If I'm who you say, you are rash to confront me."

He received a laugh choked with genuine mirth. "But we have little to lose, truly! Obey us or destroy us; it is much the same to us."

So there it was. Unfortunately, his imitation of Sha Totek must necessarily be limited. But that didn't mean he must cooperate with his would-be captors.

In the darkness Ronar raised his hands with all the theatricality he could muster. "If you would try the power of Imhotep, beware! E equals m c squared! A body in uniform motion tends to remain in uniform motion unless acted upon by an outside force! Voila!"

While his foes stood transfixed by uncertainty, Ronar launched himself at the nearest one and struck with his fist. His target's helmet flew off, giving Ronar a glimpse of a face that seemed oddly incomplete. The man gurgled and fell.

The snow crunched rhythmically as Ronar leaped aside and ran for all he was worth. He glanced back—the Nartarians were making no effort to pursue. Yet why should they tire themselves by chasing him through the snow? If they could materialize around him once, they could do it again. Nor would he take them by surprise again. How to mitigate this disaster? They were too many to fight. He might account for a few, but they were armored and heavily armed. The very attempt would spoil his impersonation—his lack of magic would be evident. Besides—if he could extract himself from this mess without more killing, that's what he would do.

Apparently the Nartarians wanted his (or rather, Sha Totek's) help in some matter. He must play along, let himself be taken, and wait for a chance to escape. This plan, logical though it was, went against his deepest instincts. Were only his life at stake, he might well throw it away in a fit of obstinacy. But there was more to it than that. He'd agreed to undertake this mission. He must swallow the bile of surrender, for awhile.

Spitting curses, he looked back again. The Nartarians were gone. The air tingled with menace—at any moment they'd reappear around him.

Ronar dashed back to the sledge and scooped armloads of snow over it and all his gear. He buried everything except the clothes he was wearing and the water bottle he wore next to his skin. He stuck an arrow in the show to mark the cache.

To abandon the possessions that stood between him and a slow death in the wilds required an act of will. He turned his back on them and floundered off through the snow. Reaching a hillock topped by a few spidery shrubs, with a frozen tributary of the Doomed nearby, he stopped and waited.

The Nartarians reappeared like figures cut from smoked glass. Ronar faced them with arms folded, looking down with stern disdain. "I have decided to look into whether I have wronged you or not," he said coldly. "Take me to your city."

Disconcerted, the dark shapes stirred. "You agree to come to Nartar?"

"I do."

"You will not fight? We would prefer it, truly. Ah, well, so be it." In unison they raised their hands. An ultraviolet aura of magic crackled about them.

Ronar stiffened in indignation. "I will help you if I can. If you act in good faith—"

But it was too late. This was not subtle magic. It blasted him to the ground, a blistering purple radiance searing his eyes and mind, taking the place of consciousness.

After an interminable interval the purple blaze condensed into a field of pulsing purple stars, through which he could see some of what went on around him. Hearing returned, filtered through a pervasive mental hiss. He noted these sensations only dully, perceiving them as a boring, pointless play, an upside-down play at that. It seemed he was being carried spread-eagled, chest up, head lolling nervelessly back. He glimpsed a Nartarian at each wrist and supposed two more must be carrying him by the ankles. It was out of the question to raise his head to confirm this theory. He peered into the slits and visors of the helmets within his field of view, trying to see what manner of men held him captive. What little he saw seemed too distorted to be believable.

His captors muttered among themselves in an amazing variety of voices: gurgling, rasping, bubbling, gasping, piping, wailing. One figure who wandered into Ronar's field of view seemed to have his head located in the middle of his chest.

It was difficult to assimilate these strange facts. Ronar tried to ignore them by looking past the Nartarians to take in the view ahead. The Glowing Hills were much nearer. He could now see that theirs was not a solid glow, but rather occurred in streaks, patches and runnels of pale green. It was an attractive color...Ronar tried to think what it reminded him of. The delicate shade of a margarita, or perhaps the glow of the Orion Nebula? No, he had it now. It was exactly the same green as the luminous face of his wristwatch. The watch with the radium paint on the hands...

That insight was enough to jar Ronar halfway out of his daze. He had vaguely attributed the glow to magic, never considering a more scientific yet even more dangerous explanation. Could these hills possibly be that radioactive? It made no sense—a planet where iron was uncommon, yet had a fair amount of gold, not to mention at least one fantastic concentration of radioactive metals.

From Ronar's inverted viewpoint the city looked like a cluster of stubby stalactites hanging from the ceiling of a luminous cave. Something new was happening—yellow sparks were pouring from the stalactites and swirling in their direction. Soon they were revealed as torches carried by the inhabitants of Nartar. Ronar's captors carried him into their midst. The din of their howling, the twisted wildness of their gestures, the stamping of their feet, the gyrations of torches trailing fire—all served to further bewilder Ronar's numbed brain. He had a nightmare impression of unfinished faces, of limbs projecting randomly from weird cauliflower growths, of shapes and structures no living thing had ever needed or evolved. It was comforting to believe these were only the delusions of a stunned mind, but it was getting harder to sustain that belief. Here were horrors beyond his own capacity for nightmare.

Dim, distorted faces wove in and out of view, taunting, reviling, showing themselves in sudden flashes of torch light. One spat a wad of slime from a jawless, rimless mouth, catching him in the face.

That was enough to awaken him fully. His sudden fury, fueled by fear of the radioactive environment, burned through the mental fog. He gave a terrible cry, kicking and struggling with all his strength. With a spasmodic flex of arms and chest he brought the two creatures at his wrists crashing together. They rebounded and went stumbling back; one released him. He might have broken away, though only into the midst of the mob, had not someone darted up and brought a cudgel down on his head, obliterating his sight and sending his consciousness floating away on waves of nothingness.

His next perceptions were of warmer air and a sulfurous stench strong enough to obscure his vision. He felt himself hauled upright, then something cool and rough against his back. Chains rattled; cold metal encircled his wrists and ankles. A weight settled on his shoulders; a lock clicked shut. They let his nerveless body sag until it was supported only by the shackles at his wrists and neck.

Ronar's outrage swam up again from the depths of semiconsciousness. With a huge effort of will he forced his eyes open and glared through a scarlet haze at the monsters around him. "Let me go!" he hissed through clenched teeth.

His captors laughed and did not let him go. Weakness washed over him again. Silence settled down. Had he been left alone? It scarcely mattered. He slumped forward, hanging from the chains, half choked by the shackle around his neck. The fires of his fury were drowned in a rising tide of oblivion.

He awoke.

Pain ran along his arms and back—a tingling, bloodless pain in his wrists, and a knotted, twisted pain in his back. He swallowed with difficulty. His head ached wretchedly. Equilibrium was slow in returning. But his memories were clear, his thoughts coherent.

And he could see. The torches mounted on the wall smoldered fitfully. Yet he could see—by the greenish glow of the walls themselves.

He was coldly certain now about the source of that eerie light. If his vision had been sensitive to the more energetic regions of the spectrum, he would have seen a brighter, fiercer, deadlier light—gamma rays, the most lethal radiance of radioactive decay. He was being bathed in radiations that must eventually kill him. He couldn't guess how long it might take—the Nartarians seemed to have adjusted to it, though he had to admit it hadn't done them any good.

Again he wondered how this area could be so rich in unstable elements when the planet as a whole was poor in heavy metals. Perhaps the Glowing Hills were extinct volcanoes which had tapped a deep-lying pocket of radioactive rock. Perhaps they were yet another impact feature, the remnant of a collision with a radioactive mass. He only knew that every minute he remained must shorten his life.

He studied his surroundings. Perhaps escaping this relic of an ancient culture was within his powers.

A brazier stood in the center of the cell. Its coals were cold; brass implements poked out of them. Nearby in the floor was a round black pit. Here and there, in racks on the walls, or leaning against them, or just lying about, were tools of pain-giving. Some were straightforward in their use, others obscure, still others intricate and devious. Other sets of manacles were bolted to the wall, though his was the only occupied set. A smell of corruption pervaded the air.

He was alone except for small rustling shapes which moved along the walls. The light was too poor to reveal what they were, but they did not appear to be rats. The only positive aspect of his situation was that he was hanging beyond their reach.

Though Ronar could guess why the Nartarians sought revenge against Sha Totek, he hadn't the time to fully analyze what had gone wrong with Nartar. He had no intention of paying the penalty for whatever sins the sorcerer might have committed.

Twisting his neck painfully, he studied his bonds. They glinted with a dull, greasy luster like lead. Unfortunately they were thick and heavy in full proportion to the weakness of their material. Unlike iron, lead chains don't rust. These looked as sound as when they were first installed, probably a long time ago.

Still, he was angry and desperate enough to try their strength. Straining to the limit, he only managed to tear his wrists. Hanging there as he was, he couldn't exert much leverage. He tried again anyway, squeezing his eyes shut, concentrating on the parting of the chain or the uprooting of the bolt, hoping the blood would lubricate his hands enough to let them slip though the shackles. None of these things happened. The failure brought him close to a fatal frenzy of frustrated rage. Recognizing the risk of giving in to madness, he pulled back from that brink.

Conceding temporary defeat, he relaxed to the extent that the chains allowed. A tense, strained laugh escaped him. He thought back to the hundreds of hours he'd spent in his previous life measuring the positions of galaxies on photographic plates, deriving their distances from red-shifted spectra, and making statistical studies of their distribution in space. Though tedious, it seemed preferable to his present captivity by the evil mutants of Nartar. His harsh laughter rang out again. The evil mutants of Nartar! He was glad there were none on Earth. Some of his undergraduate students were bad enough.

An inner voice warned against weaving toward hysteria. He forced a watchful calm upon himself. A dark zone of pain and fatigue waited to claim him, but he did not want his captors to surprise him in his sleep. He undertook a vigil. He would greet the local horrors with alertness and defiance.

But first, one last try at breaking the chains....

The pain was considerable, but Ronar had no illusions about it. It was much less than he could expect at the hands of these debased descendants of imperial Rome.

The base metal proved more stubborn than he. There would be no quick escape. He'd have to confront the mutants of Nartar on their own terms. They granted him ample time to dwell on his predicament. He hung there helplessly, his tired imagination visualizing hard radiation tearing through his body, destroying cells, scrambling genes. He knew more about the effects of radiation than the U.S. government had chosen to reveal. His knowledge had led him to avoid a trip to the Trinity site where the first atomic bomb had been detonated. It had led him to decline an invitation from his physicist colleagues to witness an H-bomb test in Nevada. It would certainly have led him to give Nartar a wider berth had he known its nature. Now he could only hang here and soak in the invisible radiance. For all he knew, his "lead" shackles might be solid uranium. Any escape might give him no more than a chance to die in solitude.

That made escape seem all the more worthwhile.

After an interminable period of introspection, something finally stirred in the corridor outside the cell. The door lurched open and a torch was thrust inside, dazzling him after the dim, deadly glow of the walls.

Several forms entered. Ronar had his first clear look at citizens of Nartar.

Carefully, rigidly, he maintained a mask of impassivity as he studied his captors. His true feelings were hard to define—they went beyond revulsion or horror until they verged on a fascination that almost transcended concepts of ugliness or deformity. He had never imagined such creatures, never dreamed they could exist. One was a short, stubby thing, basically humanoid except that it lacked a true head. Instead a low, hairless dome bulged up between its shoulders, and it was studded with eyes, about twenty of them, bright blue, perfectly human, all blinking independently of one another like Christmas tree lamps going on and off. How could such a thing live? He could barely imagine how it might be born, but how could it then survive? It had no sign of a mouth or any breathing orifice. Was a brain hidden in that distorted frame? He had the impression it regarded him with intelligence. That was chilling, to see awareness shining out of those eyes in all directions at once.

The others were likewise mockeries of the human form, of varying degrees of abnormality and functionality. Ronar was addressed by one whose hands were like bony tongs projecting from lumpy masses of forearm muscle. His sallow face was human enough except for a peculiar lightlessness in the eyes that Ronar had never seen in a living person. His voice was low and tentative, though to Ronar the reason seemed more temperamental than physiological.

"We have been watching you. Your efforts to escape have led us to consider strengthening your bonds, but they have not strained the barrier we erected to defeat your sorcery. You must feel its power. Your spells cannot reach beyond it, nor can you be reached through it. You are cut off from the Beings of Power whom you would parasitize. We are confident we can nullify any wizardry you may attempt. You are trapped."

Ronar merely looked at him, since no good answer to this occurred to him. It certainly wouldn't take much to defeat his sorcery. But at least they had him in a situation where they'd be unlikely to discover he had no magic to defeat.

Something clicked in his mind—the nature of the distinction between sorcery and wizardry? Most of the magic he'd seen Sha Totek use had involved calling upon various outside powers. Wizardry seemed to be a direct manipulation of a local magic affecting objects and natural forces, but not invoking or involving the might of other magical beings. He could see that tapping into the infinite possibilities of other universes could make sorcery more varied and all-encompassing than the nature-magic called wizardry. Probably sorcery was harder to master as well, and more dangerous to the user. If sorcery was a formalized system of effective prayer, some magical entities might still resent being called upon.

He returned his attention to the strange collection of beings before him. "Would you mind introducing yourselves?"

Tong-hands replied. "You shall not know our names. We know better than to put such knowledge into your hands. It is enough for you to know I am First Consul of Nartar."

"What do you want of me? Release me. Your grievances can be of no account when measured against the danger that threatens your world."

The consul's eyebrows raised; his tong-hands clacked together. "What danger is that? That Namirnakh shall carve out an empire on the distant Terra? It means nothing to us."

"The men of Earth could dissolve the armies of Namirnakh in fire. Then the Earthmen would pour through the Bronze Portal to overrun your world. Whether their intentions were warlike or not, no culture on this planet would survive for long. Earthmen tend to subvert and diminish whatever they do not destroy. Even if Namirnakh should win, he will then return with the means to conquer all Colibdis. Nothing could survive the combination of his magic and the weapons of Earth. Your people would be enslaved or destroyed in either case."

The consul swung his head through a minute arc, his face cold and bitter as a lightless morning. "Any invaders might approach Nartar to take a look. Once they had seen, they would beat a hasty retreat. No one wishes to invade the City of the Doomed."

Ronar could see his point. "What do you want of me?" he repeated wearily.

"We want justice! You exiled us to this place of malign magic; you made us what we are. We demand that you remove the spell of horror you placed upon us and make us human once more."

Ronar bowed his head and closed his eyes, shaken. This was what he had feared, but he must know the full truth before he could respond intelligently. He said quietly, "It has been many centuries since the Black Tower stood among you. Refresh my memory; where exactly did it stand relative to Nartar?"

They all looked at him for a moment. The blue eyes of Dome-head all blinked at once. Another mutant answered, this one with a face like a cluster of grey-black grapes, his eyes glittering between folds of flesh. He didn't flinch when sparks from his torch touched his skin. His voice sounded like it was squeezed from the lung of a butchered sheep. "It stood near what is now the land of Faerie, some two hundred miles south of here."

This startled Ronar. "I see. And why did your ancestors migrate to these Hills?"

"They—the Hills reminded them of the hills of Rome. They were attracted to their light, which they deemed a sign from the gods. Also, the climate was warmer in those days, and it was easier to farm then than it is now."

"Plus," added the consul, "as you well know, but apparently wish to remind us, they did not want to live under your domination. They were proud men, patricians and senators of Imperial Rome. They came through the Portal to escape the tyranny of a vile emperor. They resented the replacement tyranny of a mad Egyptian. And so they fled. The vengeance you took upon them was beyond reason. You have twisted us, made us the bane and scorn of the world."

A long breath rattled from Ronar's throat, pure relief, a renewal of faith. He couldn't have forgiven Sha Totek if he had really forced these people into the influence of the radioactive Hills.

He raised his head and fixed the consul with his steadiest gaze. His voice was calm and compelling. "Listen to me. No magic has been used against you. If you wish to be human, you must begin by abandoning this city."

"What, you still cannot abide our presence here? Where could we go? No people in the world would endure our presence. Would you cast us into the wilderness, to starve and freeze?"

"But it is the city itself that has done this to you! The city, and the Glowing Hills."

"How so, if not by magic?"

"It is the light given off by the rocks. In that light is also—an invisible light, that strikes at you and damages the parts that determine what your children shall be."

"An 'invisible light'? Is that akin to an inaudible sound, or an impalpable touch? Do not babble; undo your spell!"

Ronar persisted. "Do you deny the existence of the air because you don't see it? Can't you realize there are things in the world which we are unable to perceive?"

"You say there is no magic involved, but what is an invisible, hurtful light if not magic? The spell, sorcerer, tell us you will undo the spell!"

Ronar shook his head, producing a dull clanking of his chains. "There is no spell. This is a force of nature. Think! You yourselves have magic, motivation, and time. Have you ever found a way to even approach this 'spell', let alone to negate it?"

"No," wheezed the one with the tumorous face. "It has taken all the magic we could devise just to allow some of us to survive. The horror grows worse with each generation. Every woman is horrified anew at what issues from her womb."

"We have infants now," said the consul, "who do not meet even the most liberal definition of a human being. Some are things we ourselves cannot tolerate. Let me tell you a story. Recently my wife gave birth. We had not even realized she was pregnant, due to her rather irregular shape. Yet one day, something emerged from her genital opening, a thin, jointed leg, spiny enough to pain her. It slid forth joint by joint until it was over a foot long. It reached about, feeling things at random, and presently was joined by two others. The three of them waved about idly, then, after some hours, their movements became more frantic, and ceased. We tried to remove the thing, but the shape of its body made that impossible. After a few days, it mortified within my wife's body, and she died."

Ronar had no response to that.

A new voice said dryly, "Luckily, the problem will correct itself soon enough. Our population is declining; oddly enough there is a lessened interest in procreation among our people, as well as a lessened ability."

Ronar looked around, puzzled. This voice seemed without a source. His eyes lit on Dome-head. Could this mouthless creature be a telepath? If so, it was doing a poor job of reading his mind, for all but the most superficial glance would reveal he was not Sha Totek.

"You are the Magus," insisted the consul. "You can be no other. We require that you undo your spell, but we do not require that you do it voluntarily."

"It's no one's fault that you are as you are! Think, I tell you. When your people wandered north, did he—did I—try to stop you? How far do you think they would've gotten if I had?"

Tumor-face said, "Our records show that you did not try. You said there was wisdom in the placement of our Portal, and we would do well to remain in its shadow. But your malice became apparent soon enough."

"I cannot free you of a spell which does not exist. You must listen to me."

"We will kill you slowly," said the consul.

"You already are." Ronar flared up with irritation. His patience was waning. True, the Nartarians were living under the worst circumstances he could imagine, but still, there must be limits to willful intransigence. He could not forget the shower of high-energy photons and particles riddling his body with each passing second. "I tire of your persistent stupidity and pointless hostility. Release me and I will help you as best I can. Detain me further and you will regret it."

The consul returned his gaze coolly, his impassivity compromised only by a slight tremor of his lips. Abruptly he stepped forward and brought the bony tong of his hand hard across Ronar's face.

Licking blood from his split lip, Ronar favored the consul with the same gaze he normally reserved for scorpions. His contempt was like an iron bar in the pit of his stomach. Letting his passions get the better of his discretion, he spat a mouthful of bloody froth at his tormentor.

Ronar learned about pain that day. For hours monstrosities came and went, each with a new refinement of torture. A thing with a ludicrous lollypop-shaped head used a blunt implement to probe behind his rib cage. An armless being used its flexible duckbill-like snout to insert tubes in his nostrils, then blew an acrid powder into them, sending a white blaze of agony down into Ronar's shoulders. Another malformed sport had a device consisting of three wooden plugs on threaded rods. The creature inserted the plugs between Ronar's gloved fingers, then turned the screws to spread his fingers just to the point of breaking. Each mutant stripped the clothing from whatever part of Ronar's body it was interested in until he was left with nothing but boots and gloves, and those only because they were protected by the shackles.

Ronar's defense was in two parts. First, by concentrating on the pain and accepting it rather than trying to resist, it became somehow remote and impersonal, a stimulus to be analyzed rather than a source of terror. It was as if he were short-circuiting the agony, diverting it to a section of his consciousness that was less impressed than the animal part that screamed for escape. The pain was still there, still most unpleasant, but more manageable.

The second technique involved keeping a careful tally of the outrages being committed against him, and of the terrible penalties the people of Nartar must someday suffer in return.

He couldn't help noticing that no one did anything that would permanently disfigure or impair him. He suspected he was being saved for something, or someone, special.

Among the mutants only Dome-head remained aloof, watching with an enigmatic multi-eyed gaze as the citizens of Nartar vented their hatred against the one they thought had ruined them. He watched as a she-creature, a mutant covered with dozens of fleshy sacs—breasts—came before the astronomer. Without a sound she displayed a small hideous beast—a clawed, twisted thing, grey and spiny, writhing and clicking its mandibles together. Ronar thought it some huge louse until he noticed the shattering humanity of its eyes—this was her child. This alone of all he had seen brought forth a cry of horror.

His mental discipline began to dissolve, and a merciful haziness descended upon him. The torture became a meaningless sequence of lunatic faces and novel pains. It was bedlam, a waking fever dream, a miasma of sights and noises and feelings. Soon even that began to slip away. With a start he jerked up his head to find that he was alone with the consul.

"We leave you now, sorcerer, for you are to be visited shortly, and we wish you to be alert for that. But while you rest, here is something to contemplate." From a leaden box he brought forth a fist-sized fragment of metal. The glow from the walls tripled. Ronar could not escape the knowledge that here was a mass of radioactive metal of great purity. Even such a creature as the consul would not escape being burned and sickened by its proximity.

The consul brought it forward. Light followed it, glowing green on Ronar's sweaty flesh. He held it close to Ronar's genitals. Ronar could feel the heat of it. He thought he could even feel its unseen radiance pouring into the depths of his body.

The consul said, "You are intimidated by the light of Nartar. Learn now that there is nothing to fear."

A bleak, bitter despair bloomed in Ronar's breast. *They've made me one of them. Even if I live, I must never father a child.*

Although Ronar had loathed men before, the hatred now born within him was of a different order of magnitude, of a depth he had not known before. He said nothing. His kept his face impassive. He was still chained, still helpless. But upon that hapless consul he fixed a gaze as merciless as the stars. The consul could not endure those eyes. He returned the lethal metal to its box and stole from the room, leaving Ronar to contemplate the magnitude of the new concept of vengeance that had entered his mind.

Chapter 14

Corridors

Ronar fell into a stuporous half-sleep. When he awoke, keen lances of pain stung him to a state of unreal clarity. He was still alone, but he didn't know how long that would last. He didn't even know the time of day. He still wore his watch, but like the ring of Sionyn it was hidden beneath a glove. That watch would be hard to explain if the Nartarians found it. It was too obviously lit by the same light he had insisted was so dangerous. He vowed to discard it if he ever got the opportunity. It suddenly seemed like madness to wear a watch whose face was lit by radioactive decay.

Twisting within his collar, Ronar regarded the chains which held him. He didn't bother to test them again. He hadn't eaten or drunk anything in many hours. His throat was parched and burning, his body numb from lack of circulation. If he were set free this minute he'd be lucky to stay on his feet.

The Nartarians believed their magic was preventing him from using sorcery to escape. Ronar doubted how effective their spells would be against the genuine Sha Totek, but that was irrelevant. He himself had no magic—or rather, he knew no magic. Magic was apparently available to anyone who mastered a formalized, self-consistent system of manipulating it. That could be a body of spells or a set of quasi-religious beliefs. Perhaps the spirits and cosmic beings to whom Sha Totek appealed for power weren't even real—they could be only fanciful vehicles by which the sorcerer tapped the ambient magic of Colibdis itself.

But Ronar had no such spells or beliefs. He thought of the anesthetic spell he'd accidentally crafted when Mauch Chunk wounded Sha Totek. He'd felt drained by the backlash of the clumsy magic. If he tried to improvise a spell strong enough to disrupt these very substantial chains (assuming he could do such a thing despite the precautions of the Nartarians), he could easily render himself incapable of taking advantage of his freedom. Too bad. While he objected to magic on philosophical grounds, just now he couldn't afford to be too much of a purist about it.

Having nothing better to do, he found himself wondering about the nature of magic and the exact purpose of the spells and chants that evoked it. Perhaps the words and magical objects acted as points of concentration to help the practitioner maintain the rigid thought patterns necessary to bring about a specific effect. The spells must have some sort of logic behind them, or undirected magic could feed back and damage the user. Surely different schools of magic must have different ways of approaching the same problems.

The aspect of magic that made Ronar most uncomfortable was its assault on objective reality, its introduction of chaos into what on the surface appeared an ordered universe. His views on this were contradictory: on one hand he wanted a Newtonian universe of clockwork predictability, free of the intrusions of randomness or conscious control. On the other hand, he resisted the corollary that as part of that order, his own thoughts and actions must be predetermined. This brought to mind the one aspect of modern science he tried to ignore—quantum physics. Quantum mechanics stated that the fundamental structure of matter was governed by rules contrary to common sense and everyday experience. When taken to its logical extreme, this theory insisted that reality is only a convenient illusion brought about by the inherent laziness of matter on the large scale. Luckily, the unpredictability fundamental to the smallest scale of things was masked at larger scales by the statistical tendency of atoms to behave predictably over time and in quantity. The built-in unknowability of the very small was also present in larger systems, but there it was masked by improbability. It was perfectly possible for a mountain to spontaneously evaporate into space, or for a clam to transmute into a rosebush, but it was extremely unlikely.

But on the microscale, events that seemed equally unlikely were occurring constantly as part of the most basic behavior of matter. Particles could be born out of nothing, vanish and reappear at random. Even causality seemed to be violated, as particles interacted across distances where any communication between them should be impossible.

Viewed in this way, matter and energy, and even space and time, lost their semblance of reality and became phantoms, glimmers of probability that acted as they did merely because it was easiest for them to do so, not because they must. Even the densest matter was nothing but a webwork of space interspersed with nondeterministic entities flickering back and forth, in and out of existence. The hard radiation bathing him now was a result.

Ronar hissed in frustration, banishing these thoughts from his mind. He could only confuse himself by dwelling on these irresolvable matters. Illusion or no, the world around him maintained its apparent reality. This was the world he was forced to deal with.

The creaking of the cell door interrupted his feverish musings. His respite was at an end. Ronar squinted at the torches thrust into the room and at the figures who carried them.

Several were mutants, including the consul and three warriors whose distorted faces showed dimly through the visors of their helmets.

The other three were as unlike the Nartarians as was Ronar himself. They were tall and severe, clad in black cassocks and long cloaks of black fur. Their waists were tightly bound with sashes, giving them a waspish look.

The chief of these three wore an ornate iron torc. His face was proud, his eyes merciless ophidian pits. He fixed Ronar with a gaze of remote disdain. "This is not Imhotep," he said with a negligent wave of his hand.

The consul bubbled with indignation. "He can be no other! No one else bears the same aura of deathlessness."

The black one gave him a look of contempt more eloquent than any words. "You are too single-minded in your quest for vengeance. Simple possibilities elude you. To baffle us, the Sorcerer has conferred his long-life spell on this man. He is Ronar, an Earthman who accompanied our enemy until recently. He has no magic of his own, like all his ignorant breed. Did he manifest any against you?"

"We took precautions to defeat his magic—"

"I doubt you could detain either of my companions here, let alone the true Sorcerer."

One of the mutant warriors spoke up. "On the snows, before we captured him, he struck one of us down with a silent bolt of black lightning."

Ronar could not resist choked laughter. "That was my fist, you idiot."

The Consul subsided, but his brooding watchfulness showed he was not convinced.

The black one addressed Ronar in peremptory tones. "I am Kerunos lac Kai, called the Shadow of Namirnakh. You will tell me where the one you know as Sha Totek has gone."

"He has gone to Ammon to seek a tavern in which to wile away the coming time of troubles."

This brought a tiny tight smile. "He would not be so wise. You will tell me what I require."

Ronar thought carefully. His identity was now uncovered. He had no escape. He must not reveal Sha Totek's true path. Best then to seek a quick death. This Kerunos had the look of one who would not tolerate insolence. He framed a reply, but his weak command of the language did not allow the subtlety he might have wished. "You require that a stick be inserted in your ass," he said, unsure of the proper syntax.

His message got across, but it didn't have the desired effect—he remained alive. He'd misjudged Kerunos. His insult only hardened the little smile and brought a glitter to the dark eyes. The dark mage stepped forward to examine Ronar more closely. "I see our Roman allies have sought to elicit information from you in their usual physical manner. What a marvel that they thought they could treat the mighty Sha Totek in such a fashion with impunity."

"They are a desperate people. I'm beginning to like them better than you."

"Ah, well." Kerunos gave a resigned shrug and continued. "By delivering 'Sha Totek' to us, they hoped to be rewarded with a new home in Darteharn. But they will receive nothing. When Namirnakh returns in glory from his conquest of Earth, Nartar and its wretched inhabitants will be annihilated."

Ronar glanced at the Nartarians, who stood there blank-faced, having no knowledge of Celtic tongues. Except maybe for Dome-head, whose multiple eyes were blinking nervously.

"And how does Namirnakh expect to travel to Earth?" asked Ronar.

"By way of a Portal, of course. What other way is there? There, I have granted you a morsel of knowledge. Now you must reciprocate. We can encourage you in ways that are less physically debilitating than those of the Romans, but our methods take a greater toll on one's spiritual well being. Your fate is to be taken to Namirnakh for whatever use he cares to make of you. You might as well go with your soul intact. Tell us what we wish to know."

Ronar's wrath surged up in a tide that washed away any remnant of guile. Of all insults, he could least endure being treated as inconsequential. "You petty worm, you revel in your power, but you know nothing. Your magic is meaningless away from this world. It is an aberration in a greater universe of sanity. How did you travel here? On foot, or drawn by animals? Earthmen fly on metal wings. When your lord encounters them, he will find his power has been left far behind." He composed this tirade in Latin for the benefit of everyone.

The Shadow of Namirnakh was next aware of a warm stream of liquid running down his front as Ronar urinated on him. Suddenly he was no longer so amused by Ronar's defiance. He raised his hands, their flesh pallid and waxy. "Feel the power of the magic which you so disparage."

Black pulsations, like waves of shaded refraction, leapt from his hands, distorting and obscuring at the same time. Unaffected by matter, the waves found Ronar no obstacle. They twisted the space he occupied as readily as if he'd not been there.

It wasn't brutal. It neither crushed nor rent Ronar's body. Each pulsation had its momentary effect of deformation and then passed on, leaving him as he was before. But it was a worse anguish than any he'd ever known. It was indescribably sickening, a mind-blowing disorientation, a plunging, twisting chaos, like being washed in waves of insanity. There could be no defense against this, no corner of consciousness where the madness did not reach. He screamed—even that was distorted into a wavering inhuman howl.

He abruptly found and seized upon a stray thought: the Sword of Bran. How splendid it would be to feel its weight in his hand once more, to send its shining blade scything through the flesh of his tormentors! He cursed the perversity that had led him to give it up. His compunctions against killing now seemed ludicrously naive. If he had the thing now he would chop up everyone in sight. The promise of vengeance represented by such a weapon was a splendid fantasy, a focus and locking point to help him keep his sanity.

Other sensations penetrated the madness: a sudden heat in his left hand; and a strange sound, skittering, metallic, almost musical, like steel running on steel. The source fluttered around the room like the cry of a bird of war.

The sound broke Ronar's concentration, and apparently that of Kerunos as well, for the assault ceased, as did the sound and the heat. The Shadow of Namirnakh looked around briefly, then turned cold eyes on Ronar as he uttered a baleful laugh. "So, Earthman, the forces of magic aren't to be taken so lightly after all. We'll continue to explore the matter later. Now I leave you. I wish to communicate with my master, to tell him of your capture. In the meantime, make the acquaintance of my colleagues: Borna mac Dred, and Ganwydon, who styles himself the Harrier of Namirnakh." With that he turned and departed in a swirl of ebon garments.

Shaking, bathed in cold sweat, Ronar eyed the two lesser wizards as they stepped forward with malice in their pale faces. They smirked at him as if expecting a plea for mercy, but were disappointed. They resumed the assault, their power somewhat less than that of their superior, but all the worse for coming from two directions, adding a new dimension to Ronar's agony.

So relentless was the attack that Ronar was again buffeted into a dreamlike state where pain lost all meaning, and even outrage faded into a dispassionate, musing survey of his situation. His head drifted to the side; he observed the effect of the refracting magic on his chains. They swelled and stretched, twisted and contracted in unpredictable ways with each succeeding wave, just as he did himself. But the links were not parted or weakened. It was really the space they occupied that was being stressed, with the objects it contained naturally being deformed as well, conforming to the shape of the space they were in. He stared at the chains, contemplating their ghostly particles flickering in and out of space-time. In an instant of perfect perception, he saw the unyielding matter as but a pattern of forces and probabilities that need not remain as they were. What else could magic be but a means of taking advantage of the inherent quantum indeterminacy of matter and energy?

In that instant it was obvious that the continued existence of the chains was not inevitable. They dissolved into nothingness.

Ronar dropped heavily to the floor, falling back against the wall, forcing himself to stay on his feet. Now to do what must be done.

"See his power!" shrieked the Consul. "Now who can doubt he is the Egyptian?"

"Quiet, you fool," said Borna mac Dred. He and the Harrier advanced cautiously, magic radiating from them like wan, bitter ghostlight.

Again Ronar longed for the forsaken sword, wished for it with all his heart and will. Somehow he felt it near him; he called it forth with an adamant desire that could not be ignored. Again that strange ringing clamor; heat flared up on his left ring finger. A flame spurted, burning through his glove. A raw, ruby light blazed out from the ring of Eranior, banishing the sickly green glow of the walls and driving back his enemies. The ringing climaxed in a clashing, shattering sound. With a burst of white light a great sword shivered into being in Ronar's hand—Bran's sword, a shining vane of steel.

Ronar's fury, pent and thwarted until now, surged forth like a tide of arctic waters. To the magicians of Darteharn, Leonard Ronar suddenly free and armed was an entirely different thing than Leonard Ronar bound and helpless. They hesitated a fatal second before unleashing their spells. Ronar knew so such delay. His anger leaped down his arm almost of its own accord, propelling the sword in two sweeping arcs. Borna mac Dred's head jerked from his shoulders and fell into the shaft in the center of the floor, hitting bottom with a sound like a coconut. The Harrier looked after it, then looked down blankly at his own trailing intestines. He sank to his knees, toppled onto his face. Blood flowed down the shaft.

For a timeless instant Ronar surveyed the results of his butchery with a mixture of sickness and exultation that disconcerted some saner corner of his mind. But he wasn't given much time for contemplation. The death of the Darteharnians seemed to break a spell that had paralyzed the mutants. The Consul regained control swiftly and decisively. At his order the three mutant warriors drew short bronze swords and advanced. They formed an arc that left Ronar with his back to the wall—or would have, if Ronar had been of a mind to take notice of the odds against him. His freedom, gained at the expense of his conception of reality, was far too precious to surrender to this motley group of paranoid primitives.

He flung himself at his enemies with hysterical strength, quite unskillfully, but with an advantage of size and reach that let him threaten all three at once. He hammered and hacked, their blades splintering beneath his steel, their cuirasses denting and tearing like tin.

One of the warriors dashed for the door. Ronar leaped to intercept him, bowling over another in the process. The fleeing one had his hand on the door but was forced to turn and defend himself. He fell despite his best efforts. Ronar spun to engage his remaining foes. The blade felt weightless in his hand. He swung it in great reckless sweeps, making himself all but unapproachable. The Consul exhorted his warriors, but only succeeded in driving them to their deaths. One by one they fell to Ronar's maniacal death-dealing. In minutes he stood surrounded by mutilated bodies. There was a head encased in purplish gelatin; there a forearm gnarled and branched as a tree; there an antler-like structure still dribbling blood. Death had come none too soon to these twisted beings. Perhaps they welcomed the fate they'd courted when they assisted in his humiliation.

The Consul still stood unscathed. Ronar was prepared to waste no time. He strode up to his chief captor with the sword cocked.

The Consul said, "You concealed your magic and so deceived the men of Darteharn, but not me. If you are not Sha Totek, you are at least his very Shadow."

"You are wrong to the last," said Ronar. With a grimace of hatred he swung the sword in an arc that opened the Consul's abdomen. "But don't despair. Your vengeance hasn't failed utterly. You've killed me, although I haven't stopped breathing yet."

The Consul's pincer-hands plucked at his spilled guts. Overwhelmed by the imminence of his death, he didn't appear to hear Ronar's words. Soon he collapsed and grew still.

Silence reigned for a moment before a flutter of movement caught Ronar's attention. In a dark corner huddled Dome-head, quivering and blinking. Ronar leaped over the central pit and loomed over the creature with raised sword. The mutant stood shaking, not even lifting its stunted arms.

Filled with shame and disgust, Ronar lowered the weapon. "You never lifted a hand against me. You never even said a word. For that reason alone you're the only person here who I'm not convinced is insane. Don't interfere with me and I'll let you go."

The acquiescence in the swarm of eyes was unmistakable.

Ronar was distracted by a crunching, sucking sound coming from the pit. He picked up a torch and blew it back to life. Its light crept down the walls of the pit as he approached it. On the bottom, the head of Borna mac Dred was somehow consuming itself, folding in upon itself with wet rending noises, until like Ouroboros it was gone, swallowed up into nothingness. Nearer at hand, Borna's body and the remains of the Harrier began the same grotesque process. Soon only dark stains were left.

Ronar glanced at Dome-head, who had also viewed this scene. He looked at the mutant almost as if it were an old colleague.

A wry thought-voice entered his mind: *It's thoughtful of these Darteharnians to clean up after themselves when they die.*

Ronar snorted and nodded. "Remember this, the next time you start thinking you Nartarians have all the bad luck. You will not raise the alarm about my escape?"

I shall not. I saw what the Darteharnians have in mind for us. I realize we erred in molesting you. Besides, I actually find some enjoyment in life, despite my unusual appearance. I would not throw it away.

"Goodbye then."

Ronar went to the Consul's corpse, stripped off his scarlet cloak and wrapped it around himself. He eased the door open and peered into the corridor. He stood at the terminus of a long hallway lit by small oil lamps and occasional smears of radioactive fluorescence. A legend was engraved on the opposite wall: *To be punished in Nartar is to be doubly damned.*

No one was in sight. Ronar crept into the corridor, locking the door behind him. He passed and ignored other cells. The corridor ended in a T. To the right the cross corridor descended a flight of stairs. Ronar chose the left, which was wide and lengthy and gave onto a variety of shadowy chambers.

The corridors were haunted, dusty, and dead . Nartar must once have thrived, for it was large and architecturally ambitious. Now in decay, its population was a dying remnant of what it must once have been. Eerie light shone in deserted hallways where once the exiles of Rome had proudly ruled, never suspecting the true source of the power that was corrupting them.

Ronar's caution intensified as he heard a voice filtering through a door up ahead. He sidled up to listen, but the words were too muffled to make out. He might have ignored this and gone on, but he thought he recognized the voice. With utmost care he eased the latch open, placed his eye to the crack and peered in.

Kerunos lac Kai, sitting at a table with his back to Ronar, huddled over a bowl in which flickered a crimson flame. His voice was a low chant: "O my master, the moon of Teutates rises high; you bask in its glow. A Shadow is cast; it is I. Now let a shadow be cast in reverse, that as master and servant we may converse." He lifted the bowl, stood up and turned. Ronar ducked back so that not even the glitter of his eye would give him away.

When Ronar dared look again Kerunos had resumed his seat, but now the bowl was resting on a pedestal behind his back, between Kerunos and Ronar. The shadow of Kerunos was cast on the far wall, a blackness defined by the surrounding glow of the flames.

Though Kerunos sat perfectly still, his shadow did not. It swelled and shifted, expanding into a menacing form, horned perhaps, but ill defined. It filled the chamber like an inky fog. Points of light appeared in the black opacity, hovering near the location where eyes might be expected. Ronar knew with dire certainty that the shadow of Namirnakh was looking through the door and straight at him. Surely it was about to speak to him, but Ronar found that he did not wish to hear its words.

Ronar burst into the room and kicked over the pedestal with its iron bowl. The fiery liquid seeped into the cracks between the paving stones; the shadow dissipated. Someday he must thank the Despards for teaching him how to deal with the Fire of Ahriman.

The human Shadow of Namirnakh turned slowly, his eyes widening as he saw who confronted him. But his equanimity quickly returned. "So, you are free. I must assume that our hosts did not release you of their own volition."

"They did not. I have deprived my 'hosts' of any ability to regret my escape. The same with your colleagues."

Kerunos nodded bleakly. "Naturally. I underestimated you, Earthman. But I think it's understandable that I disregarded one who lacks magic."

"I have magic. Everyone does. When nothing is as it seems, why not call the resulting lunacy magic?" said Ronar bitterly.

Kerunos studied Ronar narrowly, then glanced at his blade. "There is magic about that weapon. And about the ring as well. I see. They are connected." Suddenly his eyes widened fractionally. "I recognize that blade…"

"Congratulations."

"It was carried by King Bran himself. Amazing that it still survives." Kerunos then muttered silently to himself.

"Examine it at closer range," said Ronar, plunging the steel into Kerunos's belly.

"What—?" Kerunos looked down. "But I had placed a spell of suspension upon you!"

"I chose to ignore it."

Surprise faded from the wizard's face as he choked, sank down and became still. Ronar withdrew the sword and wiped it on a wall hanging.

"I find your solutions to problems to be overly direct, even unimaginative. Your stratagems show you to be crass and callow."

Ronar frowned down at the body. "Why aren't you dead?"

"Alas, I was Namirnakh's chief servant. As such, he'll not allow my animus to depart so easily. I'm afraid I must remain here until I decompose a bit. Pay me no heed; be on your way."

"I intend to. You've delayed me long enough as it is." Ronar turned and stalked out into the corridor.

The sword had vanished at some point. He'd stabbed Kerunos, cleaned the blade, and that was his last memory of its weight in his hand. It must have faded during his surprising conversation with the dead wizard. But the garnet on his finger still glimmered with a smoky light. He did not doubt he could call the blade forth again at need. He sent a quick thought of thanks toward Sionyn for the generosity and foresight that had saved more than his life alone.

A single-minded drive to leave the city came upon him. He walked with a glacial inexorability that carried a message: here was a man to be left alone. He came to a large door which he kicked open, heedless of the boom that echoed along the corridor. Naked but for cloak and boots, he stepped out into the frigid night air. A street led between great Roman buildings with crumbling colonnades. Moonlight, reflected by patches of snow, cast a pewter glow onto brick and marble. Ronar relished the clean stillness of the night and felt somewhat revived by it. Alert as a hunting owl, he stalked between the silent structures of the City of the Doomed.

A squad of disfigured warriors sprang at him from the shadows. He called forth the sword; it shivered into existence with a clashing flare of light. The sight of it brought the mutants up short. They stared at the weaving blade, mesmerized by the moonlight that flowed down its polished face. They did not advance. Seemingly frozen in place, they scarcely moved as Ronar backed away.

The mutants attempted no further assaults, though their surveillance was ceaseless. Lurking in doorways and porticos, they stared at him as he passed. Ronar appreciated the contrast between this sullen, resigned acceptance of his departure and the exultation they'd shown at his capture. He hoped he'd never have to return to reinforce the lesson he'd taught them. He strode between ranks of watchful mutants, looking straight ahead, hiding the pain, sickness, and fatigue that made the city seem to shimmer around him.

At some point the sword slipped away again, but it didn't matter. Sooner than he'd hoped he came to the edge of Nartar. He stepped past the unwalled boundary of the grim city and stared out over the snowy plain. His shoulder blades itched as though they expected an arrow to plunge between them, but none came. Orienting himself by the stars, he trudged a weary mile before stopping to look back.

There lay Nartar, backed by the Glowing Hills, beautiful in its macabre fashion.

Ronar turned his back on it again.

The snow had been trampled into a broad track by the throng that had come out to revile him so long ago—or could it be only hours ago? He followed until it narrowed at the place where the crowd had reached him. Almost unconsciously he retraced his steps until he reached the spot where he'd cached his belongings. They had somehow seemed much more important back when he had buried them.

He sank heavily to his knees, pawing haphazardly at the snow around the black arrow. His mind wandered, wallowing in bitterness. He had difficulty concentrating on his task, or even realizing the significance of it. Nausea flowed suddenly from his brain to his gut. He pitched forward and vomited a thin dark liquid. The spasms didn't cease until long after the last drop had been squeezed out. Utterly drained, devoid of motivation, he flopped over onto his back and lay there staring at the stars. The cold seeping into his flesh muted the symphonies of pain that had been played upon him.

He had accomplished his mission—he'd deflected pursuit from Sha Totek. He'd paid a heavy price. Now it seemed he would die. No point in doing anything but lying here to await the inevitable. Dressed as he was he'd soon freeze, which was at least a clean death. That thought sustained a glimmer of bleak satisfaction.

He looked at the stars, but felt only betrayal in their distant, mocking light. It wasn't worthwhile to strive through such pain to defend a universe characterized by the essential unreality he'd so clearly demonstrated to himself in his escape. He'd lost the orderly starry realm he'd loved so dearly all his life. Let magic reign everywhere; what did it matter? If the universe was mad, someone might as well take advantage of the madness.

The cold peace of his surroundings leached away the feverish passion of his despair. A stillness settled over him, for which he was grateful. He awaited death with a calm acceptance. His mind was free to spin through dim corridors of thought where the ghosts of old ideas waited to be prodded and examined once again. He now had a clearer perception of the nature of reality than perhaps anyone ever had before. Was he so weak that the revelation would kill him? What if every scientist who confronted the inadequacy of long-cherished beliefs despaired of life as a result? He felt vaguely guilty about this lapse, but lacked the strength to do anything about it.

But the thought wouldn't leave him alone. Shouldn't he at least make an effort to adjust to his new knowledge? Surely the scientists of Earth could stand to be lifted out of the two-dimensional rut of their traditional lines of inquiry. True, a great deal was known about quantum physics, but he doubted that more than a few people had ever dreamed of its full implications. Attacks on causality were not popular even among the most radical thinkers. Even Einstein had objected to the randomness implied by quantum theory and had died trying to refute it.

A new thought, a total non sequitur, struck him. Perhaps it was the people who inhabited the universe who were worth struggling for. They were all just as trapped in this madness as he was, even if most of them were oblivious to the fact. After all, he knew himself to be genuine and worthwhile; he could only assume that others were of similar depth.

By now Ronar's despair was diluted by intense curiosity. What was really troubling him? Seen objectively, there was no good reason for this plunge into depression. His initial exposure to magic hadn't shattered him—why this gradual slide into the malaise he could now perceive so clearly?

With furrowed brow he stared up at the stars. They were not yet able to answer his questions. He wasn't himself, and suddenly he missed himself very much. Finding no answers outside, he looked within, falling into a reverie so deep that the cold was as nothing to him. His thoughts returned to the summit of the Brocken. There they remained while the stars crawled across the sky.

"What?" he said in surprise. Had someone spoken? Ronar looked about in bewilderment. No one was visible on the wide icy plain. Nevertheless, a breathless feeling of imminence, of something on the verge of change, trembled within him. Quite naturally, he looked up at the stars, waiting to see what would happen next.

A line of light was drawn across the sky. It was a peculiar light, of a kind that burned bright but did not illuminate the snow. It descended toward the southwest horizon and vanished.

Silently, invisibly, without fanfare, the stars changed. They were right again—the ineffable music of their being lost its unnatural strain. Varanu had won. The magic of Ahriman had been driven from the majestic universe of suns.

A breath trembled in Ronar's throat. Peace swept over him as at the breaking of a fever. It had been an insidious malady, gradually building, masked by the tumultuous events of his journey. But its sudden ending was like the contrast between madness and sanity. The stars were clean again, their music pure. Ronar lay there drinking in the renewed beauty of the heavens, not noticing the tear of gratitude that froze on his cheek.

For weeks now the Eye of Ahriman had been not only blinded, but vacant. Now as Ronar watched, its old malice flared up again, sweeping him and the entire planet with a merciless gaze. Then the evil subsided, and the Eye fell into a sullen, smoldering sleep.

A hushed voice said, "We won't be hearing from Ahriman again for some time. But the battle also took a lot out of Varanu. He just fell straight to Larlaninulius without even a look in our direction."

Ronar raised himself on his elbows. Sha Totek sat only a few feet away. Or rather, he appeared to sit on an invisible seesaw, for he alternately rose ten feet into the air and then sank down again, often vanishing into the snow like a ghost.

"What's going on here?" asked Ronar.

"I'm at sea. It's hard to compensate for relative motion in making this projection, and it's taxing to make it at all. But I wanted to visit you. Why are you lying in the snow half naked?"

Ronar sat up. "I'm dying."

Sha Totek raised his eyebrows. "Dying! From what?"

"Nuclear radiation. I was captured by Nartar, and I'm afraid I took too much of a dose." Suddenly Ronar felt less convinced of that. He started rubbing his chilled limbs.

"Hmmm. Well, I don't know about any new clear radiation, but has it occurred to you that I recently treated you with life-extending magic? Note that it is I, Sha Totek, the chief and oldest sorcerer in the world, who we're talking about here."

Ronar gaped like a gaffed cod. "You mean the magic will protect me?"

"Life-extension magic isn't much good if it doesn't keep you from dying, I can tell you that."

Ronar slowly rose to his feet, his head bobbing to follow the sorcerer's image. "Why didn't you tell me this before?"

"You mean before you cleverly allowed yourself to be captured by the Nartarians? I could say you didn't ask. Actually, I didn't want you to start thinking you're invulnerable. You can still be killed quite easily, but you're just a touch more resistant to ordinary wear and tear than you were. At least you are now, when the spell's still fresh."

"But I am sick."

"You won't hasten your recovery by staying out in the cold dressed in those scraps."

Ronar bent and dug out the sledge. Shivering, he pulled on ice-cold clothing.

"What did those patrician dolts in Nartar want from you?" asked Sha Totek.

"They thought I was you. Wanted me to turn them human again. I couldn't make them see reason. They tried to turn me over to Namirnakh's men. So I killed them."

"The Nartarians or the Darteharnians?"

"Some of each. I killed some of Namirnakh's top wizards, by their own admission."

"Really? Which ones?"

Ronar named them. Sha Totek was elated. "So you killed the Shadow himself, eh? Good for you. He had an immortality spell that involved mixing the semen of stags with the blood of little girls—while it was still in their veins. Maybe I should call it an immorality spell. Glad to hear he's out of the picture. I take it you've discovered the function of your ring."

"Yes. Damned devious way to get me to carry a sword, I'd say. But it saved my life."

"You can thank Gromer for that. He still hasn't quite recovered from laying down that spell—it was a big one. Bran's sword is now one of the most enchanted weapons in the world. The Spell of Encoded Matrices gives it properties other than easy retrievability."

"How in the world can the King give me that sword if it's such a cherished relic?"

"Oh, he hasn't given it up. When you aren't using it, it rests in the palace." Sha Totek chuckled. "When it vanishes they know you're in trouble. But I'm hoping you won't need it again. I'm happy to say there are no more human enemies between you and the pole. Just natural dangers, and I know how much you enjoy those. You will be joining us up there, won't you?"

"That's the plan."

"Good. Well. So, Nartar captured you. Yet here you are, still alive. By Isis! Try to avoid further trouble, will you? Whatever awaits us, I'm liable to need the help of a maniac like you."

"I'll be there."

The image of the grinning sorcerer faded away.

Ronar brushed snow off his parka, a grey fur garment with an inner quilting of goose down. He made a quick check of his equipment: the canes and skins of the tent; the binocular; bow and arrows; sleeping bag, and all the rest. With some difficulty he crouched to bind on the skis.

Before strapping on the harness he raised the binocular for a brief scan of the galaxies wheeling in the dark ocean of night.

Chapter 15

Tigermine

Although the mutants seemed defeated, they might regain their nerve at any time. For peace of mind Ronar must put the Glowing Hills below the horizon before he dared to rest. He forced himself northward despite his swimming senses.

The weather deteriorated. A north wind slid over the wasteland, bringing with it the terrible cold of the polar regions, buffeting him, making his progress all the more difficult. Banks of cloud blotted out the stars. Darkness was absolute, except in the southeast where a grey glow heralded the suns. To Ronar it seemed like weeks since he'd seen the light of day. He welcomed its coming, lover of the night though he was.

The temperature dropped until Ronar guessed it was about twenty below. His exertion helped keep him warm, but that was about to come to an end. He was ill and exhausted. The wind and clouds warned of an approaching storm which he couldn't hope to survive in the open.

He struggled on until he came to a ravine that might offer some protection from the wind. He undid the harness and let the sledge slide down into the little gully, then followed and wearily set up the tent, pushing the canes deep into the crusted snow. He laboriously packed snow around and over the tent for better stability and insulation. Though he was aching to crawl inside, flop down and sleep for a week, he knew he must take whatever precautions he could while he had the strength. He wasn't satisfied until his tent looked like an igloo. He even went to the trouble of constructing an entry tunnel with a right-angle bend to baffle the wind. No telling how bad the storm might get, or how long he'd be pinned down.

With trembling limbs he pushed most of the sledge's load into the tent, crawled in after it and lit a candle. In its warm glow, the tiny hemispherical space was an inviting refuge. He found himself frantically melting snow in a small pot. The candle took a long time to do the job, but Ronar retained the discipline to wait until the water reached a temperature his body could tolerate. He drank it down greedily, melted more, and drank again. He forced himself to eat a hard biscuit and kept it down.

He unrolled a thick straw mat and spread it over the snow. He laid out his sleeping bag, eyeing it as another man would eye a lover. Pulling it around him like a big cocoon, he waited for warmth to come back into his body.

One last task, nearly forgotten. He'd need a small hole overhead to keep warm air from building up and melting too much snow. Stripping the mitten from his left hand, he regarded the garnet ring of Eranior, glittering in the candle-light. Had he really used it to call forth that great blade? It already seemed like a dream—yet in his pocket was a leather glove that still stank where magic radiance had burned through it. He thought of the sword, imagining its weight, summoning it. He sensed it nearby; that strange metallic humming wove through the air like a giant steel wasp.

The ring spouted crimson heat; the sword appeared with a white flash and a shattering sound. Ronar was startled enough to fumble the sword and almost drop it on his head.

He used the ancient weapon to poke a hole through the tent and its mantle of snow, then let it pass back into nothingness. He blew out the candle and fell into a sleep deeper than a winter's night.

He awoke sixteen hours later. The roar of the storm was like that of a torrent of water or a pillar of flame. No light leaked in through the tunnel. He'd slept right through the day into another night.

The blizzard hadn't penetrated his haven, but he feared the wind might eventually blast the snow from the north side of the tent. It was uncomfortably cold inside. An icy draft snaked between the vent-hole and the entrance. He could close off the openings while he slept, but not while burning candles. He lit one and set about thawing another potful of snow to quiet his endless thirst. The candle gave some heat. Ronar got out of the bag and poked his head outside to check on the storm.

The wind surged in waves, sending an occasional breaker of bitter air into his refuge. He could see nothing. Needles of ice driven like tiny darts stung his face. Even here in the ravine the wind was like a living fury. This storm was awesome, pitiless, and might yet kill him. He laughed. At least the storm was without malice. It was infinitely preferable to the situation he'd just left.

Scooping snow, he piled it up in the entrance until he'd left only a small opening. He crawled back into the bag, drank more water, ate more biscuit and a bit of dried meat. Then he collapsed, exhausted again.

He awoke again, though he didn't remember falling asleep. This time he felt alert and stronger. The candle had burned out, but he had many more. He doubted he'd ever need them more than now, so he burned them freely. He still had the three books he'd purchased in Phaedra's distant bookshop. With a peculiar feeling of longing he groped for them, bringing out *Wanderings of Hamadan*. The scent of the binding evoked memories of a moment of ease and bliss. He read a few pages, but found concentration difficult.

It was very cold. Even fully dressed, protected by tent and sleeping bag, he wasn't exactly comfortable. The temperature outside must be something like fifty below. Assessing his situation and prospects, he found them bleak. Alone in this implacable wilderness, in this fearsome storm, he had only as much water as he could laboriously melt. He suffered from radiation sickness and from the effects of torture, both magical and physical. He might well die here, hundreds of miles from the nearest outpost of decent human civilization.

Why then did he feel such peace and contentment? Because he was free. He'd lived to see the greater universe cleansed of magic. He'd done his best to protect the Earth. He was safe and snug as could be under the circumstances. He knew of fates far worse than to succumb to the cold embrace of a winter night.

Grateful for cleanness and freedom, he soon slept again.

He woke up feeling well, though stiff and sore, parched and ravenous. He laughed. He was not nauseated, and his hair was not falling out. His body had shrugged off a dose of radiation that should have killed him a hundred times over. He melted and drank more of the floor of his dwelling and wolfed dried fruit and meat. He was making a good dent in his food supply. If the storm didn't subside soon he might start to run low with his goal still over a thousand miles away.

He suffered from a craving for chocolate, but as far as he knew there was none within a hundred thousand light-years.

His strength was returning rapidly. He promised himself he'd break camp and make some progress the next morning, regardless of the weather.

Ronar cleared the ventilation hole, which was blocked by fresh snow. He rapped on the walls of the tent. The snow beyond it had melted and recrystallized into an icy sheath. The tent itself was no longer needed. He worked the poles free, peeled the skin away from the ice, and rolled it up, leaving that much less work for the morning. The candlelight was brighter, yet seemed chillier as it reflected off the smooth whiteness of the ice.

The temperature continued to fall. Surely the star Kudu must have faded substantially in recent years. He doubted anyone would have settled at this latitude if storms like this had been possible in the past. What would things be like near the Pole itself?

For the rest of the short day Ronar ate, drank, tried to stay warm, and daydreamed. The blizzard's howl became no more than a background for thoughts of what he'd left behind and what might lie ahead. He steered away from the memory of Nartar—he wasn't ready to consider the consequences of that episode.

When the grey light from outside faded, Ronar armored himself against the cold as best he could and fell asleep. The candle he left burning was a stub that soon extinguished itself as its wick met the snow.

He endured a night of poor sleep but vivid dreams. The cold kept waking him up, but there was nothing he could do but huddle deeper in the sleeping bag, trying to avoid the cold spots he grew to hate in his half-awake state. The frigid air numbed his face, so he wrapped a scarf around his head. Drifting in and out of sleep, his mind prowled through restless dreams. The images were disconnected and disturbing, with an uneasy lack of distinction between fantasy and reality. Sometimes he'd wake up convinced that what he'd just dreamed was real. Sometimes he couldn't believe his present life was anything other than a dream.

At last he dreamed of the stars. A skyful of yellowish sparks crystallized before him; superimposed were the outlines of the Colibdian constellations. There was the bright hourglass of the Stars of Order; there sprawled Hamadan the legendary hero; there the Skull of Bran; there Taralorne, the Lonely Star. Near the horizon, beneath the Stars of the Cold, lurked Glorphos, the Ice Worm. It lay coiled upon the snowy skyline, its eye marked by the eerie blue glow of the planetary nebula.

The constellation raised its head and looked at him.

Ronar awoke, his heart pounding. Blearily he looked toward the entry tunnel and saw the cold blue annulus of the nebula shining in at him.

But wait—the tunnel had no view of the sky. He must still be dreaming...yes, the nebula was gone. He lay there staring blankly at the spot where it had been until sleep returned.

In the morning the storm was unabated, but Ronar grimly kept to his resolve to make at least some progress that day. He fed himself, organized his possessions, and crept from his haven into the howling wild. He gave a catlike stretch, feeling eighty percent recovered, which was about forty percent better than most men could manage on their best day. It would have to do.

The storm had camouflaged his hiding place perfectly. A knife-edged snowdrift piled against the snow bubble eliminated all sign of his presence. That much the storm had done for him.

On the other hand, when he dug out the sledge he found that his skis had delaminated in the intense cold. They were useless except as firewood. Ronar gave a subdued curse. He should have brought them inside, but they were too long to fit in the tent. Today he'd walk. If the snow was too fresh and deep he'd try the snowshoes. He reloaded the sledge and was on his way. At first the icy wind was exhilarating. It felt good to move again after days of confinement.

His environment was a grey void of blowing ice and snow, without any landmark or hint of direction. He consulted the compass. The needle was slow in settling on north. The magnetic field of Colibdis seemed weak, but it was enough to keep him from wandering in circles. He pushed on into the blizzard. The snow shortened his stride and tripled the effort of walking, even without the drag of the sledge. Nevertheless, he maintained a steady pace for hours, increasing the toll of miles between himself and civilization.

At first the wind worked against him, but as the day passed it swung from the north toward the east. Ronar guessed it was a cyclonic storm, its center somewhere to the west. The storm had plenty of fury to hand out in passing. The temperature remained polar. The wind remained a snow-laden gale.

Ronar grew worried. He was getting cold despite his exertion. His feet and face were the worst problems. These boots weren't suitable for conditions this severe. They stayed dry, thanks to the bitter cold, but they just weren't insulated well enough. He was less concerned about his face, wrapped with woolen scarves and encased by a furry hood. He peered out through slits in the wrappings. His nose stung, which was a good sign; at least he could still feel it. The sting had faded from his toes, replaced by an ominous numbness.

He walked on, though his instincts warned it was time to seek shelter. Unfortunately, he'd neglected to consider that it would be impossible to set up his tent in this gale. Unless he found some natural refuge before nightfall, to-day's walk would gain him nothing but a grave that was unlikely to be disturbed.

He was trudging on mechanically, reviewing possibilities and options, when he heard a hiss and felt a blow on his right thigh. The storm chose that moment to close in with a renewed vengeance. He could see nothing beyond a yard away.

He felt a strike on his other thigh, and a pressure that tried to bowl him over. Staggering to keep his balance, he looked down to see a great furry head clamped onto his leg. The creature's serpentine body blended into the blizzard just a few paces away, as if he were being attacked by a so-lidified tentacle of the storm.

Ronar's first impulse was to summon the sword, but an image flashed through his mind: a bolt of fire destroying an invaluable mitten. Instead he clenched his fist and dealt the creature a blow between its white-furred ears. The head drew back for a moment, eyes closed, but then its short black muzzle gaped and the creature struck again, exerting painful pressure, trying to knock him down. Ronar glimpsed rows of sharp but delicate teeth, too small to penetrate his heavy clothing. Still, enough was enough. This time he planted his fist solidly between its eyes.

The Ice Worm gave a querulous yowl and shook its head. Ronar was startled by its huge crystal-blue eyes as it came at him again.

Ronar whipped off the mitten and summoned the sword. The scarlet flash caused a moment of heavy rain. Ronar raised the weapon and brought it down toward the Ice Worm's skull. Something made him turn his wrist at the last instant so that he struck with the flat of the blade. The impact sounded like a mallet on a coconut. One enormous eye closed while the other rolled at an odd angle. A peep of dismay announced the Ice Worm's defeat. Its head thumped down into the snow. It went belly-up, revealing black scaly plates on its underside.

Ronar raised his hand for the death blow, but as he looked down at the creature he hesitated. The thing was thoroughly beaten; he doubted it would be inclined to attack again. He'd had enough of killing; let this snowfield predator try its luck on prey better suited to its dentition.

He let the sword pass back into the 'spell of encoded matrices', whatever that was, replaced his mitten and turned away.

A whir of wings and a buffeting about his face; his scarf was torn away. An instant's quiet and the flutter was back from another quarter of the storm. Ronar glimpsed a blur of white feathers. He lashed out with a backhanded blow, hitting something that tumbled out of sight. The storm was so dense he hadn't clearly seen this new assailant, nor did he bother to search. He became aware of blood running down his cheek and freezing on the tip of his chin. He could only wipe it on his sleeve and rewrap his scarf. In three steps the scene of these minor battles was lost behind him.

Not until mid-afternoon, when he'd already covered twice the distance he'd intended for the day, did he begin to hope he might find shelter. Grey spines of rock, swept almost clear of snow, meandered over the land like crude megalithic walls. Ronar walked until he found one whose south face was buried by a great snowdrift. He fell to his knees and started digging into it, but his progress was too slow. He peered around through a haze of exhaustion. Staggering to the nearest exposed rock, he pried off a large stone flake. He returned to his excavation, using the rock as a spade.

The clouds glowed the luminous purple of a winter dusk by the time his snow cave was complete. Once inside he collapsed like a dead man, savoring the luxuries of silence and windlessness.

He caught himself just as he was about to lapse into a sleep that might well have been fatal. He forced himself to exert the fantastic energy needed to set up and light a candle. Although he didn't feel thirsty, he knew he must be badly dehydrated, so he thawed and drank as much water as he thought he could hold. By the time this lengthy process was over, his body heat and the candle had warmed the snow cave to a toasty twenty degrees or so. Ronar could no longer put off checking the damage to his feet. He stripped off his boots; his toes were swollen and blistered, yellow from frostbite. They felt like hard lifeless pellets with no connection to his body.

He chewed pemmican as he tried to rub life back into his stricken toes. Eventually, lances of pain announced that the frost was in retreat. Ronar didn't flinch; after Nartar he wasn't easily impressed by pain.

The cave needed further massive efforts before it was really habitable. An irregular four-foot space wasn't sufficient, much as he wished it was.

Astoundingly, the temperature continued to drop. Ronar's sleep was even worse than it had been the night before. No position was comfortable for long. Each shift brought some part of his body into the influence of the cold leaking through the heavy bag. The muffled wail of the wind eventually ceased, bringing to mind a vision of clearing skies and heat radiating into space. During one of his waking periods he tried to remember the freezing point of carbon dioxide, but fuzzily concluded he'd be dead long before it could be reached. So far he was merely uncomfortable, not in imminent danger of freezing. But he was being deprived of rest, which could lead to his death if he wasn't careful. Was this storm an anomaly, or could he expect its like from here to the pole?

In a fitful dream he saw a television set, its screen showing only snowy static. Spinning wheels coalesced from the chaos of sparkles. The borders of the screen spread out, enveloping the world. In the midst of the wheels he glimpsed a face that seemed to encompass the universe. Its eyes were lit by a peculiar colorless light.

The sparkles thinned out, froze in place, and suddenly were stars. Before him was the dim pattern of the Stars of the Cold, dedicated to Boreas, the North Wind. Below it was the Ice Worm. It gazed sidelong at him with a blue cat's-eye of endless mystery...

Ronar's eyes snapped open. In the snow cave's entrance shone the cold annulus of the planetary nebula.

The nebula shifted slightly to the right, bringing its twin into view. Ronar looked at the two "nebulae" and knew he was in fact awake.

The eyes of the Ice Worm wove slowly back and forth, then moved slightly forward, accompanied by the soft crunching sound of compacting snow. They halted and hovered in the darkness, their roundness occasionally eclipsed by slow deliberate blinking.

Ronar fumbled for matches. He struck one and squinted against the sudden glare. The Ice Worm jerked back into the shadows of the tunnel. Its pupils shrank from lemon-sized to the size of a quarter.

Ronar lit a candle and held it before him. His other hand sought the hilt of his bright dagger.

With an interrogative trilling sound the Ice Worm advanced again. The great catlike head, big as a tiger's, came fully into the candlelight, its thick white fur clogged with ice. Its rounded muzzle was covered with short black fur, and its eyes were rimmed with black. Those eyes were a glory: huge, crystalline, colored with flakes of ultramarine and cerulean blue. The Ice Worm stared at Ronar, its whiskers twitching. Ronar was wary, but so far his soul felt firmly attached to his body, despite the warnings of the Eranians. With a tentative flutelike note the Worm wriggled the rest of itself into the cave. Its snakelike body was eight or nine feet long, as thick as Ronar's torso for much of that length. It made for a tight squeeze. Ronar huddled in half the cave, the Ice Worm in the other. At close quarters, they silently regarded each other.

For some reason Ronar did not feel menaced by this strange intrusion. The wide round eyes of the Ice Worm held only watchful innocence. He was sure this was the same animal that had attacked him. It probably couldn't imagine that he might resent its attempt to eat him—it had failed, hadn't it? Plainly it sought only to escape a killing cold.

Ronar settled back, relaxing his grip on the dagger. "Behave yourself and you may stay," he said quietly. "It's not a fit night out for man nor beast."

The Ice Worm responded with a low trill. Taking its eyes off Ronar for the first time, it began to lick its fur with a big blue-black tongue.

A hiss from the tunnel made Ronar stare hard into the darkness. He was startled to see a small white face, round as the Ice Worm's own. A young Worm? No—this visitor turned out to be more mundane, but almost as unexpected—a snowy owl. It hopped inside, feathers fluffed, head weaving, yellow eyes squinting. Ronar sat up straight. The Ice Worm glanced at the newcomer and went back to its grooming.

The owl was trailing a broken wing. Ronar felt a pang of guilt. This must be the bird he'd struck earlier in the day. Touched by the desperation that had brought it into his presence, Ronar was suddenly filled with a poignant sense of brotherhood with these fellow travelers. The bird seemed more precious and irreplaceable to him than the abstract human multitudes on the two planets of man. On this world, at this moment, the only fellowship he had was right here in this tiny snow cave.

Ronar reached for the owl. It hissed and bristled, flapping its good wing, but it did not flee or strike out. Ronar persisted, patiently offering his hands until he was permitted to touch the bird. He stroked it, murmured to it. The Ice Work leaned over and gave its back a small lick that included Ronar's hand.

Such was Ronar's confidence and sympathy that presently the owl did not resist his handling. The astronomer gently gathered it into his lap. With a bit of cane and a length of cord, he set and bound the broken wing as well as he was able. The bird might never fly again, but at least it need not die in pain.

With the owl still in his lap, Ronar looked into the glowing eyes of the Ice Worm. Hesitantly, he reached out and began plucking bits of ice from its fur, which was lusher and denser than any he'd ever touched before. "Ice Worm" this might be, but there was nothing icy about the warmth of its furry body. When the Worm was dry, its eyelids grew heavy. It arranged itself for sleep, curling into a surprisingly compact bundle. With some difficulty the owl fluttered to a perch behind the Ice Worm's head, where it immediately settled into sleep.

Ronar, shivering in his dank sleeping bag, watched the peaceful pair from the other side of the cave. Shaking his head at the strangeness of life, he half expected still more arctic refugees to arrive. At last he dropped off to sleep. He woke one more time that night to find the Worm cuddled up against him. He lay against the animal's warm, clean-smelling coils with a dreamy feeling of luxury. He couldn't help but smile. At this moment he couldn't imagine a better companion than this extraterrestrial predator which earlier had tried to eat him. Words from a half-remembered poem drifted through his mind in the last moments before he was claimed by a profound slumber. How did it go again? He remembered the name...*Tigermine. Tigermine. Tigermine...*

When Ronar awoke, Tigermine and the owl were gone, having somehow crept out from under him without awakening him. But they had left a gift: a small dead animal, a white-furred spheroid with six radial legs and no apparent sense organs. Odd as it was, when he cut it open he found blood and meat that seemed straightforward enough. Greedily he dismembered and ate the creature, not wasting a thought on the compatibility of its alien proteins with his. The meat and fat were just what his weakened body needed. He wiped the juices from his face with satisfaction.

He set about equipping himself for the awesome cold. To protect his feet he followed the example of the Lapps. He tied sheets of thick wool felt around his boots, then bundled dry straw around them. He wrapped this batting with skins, then carefully bound it all up with leather straps. With the rest of his cold-armor in place he had done his utmost to ward off the elements. If the weather could overwhelm even these defenses, he was defeated.

Outside, the fierce white sun and its somber red companion burned side-by-side in indigo air so clear and cold he might have been standing on a polar cap of Mars. The snowfield was a blinding sheet of light, fresh with new powder laid down last night. He crawled back into the snow cave, blinded until his eyes readjusted to the gloom. He lit a candle and held the lenses of his reading glasses to the yellow tip of the flame. Outside again, the smoked lenses made decent makeshift sunglasses. He bound his snowshoes to the lumpy masses of his heavily insulated feet, harnessed himself, and started off.

Ronar felt restored. He faced the wilderness with renewed confidence, keeping his pace as brisk as possible. Whatever happened from here on, it would take a lot to prevent him from placing one foot in front of the other. The fact that he'd have to take enough steps to cross almost two thousand miles of frozen wilderness seemed almost irrelevant.

There was no sign of Tigermine or the owl. Obviously, the warnings he'd received about the Ice Worms had been exaggerated. They were hardly the terrors they'd been made out to be, showing no sign of being able to hypnotize anyone. It was reassuring to learn that at least one of the dangers of Colibdis was overrated.

Ronar's stride did not falter that day, nor did it for the next eight days. Each morning he started on his way before dawn, walking all day and into the evening, especially when Sinanna shone bright. When the snow was old and crusted he could forego the snowshoes and make even better time, covering forty miles a day. The weather favored him with a series of crystal-cold but brilliantly clear windless days. He became proficient at spotting flashes of motion, stalking them with an arrow nocked, and shooting fresh food in the form of hares, ptarmigan, and Colibdian "fuzzballs". He didn't spot any large animals, though occasionally he crossed the tracks of what looked like caribou and wolves. Snowy owls were fairly common, standing their ground with no fear of the strange animal Man. He didn't see any whose wing was bound with a bit of cane and a length of string.

The morning of the ninth day didn't dawn until almost ten, when the suns began a low arc along the southern horizon. By two in the afternoon they were already setting. The Arctic Circle wasn't far north. In another week he'd have to do without the suns entirely.

They set, but twilight lingered, casting watercolor glows of rose and lavender onto the snow. Sinuous landforms appeared in the distance. The land became hummocky, covered with winding ridges roughly parallel to each other but perpendicular to his course. The nearest were mere meandering hillocks, but on the skyline was a rugged barrier that looked like a formidable obstacle indeed.

Ronar trudged on until he came to a mound some sixty feet long and eight feet high. He mounted it, digging in his heels for traction. Once on top, he hauled up the sledge and raised the silvery binocular. They weren't as versatile as they'd once been, for their focusing mechanism had frozen. Still, they showed the horizon clearly enough. The wall ahead was formed of tiers of ice and ramps of snow separated by fluted ice cliffs that caught and blended the delicate sky colors. It was more beautiful than alpenglow on the Rockies, and at least as difficult a barrier, even though it was only two or three hundred feet high.

His footing shifted beneath him. He stamped his feet into firmer snow. The ground quivered, sending sheets of snow sliding down the slope. Ronar almost toppled as well. Frowning, he scuffed at the snow underfoot. Beneath it was a layer of striated ice crystals, or perhaps—

Or perhaps fur! Ronar hopped onto the sledge and slid off the serpentine "mound". But the creature was already aroused. The round hillock at the end reared up, sloughed off its mantle of snow, revealing itself as the head of a co-lossal Ice Worm. Shaggy, crusted with ice, that head alone was at least triple Ronar's weight. Its huge eyes opened with a snap of cracking ice. It swung around to face the as-tronomer, who scrambled back. Those eyes, hovering above him, had a staggering effect on him. They were vast, liquid concentrations of life, warm and glowing, fantastic in con-trast to the immense lifelessness all around. Ronar stared at them in fascination. They grew larger; he noticed almost too late that massive jaws were about to close on him.

Ronar whipped off a mitten. A flare of crimson heat singed the Ice Worm's face, and a blast of sound caused it to flinch back. Ronar brandished the great sword. The giant Worm wasn't long deterred. Like twin moons the eyes shone down on him, more compelling than any he'd ever seen. Ronar drew back for the single stroke that must either slit the thing's throat or fail utterly. He braced himself...

"Mmmrreeeeew—?"

Both man and Worm turned to the source of that plain-tive chirp. There was Tigermine, unmistakable with the splint-winged owl perched on its back.

Ronar stood back to await developments. Tigermine, sparing him only a glance, crawled straight for the giant Worm, which appeared comically disconcerted. It slithered back a few yards, snuffling and snorting, casting covetous looks in Ronar's direction. But Tigermine was relentless. It crawled forward, its small cries growing more querulous, until the giant Worm gave up with a hot breath of exaspera-tion. It turned and crawled off into the twilight like a mov-ing wall, looking for a quieter resting place.

Letting his sword pass into oblivion, Ronar faced his savior with a mixture of relief and incredulity. He was shocked at the sound of his own voice after weeks of silence. "Tigermine! Have you followed me all this way? How did you drive that monster away?"

Tigermine's only answer was an affectionate head rub. Ronar scratched the creature between the ears. "Nice kitty," he said. The owl didn't hiss at him.

Wonder drowned out Ronar's other questions. He felt an untainted gratitude quite unlike anything in his experience. The sensation sent a tear down his weathered cheek, freezing among the frost-rimed spines of his beard. "Well, my furry friend,. I have to go see what lies over that next horizon." His voice was thick with emotion. He really had become remarkably sentimental during this hike, he reflected. He set out for the looming ice wall. Tigermine followed.

Man and Worm stood at the base of the wall some two hours later. By then full night had fallen, but even so, the sky was bright. An auroral corona radiated from the zenith, casting green and red light over the upthrust mass of ice which Ronar must now cross.

Wasting no time, Ronar grabbed the sledge's harness and started pulling, with Tigermine at his side. A snowy ramp enabled them to make rapid progress at first, but it ended in a steeper, icier slope. Even then, Tigermine had little trouble. The wide flat scales on his belly gave him excellent traction. He soon wiggled out of sight. Ronar, however, had to step carefully. The slope was slick and rounded, dropping away to an ice cliff whose accidental descent would be inconvenient at best. The smoothly fluted face of the ice wall itself offered few handholds. Ronar scowled. It would be impossibly dangerous to haul the sledge up by this route. He shucked off the harness and put a few items from the sledge into his pack. Checking that everything else on the sledge was well secured, he left it behind.

Very soon the way steepened and narrowed to a point where Ronar could go no farther, sledge or no sledge. He brought out the bronze ice ax he'd had made in Eranior. Gripping this, he chopped out handholds where he needed them, and so climbed on step by step. Bronze, as it turned out, was a pitifully inadequate material for an ice ax. In a short time the blade was flattened, deformed, and all but useless.

He caught up with Tigermine. The Worm, baffled by a sheer wall of steel-hard ice, turned around in a tiny space by pushing half his length up the wall and flopping over. He oozed past Ronar to go back the way he'd come.

Ronar was dubious. This seemed to be the final step to the summit, but it was a long one. The wall was about sixty feet high with a cornice of overhanging snow on top. It was too smooth to climb directly even with the hooks. With crampons and two good ice axes he might have made it. As in the Mountains of Twilight, he needed technical equipment, and once again he didn't have it. But he did have the claws and the rope. He took off his pack and rummaged for souvenirs of the distant south—the four gleaming nehock claws, now mounted in handles after the fashion of the Eanda. He tied the handles together to form a grapple and tied that to the rope.

His first cast dislodged the entire cornice, sending hundreds of pounds of snow rushing past, and pounds of it into his face and clothes. He stood cursing, brushing himself off, lucky not to have been knocked right over the side. The next seven tries only skittered off the edge and fell back.

The ninth cast managed to catch on something. Ronar took his chances, hauling himself up rather easily.

The summit was a wide, windy platform beneath the stars. Tigermine awaited him there, wrapped around a block of ice with the rope and grapple clamped in his jaws. Ordinarily Ronar would have been appalled that his life had depended on the tenacity of the creature's bite, but today he lacked the energy. He only laughed and tussled the furry head. How the Worm had beaten him there he never discovered.

Ronar, Tigermine, and the owl advanced to see what they'd won by their ascent. They found a vista as dauntingly beautiful as any in a dream. They had reached the continent's edge. Massive ice floes lay jumbled against this, its final rampart. The sea beyond was a reticulation of dark water and pale ice. In the distance, floating cakes of ice dwindled to mere flakes that vanished in the mists rising from the frigid waters. The Sea of Cold lay serene beneath the sweeping drapery of the auroral light. But the ice wall itself proved this was the gentlest mood of an often-furious body of water. The wall was nothing but a mass of floes driven onto the shore by countless storms, then welded together by freezing spray.

Subdued, Ronar returned to the wall's landward brink. He could barely see the sledge, far below in the multicolored gloom. He flung the hook over the side, fishing around until he caught the sledge. He braced himself against the block Tigermine had used and started hauling. Even on Colibdis the loaded sledge weighed more than three hundred pounds. Ronar was panting and very glad when the runners at last came into view.

Heart pounding, Ronar retrieved his binocular and scanned the horizon mists. No island marred the marbled surface of ice and water. Yet out there somewhere lay Hyperborea and his destination. Seeking warmth, Ronar moved closer to Tigermine. The dream-lit realm before him was a silent vastness to dwarf and disconcert even such a lover of the wilds as himself.

The time was near midnight. Fatigue made the horizon shift and the ghostlights shiver in Ronar's vision. A few feet below the ridgetop was a sheltered ledge. There, huddled in the tent, Ronar and his companions spent a last night on land. Already, the Red Plain, Thunderbird, the Skye Island, and even Nartar seemed to belong to the far side of another life, while Earth seemed less real than the shadow of a dream. He was a polar wanderer, and would remain one for as far into the future as he could foresee.

The silence was not quite absolute. Ronar thought he heard the faintest rustlings and cracklings of the aurora's phantom searchlights.

Chapter 16

In the Regions of Ice

Ronar fell into a routine more rigorous and austere than any he had ever known or contemplated. He became a creature of the ice, subsisting on what he could glean from it while still traveling miles every day, a way of life he had never anticipated while measuring the redshifts of distant galaxies.

It was worst at the beginning. Reaching the pack ice required a hard descent over chaotic slabs that had been tossed ashore by the seas. More than once Ronar had been obliged to heave the sledge overhead to set it on some tilted block, with no guarantee it wouldn't slide into an unseen crack, or even into the water.

Things got little easier after that. The floes nearest the shore were sometimes widely spaced, often unstable, and always in motion. The sledge was both a curse and a boon under these conditions. If it ever fell in with Ronar still in the harness, he would follow. Even the briefest swim in these waters would be fatal. On the other hand, when faced with a gap too wide to jump, the sledge could sometimes be pushed across to form a temporary bridge. If he ever lost the sledge he might as well jump in after it.

So he proceeded, making gains measured in feet and yards, balancing on tippy slabs, risking gaps just a bit too wide for comfort, or waiting for them to narrow.

Probably it was only Tigermine who made this part of the trek possible. The worm turned out to be as well adapted to life on the ice as on the land. He was a powerful swimmer, undeterred by the frigid water, apt to dive into any handy polynya. Half the time he'd pop back up with some creature wriggling in his jaws. Usually it was a fish, or at least something fishlike, but sometimes the sea would yield up strange lifeforms. Tigermine sometimes surfaced with a diaphanous globular creature in his mouth. These were living lattices, crystal birdcages covered by iridescent membranes, filled with fluids and jellies. Tigermine ate them with relish, but Ronar found them unpleasant. He preferred fish, which at least had a hint of blood and salt in their pale flesh.

It soon became obvious that an Ice Worm of Tigermine's size wasn't exactly a predatory terror. When he encountered a creature of any size he didn't seem to recognize it as prey. Seals basking in the fugitive sunlight didn't catch his attention, although when Ronar killed one with an arrow, the Worm accepted the meat readily enough, as did the crippled owl. Ronar had yet to figure out the relationship between the owl and the Worm. Tigermine derived no obvious benefit from the bird's presence. Perhaps he simply enjoyed keeping a pet. On land Ronar had seen the owl fluttering after rodents rousted from the snow by the Worm's passage, which might explain the bird's attachment to the worm.

One large mammal equipped to prey on seals was the polar bear. Whenever they saw one loping along, Tigermine would immediately flatten into an inconspicuous "snow bank". Ronar would stand still until the bear was gone. He had no wish for a confrontation, magic sword or no.

The character of the ice gradually changed. There were fewer open leads to straddle or circumvent, but there were frequent pressure ridges, jagged barriers to scramble over. After a while, the ice became so solid that they might have been crossing a barren land rather than a frozen ocean.

Each day's progress left the suns a degree lower in the sky. Ronar kept track of this and was able to anticipate the day when Photos failed to clear the horizon at all, while Kudu was only a red blob making a brief transit along the southern horizon. The next few days consisted of varying degrees of twilight as the suns moved around just below the horizon.

In another week they left even the twilight behind, entering a land of endless night. Time lost all meaning except as an abstraction applied to navigation. Without the suns to establish a natural rhythm of rest and movement, they traveled until they could go no further, rested as they must, and ate when the opportunity presented itself.

The weather maintained an austere neutrality that was all Ronar dared hope. The air was bitter, but at least it was calm and clear. The suns might be invisible, but they powered constant auroral activity. The endless plain of ice shone beneath shimmering curtains of pastel radiance: ghostly green, scarlet, aquamarine and gold. The flickering of the beams and streamers was the only motion in the bleakness around them.

The stars turned, Sinanna waxed and waned, and the Lever of Heaven climbed steadily.

In the spirit-light of moon and aurora, the dangers of the ice were easy to see. Polynyas were gashes of profound blackness. Tigermine always took the opportunity to slip into them, rare as they'd become, leaving Ronar to wait for his return. The food that was the usual result made the waits worthwhile. Except for these interruptions, the business of walking was so uneventful, so automatic, that Ronar glided into reveries that seemed to have no end.

When sleep could be deferred no longer Ronar would set up camp. He'd long since given up trying to drive the poles into the ice. Instead he'd reconfigured the tent into a freestanding bubble of hide held down only by the weight of its occupants. It could barely hold the man, Worm, and owl, which was just as well. It was easier to stay warm in close quarters.

During one sleep Ronar awoke to find Tigermine writhing and twisting, making little anxious bleats. Ronar reached out in the darkness to stroke the round furry head, but Tigermine would not be quieted. At last, with a panicky wail, the Worm crawled out from beneath him and slithered through the exit flap. A fading sound of fluttering feathers announced that the owl had gone as well.

Ronar lay back, ready to attribute this behavior to some perverse Ice Worm mood. His companion would no doubt return when he was ready.

But as silence returned, Ronar became aware that it was no longer absolute. Just at the edge of hearing, an eerie quaver hung in the air, suspended over a rumble that rose and fell around the threshold of audibility.

Frowning, Ronar sat up to locate the source of the mournful sounds, but they seemed to be coming from everywhere. Another attack from Namirnakh?

Ronar settled back in uneasy puzzlement. As his ear touched the wad of clothing he used for a pillow the sound doubled in volume. Ronar swept his pillow aside and put his ear directly to the tent floor. The rumblings were louder again. They were coming from the ice itself, or from beneath it, and they were getting louder all the time.

A sense of urgency overtook him. He scrambled out of his sleeping bag and lit a candle. Was the ice about to break up? Long, drawn-out cries of some unearthly sort added themselves to the mix as he laced his boots. Now he could feel a tremor in the ice as well.

Scooping up everything in the tent, he crawled out into utter blackness. A deck of clouds had rolled in, blotting up every bit of starlight that might have made it to the ground. The strange moaning filled this otherwise featureless universe, while the ice trembled beneath him.

Cursing, Ronar searched for the candle he'd just put out and managed to get it re-lit. Its pathetic pool of yellow light brought into view a ten-foot radius of ice. It was enough to show, if he'd needed the additional evidence, that the ice was heaving and flexing all around. A chorus of pinging sounds added themselves to the growing uproar.

Another new sound—the tread of heavy pounding feet. A mountainous white form loomed out of the darkness—a charging polar bear. Ronar had no time to react. It didn't matter, for the bear brushed by him and kept on going. Another form appeared. This was Tigermine, slithering over the ice with the owl astride him. Like the bear, he too fled into the night, though he did offer the astronomer a glance of wide-eyed concern.

"Wait!" cried Ronar foolishly. "What's happening? Where are you going?"

There was no answer. Ronar could only stare past the glare of his candle, trying to penetrate the darkness that hid the wider world from his sight.

A crashing rending shattering sound assailed him, rolling over him with crackings and burstings and a vast reverberation that echoed in the spaces of his skull. His jaw went slack as his imagination tried to conjure a cause to match such a cacophony. Were icebergs calving into the sea somewhere nearby? Was a submerged volcano spurting molten rock into the icewater beneath him? Were his enemies detonating lightless bombs of wizardry? Anything seemed possible in the face of that overpowering din. It was like the collision of planets of glass.

Near panic, Ronar piled everything onto the sledge, including the still-assembled tent. He pushed and dragged the sledge to the top of a nearby pressure ridge.

Of all the possibilities he had considered, nothing prepared him for what he actually saw. First, fine lines of pale light spread over the ice in a cobweb of fractures—an electrostatic glow caused by the release of strains in the ice. The pattern sputtered out, and darkness returned, but only for a moment. A green-white glow bloomed in a distant area of shattered ice. Slowly, grandly, like a planet rising over the horizon, an awesome shape brought itself into view. Black water and huge slabs of ice fell in apparent slow motion as a vast form broke the surface. A wind came up, air displaced by the emerging shape. Ronar's candle failed, but he didn't notice.

It was a glowing latticework of ribs and braces, shot through with pulsing nodules and fleeting sparks. Its visible part was basically a hemisphere, but that simplicity was disguised by huge spines, membranes, fanlike structures, and filaments trailing into the water. An array of radial spokes opened outward at the tip of the tallest spike. From the rent thus created poured a column of fluid, also glowing faintly. The cataract fell for five seconds before reaching the water. The roar of its impact rolled over the ice for a similar time before reaching his ears. When the torrent was exhausted, the creature expanded and contracted its entire volume several times, creating a rush of air like wind entering a cavern.

Finally it gave a cry, a huge impersonal sound, like the tides made audible, complete and entire unto itself, making no acknowledgment of the lesser motes of living matter that shared its universe. Slowly the creature subsided, merging with the black waters, a living moon that had risen, set, and now continued on its way with celestial inevitability.

Darkness returned. Ronar bent and groped for the candle, which he re-lit and held aloft like a forlorn spark of normalcy, all but lost in a black, cold void throbbing with immense possibilities.

He was startled back to awareness by an angry, rising hiss and a glimpse of a black wall at the fringe of the candlelight. A waist-high wave of icy water swept by, surging up around the pressure ridge. Another wave came, and then another. The last was the largest...taller than the ridge.

If I get wet, I will die.

With that thought, Ronar's reflexes took over. He grabbed the sledge's harness and leaped over the passing crest. The wave caught the sledge and tried to pull it away, but Ronar held firm. He watched the black wall recede and disappear. He was madly grateful that he'd managed to stay dry. In this cold, even wet feet could be a disaster. Then he was struck by a pang of worry for Tigermine and the owl.

The water left behind by the waves quickly froze, leaving the surface skating-rink slick. When he was sure there'd be no more waves, Ronar climbed down, hunted for and lit another light, and set the tent up again. Some of the sledge's cargo had gotten wet, but it was well-wrapped enough to prevent much harm. The stuff he'd hurriedly thrown onto it, including the critical sleeping bag, was dry. He couldn't help doing a bizarre little capering dance. His relief over his dry bag struck him as exaggerated and ludicrous, but he knew how useless a soaked down bag was. He returned into the tent and bag, laying awake for hours, awaiting the return of his friends, trembling with awareness of what was possible in this world. His fellow travelers did not return.

He woke up, still alone. Poking his head outside, he found the darkness as absolute as before. The stillness seemed to echo with the memory of the immense entity that had revealed itself just hours before.

Ronar pondered the problem of the darkness. He hadn't enough candles to burn them every step of the way, nor was it easy to keep them lit in the open air. In his careful preparations for this trip he'd somehow neglected to include a simple lantern. Had he any other source of light? The only thing that occurred to him was the magic garnet on his finger. But blinding flashes of white and scarlet wouldn't be much help in making his way over the ice. Perhaps he could persuade the ring to emit the light steadily, without producing the sword. He stripped off his left mitten and looked blindly in the ring's direction. A mental summoning of the sword produced the red light, but it all-too-quickly escalated into the white flash and shattering sound that brought forth the blade. Dazzled, Ronar dropped the weapon and let it lapse back into elsewhere. He tried again. This time he sustained the light for several seconds before his concentration lapsed and the sword leaped forth once more.

After a dozen tries he was able to command a steady crimson glow by keeping in mind a vague image of the sword rather than actively summoning it. The pure red light turned the ice field into a magical expanse of uncut rubies. Best of all, the radiance warmed him a bit. This seemed at least as useful as the ring's ability to call forth the sword.

Without a star to steer by, he was left with his compass. The needle moved indecisively, pointing north with many a quaver. He was still far from the magnetic pole, but the magnetic field of Colibdis seemed weaker than Earth's at all times.

He walked slowly, troubled by Tigermine's absence, hampered by the coating of glare ice. The ice made the sledge move too easily—it slid up and bumped him every time he slowed down. Presently he reached a rougher area of disturbed ice. He must be walking right over that globular leviathan—he kept looking down, expecting to see the creature's luminescence filtering up through the ice, but it remained dark.

He longed to see the owl and Worm. Even if they were still alive, every mile he put between him and the site of their separation made their return less likely. Yet he couldn't afford to mope around hoping for them to reappear. With a sigh he lengthened his stride, casting out loss and loneliness as best he could. Despite his resolve, the words of the poem glided through his mind like the sinuous motions of Tigermine himself:

> *...and he's happy as can be*
> *gazing on that frozen sea*

purring loudly purring proudly
gazing on that endless sea
in his lone electric palace
of Aurora Borealis
in the flickering fleeting lights
of his O so northern nights.

The hour hand of his watch swept round and round in meaningless circles. Clouds came and went, snow fell and ceased, and the wind blew more or less strongly. The auroral lights revealed ice mountains in the distance, growing more common as he went on. These were icebergs, locked in place by the winter pack ice, no doubt wanderers during the summer. Their numbers implied a nearby shore where glaciers crept down to the sea. At last, during one long march, Ronar spied a bank of mist in the far distance, a mist which hardened into ice cliffs and jutting fingers of land as he approached. The crossing of the ice had taken four weeks. Here at last was Hyperborea.

Few would have recognized the man who stepped ashore on that bleak continent. His beard was wild and full, white with frost and icicles from the moisture in his breath. His lean form had been further pared by the rigors of his travels, until now he consisted mainly of bone and sinew.

The flow of the glaciers buckled the sheet ice at their bases into pressure ridges for miles around. Ronar struggled over the ridges, avoiding the glaciers by mounting saurian-looking spines of rock that hadn't yet been ground away. These he followed inland while the stars turned nearly parallel with the horizon and the Lever of Heaven climbed the last few notches toward the zenith. The interglacial rock widened and smoothed out. The glaciers on either side diminished, until finally he hiked over an un-channeled sheet of ice blemished only rarely by weathered keels of rock. Hyperborea, or at least this northernmost part of it, was lifeless. Perhaps far to the west and south it was different.

The cold deepened even further. Despite the heat emitted by his ring, Ronar was forced to rub life back into his frozen feet every time he stopped. His toes were yellow, except where they were turning black. This was no way to travel, suffering daily frostbite, but he knew of no alternative. He fashioned a lamp to warm his sleeping quarters slightly, the fuel being oil from the seals he and Tigermine had preyed upon. Only the small flame burning in a tin cup made the tent bearable. He burned the straw in his boots as it became too sodden and compacted to insulate effectively, its smoke adding a new element of rankness to the air.

Hyperborea remained barren, offering no scrap of forage. Ronar still had some bits of meat and blubber, along with a few handfuls of dried fruit to fend off the ravages of scurvy. It was a diet barely sufficient for a man at ease. Considering the rigor of his travel, he was all but fasting. Another week of this might see him too weak to travel, or dead of hypothermia. But he sensed the nearness of his goal, and his strength did not fade yet.

Then Ronar's luck with the weather failed. A black tide of clouds rolled across the stars, and a merciless wind kicked puffs of ice needles into his eyes. Another storm would surely finish him. He trudged onward, his mouth assuming a bitter curve as he considered the possibility of death so close to his goal. In irritation and defiance he vowed to go on until his joints could bend no longer. But some part of him foresaw that simple jackhammer determination wouldn't be enough this time. He kept looking for another solution. At last he surprised himself by considering a new possibility.

After some hesitation, he shrugged and lifted his head to the wind. "Gods of Colibdis, hear me! I am ignorant of you. I don't know how closely you watch over the antics and misadventures of men. I've heard of a god of storm and cold called Boreas. I now ask Boreas to call away this storm. If I'm stopped or killed, the god Varanu may be displeased, for I have been sent here by him—although I don't yet know why."

That was all he could bring himself to say.

The wind did not abate, nor did the sky clear. The red ring-light revealed nothing. Since he'd expected nothing, he shrugged again and went on.

Suddenly the ring sizzled out like a coal plunged into icewater. A rift opened in the clouds; cold blue beams of polar light shone down, glowing in a low haze of ice crystals carried along by the wind. Here and there the crystals spun into vortices like icy dust devils. A dim figure materialized in one of the whirlwinds, a form which Ronar perceived as a man made of frozen mists, with frosty stars flickering within as the winds permitted. His hair and beard were like feathery traces of cirrus, infinitely cold and remote. Eyes peered at him from a shaggy brow—eyes deep as the winter night, fathomless as the depths of glacial ice. Words and laughter came in the guise of a sibilant wind.

I approve of you. Go on your way in the peace of the night.

A snowy owl, wings spread wide, emerged from the swirling mists, soaring straight for Ronar's face. He raised his arms to fend it off, but felt no impact.

Ronar blinked and all was gone: owl, god, and storm. He blinked again. His ears rang with what the god had said. He felt faintly embarrassed. If this weren't Colibdis he'd write off the whole episode as a hallucination induced by hardship and isolation. He was half inclined to do so anyway. Shaking his head, he went on beneath the crystal-cold clarity of the polar sky while frost-bells tinkled in the air around him.

He passed between hills subdued and rounded by the tides of ice that had ebbed and flowed over the millennia. Now only their crowns projected above the icecap. He passed among them, a speck of warm living matter in this ultimate wild.

As a boy, Ronar had fancied he could perceive the workings of great invisible wheels, strange forces interlocking to motivate the stars, generating celestial music as their byproduct. Now these feelings returned anew, amplified and enhanced by the mystic solitude of his journey. He turned skyward many a haunted look, searching for a visible sign of impending change, but finding none. The stars continued serene as always. Beneath their serenity was something less easily discerned. Hidden forces of nature were moving along paths long ordained. The wheels were turning toward some event, like the gears of a clock moving toward the tolling of midnight.

More pragmatically, a sextant reading showed that the Lever of Heaven stood ninety degrees above the horizon. The North Pole of Colibdis was underfoot. But the compass needle, though uncertain, settled at last in one direction. The magnetic pole, his destination, must still lay beyond it. Ronar continued on.

Several days later the aurora flamed up in golden waves that chased each other across a purple sky. Straight ahead, just over the horizon, reddish lights flickered. Heart pounding, Ronar got out his compass and stared at it avidly. Not only did the needle not wander, it didn't move at all—the alcohol sealed in it had frozen. Ronar fired up his ring and brought it near the compass. The heat soon freed the needle. It spun lazily on its jeweled bearing, pointing to nothing, indicating everything.

Ronar hesitated in a daze. For an eternity he had been a traveler on the ice. It was a hard life, but one he understood. Now that was over. If he went forward, he would be called upon to do more than merely walk through the cold. Ahead was change, uncertainty.

No matter how many years he might live, a part of him would always be that wanderer on the ice.

Ronar stepped forward to learn the fate of Sha Totek and of the Earth.

Chapter 17

The Grey Portal

Ronar freed himself from the sledge, strung his whale-bone bow, and crept to the rim of a considerable crater in the ice, peering in with the utmost caution. Scarlet lights leaped and blossomed from the hands of the black-robed figures at the bottom. Magic fires washed over roughhewn pillars of rock jutting from the ice, casting shifting shadows on the gouts of steam that flashed up from each application of flame. The stones were arrayed in two major groups: first a large circle of linteled uprights, and within that a horse-shoe of five huge trilithons. The layout was partially obscured by the ice, but Ronar still knew Stonehenge when he saw it.

Clearly, this was a different Stonehenge. Entombment in the ice had preserved it, while the original was a half-toppled ruin. Here, slowly revealed by each flash of fire, was a Stonehenge as it must have appeared in the days when it was new. Ronar had no doubt that Namirnakh, an Earthman, had built it. Stonehenge had been ancient even to the Roman occupiers of Britain—a monument as mysterious to them as it was to all the civilizations that came after. Namirnakh must also have seen it, and found it worth remembering.

A grim smile crossed Ronar's face. Evidently, Namirnakh hadn't included the accumulation of the icecap in his calculations. Whatever its purpose might be, the wizards would be some time in freeing this mock Stonehenge. Ronar appraised the enemy's strength. They were fewer than he'd expected, but still numerous enough. About thirty wizards in robes of black and scarlet directed their energies against the ice. Stationed around them were half a dozen huge warriors in shining black armor, their visors aimed into the night. These leaned on spears with steel points as big as spades . Slung over their shoulders were swords longer than most men are tall. They impressed Ronar as creatures to be avoided. He kept a low profile, hoping the glare of the fire would prevent the guards from seeing much beyond it.

Ronar saw no sign of Sha Totek or his allies. Possibilities sifted through his mind: they'd never arrived; they'd been destroyed; they'd been beaten and scattered; they were nearby plotting an attack. He discarded the first idea when an intense blast of firelight revealed bodies stacked like wood on the far side of the crater. He crept back from the rim and circled to the bodies. Flickers from the crater lit blackened flesh, fleshless jaws and skeletal hands. Metal ornaments were blobs of metal, while clothing was only a sooty stain on the ice. Here had been a pyre, but Ronar couldn't tell whether its fuel had been friends, foes, or a mixture. He searched for some distinctive angle of jaw or arch of cranium that would identify the remains of Sha Totek. Between his fatigue and the uncertain light, he saw his friend's face on every skull. Though his heart caught in his throat, he refused to believe that this forlorn ash-heap was the Sorcerer's resting-place. After all, this was Sha Totek—the five thousand-year-old de facto ruler of Colibdis—not some mistletoe-wielding Druid son of a bitch.

The weird incongruity of the scene arrested him for a moment—blackened bones, charred and recently ablaze, terribly out of place in the pristine landscape of Hyperborea, a land where life and death alike were little known.

Ronar abandoned the remains and crawled to survey the mock-Stonehenge from this new angle. There he saw something hidden from his former vantage—a dome, maybe eight feet high, perfectly featureless and mirror bright. It looked exactly like the magical bubble Sha Totek had erected over the Bronze Portal, except that it was golden rather than silvery. It sat on the ice a few yards from the outer circle of the monument.

Here was something to think about. Ronar saw no quick way to overcome the three dozen enemies below. By stealth and patience he might winnow them out one by one, but not in time to stop them from freeing this Grey Portal. For what else could it be but an alternate pathway to Earth?

He eyed the dome speculatively, certain it hid something that could alter the balance of power very quickly—one way or the other. Sha Totek might be imprisoned within it—or perhaps some terrible wizard imprisoned by Sha Totek before he fell. In any event, he must take the chance—he would crack that dome if it was within his power.

Ronar returned to the sledge and dumped its cargo. He paused to watch the activity below. A strange feeling of bewildered recklessness welled up within him. He grinned fiercely and foolishly. After the dreamlike grandeur of his polar odyssey, the action he was now about to take seemed painfully ludicrous.

He grabbed the sledge, rushed forward, and leaped aboard as it tipped over the rim of the crater. He hadn't ridden a sled in decades—the sudden speed as he hurtled down the steep slope took him by surprise. He shot down toward the crater's center and the Grey Portal itself. Hoarse cries of alarm rose up from around him. A blast of fire roared overhead, singing his back and choking him with steam as it struck the ice. For an instant the runners sprayed him with hot water. As he clattered along he let loose a bellow full of every violent emotion he possessed.

This speed had its advantages, such as preventing his immediate destruction, but it also deprived him of a certain degree of control. This was no Flexible Flyer he was riding—it was heading for the center of the crater and that was that. With all eyes upon him, the wizards momentarily forgot to cast their fire. Ronar shot into the warm vapor smothering the excavation and suddenly found himself in the dark.

Wait! What if Sha Totek wanted to be in that magic dome? What if he'd taken refuge in it and was even now preparing to emerge and lay waste his enemies?

No time for such thoughts. He was committed. He heard or felt himself rush past someone in the darkness.

Someone finally thought to strike up a flare. The fog diffused it into a featureless red glare. A shadow ahead—a stone! Ronar flung himself off the sledge and rolled. The sledge shot straight into an upright of the "Sarcen circle", shattering into kindling. Despite everything, Ronar still managed an instant of regret that this thing which had helped to sustain him for so long was destroyed.

Ronar had no shortage of momentum and continued on. A trilithon loomed dead ahead—could he shoot between the uprights? No, the opening was too narrow. He hurled himself aside again but his shoulder still caught the stone, knocking the breath out of him and sending him spinning over the very center of the Grey Portal. He cried out—he felt an instant of appalling vertigo as he slid through and out again.

All was confusion within the crater. Still sliding, Ronar approached the other side of the "Sarcen circle", but this time he twisted to hit an upright feet first, absorbing the impact. He regained his feet and set out for the dome. The ice was treacherous—he was reduced to taking small, mincing steps just to stay upright. At least his enemies didn't have it any easier. Neither he nor they had thought to bring crampons or anything like them.

Before the dome stood an enormous sentry, sword poised, horned helmet at least a foot higher than Ronar's head. Breath steamed from the slits in the visor at what seemed inhumanly long intervals. Ronar approached steadily, eyes locked on the blackness within the visor. The warrior seemed indecisive in the face of this deliberate advance by a small unarmed man. He didn't seem to remember his purpose until Ronar was but a yard distant. Then he raised his iron sword, but by then it was too late for him. Ronar suddenly raised his left fist, crying "Look at this!" A gout of white and scarlet brilliance erupted from his ring. The warrior howled and clawed at his visor. A shattering sound battered him further.

Ronar struck with all the force he could urge into his steel blade. It was sufficient to cut open the guard's cuirass and rip halfway through his torso. Wrenching the sword free of the toppling corpse, Ronar turned to the dome. In five seconds a dozen angry Darteharnians would be at his back. He'd have only one chance, so this one stroke must contain every bit of energy that rage and need could impart. Two-handed, he raised the blade overhead, trying to visualize all the perils and pains of life, trying to believe that a single righteous blow could destroy them forever. He focused all his will into the vane of steel that quivered in his grip, releasing all his passion in one transcendent stroke.

With a deafening *clang!* the blade exploded against the dome, shattering into shrapnel that spun away and clattered onto the ice. Ronar looked in stupefaction at the broken stump in his hands, then stared at the dome in stunned dismay.

It bore a scratch as a result of his effort.

A white light was glowing behind his eyes. He put up a hand and brought it down covered with blood from a large gash around his right eye. He barked out ragged laughter, spun, and hurled the broken hilt at his mob of enemies, striking one in the chest. They kept advancing, their haste hilariously awkward thanks to the ice. Ronar yanked out his dagger and prepared to fight and die.

Then, oddly, the assembled wizards and warriors skidded to a halt. Some of them stopped too abruptly and sat down hard. Surely Ronar couldn't appear so formidable, not to so many! But the dismay of his enemies was unmistakable in the red and green light illuminating the crater. Wait a minute—green light? Ronar looked down at his feet—he was casting a long shadow in the green glow that was waxing behind him. He turned.

The scratch on the dome was glowing a dazzling green—and it was lengthening, widening, into a fracture, then a crack, and then into a rift which emitted shafts of jade-green light that lit the bases of the clouds and dimmed the fires of the Darteharnians. Ronar raised a hand against the glare and stood back. He'd first seen this green light ages ago in Sha Totek's Tower: the All-Purpose Viridian. The radiance spread quickly and engulfed the dome, which flared like a green sun before fading into nothingness. Purple spots swan before Ronar's eyes as darkness returned. He barely made out the shadowy figure that swayed in the circle in the ice where the dome had stood.

Ronar blinked and rubbed his eyes. Sha Totek staggered forward, glanced around, and cried, "At last, my efforts against that damnable golden dome have prevailed." His gaze landed on Ronar. "And here, by an excellent coincidence, stand you. What kept you?"

"It is no coincidence. I nicked the dome and set you free, ruining the sword in the process."

Sha Totek's eyes bugged and his jaw dropped. "Nicked the dome? That dome? With a sword? Very impressive. What kept you?" he asked again, wearily. "Never mind. Great Osiris, how you've changed. Come on, let's get out of here before they can regroup."

"What do you mean? You're free now. Let's wipe them out while they're still disorganized!"

"Ronar, look at me." Sha Totek struck a pale light from his hand, forcing Ronar to look upon his wan, wasted face. "There's not a lot left here, my friend. These wizards already beat me once, and they can probably do it again. But their main concern is to get through this Grey Portal. If we back off now they may ignore us. Let's leave them to their work."

Ronar was incredulous. "Leave them to their work? Aren't we here to stop them?"

"I don't know. I hope not. We can't do it. We can't defeat these bastards, and we have no chance of destroying the Portal. That ring of stones is only a marker. The real Portal is something I don't understand. Whatever it is, it is very dangerous. Only Varanu can undo this damage that Namirnakh worked for centuries to create."

"But Varanu isn't here," insisted Ronar. "We are, because he sent us. Why would he do that if we can't accomplish anything?"

"Only Varanu can undo the damage. If he hasn't come yet, he may never. I'll try to summon him again, though I've never tried a stunt more audacious. Now let's get out of here, damn it."

But they'd argued too long to win a clean retreat. Red fires kindled around the wizards who stood ranked around the trilithons. The five remaining warriors approached on spike-toed boots. Plainly they meant to try their luck.

"I'll have to delay them," said Sha Totek resignedly. "Occupy them for a moment while I prepare something for them. Bring out your sword."

"My sword was destroyed— "

"Summon it."

"I said it was destroyed."

"I said summon it!"

Ronar shrugged and obeyed, if only to shut the sorcerer up. To his amazement and gratification, what shivered into his hand was not a broken hilt but the great shining blade, whole and unflawed.

"There you see one of the virtues of Gromer's Spell of Encoded Matrices," muttered the sorcerer. "Each smallest particle is assigned its place in the matrix, and each returns to its place when the blade lapses from the here and now, no matter what derangement has taken place in the interim. That way, the King is assured of its return even if you should decide to cast it into a volcano."

Ronar shuffled forward, wondering how long he could delay these five giants, even with the sword. More likely they would simply chop him down. Now he wished he'd gotten those sword fighting lessons Sha Totek had mentioned back in Thunderbird.

Fortunately, it was only seconds before the Sorcerer called him back. Ronar retreated from the deliberate approach of the huge warriors. He found Sha Totek staring intently at the circle of their enemies. His eyes were sunken and haggard, but alight with purpose and resolve. He swept his arms in a decisive gesture; the air temperature dropped a further fifty degrees. Ronar had to close his eyes to keep them from frosting over. He heard a splash and a number of curses and grunts. The moment of enhanced cold passed. Ronar opened his eyes.

It had happened so quickly that the water scarcely had a chance to flow. The Darteharnians were now locked in place by solid ice. The warriors immediately set to work chipping their way out with their weapons, while the wizards directed careful fingers of crimson flame to the task. A few of them had fallen when their footing went liquid beneath them. They were gone, or marked by protruding hands that clawed at the air and then grew still.

Sha Totek turned away. "Do you think we can get out of here now?"

"Actually, I'm not sure we can."

"Why not?"

"We're at the bottom of a very slick icy crater with steep walls. We'd need a rocket or something similar to get out."

"Oh, by the Nipples of Nut."

"I can try hacking out footholds with the sword."

"By all means."

But any progress made by this means was painfully slow. While Ronar was chipping away, Sha Totek asked, "What is this 'rocket' thing you mentioned?"

"It works by reaction. If you hurl something away from you, the reaction pushes you in the opposite direction with equal force."

Sha Totek said derisively, "Oh, come now. You mean if I toss a snowball at forty miles an hour, I am hurled with equal speed in the other direction?"

Ronar spared him a pained glance. "That's not exactly what I said. You have a bit more mass than the snowball."

Sha Totek looked embarrassed. "Oh."

Ronar suddenly stopped his work, let the sword vanish, and fumbled his compass out of his pocket.

"What are you doing?" asked Sha Totek. "I assure you we've already come to the right spot."

Ronar held the compass out to him. "Does your bag of magic tricks include the ability to greatly amplify the magnetism of this needle?"

Sha Totek scowled. "I neither understand nor perceive this 'magnetism' you speak of."

"Damn. Well, could you at least enlarge the needle?"

The sorcerer rolled his eyes. "You have a faulty view of magic if you think enlarging objects is a parlor trick to be casually performed."

"But can you do it?"

"I don't think so! What good would it do, anyway?"

"Oh, hell. I thought maybe if we had a powerful magnetic force we could use it to repel the sword and kick us out of here." Ronar recalled the weapon and resumed his work.

Sha Totek allowed a few more ice chips to fly while he formulated a comment.

Ronar preempted him. "I know, I know. I'll just keep on hacking."

"Wuh-wuh-wayooooooh!" Suddenly the sorcerer started to spin as wildly as an unbalanced top.

Ronar looked at him in vexed amazement. "What are you doing now?"

"Some-somebody-over there-has hit me-with-a-Whirligig-spell! Ooof!" Sha Totek fell, still windmilling furiously, and slid down the mild slope that was all they'd managed to climb so far.

Ronar forgot the sword and followed him down. "I'll grab you!"

"No-we'd-only-share-in-the-magic. I-must-neutralize—"

Ronar seized on an idea. "No! Don't neutralize a thing. I'm going to grab you." He lay down on his stomach, just out of range of Sha Totek's flailing limbs. Bracing himself for a shock, he reached out and grabbed an ankle as it flashed by. Though jarred by the impact he managed to hang on and grab the other ankle. Sure enough, they began to spin as one object around their mutual center of mass. Ronar had to hang on with all his strength against the centrifugal force that tried to tear them apart.

"Waagh! Are you trying to wring my feet off at the ankles?" yelped Sha Totek.

"Another second!" When Ronar thought they'd achieved maximum speed, he let go, not even guessing at an aiming point, as the world was a mere blur around him. They shot away from each other at high speed. Sha Totek was flung straight up the crater wall. Ronar heard him wailing all the way up, gasping as he flew over the rim into empty air, and grunting as he thumped down onto the ice beyond it.

Ronar hurtled straight at the mock-Stonehenge and the black-clad Darteharnians who were planted near it. Again he found himself desperately dodging the huge upright stones. A fireball or two scorched his heels, and an ice-embedded warrior leaned over to poke at him with his halberd as he passed. The flash and glare of the manifested Sword of Bran convinced him to give Ronar the right of way. Finally he was past his enemies and beyond the rings of stones. The crater wall remained to be surmounted. He was only halfway up when he realized he didn't have enough momentum to make it. With the rim only fifteen feet away his speed bled away toward nothing.

With a roar of frustration Ronar called out the sword, held the blade overhead, and flung it into the crater with all his strength. The sword was back in his hands before it could hit the ice. Twice more it served as his "rocket fuel", but it wasn't nearly enough to keep him from losing speed. Just as he was about to slide back down, he whacked the blade into the ice. Ronar arrested his descent by his grip on the hilt. Gingerly he squirmed around to get his feet on the guards that projected winglike from the grip. His position was still most precarious, for if he lost his balance he'd have nothing to grab onto but the sword's naked edge. Finally he had a somewhat stable perch, half lying on his back, half standing on the sword as though it were an inverted pogo stick. He twisted his head to see how far away the rim was now. It looked like about five feet, though it was hard to be sure with his eyes still dazzled by afterimages of the multiple manifestations of the sword.

Ronar drew a deep breath, crouched down, and with an all-or-nothing effort kicked off as hard as he could. The sword broke free and went skittering into the crater, but Ronar managed to scramble over the rim at last.

Dizzy, with his vision spotty and his ears ringing, Ronar wobbled to his feet. Feeling incomplete without them, he grabbed the binocular from his pile of equipment and stuffed it into his parka before loping around the crater to the place where Sha Totek awaited him. They examined each other anxiously for a moment and then broke into uproarious laughter for no reason they could have explained.

When they'd calmed down they looked into the crater to see what their enemies were up to. By now the Darteharnians had cleared the ice down to their knees and were making rapid progress.

"Those Darteharnians blasted out this entire crater?" asked Ronar.

"They sure did. Their progress has slowed, though. They're tiring, and there aren't as many of them as there were when we got here."

"What happened to your Eranian friends?"

Sha Totek sat down heavily, taking a moment to reacquaint himself with the sight of open air. He said in a grey, colorless voice, "Not all made it this far. One drowned in the Sea of Cold. One froze. Two stragglers were hypnotized and eaten by Ice Worms. I'm somewhat stunned that you were able to survive your solo journey."

"So am I," muttered Ronar.

"You admit that? You have changed. We arrived to find Namirnakh's minions already on the scene, working to melt out this Portal. The others engaged them in battle while I tried to summon Varanu. They were killed one by one, though at a high cost to the Darteharnians. Good old Gromer locked the magic of the wizards into the form of the Flame of Ahriman. They're still powerful, but no longer versatile. That damned Whirligig spell must have been a trick of one of the guards. Gromer died while placing a spell of immutability on the ice to slow them down. They trapped me while I was still trying to contact Larlaninulius, and kept me aside as a prize for Namirnakh. I should have fought and died for all the good I've done here."

"Then Namirnakh isn't here?"

"No," said Sha Totek darkly, "he most certainly is not." He closed his eyes and seemed to turn inward. "I suppose—I must try again to call up Varanu. No other option occurs to me." Ronar watched him for a moment, then sat down beside him and turned to peer into the crater.

The Darteharnians were already free of the ice and were busily excavating Mockhenge once more. Their progress was rapid; the great trilithons were almost completely exposed. Sha Totek's melting spell must have undone Gromer's spell of immutability—a serious lapse of judgment on the sorcerer's part. Ronar wondered how long he could expect his friend to go on without breaking down completely. It didn't occur to him to ask the same question about himself.

If the center of Mockhenge indeed marked the Portal, it ought to be in sight by now, but Ronar saw nothing unusual there. The Darteharnians, having finished their work, milled around, their fires guttering to desultory flickers just bright enough to show their expectant faces. Ronar found himself sharing their vigil. He wished he could just go down there and ask them what was going on. This whole business of unreasonable enemies willing to kill you was something he'd hoped he'd left behind in the war. He stared at the brooding megaliths of the Grey Portal as he'd once stared at the eclipsing Moon as it covered the last brilliant fragment of the Sun. The onset of totality then had been just as sudden as the awakening of the Grey Portal.

The door was open at last. A pale glow lit the trilithon horseshoe. A mighty wind surged from the Portal, a hundred degrees warmer than the air of Hyperborea. To Ronar it felt like a tropical breeze, thick with a scent he'd almost forgotten—the fragrance of living greenery. Here was the breath of Earth, sucked through by the thin, bitter air of polar Colibdis, flowing through a wound in space that had no right to be. It rushed up in a roaring column, dispersing the clouds, clearing a spreading pool of starry sky. The rime in Ronar's beard melted away. The cut on his face stung and throbbed.

The wizards of Darteharn passed through the Portal, stepping onto the distant world that had once nurtured their distant ancestors. But they no longer belonged there. They'd befoul an already troubled world with their magic and their heedless evil. Ronar leaped to his feet. "That's why Varanu hasn't come. This Portal hadn't activated yet. This must be the moment of disorder that Varanu had foreseen."

The Sorcerer was oblivious, still entranced; Ronar didn't dare interfere. He turned from him, stared into the crater with the realization that he possessed that most precious of gifts: the power to act. He grinned, for once without self-consciousness. After all his effort in escaping it, he flung himself back over the crater rim. Shooting down the slope like a human toboggan, he howled like a basso wolf as he passed by the weapons of the remaining warriors. The outer circle of uprights flashed by, then the trilithons loomed ahead, and he was through.

There was no sense of transition, nor any wrenching or dizziness or disorientation. He simply passed from one place to another as though the light-millennia between them were entirely absent. He got to his feet on hard turf, conscious of a weight that made him exult in defying the rigorous gravity of Earth once more. Moonlight shone down, and the great stars of Orion and Canis Major blazed like keen blue diamonds. Ronar had returned to the youth and vitality of the Milky Way Galaxy, urgent and splendid compared to the tired yellow lights of the intergalactic void.

Ronar searched the moonlit circles of the real Stonehenge for those who had preceded him. They hadn't gone far. The wizards of Namirnakh were obviously unprepared for the sudden increase in their weight. They sat on toppled stones, or crawled on hands and knees, or simply lay wherever they had fallen, their robes flapping in the gale. Wherever they were, whatever their attitude, magic was passing among them, and that was where the danger lay. Let magic gain a foothold on Earth and it might never be erased.

Ronar stared at the lightless garnet on his finger. Here on the Salisbury Plain it seemed incredible that it had ever been capable of summoning an ancient sword through some mystic dimension. But when he turned his mind to it the light came easily, and the blade followed with a thunder-crack that echoed far into the English night. He called out over the wind between the worlds: "Listen to me, you wizards! You have a simple choice. Return through the Portal at once, or die. Go back! You've shrunk beneath the measure of this world. Magic is meaningless here, and magic is all that you know."

A wizard sitting on the moon-washed face of the so-called Altar Stone turned a weary, age-worn face toward Ronar and said, "You of the arrogant eyes—don't rest so secure in your wisdom. Your mind flits from star to star in an effort to understand their gross properties, but you ignore the subtler powers that inform your own world. I sense forces here that you would not acknowledge. The reign of Namirnakh will not be as foreign as you believe."

Ronar's thoughts slid downward through levels of smallness until they flickered among particles leaping in and out of reality with an utter unpredictability that was the ghostly basis of "objective truth". Even the electrons that carried his thoughts moved and existed at the whim of these quantum forces of indeterminacy, coupling his very mind into the inherent unreality of space and time. His experiences on Colibdis had given him a look at a new, more enigmatic cosmos. Although he couldn't bring himself to like what he'd found, he feared it no longer.

"Excuse me, are we boring you?"

Ronar looked up from his reverie and turned a frosty grin on his opponent. "Not at all. But I'm afraid your intelligence is dated. I have learned something of magic in the recent past—more, I suspect, than you know yourself."

The wizard sniffed in disdain. "Then cast us out with a spell. The magic leaking through the Portal allows this."

"I haven't gone into the needless detail of formal spells. Right now the only magic you need to worry about is the spell that brings me this weapon. Get your sorry selves through that Portal, now." The great blade caught glints of a moonlight foreign to its alien steel.

"Very well. We have done enough already. We have no wish to die needlessly."

The wizards dragged themselves through the vagueness of the Portal, where they stood up and walked stiffly out of sight.

Seen through the Portal, Colibdis looked like a museum diorama. Ronar's belief in the very reality of the planet seemed to be draining away. Turning his back on the Portal, he walked slowly out of the remains of the trilithon horseshoe. The wind diminished as he left the Portal behind, but it was still strong when he stepped past the Sarcen circle to look into the night.

It was Midwinter Day. Modern Druids were present to observe the occasion, twenty or thirty of them, of all ages and sexes, goggling at him in wonder. They wore romantic-looking white robes, but apart from that they looked like teachers and bus drivers and accountants. A stout middle-aged man with horn-rimmed glasses stepped forward with an offering of mistletoe, but he couldn't bring himself to approach too closely this eerie vision—a huge, barbaric warrior emerging from a distant past.

Ronar showed them little charity. He sneered at their contrived, synthetic resurrection of Druidism and was tempted to shoo them through the Portal to learn from masters of the real thing. His harsh laughter rang in their memories for the rest of their lives, disillusioning some of the dreamier souls among them.

Ronar remembered the oblivious Sha Totek, sitting alone and helpless on the ice of a terribly distant world. After a moment's internal debate he turned and passed back through the Portal, emerging to find the Darteharnians milling about in confusion and staring skyward. Even the warriors had dropped their weapons to stare overhead. Though there was nothing to be seen, Ronar felt the same urge that prompted the Darteharnians. The fighting was over. Whatever was about to happen was outside the province of swords and halberds.

Again trapped in the crater, he walked to the side nearest the still-entranced Sha Totek and called, "Sha Totek, wake up. Varanu is coming."

The sorcerer blinked and looked down at him. "What—how do you know?"

"I can feel it."

Sha Totek got unsteadily to his feet. He approached the crater as though sleepwalking and slipped over the rim. Ronar caught him and helped him to sit up, repressing a wince as he realized how the sorcerer had declined in the past months. His body felt light and fragile as an empty cocoon. Ronar sat beside his friend. Together they awaited the event foretold by the unaccountable sense of mystery in the air, an anticipation that made every heartbeat a poignant and unforgettable moment. Turning sheepish glances upon one another, each saw tears coursing down the other's cheeks. Beaming like children, they turned to face the portentous stage-set of the Grey Portal.

With shocking suddenness their minds rotated beyond normal space, their vision expanding in a way they could never have described. They could actually see the Portal—not the mere marker, but the very rift in space-time that was the passage between worlds. Ronar's thoughts stumbled as he tried to qualify exactly what he was seeing. Looked at one way, it was a multidimensional gridwork of glowing threads delineating the structure of space, funneling into a vortex that led like an inverted tornado into deep space. Seen another way, space and time themselves became meaningless, resolving into an understructure of flickering colorless motes, with the Portal still perceptible as an indefinable flow. The one thing clear to Ronar was the strain involved—whatever this Portal was, it was being held in place by some unnatural force. The tension of it was strumming space-time like an out-of-tune cello.

Ronar looked at Sha Totek, noting the minute warping of space produced by the mass of his body. The Sorcerer was gazing at the curved column of the Portal with awestruck rapture. He whispered, "Varanu—is aware."

"Then we've won," said Ronar firmly.

Sha Totek turned a wry glance in Ronar's direction and said, "Won? Ronar, you are a very silly man. If Namirnakh had ever been serious about this Grey Portal, he wouldn't have sent so trivial a force to take it. As I feared, he merely used it to lure me from the Bronze. No doubt that Portal is under assault at this moment, if not taken already. I must give credit where it's due—not only has Namirnakh colluded with Ahriman to bring this about, he has manipulated Varanu himself to his advantage."

"I see," said Ronar bleakly.

"Don't take it too hard. A journey in which we get to see through the eyes of Varanu can't be a total waste."

As suddenly as they'd come, their enhanced perceptions were shut off, leaving a void that seemed more profound than blindness. Again the stars burned yellow and the ice glimmered beneath fugitive auroral flickers. Before them, the minions of Namirnakh stood frozen in place like smaller stones thrown up around the mock-Stonehenge. A nighthawk swept out of the Portal, tumbled like a leaf, then found its wings and floated on the updraft of Terrestrial air.

Then the howl and whirl of the wind seemed to retreat into insignificance. A majestic stillness flowed from every cubic inch of space until the universe was filled with a serene and watchful sense of expectation. Ronar's subconscious bubbled closer to the surface in these waning hours of darkness. With the sheathing around his emotions eroded by exhaustion and long privation, he sensed a profound connection between himself and everything that exists. He knew this was a truth not often perceptible to imperfect beings such as himself.

All right, he thought, *let's see how this 'god' makes order out of madness.*

Varanu did not so much arrive as become apparent, condensing out of something more fundamental than the atoms of the air.

Ronar and Sha Totek rose to their feet and stood very straight. Ronar kept his chin high as he faced this nexus of his perplexity and dismay. The visual centers of his brain perceived a mass of coruscating lights, shifting and shimmering, brilliant yet transparent at the same time. As he'd feared, these ghostlights whirled and blinked with no semblance of order or purpose. They might as well have been a swarm of blurry fireflies caught in columns of rising and falling air. Their light, though intense, didn't sting or dazzle his eyes. It illuminated nothing around it and cast no shadows. It wasn't a true light at all, merely some sort of elflight of the mind. And if he persisted in seeing a manlike form in the midst of the sparkles, surely that was an illusion too.

A voice came to Ronar as from a great distance. The voice of Varanu? No, he recognized the words of Sha Totek, filtered through ethereal chords emitted by vibrations of space and time. *Don't be afraid to look deeper. If anyone can do it, it's you.*

Afraid? The word stung Ronar's self-image as a scientist and a man. Were his preconceptions so ingrained after all that he was unwilling to confront a new way of thinking? Did he have so much at stake in his old ideas that he couldn't bear to be proven wrong?

All the experiences of Ronar's life jelled into a moment of decision. He opened his mind to Varanu and quickly noticed that the god's visible manifestation was less random than he'd thought. Beneath the twinklings and swirlings were muted fringes of light and darkness—interference patterns by the look of them, but the interference of what sort of waves? Light waves? Or something more profound: gravity waves; perhaps waves of space itself?

Mystified yet encouraged, Ronar surrendered the last of his misgivings. Ignoring the Darteharnians cowering here and there, he walked forward to mingle with the phantom lights of Varanu.

Again his perceptions changed radically, yet the changes were not disturbing or even very startling. Rather they seemed obvious and natural, though afterwards he would wonder how his consciousness could adapt so readily to such exotic modes of thought.

Time stopped, though it didn't cease to exist. Ronar felt his duration in time as an extension through a dimension foreign to his normal experience. Just as his body had finite extensions in the three dimensions of space, so it had an extension through the dimension of time. His birth and death marked the endpoints. His birth was clearly apparent, and he knew he could also perceive his "depth" in time and so foresee his death if he cared to do so. He shied away from this possibility. Ronar had seen diagrams depicting the "world lines" of objects through space and time, but they'd never seemed very relevant to everyday human reality. Now the concept was not only real but self-evident. Time contained no marker labeled "the present" sliding from past to future at some predetermined rate. All times, every moment, were equally in existence, and the word "now" was ultimately meaningless. The illusion of the flow of time from one moment to the next was an artifact of consciousness. What purpose did it serve? To bring into being a single reality from an infinity of equally possible realities....

Implications and intimations darted at the outskirts of Ronar's mind, and he reeled, staggered by the immensity of ideas he could not fully encompass. The universe trembled on the verge of exploding into universes without end, of every conceivable variation, or of blinking out into nothingness, its essential unreality uncovered by the too-close examination of a conscious mind. He drew back, searching the dispassionate wholeness of Varanu for ideas he could endure.

The Grey Portal was in the forefront of the mind of Varanu. Ronar could now see it in time as well as in space. Its origin and nature were clear. It was a wormhole, a natural bridge through space-time, of which there were apparently very many in the universe. Long ago the Newtonian motions of the stars and planets had, in their mindless way, arranged for Colibdis to pass a few billion miles from one terminus of this particular wormhole. Namirnakh had perceived this, and over centuries had devoted much of his power to drawing the twisted filament of space closer to the surface of Colibdis, guiding it along the global magnetic field to the point of least resistance, this spot, the north magnetic pole. Once it was within range of the magic field of Colibdis, Namirnakh had taken full control, using it as a conduit for magic, commanding it to seek the Earth. Like a root threading through soil, the far end had quested through space-time, drawn to Stonehenge by the force of Namir-nakh's will. But Ronar had done what Varanu could not—he'd gone through the Portal and prevented it from being anchored at that far end—an act that would have eliminated its instability and made the link a permanent feature of the universe. He'd done it by compelling the wizards to give up and return home—an act beyond the ability of Varanu, who had no direct power over sentient minds. Somehow that revelation was the most stunning of all.

Through the eyes of Varanu, Ronar saw this Portal as a wrongness in space. In themselves, wormholes were common, even ubiquitous on the scale of the infinitesimal, where they constituted much of the basic structure of space and provided routes for the smooth flow of matter and energy. But this enormous one quivered with the strain of being held in place by the magic of Namirnakh. What was magic? An expansion and easing of the mind's interaction with the quantum workings of space.

Ronar radiated questions that were lost in the crystalline depths of the mind of Varanu. Why did magic exist on Colibdis, and not Earth? Was Varanu itself truly a conscious being? What was the function of the gods of Colibdis? Did they make the rules, or were those imposed from somewhere else?

One thing was certain—whatever Varanu was, its power was unmistakable. Ronar felt forces gathering, ringing through and shining from the space around him. Ronar's thoughts resonated with a clear, splendid music made by the interaction of all worlds and times. Varanu acted, and the Grey Portal was healed, closing upon itself as gently as water parted by an idle hand.

Ronar felt reborn. His mind soared. He had found an order subtler and more fertile with possibilities than any he'd dreamed of before. The old Newtonian ideas now seemed stifling, sterile, and confining. The mechanistic universe from which he'd always drawn comfort was superficial, an illusion, and a refuge from the responsibilities of free will. How had he ever reconciled this with his own fierce independence? Was he a solipsist, thinking that the laws of nature applied to everyone but himself? If so, perhaps it was time to assume that other thinking beings had the same properties of will and integrity that he'd always insisted upon in himself. For if the laws of Newton or even Einstein did not confine the physical universe, then the mind was least confined of all. All things were possible, though some were more probable than others. The mind stood in the unique position of being able to influence those probabilities at will. Every act of magic he'd seen on this world had screamed this at him. Now at last he could listen!

Dreamily, he wandered away from the glittering nodes of light that represented Varanu. Though he barely noticed, all around him the Darteharnians cowered and wailed, the shadows within them found out by a light from which there was no escape.

Ronar went to stand beside the sorcerer. Both looked at the fading lights dancing among the stones of Mockhenge. Ronar sensed a continuing concern in his friend, a worry that seemed mundane to Ronar in his present exalted state, yet still real enough.

Smiling slightly, Ronar considered their location on the macroscale of the planet, and on the microscale, with the subatomic particles making up their bodies flickering in and out of reality, continually retranslating themselves through space according to the probabilities of quantum law. It wasn't likely that they'd both spontaneously vanish, bore through thousands of miles of space and then reappear, but it wasn't impossible, either. He looked at Varanu, whose dispersal halted under his attention. For an instant Ronar and Sha Totek felt a scrutiny that was like having their hearts laid bare before the assembled intellects of the universe. Again they felt a gathering of forces. Atom by atom, they faded from the face of Hyperborea...

Chapter 18

The Battle of the Bronze Portal

...and re-materialized in a place as real as a dream, as distant as a legend—the sanctum of the Tower of Sha Totek.

The Sorcerer gave a howl of triumph, shaking off age and care like a film of dust. Strength in monstrous quantities poured into him. He swelled with vitality, his skin glowing like oiled mahogany, his eyes flashing incendiary sparks. His tattered garments went up in a flash of fire, revealing an outlandish costume resplendent with scarlet and purple and gold. "Oh my oh my oh MY!" he shouted. "I ought to go away more OFTEN, just so I can come BACK!" He rushed to a window, looked out briefly, then levitated his way down the access shaft. An evil chuckle floated up after him.

Ronar went to a window too, though less hurriedly. He leaned on the sill, calmly contemplating the wonders he'd just experienced, while shafts of ruddy suns-light fell through dust raised by a vast tumult. He barely noticed what was happening below.

Armies were clashing on the Red Plain. Beyond the walls of Sha Totek's compound, waves of black-armored warriors, both mounted and afoot, surged up against colorfully clad defenders. The fighting was thickest near the

Bronze Portal, but smaller units fought in isolated groups on the plain between Portal and Tower. Ronar barely glanced at them. His thoughts were far away.

Non-human creatures assaulted the defenders as well. Great black Teratorns, their Riders like blood blisters on their backs, swooped and harried, sometimes soaring skyward with severed heads or arms clutched in their talons, dropping them among the defending forces. Ronar's gaze idly followed their descent.

Many of the dark warriors seemed to wield magic as well as physical weapons. Were those black pulsations the same distorting magic from which he'd suffered in Nartar? It was hard to be sure—the dust of combat made vision intermittent. Ronar squinted.

The defenders were outnumbered two to one. The Darteharnians were fond of surrounding small groups and trampling them beneath the sharp wheels of their black-armored war-chariots. Ronar's back stiffened.

Nearby, a long black shape emerged from a cloud of dust. It was a great battering ram, protected by metal sheathing and by a shimmering field of magic that liquefied any opponent who came too close. Its iron head was in the form of a leering ogre. It rolled up to Sha Totek's gate.

Ronar stirred and frowned. He became indignant, as though he'd been disturbed in a library. The ram swung against the gate with an impressive bang. With an even more impressive roar it was blasted backwards like a Fourth of July rocket, mowing down dozens of Darteharnians. Ronar gaped at the carnage.

"Ronar!"

The astronomer turned and gasped. Sha Totek had returned, his eyes ablaze with the black-diamond fire that had first impressed him so many months ago. The change was electrifying.

"Woke up finally, did you? Forget the gate. They're just a little bit too late with that overgrown dildo of theirs. Worry about the Portal. The magic there is faltering, and its defenders are being cut down. Help them. I need only a little time to prepare." Sha Totek settled into a divan, wrapping himself in shadows that defied the sunbeams that tried to pierce them. His hands flickered through gestures that Ronar couldn't follow. A webwork of forces flowed out and swathed him with dim, pure colors of blistering power. From the pulsating network drifted a chilling chuckle and a whispered "Oh my goodness, Namirnakh my old friend, you're going to get it now."

Ronar turned away and flung himself down the stairwell. He emerged in the courtyard stripped of his arctic clothing. In fact, he emerged stripped of almost everything. As a filthy half-naked wildman he returned to the heat of the Red Plain, running to the wall and up the inner stairs to the battlements.

Infantry of Eranior and Darteharn was hacking at each other at the base of the wall. Ronar called out—they all looked up to see him standing there with dagger raised as if to throw it. Every man who had one raised his shield overhead. But Ronar did not throw the dagger. He stepped off the wall and landed full on a black shield, smashing the Darteharnian who had lifted it. Friend and foe alike regarded him with consternation as he drew himself upright. He exacerbated their alarm by materializing the Sword of Bran with a flash and a clang. Before anyone could recover he had swung the steel through three enemy torsos with as many strokes. But he did not tarry long. The Portal was his goal. He loped off in that direction, leaving behind dumb-founded Eranian fighters spattered with fresh Darteharnian blood. Those who recognized the sword swore that Bran the Blessed himself had returned from the grave to help them—and recently, from the look of him.

Like a wind rushing between mountain peaks he made his way to the Portal, threading between combatant groups, avoiding them when possible. A phalanx of Greek warriors, splendid in bronze helmets and greaves, thundered by bearing huge shields and short swords. He passed a formation of Eandamen mounted on nehocks that wailed like demented air raid sirens. Warriors of all factions maneuvered, clashed, and separated like chips of colored glass in a kaleidoscope. It was a grand melee, no sort of organized battle.

The real fighting centered around the Portal, where the sounds of combat took on a new aspect. In addition to the cries of men and the clangor of weapons, inhuman howls and shrieks rose from the chaos that ringed the mirrored bubble still shielding the Portal. The metallic cries of the Teratorns added to the din as they swept over the field with bloodied talons.

Ronar looked at this carnage, called back the sword, and charged in, not bothering to think about what he was doing. Sometime later he found himself in the thick of the struggle with no clear recollection of how he'd gotten there. He remembered glimpses of black, leathery wolf-faces snarling at him from above; of pale, avid-eyed men and women whose terrible wounds leaked only a clear liquid; and of other creatures to which his whirling brain might someday assign names from Earth's mythical past. He glanced down at himself and found blood streaming from savage claw-marks on his chest and shoulders, and from smaller punctures that were numb and cold. His blade dripped a purple-black fluid that could not be human blood alone.

He arrived at the Portal just in time to see its shield blasted into shards by the massed power of the wizards surrounding it. Suddenly the Portal stood naked and vulnerable in the hazy suns-light. Ronar almost imagined he could see the Earth spinning within the Portal's black depths. A moan of triumph went up from the Darteharnians. Ronar spun around and saw no color but black clothing the monstrous horde surrounding him.

Ronar turned back to the Portal. If he made a dash for it, made it through to Earth, he might give warning of the invasion which was following—on his heels—no, that wasn't any good. Maybe he could smash down the Terrestrial Portal before too many Darteharnians could follow him through. He tensed himself to spring—

A figure lay in the darkness of the Portal. Ronar squinted; it was the recumbent form of a man, an indian by the look of him. Laying at his side was a 12-gauge pump-action shotgun, an artifact so incongruous in this setting that Ronar, despite the exigencies of the moment, could only stare at it for long seconds. He strode into the Portal, bent down, hesitated a moment, and picked up the weapon, noting in passing that its owner still lived, and was breathing in hoarse gasps. Ronar suddenly wished he had water to offer this fellow traveler.

But he had none, so he spun around and raised the shotgun at the massed wall of their common enemy. He pumped the action...

A weak, dry voice from behind: "Hey...you..."

Ronar turned. The man's desiccated lips twisted like bits of frayed rope. "What are you doing...with my gun?"

"Defending our lives," snapped Ronar. He waved his free hand at the approaching ranks of armored foes.

"Those things...are real? Damn."

"They are real. Who are you?"

"Name's Bill Hermosa. I...was tracking you...lost your trail...many times...finally picked it up again. And here I am."

"To your regret, I'm sure. Why were you following me?"

"You trespassed on our...sacred land."

Ronar nodded. "You meant to kill me?"

"No...just scare you."

"No easy task after what I've seen lately." Ronar spun, raising the shotgun. With so many targets he scarcely had to aim to blast the faces of the creatures of Darteharn. Pellets rang off glassy armor and bit into flesh. The triumph of the Darteharnians turned to ash as their wizards jerked and fell. Their line broke up and fell back in dismay.

Then the gun was empty. "Any more shells?" demanded Ronar, but as he turned he saw that the indian was unconscious again. He dropped the shotgun by his side and stepped away from the Portal. Retreat now seemed out of the question. He couldn't outrun pursuit while dragging the indian, and he couldn't leave him behind.

There was a flash, a thunderclap. "Oh, you want to die first, you evil-faced son of a bitch?" Ronar swung the great sword two-handed, sending it whistling through the air, shattering the mail of a huge horned terror that had charged him from the mob. Ronar laughed abrasively as he leaped away from the toppling giant.

The horde then came at him in earnest, midnight figures horned and fanged, spiked and plated, shimmering with the crimson nimbus of the Fire of Ahriman. They closed en masse, so many they could scarcely swing their weapons in the tangle, leaving Ronar free to hack at their front ranks.

Suddenly a bizarre figure pushed through the wall of foes. "Stand clear, you fools! I will deal with this insect." This was a small, nearly naked man with a shaved head, his body covered with grease and tattooed with ornate designs. He lifted what looked like a carved human femur, glared at Ronar, and shouted *"Ignis, flagro mani bellatoris grandis!"*

What? Why would this wizard bother to concoct his spell in Latin—

Ronar had no more time to ponder this. With a puff of smoke, flames leaped from his hands. They cracked open and spurted fluid like pieces of chicken on a grill. He shrieked in agony, dropping his weapon. It was impossible to think through such pain and horror, and yet he must. He must somehow undo this terrible damage, or die.

He studied his blazing hands with a calm born more of shock than anything else. This savage had forced heat into his hands, or had hugely accelerated their me-tabolism...something. Without knowing the details, clearly his foe had gained the effect he wanted by focusing his thoughts with a foreign language, bringing into being an utterly improbable event, the spontaneous combustion of Ronar's hands. They need not have burned—would not have burned in any place not subject to the magic of Colib-dis.

Yet magic was a delicate thing. His hands need not go on burning. They need not remain burned.

"Curse of fire, be undone!" cried Ronar—in Basque.

Gasping, half sobbing, Ronar glanced at his hands, which were again whole. He wasn't quite sure how he had done that—but he felt pretty good about it. He looked around like a bewildered boy.

"Eh?" grunted the wizard in surprise. *"Ignis, flagro..."*

Ronar manifested the sword once more and leaped forward with a wild cry. With one hand on the grip and the other on the dull part of the blade just above the guard, he sent the magician's head bouncing in the dirt with a sweep of the blade, a fate which seemed to Ronar entirely just.

The swordsmen renewed their attack, now in better order. Ronar barely managed to get his weapon between himself and a tricky thrust of a quick, wiry man who eyed his clumsy moves with contempt. Ronar caught the enemy's blade near the end of his own. A chip of steel flew off his edge.

"Parry with the part of the blade near the hilt, not the tip. Keep your weapon up. Don't give him an opening by pulling back for some grand stroke. He's too adept."

Ronar didn't dare look around to see who was issuing these instructions. It was all he could do to ward off his attacker. He was peripherally aware of fighters in Eranian dress moving up from behind him, taking some of the pressure off him, using their weapons much more adroitly than he did himself.

That damn spider-quick Darteharnian was not deterred. He kept boring in with an infuriating smirk of contempt on his face. Only Ronar's superior reach had kept him alive so far. Even so, Ronar suspected he was being toyed with.

He was proven right when with a blur of motion his opponent was upon him, having somehow stepped right past Ronar's defenses, too close now for Ronar's sword to count. Ronar made a grab for his dagger but realized even as he did so that he was too late.

Another blade flashed in and deflected the stroke that was about to spit Ronar's heart. Ronar was saved, but at the cost of his savior's weapon, which was broken. Ronar glanced aside. It was none other than King Sionyn, now himself exposed to attack while his men tried to throw themselves into position to defend him.

Without thinking, Ronar tossed him the sword of Bran. The king caught it and showed Ronar how it was meant to be used, whirling and slashing, his face calm, perfectly intent on what he was doing. If Ronar ever got the chance, he vowed, he would learn to fight like that.

The king's opponent went down; but now the enemy forces had their eyes on him alone, surging toward him and his men, ignoring Ronar, who was pushed away. The king and his party were instantly hard pressed. One of the Sons of Wut passed Sionyn a new steel weapon. Ronar called the sword of Bran back into his own hand, attacking the Darteharnians from the rear, turning their assault into a shambles. In a few moments they all lay in the dust, and there was a moment's peace.

"Thank you for giving me the chance to fight with that blade in my hands, friend Ronar," panted the king.

Ronar could only bow his head. "It's more your weapon than mine."

"Cadwaladr...summon the remainder of our army. This is where the battle lies now."

The bloody-handed captain of the Sons of Wut raised a horn and gave a series of blasts. Sionyn's small band looked around nervously as they waited for a response. It seemed to Ronar that they didn't fear battle so much as the nearness of legends such as the Tower of the Gatekeeper, not to mention the Bronze Portal, standing near enough to catch their shadows, the very gateway to Earth itself.

"You men," said Ronar. "Look out for the man lying in the Portal. He is an Earthman like myself, and he is weak and ill."

A few of the soldiers glanced around in puzzlement. "There is no such man here, Lord Ronar."

Ronar blinked. It was true. Apparently, now one man at least had come to Colibdis and returned to Earth, thanks to Sha Totek's interrupted vigilance.

Then they were beset again, a dozen men against hundreds. Ronar, cursing his amateurish use of the sword, nevertheless managed to get in an occasional swing that took advantage of the length and strength of his arms, though that strength was waning. A clamor informed him that reinforcements had arrived, though prevented from joining them by the intervening mass of their foes.

The Eranians fought with a deadly precision, the science of their attack made hot by howls and roars that sounded honest and wholesome compared to the grunts and gibberings of the motley assemblage of horrors they faced. Even the freaks of Nartar seemed preferable to Ronar—unlike them, these sickening creatures of Darteharn had been deliberately distorted and degraded by magic.

Ronar threw the sword, recalled it with the familiar crash and blaze of heat. His opponents fell back a pace, and even his allies jumped. Ronar did it again, and again, driving back his foes, dazzling them, striking while they were helpless.

"Today there is a mighty din in the halls of the palace!" cried Sionyn.

Of course it was hopeless. The ring of foes closed in again. In a moment Ronar and those Eranians who still stood must fall.

Then above the clatter of arms came another sound, a sound hot and insistent with the musical color of brass.

"A horn?" said Cadwaladr. "What nation sounds a note like that?"

Ronar recognized the tune—from the movies. Was it possible? He squinted into the distance. Mounted figures in blue and gold uniforms came charging through a fresh cloud of dust. They carried a familiar flag; the clear peal of the bugle rang from their midst. It was the United States Cavalry...rescuing them in the nick of time. Ronar shook his head, wondering whether he should laugh or cheer.

The Cavalry thundered into full view. The forces of Darteharn broke away, rushing the oncoming riders.

"Company—HALT!

"Show—ARMS!

"Commence—FIRING!"

Smoke spurted from the line of Cavalrymen. The crack of gunfire reached Ronar's ears. Darteharnians jerked and fell across the field. Ronar could only gape. The Thunderbirds had somehow produced long guns of some kind.

But apparently the weapons were single shot only, for the cavalrymen hung them from their saddles and drew sabers.

"Charge!"

And they charged.

"Forward, sons of Eranior!" cried King Sionyn.

So this horde of Darteharn was attacked from three sides: by Thunderbird, by the chariots and foot soldiers of the bulk of Eranior's forces, and by the band led by Sionyn and Ronar. It looked as if they could hope to clear the field long enough to reorganize their defense against the next wave of attackers. Ronar glanced at the Tower. Perhaps they could wrap this up before Sha Totek emerged from whatever exultant daze was befuddling him.

Then a cry, a great moan, rose up from the battlefield. Ronar looked up. A white Teratorn swept down bearing a brilliant figure cloaked in white and gold. His pale sun-god face was framed by a golden helm, from which sprang the antlers of a stag. He was beautiful in the manner of the winter sun, which glows white-gold but gives no warmth.

"By all my fathers," said Sionyn in a curiously flat tone. "That is Namirnakh."

Ronar was shocked. For some reason it had never occurred to him that Namirnakh himself might take a hand in this conflict. Nor was this bright figure at all the shadowy Persian magician he had imagined.

Ronar's next reaction was pity for Sionyn. It must have been centuries since any of his predecessors had had to face Namirnakh. It seemed unfair for the exhausted young man to be confronted with this challenge when he had been performing so well. Ronar could only hope that Namirnakh would prove less formidable than his reputation suggested.

That hope soon proved forlorn. Carrying the wind before him, Namirnakh descended on his winged steed. He gestured...a mere wave of his hand...and Sionyn and his men were laid low, barely able to cry out. The great bird landed; Namirnakh dismounted. He sauntered up to the king with a smirk on his face, bent down, and picked him up with one hand as if he were handling a puppy.

"Ah, the new young king. You're of the line of Bran, of course? You look a bit like him. I kept his skull, you know.

I'll have to see if the resemblance between you goes that deep."

He raised his other hand, fingers spread, and lowered them onto Sionyn's face. His fingers seemed to melt through the king's flesh, fingertips flattening against the skull. Namirnakh remained poised like that, ready to tear off the king's face, who could only emit a thin gurgle.

That was enough for Ronar. He might not have the battle skill of the king, but he took second place to no man when it came to confronting odious sons of bitches. He stalked up behind Namirnakh, thinking rapidly. The sword of Bran was absent; Ronar did not call it up. Instead he bent and picked up a weapon belonging to a dead man.

As he passed the great crouching Teratorn, Ronar became aware of its golden eye following him. He had no time for the beast. As the bird craned its neck to snap his arm off; Ronar plunged the point of his borrowed sword straight down its gullet, quenching the fire in its eyes. He yanked the blade free; the bird collapsed.

"Hey, you there. Get your hands off that boy. Look here, I've killed your chicken," said Ronar.

The white-gold man turned his head, noticing Ronar for the first time. "Why, so you have. And what sort of madman are you, to offend me thus?"

"The sort who will kill you if you do not obey me at once."

The pale man laughed lightly. "I shall not obey you—a filthy, nameless starveling— either now or later. I see I am not the only one who employs stinking savages on the battlefield. What argument do you make to that?"

In answer, Ronar sprang forward, thrusting the borrowed iron sword with all his remaining strength while Namirnakh was too encumbered to dodge.

But Namirnakh did not need to dodge. He tossed the king aside; with the other hand he swatted away Ronar's blade, shattering it, nearly breaking Ronar's hand.

"Oh, that was stirring, even persuasive. But before I do your bidding, let us first see how well you live up to your brave words, now that you're disarmed."

Then Namirnakh dimmed like a fair cloud darkening to storm. His face was immersed in shadow except for the stars of his eyes, which now seemed higher and more close-set than human eyes should be. A dank power flowed from him like waves of cold water. It was all Ronar could do not to run away. Somehow he managed to stand in defiance of this presence that loomed above him like a bright day gone to eclipse.

"I am not disarmed, Namirnakh."

Ronar summoned the sword, prolonging its manifestation to pour out the maximum amount of heat and light. Both were swallowed by the void of Namirnakh. It seemed a puny defense.

Nevertheless, Namirnakh flinched, the first hesitation Ronar had seen from him. A sibilant whisper: "The Sword of Bran…"

Momentarily heartened, Ronar prepared to strike, but Namirnakh's eyes flickered, and the sword changed. The blade went dull, becoming pitted with rust, while the gems in the hilt began to film over and splinter.

"That relic has outlived its time," said Namirnakh. "Let the ages take it at last."

Ronar dropped the weapon, watching as the steel decayed into a mound of reddish dust, and even the gold wire was reduced to fragments.

Naked and weaponless, Ronar sneered up at Namirnakh. "You first tried to get rid of that 'relic' a long time ago. You failed then, and you'll fail now. You will learn that even entropy is an unreliable ally on this crazy world of yours."

The ruins of the sword faded away, then flashed back into Ronar's hand, whole once more. With more than his own strength he cast the blade full into the dark nebulosity of Namirnakh, bringing forth a thin scream of pain and an outpouring of malice that buffeted him like a gale.

"I have seen you before. I glimpsed you over the shoulder of my dear, late Shadow. You are Ronar, the Earthman. A fellow Earthman, I should say."

Ronar's anger burned, deepened. "I am no fellow of yours. You have dragged me away from sanity, taken me from wisdom and plunged me into this pit of madness and blood. You have taken more from me than I will tolerate."

Namirnakh ignored this. "But—how can you be here? The last I knew, you were wasting your time in Hyperborea, you and the tired, wasted Sorcerer. And yet here you stand." He drew back, turned to study the Tower. "And if you are here…then so too may be…"

"NAMIRNAKH!"

Ronar also turned toward the source of that thunderous outcry—the Tower of Sha Totek. Namirnakh raised his hand; a lance of blistering polychromatic fire leaped from the Tower and speared him like lightning.

The echoes of that blast subsided. Ronar shook his head and opened his eyes. Namirnakh, in manlike form again, lay on the ground quivering. Leftover glints of colored fire danced through his hair and sparked out from beneath his eyelids.

Namirnakh's army gave out a great cry of dismay at this unthinkable event. They looked at the Tower and then at Ronar. The Sorcerer was beyond their reprisal, but this bearded, bloody-faced wildman was not. In unison they faced him, creatures human and vulpine, beings undead and spectral and amorphous.

Ronar glared at them. "That's right, you contemptible flock of perverted sheep, your herdsman is dead. What are you going to do about it?" He glanced over at Namirnakh. "Oh, hell. He's not quite dead yet," he said in exasperation.

For Namirnakh was flowing, changing into something like a spider made of syrupy fog. A voice came from somewhere within it, distant, and malevolent. "Not quite dead. Not now, not ever. I don't know how my old friend brought himself down from Hyperborea so quickly, but it doesn't matter. I will climb the walls of his eyrie, pluck him out and feast upon his soul."

Ronar rolled his eyes. He was getting tired of this kind of overblown ranting. That thought was soon erased by a rumbling which rolled in from afar. The Tower of Sha Totek was subsiding, sinking grandly into the earth, vanishing as smoothly as the upended stern of a ship vanishes beneath the waves. Great clouds of dust billowed aloft; chunks of dirt and rock went sailing in high, slow parabolic arcs.

Within a minute the roar faded away, the dust began to drift, and the fabled Tower was gone.

Ronar stared in stupefaction, having no idea of what to make of this. Namirnakh's man-form returned. He too stood blinking at the place where his greatest foe had vanished so unexpectedly. His minions raised a half-hearted cry of victory, but they also seemed uncertain about what was going on.

Namirnakh turned back to Ronar. "And so ends an age. The Tower, which has robbed men of freedom for thousands of years, has crumbled. No doubt its decrepit master overextended himself and has paid the price of hubris.

"I am impressed with you, Earthman. It may be that you need not die. You have taken much from me; give back but a little and I will give you life and more than life."

Angry and incredulous, Ronar said sharply, "What can you possibly have to offer me? It will take more than life to get me on your side."

"I can give you back the integrity of your seed."

Ronar was taken aback. He stared numbly into the golden face of Namirnakh.

"You fear the effect of the pale light of Nartar upon your body. Your years are half done, and you fear you have tarried too long, that you will never have a child, leaving no legacy for the future. But I am the mightiest wizard who has ever lived. Finding a single unaffected particle in your body, I can cause all others to assume its qualities, curing you. Making you a whole man once more."

Ronar tried to choke back the words, but could not. "What would you have me do?"

"Go before me as my new Shadow. Though the Tower is fallen, I sense that my enemy still lives. Seek him out. Strike him down. In return I will cure you. I will also forswear my conquest of Earth and leave it forever untouched by magic. I will spare Eranior and all other lands, contenting myself with the rule of Darteharn and Wauk. All this will I do, all this will I sacrifice, if only to see my enemy brought down by one whom he loves and trusts."

Ronar set his jaw, trying not to let indecision show on his face.

He could save the world, or two worlds. He could save himself. He could cow Namirnakh, force him to compromise and abandon his plans. Could Sha Totek himself hope to do more? Would he even oppose this alliance, knowing what it would achieve, even though it cost him his life?

No, Sha Totek would not resist. To save the two worlds, he would willingly give his life to Namirnakh.

That conviction was enough to ease Ronar's decision.

Namirnakh's human form began to expand and blacken. He grew huge and shadowed, but his godlike face smiled down at him with a reassuring light.

Ronar's face relaxed. He stepped forward slowly.

"Yes, I'll join you, Namirnakh." He extended his empty hand. His ring hand. Namirnakh reached down to take it. A moment's concentration flickered over Ronar's brow. "Here, join this."

Namirnakh flinched back; too late. The great sword shivered into being, half the blade buried in Namirnakh's torso. He screamed. An appalling gout of filth and flame roared out of his wound, blowing Ronar off his feet. The sword was destroyed yet again, this time dissolving and spraying outward as a shower of white-hot droplets.

Dazed, scorched, and stung, Ronar looked up from the dirt.

Namirnakh was bending over him as he had seen thunderstorms lower themselves onto the desert. Ronar felt an instant's intense grief, and might have wept if he'd had the time. His life was over. So many things left undone, unseen, unsaid.

And yet, could he count as a failure a life in which he'd seen Varanu?

Namirnakh whirled Ronar aloft, shook him, screamed and roared in his ears. Never, not even as a child, had Ronar been so completely overpowered. How amazing that this could happen to him! How terrifying to be so brutally reminded of his fragility! How arrogant his old conceits of strength, coming from one made of slabs of meat and sticks of bone! He fought with an insane fury, pounding at the horrid face of his killer, rocking it with blows that would have shattered any human face, kicking and punching in a frenzy. He raved and shouted, howled and cursed, as if trying to match Namirnakh's animal madness with his own.

Through the red haze he saw Namirnakh's face open up into a maw, losing its human semblance, expanding into an avid gape lined with teeth like steel pegs. A wave of reeking gases spilled out and rolled over him. Namirnakh gurgled in triumph.

"Death to Namirnakh!" A steel blade bit into Namirnakh's arm. Driving it was King Sionyn, his face streaming with blood from his forehead and cheek. "Death to the traitor! Death to the murderer! Death to the usurper! Death to the tyrant!" Each exclamation was backed up by another swift blow of the sword.

And then there were more swords, wielded by the Sons of Wut, striking Namirnakh from every angle. The Lord of Darteharnlandua roared and flailed about, Ronar still in hand. Sionyn pressed in, hacking like a maniac, cutting into that beautiful golden face.

Namirnakh dashed Ronar to the ground, stunning him.

Though his face was ruined, Namirnakh was not incapacitated. He gathered himself, swelled and darkened once more. Power flowed into him from the air and from the very planet, pushing back his assailants, surrounding him with a stunning, overwhelming barrier of black magic. His great black hands lashed out at Sionyn, cutting through the king's body as though he were made of smoke. Sionyn crumpled and did not move. The Sons of Wut howled with fury and flung themselves forward, all caution forgotten. Ronar forced himself to his feet, steeling himself against death for the hundredth time.

The earth rumbled beneath their feet. The ground erupted. Namirnakh was cast aside. Ronar fell onto the heaving surface. Slabs of earth tilted up and slid away, toppling and burying those who drew back too slowly.

The Tower's flat top emerged and mounted into the sky, carrying Ronar with it. He leaped off, fell fifteen feet, and rolled upright not far from Namirnakh. The black shaft of the Tower continued to slide skyward until it reached its original height, and then some. Teratorns flew away from it like frightened crows. The rumbling grew still louder; the ground quaked.

Shaking his head, Ronar craned his neck at the relocated Tower. The main entrance, formerly at ground level, was now at least a hundred feet up. He'd had no idea the Tower had extended so far below the surface. Now it was so tall it almost looked like it was falling over.

Smoke and a fierce golden light erupted around the base of the Tower. Its lower end emerged, a bulbous hemisphere unmarked except for an aperture from which spewed a pillar of flame. Ronar clapped his hands over his ears, buffeted back by the sound and heat. The Tower continued to ascend, rising a thousand feet. Then the flame guttered out, the Tower slowed , hesitated, and began to fall.

Ronar yelled "Run!" and followed his own advice. He looked over his shoulder. The Tower's rounded base was dropping like a blunt spike toward the earth...toward Namirnakh. The lord of Darteharn raised his arms against it, but it was futile. The hammer came down on him with a concussive blast of air and sound that sent Ronar spinning and knocked down everything within a hundred yards. Debris exploded outward. Like the heel of a giant squashing an insect, the Tower began to twist, grinding deep into dirt and rock with a horrendous screeching sound. It drilled its way down, throwing up a second pillar of dust and debris, until its uppermost windows were level with the ground. There it paused.

Ronar dragged himself upright and gingerly approached it, his ears ringing.

Sha Totek leaned out of a window, looking entirely unruffled. He caught sight of Ronar and smiled broadly. "Long have I yearned to stick it to Namirnakh in that fashion. Did you like that 'rocket' effect? I got that idea from you."

At the moment Ronar was in no mood to endure Sha Totek's smug self-satisfaction. "The king of Franior is dead," he said brutally. "If your fanciful little trick had taken place one minute earlier, he would still be alive."

Sha Totek looked crestfallen, scanning the battlefield as if seeking proof that this claim was untrue. Finding none, he met Ronar's eyes with some difficulty. "I—am sorry. I came as fast...this was the best..." He trailed off.

"You can't even say it. You know it isn't true. You've been grandstanding, showing off."

Sha Totek bit his lip. "Ronar, you are right. May gods and men forgive me."

Ronar shook his head, not in negation, but in recognition of the remorse on Sha Totek's face. "It seems inane to ask this," he said, "but is he really dead?"

"Namirnakh? Yes."

"He took a lot of killing…"

"Or rather I should say…this Namirnakh is dead. He creates these bodies in various semblances peculiar to his vanity, inhabiting them until they succumb to wear, or until he rashly exposes them to the annoyance of his enemies, such as now. When this happens, he temporarily exists in some other form which I do not know. This body seems to have been rather new, and lovingly maintained…that's going to rankle him. We can take this much satisfaction, at least. He'll be some time manifesting himself once more."

Ronar felt his heart falter for a moment. "You're telling me…that after all we've suffered…all we've lost…Namirnakh is not dead? Is there no way to destroy him forever?"

Sha Totek frowned, now thoroughly sobered. "There is no painless or convenient way to destroy one such as Namirnakh. Now I'd better put this Tower back inside the walls. This battle's not quite over, but I will soon put an end to it. Adios."

"See you," said Ronar, in a daze.

The Sorcerer ducked inside. The Tower sank into the ground. The tunnel left behind began to fall in on itself. No trace of Namirnakh remained.

Unfortunately, many of Namirnakh's followers were still as healthy as they'd ever been, and as belligerent, if now confused and dismayed.

The Tower extruded itself back into place behind its walls in an obscene-looking manner, looking as serene as if it had never moved. Ronar glanced at it resentfully. *You haven't left us in an ideal situation here,* he thought. *We who still stand could've climbed through your windows and gone with you, you idiot.*

For the Ebon Army still outnumbered the defenders. It formed itself into a line and charged.

The last thing in the universe Leonard Ronar wanted to do was swing that sword again. He had no desire to cut open living men, or living monsters for that matter. The gross brutality of death by the sword belied the aura of romance and glory that had grown up around swordplay as its actual incidence receded into the past.

Still, he ran forward to do what he must.

In the end, Sha Totek was good enough to relieve him of any further responsibility.

Every person within fifty miles heard the Sorcerer's waxy-smooth voice coming from a point just behind his or her left shoulder. Every creature on the battlefield did a simultaneous pirouette in search of the source of the phantom voice. The charging armies broke in disarray before they had properly come together.

"This is Sha Totek the Gatekeeper speaking. I'm sorry I haven't been able to perform my proper function until now, but circumstances kept me away until just recently. In fact, it's impossible that I'm here at all, but that seems an inconsequential nitpick. Anyway, I'm back now, and in control, and here's what I propose to do. You Darteharnians—or should I say, you rabble—you peat-sucking misbegotten spawn of thick-headed Celtic peasants—have once again caused far more trouble than your pathetic ambitions could ever justify. The Earth seemed poor enough to your forefathers that they fled it long ago. Why you should go to all this trouble to return to it I'll never know. I suppose it has to do with the charisma of your leader, that Persian pipsqueak Namirnakh. But you saw what I did to him. I would urge you all to heed this lesson and learn who is the real power on Colibdis, but I shall not, for two reasons: first, you wouldn't listen; second, the issue will soon be academic for you anyway. No one would call me unjust were I to kill you all out of hand. Certainly the widows and children of those brave and decent men whom you have slain would not complain. But I choose not to do so, for there has been too much death here already. To kill you would be an unworthy, vindictive act of vengeance when I can dispose of you so much more elegantly.

"You of Darteharn will not hear my voice again."

Suddenly every man and creature of Darteharn jerked a foot or so into the air. They came down clutching their groins (or the nearest equivalent) and grimacing with pain.

"Well, looks like I lied a little. I did indulge in one tiny act of vindictiveness. Goodbye!"

The army of Darteharn, every element of it scattered over the plain, imploded, its remains fluttering gently to the ground. What had been a bristling mass of fighters, monsters, and magicians was now a field of cut flowers, their foliage a soft sea-green, their petals like flakes of violet, mint-green, butter-yellow, or silver porcelain. The transformation of the Red Plain from a bleak battleground to a sea of soft beauty brought forth a collective sigh from all who witnessed it. Warriors of many nations sheathed their weapons and walked among the blooms, their footsteps sending up a fragrance of mixed mint and citrus. Ronar joined them, grateful to let the Sword of Bran lapse into its place in Eranior, hoping never to call it forth again.

Sha Totek's voice continued. "You may be under the impression that I've transformed those Darteharnians into flowers. However, that would be a gross act of wizardry in which I would not indulge. I simply exchanged them for an equal mass of flowers from a world adrift in another sphere of existence. On that world are no victims, nothing to dominate, and no magic. Let the Darteharnians spend their days contemplating the beauty of the flowers, or let them prey upon each other, as they wish. As for you, I invite you to gather the flowers. Take them to your loved ones, and to those who will mourn the heroes who've died here to protect the Two Worlds of Men. These blossoms will remain fresh for many years. For more years still will we remember what has happened here today."

Ronar looked around, uncertain of what he ought to do next. All the conflict, all the danger, were suddenly over. Somehow his mental gears were having trouble making the adjustment.

"I think I'll just sit down for a while," he said to no one in particular, and collapsed into a heap of flowers.

He awoke beneath a white expanse which he took to be an overcast sky. As his eyes focused he realized he was actually lying in a tent filled with rows of men in cots like his, sleeping, chatting, or just lying and staring.

Ronar took careful stock of himself. He was stiff, weak, and full of aches and pains. Half his body was covered with bandages. His feet in particular were heavily wrapped, and they ached. He raised his hand to his face—yes, he'd been shaved and shorn, a welcome change. His fingers encountered a line of stitches where he'd been cut by a flying shard of his oft-broken sword. But his head was clear, his limbs were all present, and his senses were sharp. He felt lucky enough.

On a table beside his cot was a bowl containing a static explosion of unworldly flowers.

Dr. Joachim of Two Suns City appeared and sat down next to Ronar's cot. "Good to see you awake, Professor Ronar. I've got something for you here..." From a satchel he produced Ronar's big silvery binocular.

Ronar took the instrument. The feel of the cool, contoured barrels brought to his mind a vision of soft evenings full of glittering stars. "Nice to see these again." His gaze lingered on them; not until this moment had he realized how much he would have missed them had they been lost. "Where did you get them?"

"From Sha Totek. How are you feeling, Professor?"

"Pretty good. I'd appreciate if you'd give me a rundown and explain each of these bandages, starting at the bottom."

"Sure. I'm sorry to say you might lose a few toes. Looks like frostbite, although I'm damned if I can see how that's possible in this heat."

"I came here straight from Hyperborea."

"And the trip wasn't long enough for your feet to warm up along the way? Never mind, I don't want to hear it. On your thighs we have some poisoned puncture wounds which gave us plenty of trouble. Vampire bites, we think, although they must have been the runts of the litter. We thought we might lose you to them for a while. Sha Totek's magic came through for you there. On your torso and shoulders are cuts, abrasions, and burns of varying severity.

You had a werewolf bite, which Sha Totek also counter-acted. A fairly deep cut on your face that I sewed up—some scarring there, I'm afraid. You lost a lot of blood. You're anemic, malnourished, and dehydrated. In short, you're one of the worst wrecks I've ever seen who still had the temerity to call himself a living human being."

"I'll get over it."

"I know that. Drink some water."

Ronar glanced at a massive brass longgun leaning against another man's table. The doctor followed the look and chuckled. "Take a look at that blunderbuss. It's twice as big as a steel gun and three times as heavy. We still have enough of the old guns to know what a rifle or revolver should look like. We got those muskets made and ourselves organized barely in time to do any good, except for setting up the hospitals—which seemed like a novel idea to the Eranians."

"If your men had been an hour later in arriving it would've been all over. You saved my life, and who knows what else."

Joachim grinned. "For these boys that's enough reason for the expedition all by itself. But I'm hoping we'll melt the guns down when we get back. Don't want everyone going around armed. Just no call for it."

"Maybe they should be stored away in case the need arises for a well-regulated militia."

"Think so? Your stock's so high in T-Bird that you just mention it and anyone who disagrees will be hanged. Or shot."

Ronar grimaced. "Well. Thanks for the care you've given me."

"You're welcome, but I can't rightly take full credit. You had your own little angel of mercy fluttering around you until this morning—made many a man around here pretty envious. Do you think I go around arranging flowers for the men? She left in a hurry when it looked like you might wake up—but she left you this." Joachim handed Ronar an envelope of scented blue paper addressed to him in a hand of graceful calligraphic perfection.

"You wouldn't happen to know what became of my reading glasses, would you?" asked Ronar.

"I'm afraid not. Would you like me to read it to you?"

"No, I'll manage." Yet Ronar hesitated while thoughts, fears, and images swam through his mind. This paper rectangle was still another Portal. Beyond it might lie a sunlit glade, a bleak landscape of cold greys, or some vista unimaginable even to eyes that had seen Varanu.

At last he opened and read the letter.

Dear Professor Ronar,

My heart is so happy that you have survived your very difficult adventures of the last several months, and that you have safely returned. It has been my pleasure to care for you as you recuperated over the last several days. Don't worry; I'll never reveal the things you might have said while you were asleep, or nearly so.

I realize that you and I parted company on poor terms on that morning in Two Suns City. At the time I did not understand why you would reject me, especially after the intimacies we had already shared following your exploit at the Despard ghost house. Since learning of the magnitude of the task which you were on your way to undertake, I realize how this must have weighed upon your noble and sen-

sitive spirit, leaving little room for the feelings of a silly girl. The cross words which passed between us now leave me feeling petty and childish. I hope that you may forgive me.

Now that this great crisis of our times has passed, defeated by your heroics, I pray that we might renew our acquaintance. Know that if you return to Two Suns you will always find a welcome with me. I believe I can promise you a pleasing stay of whatever duration.

You are a man who has denied himself many of the things which make life bearable. You strive to appear stern and remote, but I know that much of this is a harsh shelter for a tender heart. I don't know what events in your personal history have influenced you to do this to yourself, but think: here you are now, on a whole new world, unspeakably far from whatever disappointments and griefs might have scarred you. Perhaps it's time for you to make a new start. I am well qualified to help you along this path. I have no fear of sensual pleasures. I suffer no guilt from their enjoyment. Nor do I resent or regret any consequences which might arise from their pursuit. I am intelligent; this I trust you have already observed. To be seen with me is no embarrassment. My dear Professor, I am really quite decadent. I am a flower scarcely less fair than those foreign blossoms which I placed beside your bed.

I hope to hear from you soon.

Most Sincerely,
Miss Phaedra Holder

Despite all the possibilities which Ronar had imagined, the reality still took him by surprise. His cheeks and ears burned as he read what Phaedra had written. He'd never dreamed a woman was capable of using such language—especially a woman as apparently demure as Phaedra. Though taken aback, even abashed, he managed to be also pleased and flattered by much of what Phaedra had to say. The images she conjured were enough to stir him despite his depleted condition.

But other images arose to daunt him—grotesque images from a past too recent and too damaging to be ignored. Against his will his thoughts flashed back to Nartar and to the radiation that had been directed against him, invading his body, riddling his cells, destroying their nuclei, deranging their genes, especially those most critical to future generations. The magic of Sha Totek might have saved his life, but he could not risk that it had also saved his ability to father a healthy child.

He imagined the faces of the inhabitants of Nartar.

With trembling hands Ronar folded the letter and returned it to the envelope. "I cannot answer this."

"What?"

"I said I can't answer this letter."

"Well, I wasn't asking you to, but now that you mention it, why ever not?"

"I'll elaborate. Under no circumstances will I have any further contact with Phaedra Holder."

"But she's only—"

"That's enough, Doctor. I've said and heard all I intend to say and hear. Don't force me to repeat myself."

Joachim shrugged. "I assume you know what you're doing. Don't get so worked up. Doctor's orders." Looking irked and puzzled, he turned and left the tent.

Ronar did not look after him. His thoughts turned inward, where they grew chill.

At sunrise the next day Ronar got up and walked out of the tent with a stiff-legged gait on his damaged feet. Once out in the open he forced himself to walk with his normal stride, despite the pain. He would not be seen to hobble like a cripple.

All around were tents and pavilions housing the injured and their caretakers. Those warriors who were uninjured camped out in the open, awaiting the order to march for their distant homes. A wind from the west swept through the camp and brought the fragrance of the battlefield flowers.

The sight of the largest pavilion brought Ronar to a halt. Atop it flew the royal pennon of Eranior; before it stood sentinels from the Sons of Wut. Ronar approached and crafted a query in their proto-Welsh tongue. "Good morning, Sons of Wut. Whom do you house in this pavilion?"

"Lord Ronar, we stand guard over our King."

Ronar looked closer, recognizing Cadwaladr ap Dillan beneath bruises, scrapes, and cuts. "Captain. I'm glad to see you're still standing tall."

Cadwaladr nodded somberly. "Thank you, Lord Ronar. I only wish my good fortune had been universal."

"May I—pay my respects to the King?"

"Yes, sir, you may. You are brother to the King, and none have the right to keep you from his side."

Ronar blinked. "Perhaps someday—I will know—if I am worthy of his high regard." He passed into the shadows of the pavilion. The only light was the cold glow of dawn filtering in from outside. King Sionyn occupied a cot in the

center of the floor. Aside from a few items of camp furniture and some smoldering censers, the tent was otherwise
empty. Ronar approached the cot where the King's body lay
formally arranged. With a numb heart he stood looking at
the play of cold blue skylight on the King's torn face. He
looked unbelievably young, and very innocent, yet the earnest care with which he had ruled was also clear. Did he
have a queen to mourn him? So little did he know about
this young man who had trusted him, taken him in, saved
him.

Ronar lifted his ring hand and called forth the scarlet
light, giving the King's pale face a semblance of life. He
whispered, "I will wear this ring, never forgetting what you
have done, what you have sacrificed." Then he called out
the Sword of Bran, laid it by the side of the King, and left
the tent. For three days afterward he never entirely forgot
the Sword and its location, even dreaming of it at night,
never allowing it to fade away, until the tents were folded
and the King had gone home.

Sha Totek the Sorcerer leaned on a windowsill and
looked with satisfaction at the dusk settling over the Red
Plain.

The hospital tents were struck, the camps were gone,
the dead removed and the walking wounded on their way
home. Some of the worst casualties were under care in Two
Suns City until they were well enough to complete their
journeys. Sha Totek and other magicians had been able to
reverse much of the damage done to those struck down by
magic, but still, deaths had been plentiful. The Plain now
gave little evidence of that.

"I admit to surprise," said Sha Totek. "I didn't expect things to work out so neatly. True, the death of Sionyn was a blow. He was a trusty boy, wasn't he? The Eranians have had many Kings, but few who have died so well, striking mighty blows against Namirnakh himself. Now the Eranians will select a new king. We can only hope he will do as well.

"Yonder I see the Portal glittering in the last rays of Photos. Here is my Tower, none the worse for its quick trip to the nearer vicinity of the Portal. Here am I, enjoying the pleasures of the Tower and watching over a Portal, as always. Nothing has changed."

Ronar, who was seated a distance away, looked up from his broodings. "Things have changed. I have changed."

"Yes, that is true. Before our journey, it would have been you looking out the window and me lounging in the shadows. Yes, you have changed."

"I don't understand. With all we've done and experienced, how can you claim to be unchanged?"

Sha Totek chuckled. "You must realize that I'm prone to exaggerate or understate things at a whim. Yes, I have been affected by the experience. But remember, I have more millennia behind me than you have decades. After all that time you may find me a trifle jaded. Being young, you have changed more profoundly, in some ways radically, in others not at all. Tell me, do you consider it a good change, on the whole?"

Ronar considered. "I'm not sure what that means. I have been bludgeoned into opening my eyes to the truth. That was painful, but I suppose it's good."

"Why did you do it?"

"You mean why did I undertake this mission? Was it to save humanity from the evil of Namirnakh? Yes, partly. But I think at first I did it to save myself from magic. I couldn't bear the thought of magic contaminating my neat and orderly universe. Even now I feel no real desire to convert the Darteharnians to the side of 'goodness'. They can do as they please, as long as they don't try to stuff their ways down anybody else's throat. If Eranior had invaded Darteharn, you might have found me on the other side of the conflict."

"You say that, and you may even believe it, but I doubt it's really true. You've come down too firmly on the side of Varanu to feel much sympathy for Ahriman-worshippers."

"The side of Varanu," mused Ronar. "What might that be? I may not know why magic is so active on Colibdis while it's—subdued elsewhere. But I tell you, I know what magic is, more fundamentally than you do yourself. At least I can explain it to myself in scientific terms that are known if not fully explored. With Varanu, I could feel what magic is; I knew how the universe works on a deep level. But that kind of revelation is fleeting. I attained it only under the most extraordinary circumstances. You make use of magic by means of a ritualized system of spells that focuses your thoughts and provides an underpinning on logic and consistency. But it's possible to perceive the mechanisms of magic so clearly that these forces become available though a mere effort of will—even, I believe, outside the magic field of Colibdis."

"If anyone should fully realize such a state, you know what he would become," said Sha Totek.

Ronar awaited the answer.

"Well, I'll tell you—it's a three-letter word that spells 'dog' backwards."

Ronar shrugged. "If that should be a consequence of my investigations, I'll just have to make the best of it."

Sha Totek rolled his eyes. "Your humor is so dry it's desiccated, unless you're such a megalomaniac as to make Namirnakh look like a contented stable boy." He sat down to observe Ronar. The astronomer didn't notice the scrutiny.

After a while Ronar said, "I need to return to Earth for a time."

"I agree. You need a rest."

"You won't try to stop me?"

"There's no need. You won't give away the secret of Colibdis. You'll keep this planet set aside as your own personal mountaintop for spying out the secrets of the universe."

Ronar said slowly, "You might also credit me with a degree of loyalty to a friend."

"You're right. I'm sorry. I'm becoming too acrid in my very old age. Maybe I need a rest too."

"I'll be leaving in the morning, but not straight for Earth. I'm taking a little side trip first. There's something I want to see here before I leave."

"Are you going to Thunderbird?" asked Sha Totek eagerly.

"No. The other way."

"Oh. Are you strong enough to travel? Have you recovered?"

"To the extent that I ever shall, yes."

"Well then. I suppose this is farewell."

"For the time being."

Sha Totek studied the astronomer for long minutes. Finally he compressed his lips and said, "Ronar, I know you don't often solicit advice, but because of my high regard for you I'm going to offer some anyway. Don't take everything so seriously. If you fail to totally unravel the mysteries of creation, don't regard it as a sign of personal inadequacy. You are, after all, only human. Don't be so afraid of your humanity. Do something foolish every once in a while. It'll do you good."

"It seems to me that I trip over my humanity often enough as it is."

"Oh, by the Snout of Anubis! You know, when we reunited up in Hyperborea I thought you'd changed. You seemed more open somehow, better able to deal with uncomfortable human matters, healthier. I don't know how your solitary ordeal could have brought you to that, but it did. Maybe you ought to return to the ice. Because ever since you woke up in that field hospital you've been more rigid and inflexible than ever. What happened?"

Ronar only sank deeper into the shadows and turned his face away. "I'm sorry if I've disappointed you. Things change."

Sha Totek rose, spun and raised his fists in an ecstasy of exasperation. "May all the gods piss on you at once! Ronar, you walnut-headed, bladder-brained obstinate son of a scorpion! Get it out, you fool!"

Ronar raised a face taut with sorrow, defiance, and loss. "You must swear never to mention this to anyone, in even the most indirect way."

"I so swear by Varanu, whom we both revere."

So Ronar told Sha Totek about the letter from Phaedra, and about the details of his experience in Nartar.

When Ronar's outpouring was over, Sha Totek didn't know whether to laugh or cry. He could afford to do neither, since a laugh would induce terminal indignation in Ronar, while a tear would embarrass him fatally. He said, as gently as he could, "You're not about to turn into a 'mutant' yourself, are you?"

"No, it doesn't work that way."

"Umm...I doubt that Phaedra's feelings would change simply because you can't have children. Maybe she doesn't even want any! Maybe she—well—" But his sentence trailed off, words having failed him for once.

"I'm sure she wants children. Why wouldn't she? She is a lovely girl. She should have children."

Sha Totek hemmed and hawed in an uncharacteristic manner. "Leonard...I must ask you a question...did Phaedra ever actually, uh, say that she wants to pursue a formal relationship with you?"

Ronar bristled. "Not in so many words. But I read her letter—what else could she possibly mean?"

Sha Totek rolled his eyes skyward, imploring a hundred gods for guidance and mercy. "Leonard—how can I put this delicately—Phaedra is indeed a lovely girl, everyone agrees on that. But she may not be quite as—as serious as you consider her to be. In Two Suns, she has, well, sort of a reputation...in fact, I myself have... "

Ronar's expression intensified dangerously.

"Uh, I myself have heard, er, rumors, that Phaedra is inclined to..." He halted, looked at Ronar, and sighed with resignation. "I cannot escape this fate. Phaedra is known as a girl who dispenses her favors freely and willingly."

Ronar sagged back into the shadows.

At last he said, "I see. You must think me a callow fool, to have been so misled."

Sha Totek shook his head. "Oh, no I don't. I think you are a gentleman, in an awkward sort of way."

Ronar remained silently immersed in shadow.

"If it helps any," said Sha Totek hopefully, "she didn't look at anyone else but you the whole time she was here. You must have made, uh, a big impression on her."

Ronar drummed his fingers on the arm of his chair. Presently, to Sha Totek's great relief, he chuckled. Soon it escalated to a laugh, albeit a rather brittle, cynical one. "Reality I think I understand. Women are not so easy to grasp."

Sha Totek's brown face assumed an air of heavy-lidded relaxation. "Leonard, we need say no more. I'm glad you have revealed your concerns. I suspect that for you, opening up like that took more courage than fighting Namirnakh. I hope it's made you feel better."

"For some obscure reason, it has."

"Good. Now, you'd better hit the dusty trail, bed down and get yourself some shuteye. Good luck, I'll see you whenever you get a hankerin' to return to this here world."

"Good night...my friend."

When Ronar had gone, a frenzied Sha Totek set about crafting a spell. When released, it burst from his outthrust arms like an irresistible battering ram, lancing into space and blasting out a new crater on the face of Sinanna, which served no purpose whatsoever but to release some of his frustration, and very likely to offend the Moon God himself.

Sha Totek wished there were a way for a sorcerer to break an oath of silence without the goddess who oversaw such things instantly transforming him into a small multi-legged creature with a face like the rump of a hippopotamus.

Southwest of the Bronze Portal, tectonic forces had tilted part of the Red Plain toward the west. There the sea had flowed in to make a shallow gulf of that part of the Plain. Since then, sea level had fallen. It was now a brackish wetland, large in extent, alive with the myriad creatures that thrive in places of shallow water.

Ronar sat on a decaying log and looked out over the great salt marsh. The dawn light was gathering. Water-birds were stirring, flying in silhouetted flocks across the scarlet glow building on the horizon, or wading among the reeds in search of frogs, crabs, or various slithering things. The night chorus of tiny creatures had ceased, and the day song of the birds had not properly begun. Silence sighed among the reeds and over the mirror-face of the water.

And the Galaxy was still in sight.

The dawn was subdued, for this was the time of the Gloaming; only the dim bulk of Kudu lurked below the horizon. This left visible the Milky Way, which otherwise would have been lost in the glare until the slow turn of the seasons some months hence.

It glowed just above the horizon, a pinwheel of fog suspended in the purple clarity of the dawn. It spanned a distance equal to three lengths of his hand held at arm's length, and was presented at a fairly open angle.

He raised the binocular and once again scanned the ghostly majesty of the Milky Way, his home.

At high power the binocular barely revealed the pin-points of supergiant stars burning among the star clouds of the spiral arms. The vast majority of suns were lost in a haze he (as yet) lacked the optical power to resolve. As for the Sun itself, it was so humble a mote among these billions that he'd have no chance of picking it out even if he knew exactly where to look. And yet, by sweeping his glass around the outer third of the Galaxy, he knew that at some point he must have viewed the neighborhood of the Sun.

The spiral pattern was looser and more ill-defined than he'd expected. Inward from the arms was the much brighter central bulge, an absolutely featureless haze of creamy light, something no astronomer of Earth had seen before. Also previously unseen was that bulge's elongation into a bar. At its very center was a great enigma, the galactic nucleus itself, shining like a bright star, clearly visible to the unaided eye. No single star could radiate so mightily across this distance of some three hundred thousand light-years. In the binocular he could just resolve the nucleus as a tiny disk rather a point of light. What could it be? What strangeness had this fluid, living Universe arranged for the core of that great wilderness of stars?

He lowered the glasses. Kudu was catching up with the Galaxy now, overpowering it until it looked like a breath of fog on a windowpane. Soon it would be gone.

He shivered from the coolness of the morning air, and from his knowledge of the unity of that distant galaxy, the dabbling water fowl, and his own mind in the all-pervasive web of reality that contained them all. Once, he had taken comfort in the "knowledge" that the stars would continue, unchanged, in their uncaring courses regardless of what might befall him and the rest of his race. How foolish he had been!

THE END

Appendix

Leonard Ronar: a Brief History

Once upon a time there was a maladjusted teenage boy who liked to draw superheroes and write stories about them. One day he invented an astronomer-adventurer who was so much better than anyone else that he did whatever he wanted. He never questioned his motivations or the rightness of his actions, never doubting that any opposition must crumble before his righteous superiority. In other words, he was pretty much the opposite of that teenage boy, except for the part about imagining himself to be a superior being.

This character was more intimidating than Batman, stronger-willed than Green Lantern, more hardy than Aragorn, more austere than Solomon Kane, and grimmer than Conan. His sweaty, torn-up shirts were stinkier than those of Doc Savage. He rarely shaved, and this was a decade before another stubbly scientist-adventurer, Indiana Jones, came along.

His name was Leonard Ronar. Leonard, because the teenager thought that name sounded strong yet also somewhat nerdy and offbeat (plus he liked Leonard Nimoy); Ronar because the teenager knew of a Marvel Comics villain called Ronan, which he thought was also a strong name, especially with that vaguely science-fiction "ar" syllable replacing the "an". Radar, Sonar, Ronar.

Ronar, Sha Totek, and their basic milieu and storyline all existed by 1972, possibly as early as 1970, when I was in the ninth grade (oh...that teenage boy was me; surprise!). Their influences were many, and probably more obvious than I wish they were. They include Tolkien, Robert E. Howard, and Edgar Rice Burroughs's Mars books. In more recent years a bit of Jack Vance may have crept in as well.

I like to think that Colibdis, populated by enclaves of various ancient civilizations transplanted there and remaining mostly intact, is a concept original to me.

In high school I drew a few pages of a Ronar comic strip. This story, called "The City of Wraiths", concerned Ronar and a large talking bird named Albianor as they trekked through a tropical jungle on their way to the City of Wraiths, built on the side of a volcano. There Ronar retrieved his spaceship, which had been hijacked by the wraiths, incidentally managing to destroy them and their city in the process. Drawing the story on big pieces of paper using a ballpoint pen turned out to exceed my then-limited patience, so I resorted to writing a prose version which I may have actually completed. This story was partially serialized in *MErcury,* my high school newspaper. I say partially because only two chapters appeared before the whole newspaper staff exhausted its meager supply of discipline and stopped publishing. Thus my fellow students at Maine-Endwell Senior High never did learn the fate of Ronar and his feathery pal. If any of them are reading this now, I can at last end the suspense: they won.

During the following years I wrote a number of Ronar novellas and short stories, the plots of which I may recount in a future appendix. In college I submitted one of them as a project for my creative writing class. The professor, feminist science fiction writer Joanna Russ, said it was fairly well written, but remarked that reading about Ronar was like reading about the adventures of a jackhammer (actually, for this story I called him Lucas Ray, for fear that someone might steal his true and obviously precious and valuable name). Ms. Russ was certainly correct. At that stage Ronar wasn't much of a character. He just stomped and smashed and slashed and glared his way through any obstacle. He had few discernible emotions or traits other than sheer relentlessness.

In 1982, having at last moved into my own apartment, I decided it was time to put some discipline into my writing and write a novel. The obvious choice of subject matter was Ronar's first exploit on Colibdis. Using first a manual and later an electric typewriter, I typed the first version of the novel now in your hands, under the title *The Grey Portal*.

Those early drafts had a very different opening than the current version. To make sense of it I need to describe an early incident in Ronar's life. In 1941 Ronar was unwilling to be drafted or to enlist in the military. In his youthful arrogance he was convinced that he was too special to take orders like some common soldier. On the other hand, he was always ready to develop a massive case of indignation over acts of bullying and conquest. He wanted to take part in the struggle against the Nazis, but only on his own terms. He wound up sneaking into Nazi Germany, where he lurked in the countryside, spying and committing various acts of sabotage and disruption. For part of this period he posed as an officer in the Waffen SS, where he actually fit in rather well. Eventually he made his way to the German rocket base at Peenemünde, where his disguise was finally penetrated and he almost became an unwilling experimental subject in manned rocketry. He managed to escape but was forced to flee the country.

The Allies became aware of Ronar's stint in the SS. Having no clear information to the contrary, they assumed he actually was a Nazi and not an infiltrator. Since Ronar was too proud to explain his actions, he remained under suspicion as a war criminal. Under this scenario, "Leonard Ronar" was a false identity (his real name was thus unknown), which he assumed to evade pursuit.

In the first draft of *The Grey Portal,* American law enforcement had finally caught up to Ronar and had tried to arrest him in Tucson. Ronar fled to Kitt Peak in his jeep, chased by motorcycle police. He managed to delay them by creating a rock slide on one of the switchbacks up Kitt Peak. Arriving at the observatory, he set off on foot into the southern mountains, confident he could evade any pursuit in the wilds and escape to Mexico. Ronar discovered the Bronze Portal along the way.

My intention was to begin the story with a "hook", hoping to grab readers. I also wanted to portray Ronar as a man of action who might plausibly pick up a sword on another world and succeed in a series of adventures.

The main theme of *Portal* was obviously Ronar's coming to terms with a reality and a way of thinking different than the one he prefers. At that time, the writings of physicist Paul Davies were illuminating me about the profound implications of quantum physics. His books changed the way I view the world and also showed me something that I had thought impossible: a real, scientific basis for the possible existence of telepathy, telekinesis, other forms of paranormal phenomena, and "magic".

By 1985 I was living in Chapel Hill, North Carolina, where I bought a Macintosh computer for the sole purpose of revising *Portal* without having to type out multiple drafts. I laboriously entered it into MacWrite and began a very long process of revision which may not be quite complete even now.

At some point I became dissatisfied with the book's opening. I decided I preferred a quieter, moodier opening that would show Ronar as a more-or-less ordinary astronomer, albeit a restless one who yearns for something new and different in his life. As I now see it, Ronar did in fact invade Nazi Germany as a youth, but his exploits there were less extreme than what I had envisioned, and he didn't get into any lasting trouble over it. This new opening was an important part of the de-jackhammering of Ronar, in which he gradually became more vulnerable and complex.

In the late 80s I began submitting *Portal* to publishers. In 1988, during a spell of living in the California desert, I received a phone call from an editor at one of the first publishers I tried. He said my novel was fresh and colorful and that they wanted to publish it.

That may have been the high point of my life. I was young, I was getting high-end illustration jobs, and now it seemed I would even be able to sell and publish my writings. I foresaw a great creative career ahead of me. Soon after that I returned to New York, where I awaited further word from this publisher. After a few months there was none, so I contacted them to learn why not. I was informed that although almost everyone who read the novel thought it was worthwhile, their senior editor had decided it had too many problems and that it wasn't worth the effort to fix them. The editor said that his decisions were sometimes overridden in this way, and he'd never really promised me anything, and wasn't it too bad, and goodbye.

I was pretty disillusioned by this. Over the next few years the novel was rejected by all other science fiction publishers. Since then I have massively revised and rewritten the whole thing several times over. The current version is, I believe, far better than the one that was nearly published. But in the intervening years publishing has changed. It's now even more difficult for new writers to find publishers, as the corporations that own them demand big results and profits from every book.

As I exhausted my options one by one, I was forced to admit that I might never be able to publish this or any of my novels. It may be that self-published editions like this one are the only form these books will ever take. Since I'm unwilling to concede that my novels are unfit for reading, I will at least give them at least this much chance to survive.

Two sequels, *The Astronomer Who Hated a God* and *The Astronomer Who Gave Back a Crown,* complete Ronar's story, though many blanks remain which I may someday fill in.

I hope whoever reads this will agree it was worth the effort and tenacity I've invested in writing it.

Joe Bergeron

February 5, 2011

www.ingramcontent.com/pod-product-compliance
Lightning Source LLC
Chambersburg PA
CBHW071637260626
47170CB00001B/139